Doubt Not, Cousin

Doubt Not, Cousin

BARRY S. RICHMAN

OYSTERVILLE, WA

◇◇

"Mr. Richman in *Doubt Not, Cousin* introduces a distinctive and unapologetically male voice to JAFF, rendering beloved characters recognizable but also original as he adapts them perfectly to the circumstances of the novel. From the gritty opening scenes to Darcy's and Colonel Fitzwilliam's brotherhood to the elegant portrayal of Lizzy and Kitty's character development after a tragedy, *Doubt Not, Cousin* stirred my emotions and captured my interest throughout the story.

— Cherith Boardman
author of *Mistaken Premise*

◇◇

DOUBT NOT, COUSIN

ISBN: 978-1-68131-071-8

Cover design by Janet B. Taylor
Front cover images: *Lieutenant General William Stuart, 1778–1837* by Henry Raeburn (1756–1823); *Portrait of Eugène Delacroix* by Thales Fielding (1793–1837)
Back cover images: *Duel between Alexander Hamilton and Aaron Burr (July 11, 1804)*, illustration after the painting by J. Mund; *Miss Juliana Willoughby, 1781–83* by George Romney (1734–1802) from Shutterstock

Edited by Don Jacobson and Ellen Pickels
Book layout and design by Ellen Pickels

Published in the United States of America

For Senar, my thirty-year heart of hearts,

...Non est Dubium.

Table of Contents

When I am dead, my dearest,
Sing no sad songs for me;
Plant thou no roses at my head,
Nor shady cypress tree:

— Christina Rossetti, *Song*

Let your plans be dark and impenetrable as night,
and when you move, fall like a thunderbolt.

— Sun Tzu, *The Art of War*

Overture

Fanny Murray's Bawd House
London, December 28, 1781

Two men were bent over a card table, drink glasses half-empty. Whiskey fumes intertwined with cigar smoke as both rose to the ceiling. A window was ajar, allowing a cold breeze to waft around the closed burgundy curtains. The moving air roiled the haze, but like the tide, the ebb and flow were ever changing. Cards lay face down in front of the players; the tabletop's green baize was marred by ashes and drink stains.

"Vingt-et-un. House wins, gentlemen," stated the dealer, a man with narrow, beady eyes.

Neither of the two players looked up from the felt, their mutual lack of motion indicative of the hand's outcome.

"Are you able to cover your vowels?"

"Not immediately," admitted the young man, the insecurity in his voice sounding the antithesis to his suitably aquiline nose.

"And you?"

"No," confessed the obese man sitting next to him whose claret-colored stain, evident on the left side of his neck, disappeared into his double chin. His left hand rested on the table as it, too, bore the mark except for the upper half of his pinkie finger, which was missing.

The dealer grimaced, baring silver-capped teeth before he lifted a hand to summon a reed-thin, dark-suited man. After a whispered conference, the card pusher rose and left the table. His sepulchral master slid into the vacant seat, folded his hands on the table, and leaned forward. "You admit your dibs are not in tune,[1] yet you continue to wager with our money. Credit is a courtesy we extend to gentlemen with tangible assets. Both of you are on the rocks in our books.

"You, my young lord, have expectations, but who knows how long your father will continue to live, let alone permit you to beggar his lands. We could not afford to have you experience an embarrassing refusal."

He turned his attention to the corpulent punter. "You, sir, are already in possession of an estate and can deed us acreage to redeem your vowels. However, we are but creatures of town and not agriculturalists. Our business demands that our wealth must be more easily transportable in nature. We would have to resell the land at a discount, and who but your neighbors would be willing to purchase? No, no—that would not do."

The two men kept their eyes on the cards in front of them.

"The house cannot grant further considerations. What do you gentlemen propose?"

The young man cast a side-glance at the obese man beside him; the latter nodded to the former. "I know of an opportunity."

"What do you require?"

"Legal documents that will pass muster in the Courts of Chancery."

"Not complicated. Of what sort?"

"Inheritance codicils."

1 To be in a poor financial state. Find oneself on the rocks: to have no money; to be in debt.

"Stipulating...?"

"That a neighboring peer will serve as a regent-in-trust until the estate heir reaches majority."

The dealer smiled knowingly. "How long to take stewardship?"

"As regent-in-trust, a short time after the decease of the master—seven years later, as owner-in-trust."

"How quaint. Pasteboard opponents apparently are partnering outside of these hallowed hells. How are you to satisfy your debts without selling up?"

The obese man cast a sideways glance at the young man next to him; the latter, eyes wide in surprise, shook his head. The former ignored him. "We shall rotate out the current crop of barley."

"What will become your main crop?"

The rotund man, eyes hooded, licked his lips. "Roses."

"Of what variety?"

"English."

The manager narrowed his eyes. This was not something he was eager to pursue. He imagined the gentlemen upstairs would likewise wish to remain uninformed. *Gold's glint washes clean the mud of its origins.* "What would entice us to accept this offering?"

"We would offer you future considerations—say a finder's fee of 15 percent in perpetuity."

"We shall require the consent of a guarantor. I am sure you understand."

"Yes," the stout debtor continued. "A Fitzwilliam will guarantee all debts on your ledgers."

"Which Fitzwilliam?"

"A Matlock Fitzwilliam."

"To my knowledge, neither the earl nor the viscount would be your patron."

"You are correct."

"Of whom are we speaking?"

"My betrothed."

The factotum narrowed his eyes again. This had now become something he was eager to pursue. "You, sir, are as yet unmarried."

Eyes cracked open above a smile that slashed through fat cheeks, as crooked yellow teeth glimmered in candlelight's dimness. "The earl signed the settlement papers earlier this day."

His eyes crinkling, the underboss sucked his upper lip under the bottom, reversing the movement several times, as he savored the moment.

"I believe we have an agreement, gentlemen."

Act One:

Foundations and Cellars, 1782–1799

Chapter 1

Canterbury, January 3, 1782

Thea Cavendish sat in the parlor with her mother. The conference was being held to air Thea's defense of her upcoming betrothal to a sixty-year-old man.

"Thea, I cannot agree with this decision. You are not yet seventeen! It is unnatural. You are not without means, dear," her mother begged. "I implore you not to waste yourself on a man old enough to be your grandfather."

Thea refrained from sighing; it would be rude, and she was fond of her mother. Since her father's accidental death, the dowager marchioness had become overly protective.

"Mother, surely *you* are not questioning His Grace's decision?" Thea's choice to marry had been hers and hers alone.

Her mother tried a different, more honeyed, tack. "Darling, you are the granddaughter of a duke. There are alternatives. Let us look close by. What about that charming young man in Derbyshire? His estate is enormous. You will be quite comfortable and within a day's carriage ride."

"George Darcy? Untitled George Darcy? George *D'Arcy*, the Frenchman?" Thea declared in mock affront, her hand theatrically rising to her throat.

Thea thought George Darcy to be quite handsome, but he only had eyes for her dear friend Lady Anne Fitzwilliam. No one would get within an ames-ace[2] of those two. Who would have believed that the Earl of Matlock would consent to a love match, even if Cupid's arrow had pierced a heart with the convenience of an income of £9,000?

"Mother! You would never allow me to be sold to a farmer, even one with flocks numbering in the tens of thousands. A sheep farmer? *Really!*"

Theodosia Cavendish, even at sixteen, understood that her betrothal, unlike that of her friend, was to be a business transaction. Her grandfather approved of her plan. She was a smart, direct young woman, uncowed by what others thought of her. She was born with dark chestnut hair, complemented by mahogany eyes with long, thick black lashes, and Gainsborough would memorialize her dark beauty when painting her wedding portrait. The commission had already been given by her future family, the Manners-Suttons, to the master who would begin after the signing of marriage articles later that day.

Thea understood her upbringing and her value as political currency. She did not begrudge her grandfather for it one jot. Rather, she embraced his vision for her, which endeared her to him: William, the fourth Duke of Devonshire. Although the duke would never own to having tender feelings, he relished being wrapped around his darling granddaughter's delicate, cunning little finger.

Thus, she accepted a marriage of convenience to Lord George Manners-Sutton, third son of the Duke of Rutland. That clan wanted a connection to the House of Cavendish. Their goal was not more power; of that, they already had a surfeit as evidenced by their success

2 The slightest margin or degree; in close proximity.

in placing young Charles into consideration for the Canterbury archbishopric. No, their goal was the maintenance of a principle. The finest families presented stability through alliance, especially since Culloden.[3] How else was a country to keep its place on the world stage?

Thea Cavendish loved her grandfather. Still tall and fit, he wore his silver hair full and crown-like. To all and sundry, he was abrupt, cold, aloof, and disdainful. He never considered the opinions of others, as his pride—in his own *opinion*—was no fault but rather an innate virtue. His little dumpling, however, was not everyone else.

A knock on the door and Quince, the Manners-Sutton butler, pompously announced the addition to their party. "His Grace, the Duke of Devonshire of Chatsworth, Hardwick, Bolton, and Lismore."

"Quince, I have told you repeatedly, he is just Grandpapa. Why do you not heed me?" teased Thea, just as pompously.

The duke entered the parlor, distaste written on his face as he perused the furnishings. The dowager's eyes narrowed, but she made her curtsy nevertheless. The duke nodded without looking as he continued in his same disgruntled attitude.

Thea cleared her throat—loudly—and whistled a short two-tone sound like a small bird in a tree on a summer day. Her mother scowled. Quince tried to maintain his neutral demeanor but winced. The duke's laughter filled the room. He turned and opened his arms wide, his smile stripping twenty years from his face. "Ahh, now I may breathe. Come here, my darling, darling girl."

Thea stepped into his arms where he engulfed her in a hug. The duke enveloped her with the familiar scents of her childhood up north—citrus, oak, and cherry tobacco—smells of home.

"Let us sit," commanded the duke. He pulled Thea down next to him on the settee and nodded to her mother.

"Tell me, Your Grace, are you pleased with our current plans?"

---

3 The Battle of Culloden was fought on April 16, 1746, when the Jacobite army of Charles Edward Stuart was decisively defeated by a British government force. It was the last pitched battle fought on British soil.

asked Thea.

The duke inclined his head in acknowledgment of her wish to address business. "Aye. Your future relations are acceptable, the settlement articles are acceptable, and your betrothed is acceptable.

"Well, what more could a girl look forward to than that?"

The duke's eyes narrowed. "I thought we were discussing business."

"Of course, Grandpapa."

The duke, distaste on his face, addressed his son's widow. "Madam, you are free to attend to your own pursuits."

Thea placed her hand on her mother's arm to soothe her. "I shall join you soon."

The lady stood, curtsied, and departed. The doors to the parlor closed, leaving the duke and his granddaughter alone.

"Your mother does have the right of it, as much as it pains me to admit."

Thea was put out to have her decision questioned by the very man who had educated her in the ways of the *ton*. "Sir, do you doubt I have not considered every aspect of this venture?"

The duke dismissed her display for what it was: youthful petulance. "I find my patience fails when you lower yourself to the mundane, which *you* most certainly are not. I must insist you cease."

Thea took a cleansing breath. "Your Grace, the ends justify the means. The distinction of my final consequence will include, at a minimum, connections to the houses of Devonshire, Rutland, and Matlock."

The bishop of Leeds, Lord Robert Sutton, brought the connection to the Langston family. His Yorkshire offspring, daughter Penelope Sutton, was the wife of Hugh Lambert. His Derby offspring, daughter Eleanor Sutton, was the wife of Lord Simon Langston. Lord Simon was the father of Lady Audrey, the soon-to-be Viscountess Hopton. Her betrothed, Viscount Hopton, was Lord Henry Fitzwilliam, the future Earl of Matlock.

Neither she nor the duke lowered the value of the discussion by mentioning untitled future connections, regardless of their wealth.

The duke nodded approvingly. "Excellent. What are a few years of inconvenience to a lifetime of independence? Now, where were we, my dear?" he asked.

Thea grasped his hand and used her forefinger to trace shapes in his palm.

The duke genially smiled, used to his granddaughter's ways. "You will not distract me, dumpling. Tell me about the Thomsons' ball. I understand you had a fine time as you eviscerated another poseur."

Thea laughed in her throat, a sound one would describe as sultry, had she not been a Cavendish. She was, so it was not. "That would be Lady Catherine Fitzwilliam, soon-to-be de Bourgh if the Matlock coffers can cover the settlement demanded by her future relations. Dismal it is that the earl must approve robbing Peter and giving this theft to Paul."

"I assume you refer to Lady Anne as Peter and Lady Catherine as Paul? How biblical of you."

"Quite."

The duke narrowed his eyes. His forefinger, which had toyed with his upper lip, now pointed at her. "Let me caution you, my dear. Viscount Hopton, Lord Henry, is his father's son, only more vigorous and much more calculating. Despite his elder sister, he owns advantages that you currently do not."

Thea scowled. "I once heard a very vulgar verse while standing for a fitting. Madame Cherbourg's assistant must have been part deaf to have spoken so loudly, but to this topic it signifies."

"Astound me with your wit, my darling girl," challenged the duke.

"Balls, said the Queen." Thea paused. "If I had two, I would be King!"

Thea enjoyed the shock on the duke's face. He coughed, his fist to his mouth.

"My, what a saucy observation."

"But apropos, Grandpapa."

"Yes, I daresay it is."

"Nevertheless, I shall heed your counsel, well given as it is, and *try* to temper my disapprobation of Hopton's unsavory elder sister."

"Thank you, my dear. One never knows when bridges, however lower they may be on the mountain, may benefit a needful explorer," counseled the duke as he clasped his granddaughter's fingers in his palm, raised her hand, and gave it a paternal kiss, ending the lesson.

Westfield, Kent, January 5, 1782

Lord Henry Fitzwilliam escorted his betrothed, Lady Audrey Langston, from the dance floor toward the refreshment tables. They failed to make much progress as attenders at Lord and Lady Westfield's Twelfth Night ball stopped them to exchange greetings, compliments, and perfunctory on-dits. The couple played along. They knew future friends from superficial sycophants. A few more steps and the future of the Matlock earldom encountered a personage for whom they desired to attend.

"Viscount Hopton, Lady Audrey, you continue to set the standard we poor mortals struggle to follow."

"Lady Theodosia, your fabled wit is ever in competition with your sparkling presence. I know not which to compliment first," replied Lord Henry.

"I shall gift your compliments to your spectacular betrothed. Lady Audrey, I do hope you received my invitation for tea. It is a treat to have you in Kent."

Thea turned to the viscount. "How does the earl fare?"

"His last days are nigh."

"Please accept my condolences. What are your immediate plans?"

"We return to town after the ball."

Thea turned to Lady Audrey. "How unfortunate for your admirers."

"Thank you, Lady Theodosia. As you know, my betrothed and I have journeyed here to support the impending nuptials of his elder sister."

Thea could not help but smile. Before she could present her planned empty compliment, an unpleasant voice interrupted them.

"Well, Thea, I see you without your soon-to-be once again. One would not think the late hours so daunting for such a virile specimen."

Thea heard the gasps but kept her eyes on Hopton, whose lips had tightened. She focused on the higher-ranked man in front of her. "Well, Cathy, I see congratulations are in order."

"You may address me as Lady Catherine de Bourgh upon our next encounter."

Thea turned to her adversary. "Why would I do that, *Catty?* Ladies are courted, accept proposals, and have settlements laid upon them."

Thea turned back to Lord Henry. "Livestock are evaluated, negotiated over, and sold."

The gasps were explosions, and Lady Catherine gaped as Lord Henry interceded.

"My dear, I believe my elder sister requires some moments in the ladies' retiring room. Please render her your exquisite assistance."

Lady Audrey escorted a stumbling Lady Catherine away, their departure trailed by murmurs and finger pointing.

"Thea."

"Yes, Henry?"

Hopton smiled. Thea realized her grandfather was, once again, correct. This man had advantages she could, and would, recognize.

The astute gentleman leaned in. "I applaud your future. Please remember Audrey and me as allies."

Thea placed the tip of her fan against the gentleman's shoulder. "Never doubt that you and Audrey shall be such for me as well. And as much as I adore a midnight spectacle, I do not envy the fireworks this evening."

The viscount tilted his head back and laughed. "My goodness, Thea. You do get to the essence of these exchanges rather directly, I daresay."

Thea allowed herself a brief blush as Viscount Hopton kissed her hand.

Rosings Park, Kent, April 1782

The fat man—a claret-colored birthmark evident on the back of his left hand, neck, and chest—sat naked in an overstuffed chair in his bedroom suite. He gripped a tumbler full of whiskey, a half-empty decanter on the adjacent table. Across from him sat his bride, dressed in a chemise and dressing gown. Her distaste was evident.

"Well?"

"All in good time, my dear wife. Would you like a drink? I believe you will require one."

"You are disgusting. Let us get this over with and speak not of it again."

"Oh, I think you will beg for several drinks once we finish our… conversation."

"I forbid you to speak to me in such a manner! I am your wife and the daughter of an earl. Mind your manners, sir."

The obese man tutted, which caused his chin wattles to oscillate with the nodding of his head. "You may refer to yourself as you like, but know that, now and forever, you are my property."

"How dare you!"

"The viscount sold you to me because I was the lone buyer. Accept this fact. You will sleep easier."

"Henry did not sell me. My dowry is in the estate coffers, as it should be. You have settled upon me the manner in which I shall live should you predecease me, which you will."

The bulky man drained half the contents of the glass in his hand. "Yes, no, no, and we shall see."

"What is this gibberish you speak?"

"My dear wife, the Fitzwilliams—or should I be more specific, Viscount Hopton—sold you to me. Would you like to see the bank draft? It is twice the amount of your vaunted dowry. Your angelic sister, Anne—now there is a flower I would like to pluck—sacrificed her dowry so that I would take you in her stead."

"You lie!"

"Had you any proficiency for figures, you would have known that you will have nothing should I predecease you. Nothing. All that is mine will go to our firstborn as stipulated in our marriage settlements."

"You are an animal. You sicken me. I…I…I shall never consent to such an arrangement."

"Yet your family has. So let us begin this business and get on to more important matters."

He stood and loomed over a cowering Lady Catherine de Bourgh.

"I have heard tell of mothers advising their daughters to lie still and it will end quickly, the pain but brief."

She nodded her head. He handed her his glass half full of whiskey, which she took from him with a shaking hand.

"Those mothers were very, very wrong."

"Sir Lewis, please…please do not hurt me."

"Drink deep and imagine yourself as Julian of Norwich, my dear."

Lady Catherine drank down the false idol of courage. Tears trickled down her cheeks, a precursor to the nightmare he intended that she never forget.

He leaned forward and whispered in her ear. *"All shall be well, and all shall be well, and all manner of things shall be well."*[4]

4 Julian of Norwich (1343-1416) was an English mystic of the Middle Ages. Her writings, now known as *Revelations of Divine Love*, are the earliest surviving English language works by a named woman. She wrote of Christ, not as a saint but as a literal mother. The use of her words is the antithesis of their meaning.

Chapter 2

Chalk Farm, Yorkshire, June 1782

Two gentlemen stood back-to-back, the pistols in their hands pointed skyward. Upon hearing the command, they would move to their marks—two stakes pushed into the ground five yards away. Ten yards to their flanks stood their seconds, a surgeon, a priest, and the master of the field.

The root of the engagement was an insult to the honor of the Grafton dukedom—tenuous at best but something that can happen during a gathering. Felicity is usually restored by cooler, more senior heads, but this was not to be the case. Unfortunately for Mr. Hugh Lambert, his opponent, Baron Andrews Davies, an aficionado of the *code duello*, was the duke's proxy. It was likewise unlucky for Baron Davies that Mr. Lambert, a most inflexible gentleman, was unlikely to cry off.

Lambert was unknown to the baron or his sponsor, the elderly duke. But for a late petition by the marquess to his father's hostess, the situation would have remained as such. However, thanks to the heir's intervention, Lambert and his wife received a last-minute invitation to the duke's house party. The billet was accompanied by a handwritten note claiming a secretarial oversight. Since they lived nearby—Tang Hall outside Yorkshire, but a day's carriage ride away from Broadmoor—Mrs. Penelope Lambert penned her acceptance.

As with all house parties, daily activities saw the men separated from their spouses. Mrs. Lambert rubbed along well with her counterparts. Her husband, however, did not. The difference in the attenders' proclivities became apparent after the first night's dinner. During the separation of the sexes, the duke and his sycophants dove deep into their port and brandy. Mr. Lambert abstained. The baron ignored Mr. Lambert's second polite refusal as the marquess looked down his suitably aquiline nose at their plebeian guest.

Despite insistence that a guest show good manners by joining his host, Mr. Lambert, who preferred moderation, refused to be manipulated by the peer, and he let the party know he preferred not to compromise his moral code to placate the vanity of a new acquaintance. The duke, his son's manipulations in his ear, roared his drunken outrage and called into question Hugh Lambert's honor. Lambert refused to rise to the duke's provocations as he was on the far side of sixty-five. The duke demanded that the baron be his proxy, which the baron accepted, rabid for the opportunity. Davies immediately called out Lambert.

Lambert, even if he had had a hint of flexibility in his character, which he did not, chose not to refuse the baron's challenge. The barrage of affronts had been too much for him to ignore. The potential duelers, to be accompanied by their seconds, scheduled a meeting in a se'nnight to agree upon weapons and terms. Mr. Lambert collected his wife and left that same evening.

Once home, Lambert sent an express to a connection he had made at his university. Although the other gentleman was a few years younger, they enjoyed each other's company. Their friendship continued despite Lambert's decamping Cambridge to assume his estate after his father's sudden death. The pair continued to exchange informative letters—Lambert's of his growing family, his correspondent writing of his service to the King. Lambert's express asked his friend to assist him in a matter of honor. The army officer, accompanied by a surgeon, arrived on horseback a few days later.

Negotiations with the baron and his second deteriorated to a nonplus point, as the aristocrat longed to fight regardless of the consequences. The magistrate, a second son to an estate owner, had accepted the position due to a lack of interest from the local landed gentry and, thus, was not beholden to the duke. Despite the baron's demand that both parties be absolved of culpability, the magistrate set aside his inclination to enforce the law and agreed to serve as master of the field. A veteran of England's earlier conflicts, he chose an unoccupied and secluded farm with a meadow surrounded by trees. All that remained was for the challenged party to choose his weapon; for Lambert, that would be pistols. The baron never considered himself to be in any danger even though his preferred weapon was a rapier.

Davies was of medium height, lean of build, and sported dark hair and brown eyes. One could not forget meeting him, for he constantly spoke of his rank, his connections, and his passion for dueling. He proudly sported a vertical two-inch facial scar earned the previous year. His opponent later yielded but not before the baron left him having to use a cane to walk.

Lambert, on the other hand, was most unremarkable. He was of medium height, medium build, and had neutral-colored hair and eye. None of the house party knew of his wife's connections to the aristocracy and the upper reaches of the Anglican Church, connections that were never trumpeted.

Enjoying the field of honor and its pageantry, Davies was convinced that it was an important part of a gentleman's credentials. The more challenges made and survived, the greater the nobleman. Although his prowess with bladed weapons was far superior, he felt that, in this situation, due to his reputation alone, his opponent would yield, offer a forfeit, and make recompense. His last five duels had ended in this manner without a single drop of blood. He had been told that his opponent was a provincial sheep farmer who spent no time in town. Davies dismissed any thoughts of a poor outcome for himself.

That sheep farmer had a natural ability with firearms. He was unmatched at trap shooting, a sport in which neither the duke nor the baron could take part, much less describe. Lambert's gamekeeper had never recorded a scoring of his employer with more than a single miss for every twenty game birds released. Although he did not own a set of dueling pistols, his coach and saddle horses each sported a working pair. He never failed to hit his targets with the notoriously inaccurate unrifled weapons.

Lambert regulated his emotions as he prepared to defend himself for nothing more than a thoughtless declaration in the wrong company.

Lambert's second stood to the side of the field. He recognized the danger of the situation but felt helpless to do more than secure his friend's safety.

The master of the field inquired of the combatants' readiness.

"Ready," confidently answered the baron.

"Ready," responded Lambert, his voice flat.

The master of the field inquired of the duelers' seconds whether all was in order.

"All is in order," responded the baron's second.

"All is in order."

The master inquired of the duelers' seconds whether either side wished to forfeit.

"Nay," sneered the baron's second.

"Nay."

The master then inquired of the duelers whether either principal wished to delope.[5]

"Nay," answered the baron.

"Nay," responded Lambert.

The baron frowned. Lambert's expression remained unchanged.

"Duelers, take to your marks."

Lambert walked the five yards to his mark, turned, and faced his opponent with his pistol pointed at the ground.

The baron hesitated for a moment, his eyes swinging back and forth between his opponent and the sideline participants. He walked to his mark, turned, and faced his adversary.

"Cock your weapons."

Two distinct clicks added to the tension.

"On my mark, aim at your opponent, but do not fire. Seconds, prepare to defend your principal."

Four pistols rose to the eye level of each armed man. The baron and his second sighted on Lambert. Lambert and his second, making sure he was standing within arm's reach of his counterpart, sighted on the baron.

"On my mark, principals may fire. Seconds may fire if the principal fails to wait for my mark. Seconds ticked.

"Fire!"

The baron flinched. Lambert did not. His shot flew true, hitting the baron in the center of his chest.

The baron, knocked backward, fired his pistol. His shot missed its target.

The baron's second, having lowered his arm, raised his weapon, and sighted on his principal's opponent.

Lambert's second put his pistol to the head of his counterpart and fired.

The baron's second fired his weapon as a reflex to a mortal injury. His shot hit Lambert in the stomach. Lambert's second lowered his

5 The practice of wasting with deliberation one's shot in a pistol duel in an attempt to abort the conflict

arm and dropped his pistol to the ground, his jaw tightly clenched as he looked over at his friend lying on the ground.

No one moved. No one spoke. When the clouds of smoke dissipated through the trees surrounding Chalk Farm and the remaining witnesses recovered their senses, the master of the field surveyed the carnage, trying to assess the degree of the disaster at hand. From the first shot to the last, less than five seconds had passed. Gazing around, he looked to the sky and exclaimed to no one, "Bloody hell, this, this… bollocks!" He swiped at his clothing.

"Doctor, please see to the wounded."

He turned to Lambert's second. "You did well to act in defense of your friend."

"Not well enough."

"No, I daresay. Who knew the baron had such dishonorable associates?"

"The baron?" Lambert's second offered doubtfully.

The surgeon returned. "Neither lives."

The master of the field pursed his lips. "Let us ferry the bodies away. Maybe we can salvage something of the day. The baron's carriage is at the east end of the field."

"One moment, Magistrate," demanded Lambert's friend.

He examined the corpse in front of him. The second's shattered head was tilted back, chin high. His mouth hung open; silver-capped teeth on display. The army man ignored the macabre and searched the body for the mundane. He found two additional pistols before discovering a note. One line jumped out and explained the past several minutes.

… should the baron fail, you will prevail. Lambert must die…

He stuffed the missive into his boot top and moved to the baron's carcass. He searched that corpse and found a blood-covered letter in the peer's inner pocket.

He also slid that into his boot and returned to the others.

"Well?"

"No final instructions on either body. I spoke with my friend before this…tragedy. Let us continue."

They carried the baron's corpse and that of his second to the aristocrat's carriage and laid them inside. Neither the driver nor the horses were anywhere in sight. Lambert's second, the parson, and the surgeon remained silent, allowing the magistrate to lead.

The master of the field looked across the meadow and gestured to the remaining carriage, its driver having likewise fled the scene. "Let us continue with the unfortunate Mr. Lambert."

The surgeon and Lambert's second carried the dead man. Upon their approach, they all saw the bullet hole in the lowered window curtain. Lambert's friend shook his head at the errant shot. The two men lowered the body to the ground.

Lambert's friend stepped up and pulled open the carriage door, then jumped back in horror as Mrs. Lambert tumbled out. Her blood was everywhere.

The surgeon applied a pressure bandage to her neck, but his efforts were for naught. The magistrate and the priest gawked at Penelope Lambert's body in shock.

Movement on the floor of the carriage caught the eye of Lambert's second. Stepping closer, he reached under the carriage seat and assisted a small girl from within.

Captain Thomas Bennet, decorated veteran of the American rebellion, stared into the unseeing, violet eyes of the Lambert's eight-year-old daughter Madeleine. The child's gaze, so terrifyingly vacant, bore a look that would haunt him for a decade.

"Come with me, my child," he whispered. He offered his hand, which she grasped tightly.

He lifted her out, and she wrapped her arms around his neck, burying her face against him.

"Magistrate," growled Captain Bennet, his voice steely.

"Sir?" he answered, snapping to attention at the sound, a bewildered look upon his face.

"You once wore the King's scarlet, did you not?"

The magistrate nodded several times, his eyes wide. "Yes, sir."

"And you continue to serve the Crown. What are your intentions?"

Bennet was annoyed by the surgeon and the rector. They resembled a pair of caged canaries, swiveling their heads back and forth between himself and the magistrate. He felt weighted down by every stone of his own guilt as he held his friend's daughter in his arms.

The magistrate sighed in despair. "An illegal duel, a family destroyed, and a child orphaned. Are you suggesting we be less than forthcoming, sir?"

Captain Bennet could sense the wariness in the man's reply. "I am *suggesting* something underhanded is at play. I am demanding we protect this child. I am also confirming we are all complicit."

"What do you propose?" asked the priest.

"Magistrate, we shall leave this field and the unfortunates in your hands. We shall not exchange introductions nor correspond. The parson and I shall see to the child. Need more be said, gentlemen?" The crown official acknowledged the terms and walked off.

Once at his horse, Captain Bennet turned to the surgeon and the pastor.

"Must I explain how precarious is this child's welfare? I have written confirmation from her father's hand that she is the heiress of Tang Hall and is, as of this moment, worth thousands a year."

Captain Bennet turned to the surgeon. "My friend, I implore you to return home and remain mute about all of this. I shall contact you later."

"As you wish."

Captain Bennet waited as the surgeon departed. "Wells, you and I must secure this child's well-being. As I stated earlier, there is something amiss here. I suspect villainy, and we *will* sacrifice our comforts to ensure her safety."

"Why are we not seeking out her family, sir? Is it not their Christian duty to take in the young child?"

Bennet spoke in measured tones, his friend's warning in their last conversation predominant in his thoughts. *Trust no one.* There were other lines he had read in the metal-mouthed man's note that concerned him.

He cautiously continued, "Their duty, perhaps, but whether or not they would undertake it in a Christ-like manner is an open question. In this instance, I would be remiss to make such a snap judgment until we sift through the intelligence at hand. Will you grant me a reprieve to verify her safety, my friend?"

Together, they rode off—Reverend Wells in his gig and Captain Bennet atop his mount with Maddy Lambert's face buried in his chest.

"All will be well, child," he whispered repeatedly. He kept up a constant prattle as they rode, including narrating Robinson Crusoe's tale from memory. Bennet shook off the chills as he imagined this sweet girl as a castaway.

An hour and a half later, the group pulled into the parsonage at Flaxby Knares. Thomas dismounted, then helped down his friend's daughter. He reached into his saddle kit and removed a cloth bag secured with a tie-string. Holding Maddy's hand, he entered the parsonage and urged her to take in her surroundings. She remained unresponsive. They sat together on a thread-worn sofa as they waited for their host to join them. Minutes later, he did, sitting in a rickety chair a few feet across from the pair.

"Wells, what have we to feed this brave young lady?"

The parson smiled. "We shall have a hot meal upon our table as soon as the local girl comes by."

"Excellent, my friend. Is that not good, Maddy?" Thomas lifted her chin with his finger, once again taking in her astonishing violet eyes, still moist.

Maddy looked blankly at him although her tears now sparkled on her lashes and cheeks.

"Yes, excellent provisions for our excellent princess!"

Thomas smiled at the parson's exuberance; the child did not.

The two men chatted about everything and anything, avoiding the day's tragedy. As they spoke, Maddy's fatigue showed. Thomas took her by the hand, the cloth bag in his other, and led her to a bedroom. He helped her take off her shoes and made her snug under the covers. She stared at him in silence. He opened the cloth bag and removed a small doll, then set it on the bed next to her. When she made no effort to embrace the offering, he placed her hand upon it. She closed her eyes and quickly dropped off to sleep. He left the door ajar.

"She sleeps?"

"Yes, she does."

"How may I be of service, Bennet?"

"I require time to read through some papers, Wells."

"Certainly. Follow me."

The parson led his guest to a small, cluttered study. Captain Bennet sat in an available chair, pulled the documents from his boot, and settled in.

Accustomed to ascertaining the relative importance of information, Bennet returned to the letter he had found on the baron's faithless second's corpse. Bennet's uneasiness turned into a chill that seeped deep into his soul, one that confirmed his caution. The death warrant issued for Lambert had been worth £1,000 if the killer had been successful in leaving the field.

No doubt this denizen of the Seven Dials assumed that the baron would finish Lambert, leaving him to put paid to the medico, Wells, and me. He could have disposed of the baron at any moment and claimed his reward from his employer. He did not bargain for the actual outcome.

Bennet turned to the unopened letter liberated from the baron's body. Reading around obscuring bloodstains, his eye passed over the platitudes assuring the dead man of eternal gratitude for loyally standing in the Grafton interest. What caught Bennet's eye, though, was the unexpected signatory: Marquess Bradford, rather than his father the duke, who by Lambert's account had been the aggrieved party.

Now, why would the old man's son be involved in this affair? His father is no doddering fool. He would have written his surrogate. Yet, the pup is affirming the dukedom's debt to this aristocratic fop. This might be a candle that will shed further light on today's goings-on.

A chilling phrase riveted him. "*...a Matlock Fitzwilliam guarantees the scheme...compensation after your agreement for the estate is penned...*"

A knock on the door broke through the brown study into which Thomas Bennet had fallen. He blessed the intrusion.

"Bennet, dinner will soon be served."

"Wells, please join me."

The priest moved several tomes off the remaining chair before doing so. He rubbed his left arm as he settled back.

"I shall not burden you with the origins of today's heinous acts. I shall only, upon your word sworn on the name of our Almighty, task you with the safety of the young lady. Do not inquire as I shall not be forthcoming. Know that the child is in mortal danger and must be hidden for a time until I can assure her safety with honorable family relations."

"Surely, you cannot mean her relations are suspect? Bennet, by your own words, her family is of the first circles!"

Captain Thomas Bennet narrowed his eyes at the parson until the man fidgeted.

"Wells, you know of me and my family. You studied at the seminary with my younger brother, God rest his soul. You have dined at Longbourn's table. It is why I contacted you when I received Lambert's express regarding this horrible business. I know I am not Solomon, but do not doubt me. This child is in the unfortunate position over which he presided. Maddy, though, will not receive a reprieve as did the biblical baby."

"What…what do you propose, sir?"

"You must take her in hand for the time being. Located here in the wilds outside of Leeds is the next best thing to taking her halfway around the world. The Lamberts must vanish for a time. If they are unseen, the assumption will be drawn that they have decamped, been kidnapped, or whatever the chinwags assume."

The strategist stood.

"I shall return once I am better prepared to assure her safety. She must remain out of sight. Can you do that, Wells?"

"Aye, I can."

"Good."

Rain extended a pleasant visit by friends from the neighboring shire. The rector debated *Romeo and Juliet* with Mr. and Mrs. Eriksen; Mr. Wells defended young love's premise. The Eriksens took the opposing position—that of a pair of young people manipulated by politics and powerful parents. The godly man struggled not to show his rising discomfort—with both his friends' unpopular opinion and the pain pulsating through his left side.

At dinner, the parson gave in to the persistent ache, rubbing his chest as pain radiated up his left arm. He allowed Eriksen to help him upstairs where Mrs. Eriksen fluffed his pillows to ensure his comfort. Her husband placed a chair next to the bed.

The parson grasped his friend's hand. "You must help me, Eriksen."

"Anything, Wells. Just ask."

"He, who is greater than all, has not blessed you with children. I see it as the Lord's will. Do you not agree?"

"I find my love of our Lord as strong as ever, despite the trials he puts us through."

"Yes…yes. For he now blesses you for your piety."

"Whatever do you mean, Wells?"

"My niece Maddy. She is but an orphan these few days past and is still shaken by the loss of her parents. I am entrusting her to you and your wife."

"Wells, you cannot be serious!"

"I have not much time left. I beg you to open your home and your heart. She will have no one when I am gone. No one. Will you allow me to meet our Lord with this burden?"

Eriksen squeezed his hand. "No, Wells, I will not. Let me speak with my wife."

"Thank you, my friend. Send Maddy to me. I want to fall into her beautiful eyes as I leave this world."

Wells looked up at the ceiling. The chair scraped the floor. Footsteps receded. He closed his eyes. Light footsteps indicated a child approached, then a small, warm hand grasped his.

"Uncle Wells, is your time nigh?"

"Yes, my dear, I am afraid it is. I shall be with your mama and papa before long."

"Captain Bennet has not yet returned."

"He will, Maddy. He will. He is the best of men."

The rector turned toward her.

"What am I to do?" she whispered.

The parson felt more pain in his chest. He tightened his grip.

"You are Maddy Wells. You are Eriksen's niece. You must protect yourself. You are Maddy Wells."

"I am Maddy Wells."

"Captain Bennet will find you. If not now, in the future."

"Captain Bennet will find me."

"Forgive him if he is late. Promise me. You are Maddy Wells."

"I shall forgive Captain Bennet, I promise. I am Maddy Wells."

Wells again looked up and away from the girl and saw light. Glorious light. He slid away, a beatific smile on his face as the Lord greeted home his good servant.

Maddy held the parson's hand until Mrs. Eriksen came for her. The three left for Lambton the following week.

A fortnight later, Captain Bennet dismounted from his horse in front of the rectory. He looked about. All was not as it should be. He knocked on the door. No response. He pushed on the panel and discovered it unlocked. The house was vacant. He searched every room. Nothing. Nothing remained of his friend or Madeleine Lambert. His one consolation was that there were no signs of violence. He searched the chapel and the churchyard. In that latter location, he found a freshly turned grave, too large for a child.

Ah, Wells, I fear you carried out my pleas too thoroughly. You took Maddy's secret to the grave. How I wish you had left me a clue as to her whereabouts.

Frustrated, he remounted his horse and rode off with two unseen companions: fear and anger. Fear for Maddy's safety and anger at his own impotence. Undergirding these pair of feelings was the ashen taste of his failure to his murdered friend, now gone these past weeks. Worst of all, he was no closer to the truth of *why.*

Chapter 3

Rosings Park, Late November 1782

The obese man loomed over his wife. She was still abed with the last remnants of childbed fever. He addressed the young nurse sitting in attendance.

"Leave us."

She hurried from the room.

Sir Lewis de Bourgh sat in her chair and looked at his wife. He took up her hand and patted the back of it. Lady Catherine de Bourgh slowly opened her eyes and turned her head. "So, I have died and gone to hell."

"They made you of much sterner stuff than that, my dear."

He saw her eyes focus. Now was the time. "I am leaving."

"Thank the Lord for small miracles."

"Thank you for our daughter, should she live."

"She will. She is a Fitzwilliam."

"Yes, I agree with you. Anne de Bourgh is certainly of the Fitzwilliam bloodline."

"No! My daughter will not bear the name of my traitorous sister."

"She will, and she does. You have been abed these two weeks with fever."

"You are a bastard."

"If I am, your vaunted connections are worthless."

His wife closed her eyes.

"Not yet. We have business to discuss."

"What do you want of me? I am near dead from your…ministrations."

Sir Lewis could not help but smile. Though he liked his delicacies much younger, he had enjoyed the earl's daughter as if she had been livestock.

"I am leaving. You are rid of me. I am to be found dead in the next day or two. Do you understand?"

"Yes," she whispered, her fear evident.

"You will continue with all of our schemes."

"As you wish."

"Know this, wife. Anne inherits everything. Everything! You will have rights to the dower house but nothing else! Anne de Bourgh is mistress of Rosings."

"Henry would never agree to such terms from one like you."

"Your brother does not know me as you do, does he?"

Sir Lewis squeezed her hand until she whimpered. She would not question his contrivances.

"Do not make me return, Catherine. It will go poorly for you."

"Begone [illegible]

"Remember my requirements, wench. You do not want the Ouroboros[6] to complete its transition."

His beleaguered wife goggled at him. "I shall do as you say."

"No. Not as I say. As I command. Do not be remiss in this. You will continue to send the Lambert correspondence through my agent

6 The symbol for eternal cyclic renewal; a serpent or dragon eating its own tail leading to death, then rebirth

to Lady Audrey. Exactly as you have. For many more years. Do not falter, for I am omniscient."

Sir Lewis squeezed her hand again, relishing her pain.

Three days later, a wan Lady Catherine de Bourgh received the magistrate and the coroner. She did not invite them to sit.

"Lady Catherine, we bring grim news."

She glared at the magistrate. "Speak, man. I have not all day for your melodrama."

"A villager discovered a destroyed carriage burned and discarded off the main road past Bromley. The horses were nowhere to be found."

"Why would this bring you to Rosings? Out with it, man."

"A body, well, the detritus of the carriage contained what remained of a body."

"And? Do I have to pull the conversation from your person?"

"The remains displayed a certain past injury. We would not want to postulate of Sir Lewis, but would you offer…?"

"For my sake alone, stop blathering. Sir Lewis was missing half the small finger of his left hand. Are you advising me Sir Lewis perished in the carriage fire?"

"Yes, milady."

Lady Catherine stood. "You may consider yourselves dismissed. My man of business will contact you regarding the funeral arrangements. I must see to my mourning clothes. Find your way out."

The funeral of Sir Lewis de Bourgh was attended by the magistrate, the coroner, and four purchased pallbearers. No others. The delayed death announcement left no option for Lord Henry—the new earl—and Lady Anne but to send letters of condolence to their sister. They were returned unopened.

Matlock House, January 1, 1783

Lady Audrey felt something tug within her body. She grasped her sister's arm.

"What is happening, Anne?" gasped the countess, wincing as she adjusted her position.

Lady Anne Darcy frowned and turned to the midwife and accoucheur. Neither returned her notice as both were intent upon the countess's lower body.

"Careful now, slowly...slowly. Turn him in opposition to the cord... not that way, in reverse."

The countess moaned. She squeezed her sister's hand savagely, as another pain gripped her. Lady Anne gasped with her.

"Towel! Give me another towel. Rub him...rub him. Briskly now... mind his neck and head."

A snipping sound and the accoucheur walked across the room. He whispered to a nurse, who rushed from the room.

"Easy now, milady...easy now. We shall take our time, we shall... prevent fever, we *will.*"

A physician rushed into the room, an additional nurse close on his heels. Both bent over the bassinet, having joined the accoucheur. The three whispered amongst themselves, the accoucheur's arms pumping back and forth.

A croak wafted up, and the three medical people stood up straight and smiled. Lady Anne noted their newfound confidence, leaned over her dear friend, and whispered in her ear. "Newborn twins are so impractical; they require twice the attendance."

"So true, I daresay," slurred Lady Audrey. She drifted off to sleep.

Lady Anne reached over and brushed the hair off her forehead. "I posit no one save the indomitable Countess of Matlock would dare challenge both Mother Nature and Father Time. Who but she would birth twins on either side of the New Year? Sleep. We shall attend your sons on the morrow."

Henry Fitzwilliam, the Earl of Matlock, scowled at his housekeeper. George Darcy, his brother, sat in the adjacent wing chair.

"What are you saying, Mrs. Hudson?" the earl demanded.

Darcy frowned. He never agreed with the earl's treatment of servants.

"The second child has had difficulties."

Darcy noticed she did not smile as she had when she delivered the news of the heir's birth.

"What difficulties, woman? Do not spare words!"

Darcy poured oil on the waters. "How fares the countess?"

Mrs. Hudson smiled. "She is exhausted, Mr. Darcy, but resting comfortably. Lady Anne has taken herself off for bath and bed."

"Excellent. Dare I inquire as to the problems encountered by the second babe?"

"The physician will explain the details. Master Richard has had a difficult birth. He lives but has had struggles unkind to one so little."

Darcy put his hand on his elder brother's arm. "Thank you, Mrs. Hudson. Please ask the physician to join us."

The physician joined them in quick order where he outlined a short list of complications. The umbilical cord, previously wrapped around the babe's neck, may have caused damage to his voice box. There was also a chance of other injuries. He finished his report with the hope that time and care would mitigate some of the infirmities.

The earl, eyes hooded, looked to his brother. Darcy attempted to relieve the tension.

"Twins are so practical, as they always have a spare."

"So true, I daresay, so true!"

Darcy reached over and removed the glass from Lord Henry's hand as he yawned and laid his head against the back of his chair. The new father turned to his brother. "Let me tell you one, my friend. Twins are God's way of saying, 'One of you is a rough plan.' Yes…"

Darcy saw that the earl was asleep. The long hours had taken their toll. He leaned his head back. George Darcy, a pious man, prayed in silence to the Lord not to take offense.

Little did the four of them realize that the Almighty heard their jests and found no humor in them.

A month later

A ruckus outside his study door caused the earl to look up. He recognized the voice.

"I will *not* wait like some common trollop. Open the door!"

The door flew open, and his older sister stepped through.

The butler intoned, "Lady Catherine de Bourgh."

"Thank you, Smythe."

The earl waited out his sister. He did not wait long.

"Well, stop acting like a parsnip, Henry. Offer me a chair."

"Join me, Kat."

"Do not ever, ever use that atrocious appellation with me!"

The earl briefly closed his eyes and exhaled. "Sit, Catherine."

She dropped into the nearest chair, distaste written on her face.

"Why the sour expression, sister?"

"I should have been earl. I am the eldest. Male-only primogeniture is unnatural and against the Lord's will."

"Yet, it is the law of the land."

"Were I Queen, I would dismiss the silliness of it."

"Alas, you are not."

His sister harrumphed.

"What brings you to town?"

She pulled a document from her large reticule. "I have come for reparations."

"Reparations, you say?"

"Yes, Henry. Reparations. Reparations from you—you who sold me to that animal."

"Catherine, I did not sell you. You have a respectable set of marriage articles, ones that will provide for you and Anne comfortably, whatever the future holds."

"Your account differs from that of Sir Lewis."

The earl pinched the bridge of his nose. He sensed a headache nearby. "Catherine, I shall not argue reality with you. What is it you want from me?"

She pointed the document in her hand at him. "This is a contract for the betrothal of your heir to mine."

The earl blinked. Twice.

"A cradle betrothal? Between Langston and Anne?"

"Yes. It will be a most excellent match. The combining of two great legacies. Two children descended from the same noble lines. Their fortunes are splendid."

"Why not Richard? As a second son, he would benefit more and not be distracted by managing other estates."

"Spares are cannon fodder. Nothing more."

The earl pursed his lips, his affront contained.

"Should you refuse, Henry, I shall sever all connections between Matlock and Rosings henceforth and in perpetuity."

The earl took a deep breath and smiled. "I see we have like purposes, sister dear."

Lady Catherine smiled as Lord Henry offered his hand, palm up. She placed the contract into it, but frowned as he leaned over to his right, dropped it into a drawer, and locked it.

"What are you doing?"

"Agreeing with you, Lady Catherine. All connections between us, henceforth, and in perpetuity, are severed."

"Whaa…whaa…?"

"Smythe!"

The door opened. "Yes, your lordship?"

"See Lady Catherine de Bourgh out for the final time."

Fingers snapped. Two footmen flanked the woman, grasped her arms, and lifted her into the air.

"Do not touch me!"

The earl held up his hand. The footmen stilled, his sister's feet dangling above the floor.

"Do not think to try the same with our sister Anne should she birth George an heir. I shall write to Darcy as they cart you out of these halls for the last time."

The earl watched the bane of his existence exit his study door. He shook his head and returned to his letters.

Chapter 4

Lady Audrey Fitzwilliam stared at her child, not understanding why her little Richard never cried. Never.

The midwife had been surprised when the newborn did not unleash the expected lusty wail announcing his presence to the world despite the difficulties encountered during his birthing. The wet nurses reported they had never seen as silent an infant. The day nurses talked of the quiet of the younger twin's private nursery. Yet, the child was not mute.

Richard cooed and giggled when prompted. His perfect little hands and feet wiggled when left unencumbered. As he grew, he crawled all about the carpeted floors. He learned to pull himself up much earlier than his elder twin did. The earl himself bragged of little Richard's strength, fortitude, and singular focus. He boasted that the child would not want to be distracted by crying.

True, Richard did not cry. He did not cry even when he was hungry. Had it not been for a keen young nurse noticing a slight weight loss, the child's parents would have missed the life-saving revelation that

Richard's feedings had to be scheduled, as he would alert no one to his suckling needs. Thus, the Fitzwilliam "spare" nursed on a set program, happy to drain the provided nourishment reservoirs without making a fuss. At all. Ever.

Physicians were called and examinations were conducted. London expert after expert weighed, measured, and prodded the child. All departed professing bewilderment. None returned.

Fearing gossip and its accompanying scandal, the Matlock earldom ensured that the London medical community understood the ramifications should their son's evaluations be discussed in any manner. Lord Henry Fitzwilliam, powerful in the House of Lords, supplemented his influence by serving as a senior advisor in the War Office. None desired the wrath of a war counselor.

Four years and much angst later, a young army surgeon, recommended to the earl by a trustworthy connection, arrived at Matlock House to examine the four-year-old child.

March 1787

"Mr. Burton."

A wiry man walked with purpose across the parlor, his posture ramrod straight. His arms hung at his sides—his right hand empty, his left carrying a black leather medical satchel. His light hair was short, and gold-framed spectacles were perched upon his patrician nose. He had been raised a gentleman and was comfortable in the current setting. He paused and waited for the aristocratic couple to take notice of him. Once the niceties had been completed, a young redheaded nurse entered the room and delivered her charge to the surgeon. He appeared quite comfortable as he briefly communicated with the child. She seemed reluctant to leave. The medico regarded her with kindness.

"He will be well, I assure you."

Nurse curtsied and departed. The earl and the countess stood.

"If possible, I would like for you to remain. It reduces speculation."

The earl and the countess returned to their chairs, unsure of what to say. The surgeon began his examination. He sat Richard upon a coffee table and opened his bag.

At first, the evaluation mirrored those made by the other London physicians. Seeing that, the earl and countess prepared themselves to accept another wasted afternoon. Yet, after measuring, weighing, and handling the child, this surgeon deviated from evaluations conducted in the past. He spent a considerable amount of time looking at and touching the boy's tongue. He compared it to his upper and lower teeth repeatedly. He used a set of calipers to measure the length and depth of each furrow. He opened a journal and made precise, miniature drawings of the scars. He showed them to his patient as he completed each one and asked for his opinion. The two exchanged whispers. At one point, the surgeon inclined his head; the boy nodded several times. They recommenced whispering, their heads nearly touching. The earl and the countess looked on in wonder, exchanging glances between themselves.

The surgeon next sat the child on a settee. From his bag, he removed a small jar containing clear fluid and thin needles. He set this on the side table next to the boy who watched the surgeon dispassionately.

"The best Damascene steel sewing needles in neutral spirits," offered the surgeon to the couple. The earl's eyebrows neared the top of his forehead.

Mr. Burton knelt until he was at eye level with his patient. The boy's parents watched him whisper to their son and receive the same in return. The surgeon removed a large black cloth, reassured the child all would be well, and blindfolded him. Opening the jar, the surgeon removed a needle and scratched it down each bare leg without breaking the skin. A pink trail remained. The patient displayed no reaction.

The surgeon next removed the child's shoe and stocking. He grasped a bare foot in his hand. He leaned over and whispered again into his patient's ear. Richard nodded back in return. He removed another needle, then looked at the countess briefly. She blinked. He pushed the needle deep into the child's heel. The boy moved his head down as if looking at his foot through the mask but made no sound. The surgeon carefully eased the needle out and checked the heel for blood. He found none. He removed the blindfold, replaced the boy's stocking and shoe, and congratulated young Richard on his bravery. The child looked up at Mr. Burton and smiled.

The earl was doubly stunned, both by the ordeal he had assumed his son had undergone and equally so by Richard's reaction. He looked at the countess, who had her right hand over her mouth; her left gripped the sofa's arm. Her expression showed her agony, and her eyes were filled with tears. She reached out to her husband for comfort. The earl encompassed her trembling hand.

Mr. Burton bowed to the earl. His examination was complete, but he remained silent.

Matlock called the butler into the room. "See that Richard is served his favorite treat. He has done very well—very well, indeed."

"Yes, my lord." Smythe closed the door. A few moments later, Richard's young nurse entered and swept up her charge, humming a melodic Irish ballad. Richard's little arms wound around her neck. The door closed, and silence again settled in the room.

The earl put the question to Mr. Burton, not arrogantly but in a quiet, hopeful manner. "Well?"

"I shall require time to conduct some rather specific research. For now, I can extend a hypothesis."

"Please do."

"Your son does not feel physical sensations like others. This is clear in his minute reaction to painful stimuli."

The surgeon nodded to the couple to ensure their understanding. They both replied in kind.

"There is more evidence as seen by the scarring on his tongue. The teeth marks match his inner mouth shape. I conjecture he chewed his tongue while teething. I speculate his weight loss, coupled with his failure to demand to feed, also stems from this high, or in my opinion, indifferent pain threshold. His diminished response to pain concerns me." Mr. Burton gestured with his forefinger in the air. "He must be taught that blunt trauma is a danger to him. Pain is our body's warning mechanism. Your son, as he grows, will not acknowledge the everyday bumps and bruises children encounter while playing."

"Pray continue," directed the countess, her focus on the surgeon.

"I should like to spend more time with the young master in his familiar environment. Together, we shall develop a protocol for him to self-assess throughout the day. We desire to prevent smaller incidents from growing into larger injuries. The French have a name for this protocol."

The earl curled his lip curl in disgust. "Odious lot. You have my permission to speak the words, sir, as this is your area of expertise. What is this practice you are describing?"

"The French use the word 'triage.' We shall instruct the young lord to continuously self-triage throughout the day. It will become second nature to him."

The earl nodded.

The surgeon continued. "I would also recommend that family and staff begin the courtesy of *requesting* physical contact rather than initiating it."

"Even his mother?" the countess blurted, then covered her mouth with her hand.

"I believe individual family members will find a happy balance." The surgeon returned the countess's smile.

She continued. "Is this indifference to pain related to his slow development to speak?"

"I believe not, your ladyship."

"What prompts this opinion?" she inquired.

"Your son Richard, if I may, is not reticent to express an opinion or an observation in the short time we have spent together. He *chooses* when to speak and how much. As time passes, he will become more comfortable and, therefore, will speak more. He is aware that the scarring on his tongue delays, but does not prohibit, speaking normally. What that manner is, only time will tell. He is alert, bright, and strong—quite strong. He will adapt."

The countess relaxed, a slight smile playing around her mouth.

The earl stood. "Mr. Burton, see my man of business today. We welcome you as a Matlock retainer."

"Yes, Mr. Burton. You have lightened my heart. Please join the earldom," invited the countess.

Mr. Burton nodded his assent. "Thank you, your lordship, your ladyship. I shall."

"Smythe." Again, the Matlock butler entered the study. "See to Mr. Burton's comfort and requests." Mr. Burton bowed and exited the study. Lord Matlock resumed his place.

The earl looked at his wife and opened his arms. She nestled in, laid her head on his shoulder, and succumbed to his embrace. Together, like their youngest son, they sat in silence.

Three days later

Letter to Thomas Bennet from David Burton—

My friend,

I hope this missive finds you and finds you well.

I endeavor to learn as much as I can, providing service and care for those who can see past their prejudices regarding physicians over surgeons. I know you will appreciate the irony that the tailor population continues to outpace that of the Quality, mayhap upon this peccadillo alone!

Your instruction to an introduction to the F_________ family of

M______ succeeded, as you described. The results of the endeavor you cannot imagine.

My introduction to the E & C of M was perfunctory, although I admit surprise that the C of M has the same eyes as the child. The very same. It is quite astonishing!

I cannot support your belief the family is involved in this nefarious business. I have spent days with their younger son who has unique and captivating health matters.

I shall keep my ears open as I have accepted the offer to join the earldom as a medical retainer.

Keep well. Advise me further as you learn more.

David Burton

Chapter 5

April 1787

Lady Audrey Fitzwilliam commiserated with Lady Anne Darcy about the trials of multiple children. A sumptuous tea tray remained untouched. Sitting side-by-side on a comfortable sofa, Anne held her sister's hands as she absorbed her laments.

"Anne, how wrong I was in my assumption that the ease of raising twins would be solved through the purchase of two of everything. Langston and Richard are as opposite as if they were two children from unrelated families."

Anne shook her head, not in censure but in sympathy. "Audrey dear, what has anchored such an opinion in your mind?"

"Langston is the quintessential viscount. He owns the Fitzwilliam light hair and blue eyes. He cries out his wants. He has already molded his nursing staff to his whims. He is a darling. His cherubic face is everything happy. There is no doubt he is the future of the earldom."

Anne grinned at her best friend. *What mother does not boast of their*

heir? "What of Richard?"

Audrey sighed. "I do not know what to do, Anne. Richard, with his dark hair and his near-black eyes, is everything opposite considering his Fitzwilliam and Langston roots."

"Oh, Audrey, neither you, nor I, and certainly not these men posing as healers, could ever possibly understand the will of the Almighty. To think so is inane. But do go on, dear…what of Richard?"

"Richard neither cries nor babbles. He makes sounds, little grunts, when he wants attention, but I cannot describe it…he seems to bask in silence. He sits in solitude and observes. Other than his nurse humming to him, which makes him smile, he remains quiet. It is quite disconcerting."

"A quiet child? This is your complaint?"

"You are not attending me, Sister. I am speaking of Richard's singularity in everything he chooses. Take his clothing. He refuses to wear anything not resembling a livery. The more military, the more accepting he is of the garment. One nurse refused to accommodate him, so he passed the entire day in the nursery in his smalls!"

Anne laughed, her musical tone clearing the angst from her sister's brow. "Audrey dear, indulge the child. It is whimsy."

Dissatisfied at her sister's dismissal of her fears, Audrey resorted to pouring tea and changed the subject. "How fares William and his riding lessons?"

Mrs. Demelza Benson, the name by which her employers knew her, sat in the most comfortable chair in the nursery. She read aloud from *The History of Little Goody Two-Shoes* to her charge, Langston Fitzwilliam, the future of the Matlock earldom. The child listened yet would look off to his toys longingly. Entertaining a four-year-old who recognized his privilege was difficult.

"Master Langston, what do you think of Miss Margery's adventures?"

"Girls are boring."

"Oh my, whatever shall you do with your sisters?"

"I did not ask for sisters. I already had a stupid brother."

"Master Langston, please do not use such common language regarding Master Richard. You are a Fitzwilliam, sir."

"I want another story. Find me another story!" he demanded.

Spoiled child! Wants for nothing and yet demands everything. "Very well, Master Langston. Let us to the library to look for something more entertaining."

Mrs. Benson held out her hand, expecting compliance. She was disappointed.

"I am not a baby. I can walk by myself."

"As you wish."

The pair walked to the library in silence. Upon entering, Mrs. Benson saw they were alone.

"Behave yourself while I find a tale to entertain us. Mind me now, young man!"

She was pleased to see the heir sit properly.

Perusing the selection, she found a treasure, which she pulled from the well-populated shelves: a bound collection written by Charles Perrault, containing *The Sleeping Beauty in the Wood* and *Tales and Stories of Times Past with Morals: Tales of Mother Goose.*

"Master Langston, I have found our next few weeks' entertainment. I believe you will be well pleased. Let us back to the nursery, enjoy a cup of cocoa, and settle in."

Langston jumped up. "Cocoa. I want cocoa!"

The pair returned to the nursery, and Mrs. Benson pulled the bell cord. A young maid appeared.

"A cup of cocoa for the master, Amy."

"Yes, mum."

Mrs. Benson settled into her chair and began reading.

"Once upon a time, there lived a king and queen who were grieved, more grieved than words can tell because they had no children..."

Mrs. Benson read until the young heir fell asleep. She wondered how long she could continue fooling the staff. They had no idea she was not Mrs. Demelza Benson but Mrs. Hannah Berenson, a widow with no living family or prospects. Her perfect credentials were forgeries, given to her by a protector she called "Uncle." On her half day, she spoke with the heavy man about what passed beneath Matlock's eaves. He seemed quite interested.

When she asked why he had aided her, he would smile and remind her to enjoy the condescension of the Great Lady. She once remarked that she had yet to thank the countess, but he informed her he worked for another. He never did tell her the Great Lady's name and insisted she make the best of the position until they discovered her fraud, for when that occurred, she would return to his employ at the house behind St. James's Street. So, she did and would continue to do so until she had to leave and seek another situation.

Chapter 6

Pemberley, May 1789

Lady Theodosia Manners-Sutton and Lady Anne Darcy, arm in arm, strolled the luscious lanes of Pemberley's gardens. The two ladies formed a pretty pair; their colorful pelisses and gowns were complemented by the more subdued livery worn by the trailing footmen.

"I am delighted to have you at Pemberley, my dear Thea. It has been too long since we have spent time together not encumbered by mourning weeds."

"I cannot disagree with you, who are one of our Lord's earthly representations, can I?"

"Ever the provocateur, I daresay. Goodness, you do enjoy poking at the Lord and tempting fate, my friend."

Thea stopped, forcing Anne to do the same. A glance over her shoulder warned the footmen to stay back. Thea leaned closer. "Speaking of tempting fate, dear Anne, I see your hand wandering to your waist.

I hope that it is merely indigestion and not the alternative."

Anne looked perplexed. "You truly expect me to discuss such private matters here in the open garden? Surely, you jest."

Thea harrumphed and continued walking. "Nothing more need be said, I fear. I am not reluctant to remind you of the secrets we shared in Canterbury when you came to pay your respects to my late husband."

"Thea, nobody else is like you. You are unequaled in wit, intelligence, and connections. Had you lived two hundred-odd years ago, we would read of *you* rather than that verbose little Italian man every politician deems to revere."

Thea threw her head back and laughed, producing an incredible throaty, sultry intonation that had the footmen bow their heads and look at their shoes lest they be seen gawking at the sheer sensuality of the sound. They would whisper of it when in private but define it as pleasing, as a Manners-Sutton née Cavendish would never consent to a bawdy description of their person, and Lady Theodosia, of course, was a Manners-Sutton née Cavendish.

"Imagine, my dear Anne, these masters of the universe planning, talking, and failing in their negotiations because they never understand Theodosia Machiavelli. How droll!"

Anne laughed. "How I have missed our little tête-à-têtes, Thea."

They walked for another hour before returning to the manor house right before the sounding of the dinner gong.

The meal was an intimate and merry party. George Darcy was solicitous of both ladies, allowing them to lead while he sat back and waited for the conversation to come to him. Well acquainted with Thea Manners-Sutton, he knew that there was no way to escape being cut by her rapier-like wit. Darcy could not help smiling to himself, recalling the setdowns that had eviscerated his wife's elder sister, Catherine, time and time again.

Even avoiding engagement did not spare him of Thea's thirst for repartee. "I see you woolgathering, George. Dare you share your pleasant musings?"

"I do dare," he replied, hoping for gallantry. Anne's melodic chuckle drew him into her song, and his gaze snapped away from their guest to his wife.

Thea sipped her wine, eyes bright with provocation. "I do not understand why you two ever entertain. Your fixation on each other is adorable. Even the cynics of the *ton* comprehended as such the first time you, George, solicited a dance from Anne. It gives me hope for the future of your heir to see such amiability between his parents."

Darcy remained silent, unsure how to answer. Anne reached over and put her hand on his arm. He visibly flinched.

Thea scowled. "Surely, you share your story, your history, your passion with William."

George Darcy's face turned to stone. "Madam, you must refrain from commenting on matters so personal. I respect your long-standing friendship with my wife, but I ask that you observe propriety when toying with our privacy."

Anne Darcy stood. "Come, Thea. Join me in the music room. I believe Mr. Darcy has work to complete."

Darcy watched the ladies glide from the room. He did not know how he lost control of the evening, but he signaled to a footman, who cleared the table. Darcy, though, forwent drinks and cigars, choosing to go to his study as his wife suggested.

In the music room, Thea turned on her friend, quivering in anger. "I do not understand, nor can I condone your husband's negligence toward your son's emotional education. This indifference cannot continue."

"My dear Thea, I do not have your independent streak nor means to allow me the freedom to dispute my husband. I take my marriage vows, sworn in front of the Almighty, quite seriously. I am not saying you did not, but you are your own mistress thanks to generous marriage articles that I, unfortunately, could not demand."

Thea sighed. "Yes, I commiserate with you that your brother had to bribe a fraudster to claim your elder sister's hand and you—your dowry—became their victim."

The shrug in Anne's voice echoed throughout the room. "What is past is past, my friend."

Thea stopped pacing and sat next to her friend. "Anne, you must not let your son continue the Darcy ancestral reserve. It stinks of disdain, as if all Darcys are above their company. Promise me you will intervene."

Anne looked at her friend. "Whatever do you mean? William knows how much I love him. I enjoy spending time with him."

Thea shook her head. "No, Anne. The affectations of this male-dominated society will repress your son's heart and stifle that which makes him so unique and attractive. I beg you to attend to him more. I realize your husband is of a mind to adhere to those outdated and harmful forms of ignoring a child until one perceives him as a rational being."

"Thea, do not mistake shyness for complacency."

"Were it complacency, I would call it so. I may grant you 'reticence.' Either in this matter is unwelcome—more so, intolerable."

"I understand your point and admire your courage, so I shall agree upon a condition."

"Anything, Anne. I am yours to command."

Anne laughed, her aria once again calling out to her partner.

Thea closed her eyes and shook her head. Time, like the tide, waited for no man. None of them knew how precious and short a loved one's life might be. Childbirth, even for the healthiest, was a woman's greatest danger. Anne's history of failure to carry another child made her more of a future victim than other women were. Thea refocused on her friend as she cleared her maudlin thoughts.

"Should you ever learn of William's doubt and his eschewing his own heart, you must take him in hand. Promise me." Thea looked her friend in the eye as the door to the music room opened.

"I promise."

Lambton, the next day

The Manners-Sutton carriage drew much attention; its pristine, gleaming black surfaces reflected the spring sunlight in all directions. Thea and Anne toured the village shops, making purchases all along the High Street and generating goodwill.

"What a delightful tearoom," remarked Thea, looking across the street.

"Yes, I adore the décor. My husband assisted the owners, and they have made quite the success of it."

"Excellent. A quick stop in the bookstore, followed by a splendid tea tray. What a lovely thought."

The ladies crossed the street, led by one footman, flanked by two more, and trailed by a fourth. Thea looked at her mob of guards. "We have made quite the spectacle of ourselves. Portman, go inside and remain out of the way. You three may post yourselves outside and around the back." Portman entered the shop, looked around, then nodded to his mistress.

Thea noticed Anne shaking her head, assuming it was more in humor than dismay. Anne would wither if forced to live in Thea Manners-Sutton's aerie. Thea was the first to admit that wealth, when taken seriously and managed responsibly, made one uncomfortable. In her opinion, the more wealth, the fewer comforts. Thea herself had *no* comfort as her connections, wealth, and influence were of such elevated proportions. Yet, with eyes wide open, she had entered that realm—entered it and embraced it as no woman, nor most men, ever had before.

Anne followed Thea into the bookstore. They browsed and chose a few volumes to purchase. The shopkeeper, having run out of twine, turned to the rear and asked for more. A young girl with brunette hair, showing the first hints of womanhood, handed the man his request. She kept her eyes down, respecting the Quality.

"What a lovely daughter you have, sir," remarked Thea.

"My niece, my lady," he replied.

"Anne, may I have an introduction?"

"Thea, this is Mr. Eriksen. My husband claims no one can procure new editions better than he can. I have not had the pleasure of meeting his niece."

Anne turned to the bookstore owner. "Mr. Eriksen, allow me to introduce you to Lady Theodosia Manners-Sutton, of London."

Mr. Eriksen bowed low. He rose a bit unsteadily, then gestured to his niece.

"It is an honor, my lady. It is my pleasure to introduce my niece, Maddy Wells." The young girl curtsied, keeping her eyes down.

"Maddy, this is her ladyship with Mrs. Darcy."

"Thank you for the introduction. Might I ask to enjoy the complete beauty of your niece, sir? She is a well-mannered young lady. What can we do to entice her to gift us with a smile?" asked Thea.

"Give our noble guests a smile, will you not, dear?"

The young lady, hands clasped in front of her skirt, looked up and smiled, her violet eyes illuminating her face. Anne Darcy gasped.

Thea's eyes narrowed, and her ire was instantaneous. "Portman!"

Thea shifted her gimlet gaze to the bookseller, satisfied by the immediate loud whistle. Heavy boots stomped into the shop, and the breathable air thinned as the odor of men—large men—invaded.

"Mistress?"

"Send for the magistrate."

"Yes, mistress."

Footsteps pounded away. The door slammed shut.

Thea continued to glare at the bookseller, his eyes open as wide as his mouth.

"Mr. Eriksen, we must have a conversation."

"Must we, milady?"

Thea heard confusion, not fear. "We must. Where may we sit?"

"Our rooms are above the shop. Not to your standards, milady, but I offer them freely."

"That will do. Portman."

Portman grasped the bookseller's elbow and allowed him to lead them to a staircase at the back of the shop.

The party marched up the steps. Another footman, his pistols evident in his wide belt, remained at the bottom.

The four principals seated themselves, Portman standing behind the young lady and her uncle.

"Mr. Eriksen, tell me of your niece."

"Maddy?"

"Is it Maddy? Or is it something more formal?"

"It has always been Maddy, milady."

"Has it? And for how long has it 'always been' Maddy?"

"Well, everyone knows, milady. Maddy came to live with me and me wife—Lord rest her soul—when her uncle died."

"Her uncle, you say?"

"Yes, milady. Her uncle."

"And who was this uncle?"

"He would have been the Parson Wells, milady."

"Mr. Eriksen, I must insist that you expand upon your answers."

"Of course, milady. I did not aim to be difficult. 'Twas Reverend Vernon Wells of Flaxby Knares, who passed on all these years ago. He bade me wife and me to take Maddy in hand, them being his final words. Him being me good boyhood friend, we could do no less."

Thea turned to the girl. "Miss."

The young lady, hands clasped in her lap, did not look up.

"Miss Maddy, please pay me respect and look at me."

Maddy looked up, wet amethysts glowing through her tears. Thea saw a young Audrey Langston.

"What is your name, child?"

"Maddy Wells, mum."

"You are sure of this?"

"I am Maddy Wells, mum."

"Who are your people, Maddy Wells?"

The young lady shook her head.

A banging noise below was followed by thumping on the stairs.

"Mistress."

"Yes?"

"The magistrate is at 'is estate."

"Thank you. That will be all."

Thea's anger abated. *What would scare a child to the point she denies her heritage? Well, this is not the time or place.*

"Mr. Eriksen, I ask you to forgive my severe approach to this misunderstanding."

"Think nothing of it, milady."

Thea turned to the young lady.

"Maddy, should you ever require assistance, know you only have to send a message to Mrs. Darcy at Pemberley in my name. Do you understand?"

"Yes, mum."

"So that I may earn your trust, I will not reveal your exact location, nor will Mrs. Darcy. Should you leave here, you or your uncle must inform me."

"Yes, mum."

"Portman, prepare the carriage."

Thea kept staring at Maddy as her guards stomped down the stairs.

"Maddy, you are not alone. When you are ready, know that I shall move heaven and earth to bring you back to your family. Your relations miss you and love you, child."

Maddy kept her eyes down, acknowledging nothing.

"Good day, Mr. Eriksen. My man of business will send you our purchase requests in the future. Thank you for your attendance."

"Thank you, milady."

Once the carriage cleared the town limits, Anne reached over and gripped her friend's hand.

"Thea, tell me all. Leave nothing out."

Thea took the walking cane from the sideboard and rapped the carriage ceiling. The carriage coasted to a halt. Portman opened the door and offered his hand. Both ladies accepted his assistance out of the carriage, then walked down the road, heads together, whispering.

Portman followed a short distance behind. His hand never strayed from the pistol in his belt.

The ladies returned to Pemberley quite late—the sun had nearly dipped entirely behind the Peak. Thea requested a tray for dinner, sending a note of apology to her hosts. She had many letters to write. Anne would entertain her husband in the music room, singing to keep his mind off their late return from the village.

Maddy watched through her bedroom window as the *Regal Lady* and Mrs. Darcy entered the carriage. She worried about the future, her fears once again flaming to life. She hugged a ragged doll to her breast.

"Come save me, Captain Bennet," she whispered to herself, hoping against hope. "Save me, please."

Suffolk, August 1789

"Reggie" Hurst was not a firstborn son. Raised a gentleman, he took after his father far more than his older brother, who quickly cloaked himself in the behaviors of those whose incomes were assured through the birth order lottery. Like his father, Reggie was intelligent and passionate about his future, though unburdened by inheritance concerns. Also akin to his father, young Hurst was a patriot, loyal to King and country. Reggie did not desire a scarlet coat, a traditional destination for second sons disinclined to don a barrister's robe in favor of more active pursuits. He, though, had been enough of his father's child to watch and listen to the comings and goings at their Suffolk estate to accept that there were other avenues open to him. He bearded the old lion in his study.

"Join me for a game of chess, Reggie."

"Gladly, Father."

They sat down at the board, his father taking white, a rarity in their match play. Several exchanges in, Reggie was confused. His father seemed to be playing a different game.

Reggie sat back, closed his eyes, and reviewed his father's moves. Something niggled at him. He studied the board and realized his father's aim. He made his next move and smiled as his father pursed his lips.

The game continued. Upon the eleventh move, Reggie jumped his knight over a wall of pawns and captured his father's queen. "That is mate, father."

"My king remains, Reggie."

"Ah, but you have been playing otherwise, sir. I understood so upon your fourth move."

"Very good, son. Very good. I am quite pleased with your discernment. Call for tea. I have some letters to write."

Reggie enjoyed his father's praise and subsequent attention that day. He did not know that his father agreed with his son's view that there were other ways to serve the Crown. An influential gentleman, his father presented him with an invitation to an exclusive house party—one attended by a group of gentlemen in a private home below Cambridge. Reggie understood it to be Cambridge because that is what he was told; his hosts had conducted his entrance into the estate under cover of darkness. Since the location was of no importance, he cared not regarding the accuracy of the revelation.

The carefully furnished manor provided no sign—not the

architecture, furniture, or artwork—of the identity or history of the owners. He spent a week speaking with gentlemen of all shapes and sizes. He knew he was being observed, but it was not until the third day that he understood the way they were evaluating him. So, he embraced the opportunity with fervor.

He listened more and spoke less. He prompted conversations with one group by relating altered bits from another. He planted quips in one conversation and then waited to hear them repeated. Invariably, the bon mots were spoken as if they were original offerings from other guests. He never tipped that the reference was supplied by him. Days later, they rewarded him.

The seventh day of the house party saw him awakened at dawn by the house under-valet. He acknowledged the extraordinary morning reveille, completed his toilet, and thanked the servant for his attendance. In the dining room, every gentleman with whom he had met and spoken throughout the week was present.

A footman helped him into his chair, and another served him all the foods he enjoyed from other sittings. *They have watched me, as I thought.* He tucked into his food, the meal a welcome perquisite of this foray into the unknown. Conversation ensued, and Reggie was an active participant, ensuring he addressed each of his tablemates by name, including any and every tidbit of information he had gathered during the house party. After the host signaled for the footmen to depart, none of the diners rose. The last servant from the room closed the doors behind him. After half a minute, three knocks followed by two more rang out. The host, having looked to the doors as the knocking began, refocused down the long board and appeared to be taking a straw poll of all the diners except Reggie.

He was intrigued as he was obviously the subject of their deliberations. He recalled a pamphlet about the Wars of the Roses. *Glad I had some toast,* he mused, recalling enemy emissaries remaining unharmed after bread had been served.

The host addressed Reggie. "Hurst, we would like to know your impressions of the house party."

He seemed to have passed muster if they addressed him by the familiar "Hurst." He paused. "Although it is a hypothesis, I believe I have been—am—under scrutiny."

"And does your hypothesis offer insights?"

Hurst believed that the host wore a pleased expression on his face. "I daresay, it does, my lord. And may I express that it is my honor to make your acquaintance, Sir John."

"Well done, Hurst, well done. You are correct. I am Sir John Beckett."

"May I surmise the Home Office has hosted me for this extraordinary event?" asked Hurst, now most confident in his hypothesis.

"You may. Please refer to me as 'C.' These other gentlemen, all from the Drey, are pleased to welcome you." All the diners stood and bowed, one of the crowd applauding while another smiled and made a pistol with his forefinger and mimed shooting.

Hurst bowed to both sides of the table and reclaimed his seat. Beckett waited for the multitude to quiet. "We are going to send you home for a fortnight so that you may take your leisure. A courier will deliver your instructions. Expect to be away from home for quite a while, my young friend."

"Of course," affirmed Hurst.

The gentleman who had made the pistol gesture cleared his throat. Hurst acknowledged both the spoken messenger and the unspoken message. "I understand that the utmost discretion is required, gentlemen."

"C" led the way to the parlor where the men broke into smaller groups. Hurst circulated, listened, and collected information. That afternoon, he stepped into a carriage and headed back to his family's estate. He found he enjoyed the "games" as his new superior, the finger-pistol gentleman, referred to them.

Hurst spent the next six months traveling from house party to house party, playing the part of a son of the *ton* but taking part in few of the expected activities. Instead, he trained with military men, intelligence operatives, martial arts masters, cryptographers, and field agents. Contrary to his status as a gentleman, Hurst also observed senior members of the Bow Street Runners. While working with those men, he helped solve a kidnap-for-ransom scheme.

Kidnapping was a misdemeanor under common law. The guilty, if captured, were liable to be fined at the very worst. Without the deterrence of a felony classification and its severe punishments, debt-ridden estate owners or tradesmen would hire thugs to abduct and hold unprotected heiresses. The ensuing threat of scandalous compromise would lead to marriage and the floating of financial hulks on the women's dowries. These were the essentials of the Aronson case. Someone wished to take advantage of this family of wealthy Jewish merchants who stood astride London's precious-metals trade.

The patriarch, Abraham Aronson, hired Bow Street to recover his sixteen-year-old daughter Rivkah, who had been missing for four hours. The Beak and his minions listened most intently, never once considering his concern frivolous. Mr. Aronson had retained *every* runner working for Bow Street. A large bag of silver coins ensured the full attention of the fabled investigators.

Hurst joined the initial conversation with the family. He learned that Rivkah's day-to-day routine never wavered. She was a dutiful daughter and observant *meydl*—an unmarried Jewish woman. The Aronson family had no known enemies but offered three surnames in their business circle known to be facing financial woes. Hurst listened to the investigators put a plan together to follow the members of those families. They hoped to recover Rivkah quickly. The words "dutiful" and "observant" had plucked a chord in Hurst's ear.

Hurst cleared his throat. "May I make a recommendation?"

Bow Street's top man nodded as he was the sole person who knew with whom Hurst worked.

"This being Friday, station your men within sight of the windows of the suspected families. The one *not* observing the Sabbath will most likely be your culprit."

Eyes widened at Hurst before exclamations of "By Jove," "Good show," and "Right bugger, that one" filled the air.

That evening, a shaken Rivkah Aronson slept in her bedroom, no worse for wear. She would adapt to her new life: being escorted by two exceptionally large footmen everywhere outside of her home.

By this time, Hurst had built up webs of connections, which he believed was the intent of his superiors. The Aronson Affair added both Bow Street and the Silver Exchange to his collection. The commander of the Bow Street Runners sent a note to Hurst's superiors.

Not two hours after the reduction of the kidnappers, Hurst received an express regarding his next assignment. An earl was waiting to speak with him.

Chapter 7

Matlock House, March 1790

Mrs. Demelza Benson sat in the most comfortable chair in the nursery, listening to her charge read from *The Right Pleasant and Diverting History of Fortunatus and His Two Sons.* Langston Fitzwilliam read in a slow and ponderous manner. It was her opinion that he had the same reading difficulty her younger cousin Miriam Berenson exhibited.

"I demand a story—one I have never heard. These books are boring."

Mrs. Benson closed her eyes and recalled several of the Germanic stories her mother told her brother to scare him into behaving properly. During the following weeks, instead of the Matlock heir improving his reading, he sat rapt in gleeful horror, immersed in the Germanic lore of revenge and retribution of oppressed families.

Hannah Berenson told of the *dybbuk*, a disembodied human spirit wandering in agitation until it could find succor in another human body, driving the host into madness. She told him of the murderess

Lilith, the first woman created by the Lord—even before Eve—who killed women in childbirth and stole their babies. Over and over, she told him of the Golem, a silent, emotionless monster that was unable to be hurt but would kill young, wealthy children for misbehaving.

The Matlock heir sat fascinated by the stories but obsessed upon them when alone. He demanded candles remain lit as he retired at night. He would never admit his fears—or his nightmares, when he remembered them, which were few and forgotten.

The kitchen at Matlock House was in a snit. Cook, snarling at everyone, had a bee in her bonnet.

"Lazy slatterns, get yer 'eads up 'n' wipe 'em down right," she shouted. Undercooks and young footmen leapt at her command as everyone was aware of the party of three in the Matlock parlor—a more august assembly of ladies not seen in a decade.

The Countess of Matlock had finished receiving her calls for the three-hour portion of her Thursday. Gone were the vainglorious baronesses, viscountesses, and countesses.

The flocks of the Royal Menagerie sported fewer feathers than today's visitors wore, mused Smythe, the Matlock butler. The more influential ladies remained to relax in each other's more acceptable companionship.

Audrey Fitzwilliam sighed and relaxed back into her chair, comfortable with her company. Anne Darcy still wore a smile of amusement, the utter obsequiousness of their earlier visitors a lasting diversion. Theodosia Manners-Sutton sat in the chair of honor, enjoying the rare opportunity to spend time with women of wit and compassion, as she viewed her two friends.

"How are your boys, Audrey?" asked Thea.

"Langston is with his father, touring Ashdale. Henry insists on educating his heir to be ready to manage the estate sooner rather than later."

Anne Darcy added, "George has the same plans for William, though I would rather he spend the time getting to know his son's character rather than planning his future."

"And your other son? What of him?" Thea asked Audrey, leaning forward when she saw the countess render a small smile.

The countess rang the bell on her side table. Smythe entered the parlor and inquired, "Yes, your ladyship?"

"Please have Richard come to pay his respects."

"Very good, my lady."

A maid entered the parlor with a tea tray loaded with finger sandwiches and fruit. The ladies served themselves and compared tastes as they waited for the youngster to make his appearance.

A knock on the parlor door alerted the ladies to an arrival. Smythe stepped in. "Master Richard Fitzwilliam."

Thea Sutton watched the young man walk into the parlor, head swiveling back and forth, taking in the company. He walked to his mother stopped and bowed. She nodded, acknowledging his gallantry.

Richard next stood tall in front of his aunt, Lady Anne, and bowed. She, too, nodded, acknowledging his gentlemanly manners.

Richard finally moved to the third woman. He turned his head to look at his mother, waiting for her to start the introduction.

"Richard, allow me to introduce you to Lady Theodosia Cavendish Manners-Sutton, granddaughter of the Duke of Devonshire, cousin to the most reverend primate, the archbishop of Canterbury, and cousin by marriage to my Langston family of Yorkshire and Leeds. Thea, my son Richard."

Thea Sutton held out her hand, admiring the dark-haired, dark-eyed young man with the perfect manners. She noticed he was dressed in subdued military regalia, an affectation that suited him quite well. She allowed Richard to grasp her hand and bow over it. Without releasing it, he lifted his head and locked eyes with her, his coal-blacks staring into her mahoganies. He whispered a polite, "Your Grace."

Thea made an immediate judgment: this young man would receive her approbation. "Lord Richard." She nodded in acknowledgment.

Richard stood straight, released Thea's hand, and nodded at his mother. He repeated the action to his aunt. Turning back to Lady Manners-Sutton, he bowed again, turned, and exited the parlor.

Lady Matlock looked at Thea, who had opened her fan and was putting it to good use. "Are you well, my dear?"

Thea understood the question was not of her health, but of her opinion. "Yes, I daresay I am. Your son Richard…"

"Yes?"

"Your son is…extraordinary, Audrey."

Audrey looked at her sister and saw the same pleased expression on her face that she herself felt. Richard had made quite the conquest, earning the approbation of one such as the exalted Lady Theodosia Cavendish Manners-Sutton.

Lady Audrey and Lady Anne raised their teacups to their guest, and the three ladies continued their visit.

A week later

The surgeon wrote in his journal as Richard practiced his triage protocol. Burton watched his charge from the corner of his eye. "Try closing your eyes. Allow your other senses to note any differences. Do not depend upon your vision alone."

Richard closed his eyes and continued touching each finger to his thumb, over and over five times. He repeated the action with his left hand.

"Remember, it is your extremities that will alert you to an injury."

Richard nodded his understanding.

Burton set aside his quill. "Please remove your shirt."

Richard disrobed.

"I am going to examine you. This will be tactile. May I?"

Richard nodded.

Burton slid his hands over the boy's shoulders and along each arm. He dug his fingers into the armpits. His patient did not respond. Completing the anterior examination, Burton turned Richard around. "Were you aware of this mark?"

Richard shook his head back and forth.

"Verbal, please. We are in protocol."

"No."

Burton had his suspicions. "Have you been in the schoolroom with your brother lately?"

"Yes."

"Was this bruise from planned physical activity?"

"No!"

Burton paused. His patient was quite defensive of his family. *It is only a matter of time before verbal evolves into physical.*

"Please be aware of your surroundings, more so when it comes to people behind you. You will not acknowledge them as an injury threat as others do. You must consider the consequences when others place themselves behind you in the future."

"I shall."

"Such caution will serve you well at Eton."

"I shall not attend Eton."

"No?" asked an interested Burton.

"No."

Burton waited. As his patient offered nothing more, the medico reverted to protocol.

"Your toes, please."

Burton watched his patient's feet. It was difficult to see the toe movements inside his riding boots.

"I am not satisfied."

Richard looked up.

"We shall have to remove your boots."

Richard shook his head. "My batman is not here."

"Your batman?"

"Yes. My batman."

Burton smiled. "Do you have a batman?"

"Not yet."

Burton held his opinion. A valet served the son of an earl. A batman served a military officer. *Interesting.*

"I shall serve as your batman, Lieutenant Fitzwilliam."

Richard shook his head. "Captain."

"Captain?"

"Captain."

"Well, Captain Fitzwilliam, please sit in the chair and lift your leg."

Richard sat and lifted his booted right leg. Burton straddled his leg, his posterior facing the seated young man. Richard snickered.

"This is how we did it in camp. Please pay attention." The surgeon looked over his shoulder. "Place your other boot against my buttocks, Captain."

A booted foot pressed his hindquarters.

"Now push against me with your left foot while pulling out your right. There we go…a bit more…excellent."

Richard's stockinged foot dropped to the floor. Burton handed him his boot.

"One more, Captain."

They repeated the process for the opposite boot. Richard giggled when he placed his stockinged foot against the medical man's derrière. Once his foot was free, Richard accepted his other boot and removed his stockings.

"Place your ankle on your knee. Use either hand to push back against each toe. Use your toe muscle to counter. Like your fingers, five times each."

Richard used his left fingers to pull back his right toes repeatedly, then switched ankles and performed the same task.

"Excellent, Captain. Take advantage of any bootless state of undress to repeat this exercise. Without a functional toe, you will not competently walk or, by your desired future, ride."

"I understand..." A throat cleared. Richard stopped speaking and became still.

"Master Richard, your history tutor awaits your presence in the schoolroom." Richard picked up his boots, nodded to Burton, and followed the Matlock butler into the hall.

David Burton sat down and continued writing in his journal.

...repetitive practice has nearly achieved the unconscious need to perform triage exercises in RF's daily, if not hourly, life. He absorbs his lessons and has yet to repeat any errors in judgment. He is unlike others with his condition I encountered on the battlefield. He is aware he is not invulnerable. I have high hopes for a healthy future for this extraordinary young man...

Chapter 8

April 1790

Langston Fitzwilliam screamed from another terrifying dream. He sat up in bed, hands to his head, blind to his surroundings. His terrified yells escaped through his room into the corridor. His night nurse hurried to him, careful not to drop her candle. Placing it safely out of reach, she sat on the bed, hugged her charge, and rubbed his back until his cries tailed off into whimpers. She laid him back down, secured his coverlet, picked up the candle, and left. The bedroom door remained open.

Langston was roused very early by his morning nurse. The young viscount was tired but did not recall he had had a nightmare.

He joined his twin brother at the dining table in the schoolroom. Such was a rarity as the heir tended to sleep in; the spare greeted the dawn each morning. Richard ate his meal silently. He gave his brother's entrance no notice. Langston ignored him as he considered his younger twin brother "cannon fodder," a term he remembered overhearing from one of his father's stuffy old friends.

Langston sat down to a prepared plate. After taking a couple of bites, he turned to Richard. Richard stared back, unintimidated, a blank expression on his face.

Langston choked on his meal. Fear. Overwhelming fear. He jumped up violently. His chair crashed to the floor behind him. Frantic, he looked for assistance, but no one came to help him. Crazed and finding breathing difficult, Langston grabbed a fork off the table. His younger twin continued to stare at him, emotionless. With a shout, the viscount stabbed the utensil into his brother's hand where it rested on the table. The tines sank in deep and lodged in the bones. Richard looked up at him with an upraised eyebrow but remained silent as blood welled up from the wounds.

Langston pointed at his brother. The night terrors crashed back into his psyche with hurricane gale force. His breath came back, so he screamed. He wailed. "He's a golem…a golem! Uh, uh, uh…"

Langston collapsed to the floor, hugging his knees to his chest, and rocked back and forth, whimpering over and over, "Save me…save me…save me…"

A door slammed against a wall as Langston felt a blanket wrap around him. He was lifted from the floor. He sensed it was Smythe, but the Matlock butler had never touched him before.

"Find Mr. Burton!"

Langston closed his eyes and fainted as he was carried away.

The remaining staff stood in place unmoving, bewildered at what they were to do. They stared at each other and not at the young child. Richard continued to sit at the table with a fork lodged in his hand. He alone fixated on the offending item.

Richard's nurse entered the dining room and, with hesitance, extended her hand, silently asking permission to touch him. He gave her his injured hand; the fork standing tall for all to see and allowed Siobhan to lead him out of the room, and back into the nursery.

The earl looked up at the soft and tentative knock. *Not a Smythe knock.* His hackles rose. "Enter."

A footman he did not recognize hesitated at the door.

"Out with it, man."

"Your…your…your lord…lordship…"

The earl could not help himself, his frustration spilled over into his voice. "SMYTHE!"

Smythe appeared, scowled, and snapped his fingers. The young footman ran off. "My lord, we have had a most distressing incident."

"Have we?"

"Yes, my lord. The viscount has had a troublesome encounter with his brother. Lord Hopton has fainted. Master Richard was injured. Mr. Burton has isolated the heir from his brother and is ministering to them both."

"Where is the countess?"

"We expect her ladyship to return within the hour."

"Have her lady's maid attend her while we sort this out. Her chambers would be best."

"Anything else, my lord?"

"Gather the heir's staff so Mr. Dolan may learn more of this dispute."

Smythe returned an hour later and led the earl below stairs and into the staff common room. All scrambled to their feet, their apprehension apparent. No one spoke or whispered as they stared at the earl.

"With whom are we meeting?" he inquired.

Smythe introduced each nurse, footman, and tutor—ten in all. The earl sat and nodded to Mr. Dolan, his man of business.

A nondescript, lean man, Mr. Dolan donned a pair of spectacles and pulled out a journal. He asked numerous general questions of each servant present; their answers spoke to the repetitive nature of the inquiry. The earl held up his hand.

"Yes, my lord?" asked Smythe.

"Release all back to their duties, save Mrs. Benson."

Smythe complied.

"You have not been forthcoming, madam."

Mrs. Benson looked down at her clasped hands.

"Smythe."

"Yes, my lord?"

"Fetch Bill."

"*Bill*, my lord?"

"Bill!" barked the earl.

Bill Steele worked in the mews, always remaining at the back of the house. He never came inside, even taking his meals in the laundry shed. He kept to himself and away from the servants' floor. At more than six and a half feet and nineteen stone, he was the largest man most would ever see. Burn scars that covered the left side of his face and hands were most repulsive. Yet, horses responded well to his gentle touch, soothing voice, and genial manner. The other grooms respected him for his ability to lift anything and everything, although they made sure to avoid him otherwise. Richard adored him as he always had a piece of hard candy to reward his never-ending questions, and the giant seemed to be the only person the young lord allowed to pick him up and place him upon the different mounts in the stalls. Bill revered the Fitzwilliam family; they gave him employment and board when no others would, for Bill was a pariah everywhere but in the Matlock House easement.

Mr. Dolan glared daggers at Mrs. Benson as Smythe left through the door leading to the mews.

The earl continued to stare at Mrs. Benson, who shook from crying silently.

A minute later, a door opened, allowing but a brief bit of daylight to flow through. Then, the doorway went dark. A scarred mountain walked into the room.

Mrs. Benson gasped. She then fainted.

"Well done, Bill," granted the earl.

"Your humble servant, your lordship," he rasped.

Smythe revived the woman by passing a bottle of smelling salts beneath her nose. She glanced warily at the earl.

"Confess all and you will avoid the gallows. Bill?"

Bill walked behind her and put his massive hands on the back of her chair. His knuckles brushed her shoulders. She shuddered, took a halting breath, and confessed, never looking up. Mr. Dolan scribed her statement that included her true name, Hannah Berenson, her owning fraudulent references, and her reporting the house's activities to her patron, her "uncle." She could not name him. She described him as stout but not overly fat. She had noticed no distinguishing marks on his person. He always wore a hat.

The earl nodded. Bill fisted his hands. Hannah Berenson—no longer "Mrs. Benson"—recoiled and completed her tale.

Mr. Dolan added her admission of the patronage of the nameless "Great Lady." Berenson tearfully vowed that she wished she could offer more, but she was dry.

The earl looked splenic. "Keep her isolated in her chamber until we learn more." Smythe led the quivering woman from the room. Mr. Dolan left with Bill.

The earl returned upstairs and sent word that he awaited the countess in her sitting room. She joined him minutes later, smiling her surprise. Two sentences later, her happiness—but not the shock—evaporated. She flew toward the nursery and her children. For another hour, the earl watched his wife pace back and forth in front of a closed and locked nursery door. Every time a cry broke through the thick oak panel, she stopped moving until peace was restored.

Smythe rounded the corner to ask whether the couple desired any refreshments. Lady Matlock shook her head and continued her march. The door rattled in its frame as the deadbolt was slid back. The countess glared at the earl, ready to take him to task for his laxness in ensuring the boys were protected. The door's opening stalled her reprimand.

Mr. Burton stepped out and closed the door behind him, implicitly barring admission to the lady.

The Matlock medico spoke in a low voice. "The viscount is resting. I have given him a mild draught. I doubt whether he will remember what happened. Master Richard's injuries, while bloody, are more disquieting than dangerous. With Miss Siobhan's assistance, I removed the fork and cleaned the punctures. I fear that I used a few drams of my lord's best brandy. If they do not fester, they will heal with only the most minor of scars. There is more, but I would prefer not to share it with the hallway. May we confer in private?"

Lady Matlock led the men to her sitting room and dismissed her lady's maid with a look.

The three of them conferred for an hour, and when it ended after tears, anger, threats directed at others not present, and considerable dismay, Mr. Burton departed. The Fitzwilliam family was destined to be fractured. The twins could no longer live together; one had attacked the other, and it was only a matter of time before that boy would defend himself, probably in a lethal manner. Richard would live at Ashdale, the Matlock estate in Derbyshire. Langston had to remain in London where he could be examined and treated. During the summer, when town's miasmas became especially dangerous, Langston would go to Ashdale while Richard spent those months somewhere else, possibly with his younger cousin at Pemberley.

The countess stood and began pacing again to incinerate her frustration. The earl channeled his fury into the contemplation of a glass of brandy. Lady Matlock could not shake the lingering thought that she had been a bad parent and was being punished. How she wished for Anne. Her goodness and tranquility would be a comfort. But that was impossible; Anne was in her confinement at Pemberley. Audrey closed her eyes, her cousin Penny coming to mind. If not Anne, then Penny would have been perfect.

Where were her Lambert cousins? Penny, Maddy, even the resolute

Hugh. Never-ending travels. Plans changed on what seemed to be a whim. Who were these men to rend apart families so heartlessly, so thoughtlessly? WHO! Lady Matlock stopped in place and spun around to face her husband, her right finger in his face, her left fisted on her hip.

"Hear me now, Henry Fitzwilliam!"

The earl gaped up at his wife. She had never spoken to him with the controlled fury she showed at that moment. This new version of his wife frightened him.

"This nonsense from the North must stop. Infrequent letters. Sudden trips abroad. Frequent changes of plans—for years? Langstons do NOT miss weddings or baptisms! Something is amiss. It must stop immediately, I say! An outsider has breached our family felicity and rendered harm. Irreparable harm. It will not do! Find my cousins. Find them and bring them back to the fold. You WILL attend to this, AM I CLEAR, sir?"

The Earl of Matlock adored his wife and worshiped her unique violet eyes every chance she allowed him. He immediately capitulated.

"Yes, dearest," then admitted he already had started the search for the answers she demanded. She thanked him, then asked him to put every servant through a rigorous examination to root out any other similar foolishness lurking near her children. He agreed.

Neither noticed the small, bandaged hand that closed the servants' door, which had been ajar.

Chapter 9

"Sir John Beckett."

The earl stood to welcome a most secretive man. Matlock knew that Beckett led the kingdom's internal intelligence service. Sir John was not a man to treat lightly.

The earl felt he had seen him before, although he could not be categorized as memorable. Beckett was of medium height, medium build, and neutral-colored of hair and eye. *I would forget him in an instant if I had not an earlier acquaintance. He is the human equivalent of smoke.*

"Good afternoon, Lord Matlock. You summoned me. How may I assist you?"

The two men sat. The earl did the pretty and offered refreshments. The intelligence chief declined and sat silent, waiting for the aristocrat to begin the proceedings.

"I have two personal matters upon which I need your assistance."

Sir John nodded.

"I believe something nefarious has occurred with our Lambert cousins."

"Mr. and Mrs. Hugh Lambert?"

The earl could not keep his eyebrows from rising. "Yes, the

Lamberts of Tang Hall."

"The Yorkshire daughter of the bishop of Leeds."

"Yes."

"What is the situation?"

The earl took a moment to recompose himself.

"The Lamberts failed to attend our wedding in April, '82, citing business interests. They never stop traveling. They change their plans upon every inquiry. We have had no correspondence from Hugh nor their daughter Madeleine."

"Anything else?"

"I have had a letter from a close connection that fears for Hugh and Penny. There is a suspicion that young Madeleine is the ward of a family in trade in a northern shire."

Sir John looked directly at the earl. "A close connection, Lord Matlock?"

"Yes, Beckett."

"May I *inquire* of this connection?"

"You may."

"You are being less than forthcoming. May I inquire why?"

"The communication is from Lady Theodosia Cavendish Manners-Sutton."

Sir John's eyes widened. "One needs to tread carefully when invoking that lady's name."

"I agree. I may be an earl, but I am a sparrow when it comes to the eagles in her aerie."

Sir John held up his hand. "Thank you. I have heard enough to turn my eye to your difficulty. What is the second matter?"

"A nurse infiltrated our staff with forged references provided by a patron. The nurse refers to her patron's sponsor as 'the Great Lady.' She is more fearful of retribution from this lady's ire than any punishment a magistrate would mete out."

An intrigued Sir John nodded. "Hmm...Lord Matlock, I am going to send a young man to see you. Do not let his age lead you to believe

I am not taking this situation seriously. The gentleman has one of the sharpest minds I have encountered in many years." He fished a folded paper from his waistcoat and handed it to the earl.

"Let us see what he stirs up, shall we? Until we can classify either of your complaints as a crime against the crown, he will report to you as you will support him."

"Of course, Beckett."

Sir John stared at the earl. He cleared his throat. "Lord Matlock, allow me to be frank."

"Please do."

"You want answers. Answers do not come without cost. Be prepared to see these things through, no matter the consequences."

The study door opened, and the countess stepped in. "Cousin Hugh!"

Sir John stood and bowed.

A startled Lord Matlock recovered himself. The countess was correct—Sir John bore a striking resemblance to their northern cousin.

"My dear, this is Sir John Beckett of the Home Office."

"Oh dear. Forgive me." The countess glided over and extended her hand to the knight. "I am pleased to make your acquaintance, Sir John."

"Likewise, madam."

"Thank you for seeing us. I trust you will be able to assist my husband," she replied, casting the encounter as personal, not political, while emphasizing a level of interest on her part.

Sir John bowed and exited the study.

The countess glanced down at the paper he was holding. "What is in the note, dear?"

"The name of a young man who will assist us."

"What is his name? Do we know his people?"

The earl unfolded the message. "A Mr. Reginald Hurst."

A WELL-DRESSED GENTLEMAN WALKED TOWARD THE EARL, BOWED, and waited to be addressed.

"Good morning, Mr. Hurst."

"My lord."

"May I inquire as to your knowledge of this endeavor?"

"You may, sir, but I may choose not to answer. I would prefer, with your indulgence, to listen to your tale."

"My word, you give your opinion rather decidedly for so young a person."

"Yet, I am standing here ready to assist you, your lordship."

The earl sized up the crown agent. He noticed neither conceit nor pride.

Nodding toward a chair, he began after Hurst sat. "Very well, let us begin."

The earl picked up a document and read a chronological list of names, events, and letters received. He held up the correspondence his wife had received from her cousin before they failed to show up for the wedding, as well as those received during their extended travels. The earl stopped talking as he noticed the young man was taking no notes.

"Have I bored you?"

"Why would you ask that, my lord?"

"My man of business takes notes. My stewards take notes. My solicitors take notes."

"Yes, I agree they would. But, my lord, we are embarking upon a mystery, not a specific task with a known and desired end, are we not?"

The earl sat back, his cheek upon his fist. The young man was correct and astute. "I shall grant you that, Mr. Hurst."

"'Hurst,' please if you would be willing."

"Hurst?"

"Yes, Hurst."

"Very well, Hurst. Where do you propose we start?"

Hurst's eyes gleamed. "Where every mystery starts, your lordship: at the beginning."

Chapter 10

Hurst and Bill arrived by post in Yorkshire six days later, put down at the inn, and rented horses at the livery stables. At sunrise the following morning, they rode to Tang Hall.

Hurst dismounted at the front door and handed the reins to Bill. He was surprised no one challenged them en route from the gatehouse. He pulled his walking stick from his saddlebag, adjusted his clothing, and knocked on the door.

Repetitive raps later, the door opened. A ragged-dressed footman blocked the entryway. "Waddya want?"

"I am here on Lambert family business."

The hired hand made to shut the door. "Dun know 'em."

Hurst shoved his boot into the gap between the door and jamb. "Bill."

The door slamming into his nose erased the footman's terrified look. The giant led the way into the dilapidated building.

"Let us have a conversation with our greeter."

The man's futile attempt to scrabble across the floor to avoid Bill's reach was pitiful. Bill grabbed the man's lapels and hauled him into the nearest chair.

Hurst affected quiet disinterest. "Your name?"

"C-Con…Connor."

"Is Mr. Lambert your employer?"

"Who he be?"

Hurst snapped an impatient look at the footman. "Mr. Connor, if you are not in the Lamberts' employ, who and where are your employers?"

"Dun have nun."

It was as the countess feared. "I see. Bill, have this man take us to the study."

Bill snarled, hoisted the unfortunate object of his attention out of the chair, and squeezed the man's shoulders. His flesh was crushed between Bill's calloused hands and unforgiving bone.

The whimpering man led them to a hall on the left, down two doors, and pointed right. "Cain't open the' door."

"Excellent. Bill, please see what you can do."

Three kicks followed by a shoulder press, and the door was ripped from frozen hinges and reduced to firewood. A dusty room opened before them, ready to reveal its secrets. Hurst sat behind the desk; Bill pushed Connor inside, grabbed two chairs, and tossed Connor at one while he dropped into the other, a twenty-inch belaying pin in his lap.

Hurst smiled. Bill was a treasure.

Hurst pried opened all the drawers. He pulled out letters, notes, contracts, and journals and placed them on the desktop.

"One more moment while I look through the bookshelves."

Hurst pulled accounting ledgers and placed them next to the correspondence pile.

"Bill, would you mind accompanying Connor to the kitchen to dredge up some tea? I have a bit of reading to get through while we still have light."

Bill grabbed Connor by his upper arm, lifted him into the air, and dumped him upon his feet. Hurst was already flipping through journals, ignoring the whimpering that receded as the two men departed the study. Bill returned later with tea—and without Connor.

A half-hour before sunset, Hurst closed the last of the accounting ledgers and looked up.

"Let us depart, Bill. No need to invite trouble."

Hurst and Bill departed Tang Hall without incident, Hurst again bothered by that fact.

Matlock House, nineteen days later

"Mr. Reginald Hurst."

Hurst bowed to the earl and took the seat offered. The earl was touchy and did not mince words.

"What have you learned?"

"We continue to search, my lord, but...information is sparse."

"Sparse?" echoed the earl.

"Yes, my lord. Sparse." Hurst did not smile as he repeated himself.

The earl's impatience turned to anger. "How can the disappearance of a prominent family, en masse, be sparse?"

"You have read my report, my lord?"

The earl glared at Hurst antagonistically.

Hurst bowed his head in recognition of the earl's status. "The Duke of Grafton remembers nothing of the Lamberts' attendance. Others remember Mr. Hugh Lambert accepting a challenge from Baron Andrew Davies, issued for unknown reasons. Our information regarding the baron confirms his proclivity to manufacture reasons to duel. The Grafton staff we located confirmed the Lamberts left the house party that same evening."

The earl's choler settled.

"The Lambert staff confirmed the master dispatched an express rider who returned within the week. An interview with the express rider informed us of an army officer and a surgeon returning with him."

"Yes, yes." The earl's impatience returned. "Your report said as much. What else?"

"I have conducted an additional interview with the express rider. I now have a thread to pull."

The earl's eyebrows rose. "And…?"

"Your lordship's involvement is required."

"In what manner may *I* assist *you*?"

"War games."

Horse Guards, London, June 1790

Lieutenant Reginald Hurst reported to Captain Thomas Bennet. It took no less than fifteen minutes in Hurst's company for Bennet to recognize that the new man was not at all what he presented himself to be. The captain kept his own counsel and bided his time. He did not believe in coincidences. Lieutenant Hurst's reporting for duty at the onset of his forays into the misdirection phases of his work was suggestive.

Bennet had become inured to the dearth of imagination in the officer corps. The distinct lack of finesse, the propensity for frontal attack, and the failure to understand binary planning and execution frustrated the bibliophile-turned-strategist. Extraordinary, insightful commanders such as Brigadier General Foote were rare. Thus, Hurst quickly caught his attention. No one thing, no one action gave the man away; rather, it was his competence on top of his unmaskable intelligence.

One evening, Bennet reviewed the results of a planned exercise to misdirect a colonial militia into an incorrect identification and attack another troop of allies. Bennet had planned for the colonials to find planted intelligence, act on it, and capture unacknowledged affiliated militia, the goal being to delay the merging of forces to allow the Horse Guards to escape.

Hurst executed an alternate plan where the Horse Guards destroyed the captured allied militia, then having superiority in numbers, skittered away with extra munitions. No other officer ever deviated from a command plan. None had the presumption, the courage, nor the ingenuity. This series of decisions allowed Bennet to understand what Hurst was and from whence he came.

Both plans resulted in the same outcome; they differed in the means. That, Bennet realized, was the fundamental difference between him and Hurst, not *Lieutenant* Hurst, as Bennet now understood for whom this "shadow" worked. The captain had enjoyed the like-minded, astute Hurst. However, that pleasure was tempered by the knowledge that command would not appreciate any interference from the Home Office or any other internal intelligence department.

Hurst, unperturbed when Captain Bennet mentioned it was time for the cuckoo to depart, thanked him for the education and wished him the best. He added Captain Thomas Bennet to his list of connections. Hurst never burned a bridge.

Matlock House, August 1790

"Captain Bennet and Mr. Hurst," announced Smythe.

The two men bowed to the earl, who returned a respectable bow rather than his usual head nod reserved for those of lower status. This prompted raised eyebrows from his guests. With a hand gesture, the earl indicated chairs for the men to sit upon which they did, also in unison.

"Gentlemen, thank you for coming. The countess and I require your special talents. We have had an incident. A nurse, using forged references, made it onto our staff. The countess is concerned this creature may not be the only one."

The two men looked at each other, deciding who would lead. Hurst nodded to Bennet.

"My lord, before getting the necessary background intelligence, what are your fears?"

The earl, affronted for but a moment, realized the man's true intent. "We worry these imposters have gotten close to our children and left dissent within our current staff."

Bennet nodded. "Is there a time limit, my lord?"

"No time limit, no budget constraints. I expect results."

Bennet looked at Hurst, who nodded. Bennet turned back to the earl. "We shall return with a plan within a se'nnight, my lord."

The earl nodded. "Smythe will see you out."

Hurst took Bennet to White's where he secured a private dining room and sleeping accommodations for the duration of their collaboration. Once their meal had been served, they paid an extra shilling for a footman to stand post outside the door.

Bennet opened the conversation with a warning look. "Let us concentrate on the means—rather than the ends of which you are so fond."

Hurst guffawed. "Still vexed by that?"

They talked long into the night and wrote out plans before retiring. The next day, Bennet received orders via military courier assigning him from the War Office to Whitehall. The intelligence pair worked day and night, as Bennet demanded they take breaks every few hours to get physical exercise, attend entertainments, and do anything unrelated to the assignment to allow refreshment of their thinking.

The following week, Bennet and Hurst reconvened with the earl. The intelligence officers amazed him with the originality and detail of the enterprise. He approved every recommendation but reserved the right to influence the events after the primary target, the "uncle," was in chains. No objections were voiced.

The intelligence officers began the next morning. The plan was for Hurst, as a gentleman, to question the upper floor servants and work his way from the top down. Bennet, as a uniformed officer, started below stairs and would work from the bottom up.

Hurst started with the earl and the countess. Following the aristocrats were Smythe, the housekeeper, Cook, and the countess's lady's maid. Hurst finished the day with the earl's valet and Mr. Dolan, who had attended from his offices in Lincoln's Inn.

Bennet began with the under-footmen, scullery maids, and footmen. Rather than ask for their opinions, he manipulated each servant to privately tell him who they felt was not loyal to the family. He did not ask why. In between interviews, he pulled out a list of surnames, adding tic-marks beside each servant mentioned.

The interviews continued as such for a se'nnight, as Matlock House employed a few dozen servants of one type or another. On the tenth day, Hurst and Bennet sat together on a bench in the mews, surrounded by hay and horses. With the thought they may be overheard, Bennet inquired of Hurst's apparent disinterest in security.

"Bill is grooming the horses today," offered Hurst.

Bennet looked at his list. Bill Steele had not a single tic mark.

"Odd that," remarked Bennet.

"Do tell."

"Your Bill has not a single detractor."

"I would think not. He is Matlock's most loyal servant."

"Let us speak to this Bill, if you please."

"Bill," shouted Hurst. He glanced at Bennet to catch his reaction. He was not disappointed. Bennet's head tilted up as his eyes opened shockingly wide and moved skyward—up, up, and up!

"Hurst." Bill nodded.

"Bennet, allow me to introduce Bill Steele. Bill, this is Captain Bennet."

Bennet stood slowly. "Bill, may I ask you a few questions?"

Bill nodded slowly.

"We are assisting the earl on a private matter," explained Bennet.

Hurst and Bennet spent the next thirty minutes in near dismay as they learned more about the service population at Matlock House from Bill than they had garnered from the other servants over the past fortnight. When asked about the heir's nurse and her half-days, Bill described a portly gentleman's horse. He had seen the pair together briefly earlier in the year. Hurst rubbed his forehead, as did Bennet. Both rued their oversight. They thanked Bill and resumed looking at Bennet's list. Five names stood out as candidates with suspect loyalties. Bennet wrote those names on a separate page. They went to see the Matlock man of business.

"How may I assist you, gentlemen?"

Bennet handed Mr. Dolan the list of five names. "These individuals, statistically more so than the others, have made quite a negative impression upon their fellow servants."

"We should like to see all of the papers you have regarding their employment, especially their character letters," added Hurst.

"One moment, gentlemen." Mr. Dolan rose, moved to a cabinet, and opened several drawers, removing banded bundles of documents. When he confirmed the five bundles matched the names on the list, he handed them to Hurst. "The large table in the adjacent room will serve well. Godspeed."

They spread the documents across the table, side-by-side and organized by content type. Both men shook their heads at the audacity of the patron. Three of the five servant references were identical in penmanship. Forgeries! Hurst went to fetch Mr. Dolan as Bennet studied the documents' calligraphy. He discerned a well hidden but subtle feminine quality to the script.

Mr. Dolan's reaction to the three documents was as expected. He thanked the intelligence agents and let them know he would immediately compare every piece of correspondence in his possession for like abuses. The weeks had been eventful but, in the end, disappointing for their further investigations.

Three weeks from their first meeting, the two intelligence agents sent a message requesting a meeting with the earl. They received a verbal answer from a footman who directed them to enter the house through the mews.

The earl and the countess sat in the parlor, each door with a liveried footman standing post.

Smythe announced them. "Captain Bennet and Mr. Hurst."

Lord and Lady Matlock watched the men walk to the center of the room and bow. They nodded their acknowledgment. "Please present your summary, gentlemen."

Bennet led. "A full and exhaustive report is available to you, Lord Matlock."

"Thank you. Proceed."

"Of the thirty-seven individuals classified as staff in one form or another, we identified one male and two females as a threat to Matlock House."

Hurst added, "We shall continue the investigation into the forgeries, my lord."

The earl sighed and grimaced. Lady Matlock tilted her head up. "How sure are we of the malcontents?"

"One hundred percent, my lady," Bennet stated. "There is *no* doubt about their forged references. Once presented with their perfidy, confessions were easily obtained. All are in our report."

Lady Matlock stood with Lord Matlock following suit. She squeezed the earl's arm and nodded to Bennet and Hurst.

"Thank you for your hard work and loyalty to our family, gentlemen." The countess exited.

The earl ignored Bennet and addressed Hurst. "As there was *no* doubt, I assume that the 'uncle,' against my wishes, is not in chains?"

"No, my lord. Unfortunately, circumstances prevented us from entertaining your request. Please accept our regrets. Our physical pursuit of him led to his demise, most likely at the hands of his associates. Know that we shall continue to pursue the original fraudster's claims."

The earl looked at Bennet.

"Do you have reservations, Captain?"

"None, Lord Matlock."

"Smythe," called the earl. "Please see that these gentlemen leave incognito."

Bennet and Hurst followed the butler through a servant's door, down the back stairs, and out into the mews.

They turned to leave but stopped upon hearing a throat clear. It was the Matlock butler, who bowed deeply. "Gentlemen, your service speaks for itself."

Matlock House introduced three new servants below stairs the next day, advising all to remember their loyalty.

Chapter 11

Ashdale, September 1790

"Mr. Burton."

The earl looked up from his letters. He liked the young man who had brought calm, good sense, and hope into the earldom.

"Good morning, Mr. Burton."

"Good morning, Lord Matlock."

"What pearls of wisdom today?"

Mr. Burton smiled and produced a pamphlet. "This is information for a type of unspoken communication. It describes a silent language of finger and body signs based upon the writings of Charles de La Fin from 1692."

The earl was intrigued. "Pray explain."

"As your younger son seems to prefer observation over speech, I believe this would be a way to allow him alternatives to better express himself."

"Anything else?"

"I feel he would give much attention to this subject as it is singular in the manner of other…unique topics that capture his interests."

The earl leaned back and placed his cheek on the knuckles of his fist, elbow on the chair arm. "In short, Richard may stop obsessing over insane and dangerous cavalry tactics from centuries past and learn alternate communication skills to allow for a closer relationship with the countess and myself."

"Indeed, your lordship."

The earl nodded. "Who is this teacher of…what was it…silent communication?"

"He is Friar Peregrine Ambrose Abbott."

The earl's lips rose in distaste. "A Frenchman *and* a Papist priest?"

"No, your lordship. An ordained Anglican priest who does not report to a bishop."

"Well, let me contact our cousin, the bishop of Leeds, about this abbot. He will have the answers we seek."

A stout, jovial man stood in the schoolroom's doorway.

Richard sat at a desk stacked high with books. To his left, from the bottom up, was Homer's *Iliad*, Thucydides's *History of the Peloponnesian War* and Sun Tzu's *The Art of War*. To his right were Aelian's *The Tactics of Aelian,* Golding's *Martiall exploytes in Gallia,* and Cruso's *Military Instructions for the Cavalrie.* He was currently obsessing over a military history pamphlet about the Hun nomadic riders, Barnet's *The Theory and Practice of Modern Wars.* He felt a calling.

Richard sensed a presence to his left and looked up at his visitor, neither recognizing him nor understanding why he had a caller as his time during his lessons was his own. He did not expect his next tutor until later.

"Good morning, my lord."

Richard shook his head back and forth.

"I fail to understand you, my lord. Is it not a good morning?"

Richard shook his head back and forth again.

"It IS a good morning, my lord?" asked the man again, smiling.

He nodded.

"So, it is a good morning?"

He nodded again.

"You are not the viscount?" queried the man, hairy eyebrows wrinkling.

Richard opened his eyes in a wide, comical way, nodding exaggeratedly, diverted by the funny man.

"Ah," exclaimed the man, clapping his hands together, "you must be Master Richard!"

He nodded, indicating the man was at last correct in his assumptions.

The man spread his hands wide as if he were going to take flight. "Wonderful! I am Friar Perry, and we are going to have a splendid time!"

Richard could not help himself. The man's joy filled the schoolroom. He laughed aloud, the first of many joyous hours spent in a lifetime of tutelage and friendship with the affable teacher of unspoken communication.

A letter to Thomas Bennet from David Burton—

My friend, I write again in the hope you have found answers to your questions and that your duties keep your keen mind occupied.

I presented the E of M with a pamphlet describing unspoken means to communicate—this medium being taught to the deaf and silent. Since RF seems more at ease communicating through head and facial gestures, this alternative would seem to be in his best interests. How little I underestimated my contribution!

A Friar Peregrine "Perry" Abbott is an itinerant teacher of "signing" or, as de la Fin writes, a silent language. He uses different parts of the body to show letters as well as shapes, with the fingers on the hand to make vowels.

RF took a single day to grasp his teachings and now has given up speaking unless prompted! He and I have had whispered conversations, myself reminding him of the need to speak in a verbal manner regarding his health as well as what propriety demands. He took my censure with goodwill.

I shall not bore you with details regarding this young man's innate intelligence, instinctive awareness of his surroundings, or assured self-confidence. And he at such a young age!

David Burton

Horse Guards, January 1791

"Enter."

Captain Thomas Bennet, although officially captain in the King's service for just a few more minutes, strode into Major General Foote's office.

"Sit, Captain, sit. Join me in a drink to mark your selling out."

"Yes, sir."

Thomas sat across from the general, waiting for the sage counsel that was sure to come.

"I suspect it quite surprised you to hear from the Courts of Chancery."

"Yes, General, I never expected to inherit and manage an estate."

"Your elder brother worked with your father learning to manage an estate whereas you did not."

Thomas nodded, unsure where the general was going.

"I surmise you took part in few of the important day-to-day tasks required to ensure a prosperous estate."

"You are correct, General. I know nothing of what my brother learned."

"I do not sit in judgment, Bennet. Tell me of your boyhood."

Thomas leaned back in his chair and crossed his legs.

"I loved to read. Nothing bored me, although I favored histories and philosophies. I found I had a natural ability with languages and put it to good use by reading the classics. I read and then tutored at Oxford. My future hope was to become a don. Rising to warden was beyond my reach given the paucity of my connections. I sat for the entrance exams and spent several weeks making favorable connections with my classmates. I enjoyed the collegiate atmosphere. I spent two weeks undecided whether I would sit for history or philosophy."

Thomas looked down at his hands. "Everything became moot when my father retracted his support, his reasons for which he never did elucidate. I recognized I was a second son to a country squire, and I accepted the conditional support my father offered. Thus, the purchase of a lieutenant's commission in the Regulars."

The general raised a finger in the air. "Where you reported for duty and found yourself quite satisfied and challenged pleasantly. You earned your step on sheer talent. You became proficient in weapons training, fencing, and military tactics. Your nimble mind and logical thinking made you successful in wartime subterfuge, planning, and leading psychological operations, and in short order, you were directly reporting to the Horse Guards."

"General, you have summarized with accuracy the latter years of my life. To what do I owe this honor?"

"Bennet, you are a reserved and thoughtful officer, having spent more of your youth with books rather than other boys. You have enjoyed the quiet camaraderie of a few of your fellow officers, as your assignments prohibited any open friendships. I encouraged you to make and keep astute connections, which you have, including to a powerful aristocratic family."

Thomas knew not to ask questions. General Foote delivered counsel; he did not explain why. "The Horse Guards' loss is your family estate's gain."

"General, as much as I would have liked to remain in the King's service, Bennet males have occupied Longbourn for four centuries."

"Yes, you must accept your inheritance. I am taking this time to caution you. I am well versed in what will next happen to men like you. You are, without doubt, one of the finest minds I have had the privilege of commanding."

Bennet nodded in acknowledgment of the unexpected compliment.

"Captain, you will find yourself unsatisfied with the repetitive, unchanging day-to-day needs of the estate. This will lead you to become careless in understanding and improving the estate finances. You will revert to your previous wants, that of a book lover."

"That is quite an unhappy future you paint, General."

General Foote leaned forward, his eyes narrowing. "Do not think I am unaware of distractions that clouded your performance for several weeks upon your return from your foray north."

The general leaned back in his chair. "Captain Bennet, as my last command to you, I order you take your armorer and batman from service and employ them at your estate. The Navy has a fine tradition of officers giving followers lifetime sinecures. Maintain your physical training and continue writing your psychological plans. Find a good woman, have children, and make your family your mission."

Bennet scrambled to his feet as the general had stood and put out his hand. Thomas reciprocated, feeling the steel in his commander's grip, his words—of the same consistency—having been delivered just as effectively.

"Good luck to you, Captain. I hope you vanquish those burdens you have placed upon your conscience."

Ashdale, March 1791

An eight-year-old Richard Fitzwilliam rose at the urging of his nurse, Siobhan, an Irish girl with a mellifluous voice who had cared for him since his birth. Smiling, he rose without fuss. Siobhan clucked her tongue out of habit, though not because her charge frustrated her. Richard quite spoiled her with his *regimented* everyday behavior. The young lad tilted his head and raised an eyebrow. Siobhan began humming his ritual morning nursery melody, which she had found odd; lyrics did not interest him—just melody—a precious secret she kept to herself.

A knock on the nursery room door broke the regular morning routine. Siobhan looked up, and Richard stilled. The door opened, admitting the Ashdale butler.

Eyes cast down, hugging Richard's back to her front and feeling defensive, Siobhan acknowledged the senior staffer.

"Good mornin' to ye', Mr. Clarke," she replied in her characteristic Irish lilt.

"Good morning to you, Miss Siobhan."

Siobhan feared the senior staff. She remembered the disdain on their faces when she brought the young master's weight loss to their attention. The following week, they started a feeding program and journaled each wet nurse and her time with the child.

"His lordship and her ladyship expect Master Richard to join the table this morning."

Clarke turned, nodded to the child, and waited.

Siobhan tried not to fret, as she feared for Richard. Her own security never crossed her mind, so deep was her care for the boy. She knelt in front of her charge, tightened a frog here, and adjusted a waistline there. The young woman stood and held her right hand out for his. She waited a few seconds, surprised her hand remained empty. She looked down.

Richard shook his head, smiling.

Siobhan's eyes filled, acknowledging the change. She, too, nodded and turned to tidy up the nursery, every horror she could imagine racing through her thoughts. She felt a tug on her dress and looked down.

"I shall be fine. I have you and Clarke," whispered her charge.

Siobhan knelt and asked with her eyes whether she may hug him. Richard nodded, and she did. He reached up and patted the back of her shoulders once, twice. Siobhan sniffled and, grabbing his shoulders, extended her arms, forcing Richard to take a step back.

"Off you go now. Mind your manners."

Richard nodded. Siobhan held out her left hand, which prompted Richard to place his right in hers. It was their custom. Siobhan took Richard's right hand and kissed the fading furrow of scars as she did each morning after he finished dressing.

Clarke watched the little drama impassively, giving away nothing of his feelings. If asked by the countess, he would recommend the lass continue as a nurse for the two Fitzwilliam girls. A short note to Smythe would be just the thing.

Richard approached. The butler admired the young boy's composure. *He will grow to be an exemplary Englishman.*

"Please follow me, Master Richard."

The earl and the countess were breaking their fast in the small dining room.

"Master Richard Fitzwilliam."

Richard walked into the room at a measured pace. He surveyed the room, taking an inventory of the occupants. Ignoring the sideboard full of food, he stepped to his father's side and bowed. "Good morning, your lordship."

He turned to his mother, bowed again, stretched to stand taller, and smiled. "Good morning, Your Mothership."

The countess's musical peal of laughter filled the room. The smiling woman reached out and hugged her child. The earl guffawed.

Richard returned her motherly embrace and inhaled her lily of the valley scent, the unmistakable perfumed signature of his beloved mama. The earl pointed to an empty setting to his right and he himself rose to fill his son's plate. The earl and the countess led the familial conversation, asking Richard questions suited for a boy his age. All required nothing more than a "yes" or a "no" answer.

"Richard, do you find your lessons interesting?" asked the earl. Richard nodded.

The countess dabbed her lips with a serviette. "Dearest, are you getting enough snacks? Does Cook keep your favorite cakes available?" Richard nodded.

"Mr. Burton reports that you have been consistent with your triage exercises. Are they difficult?" asked the earl.

Richard shook his head, indicating the process was not. Richard tilted his head and looked at his father. "Why?"

He noticed his mother trying not to wince at his scratchy voice.

The earl shook his head back and forth several times, in a dramatic fashion, his eyes opened quite wide, his lips pursed in a funny way.

Richard covered his mouth as he snickered. The countess giggled musically; the earl joined her with a booming, natural laugh.

Then he sobered. "Richard, I understand from your reading master that you are interested in the kingdom's military history. This is something few find engaging, yet you do."

Richard nodded, noticing the frown on his mother's face.

Lady Matlock calmly folded her napkin, indicating that the meal was over. She stood and bid her husband and son *adieu* and *bon chance.* After three steps, she stopped, turned, went back to her son, knelt, and placed her hands on his shoulders. "Make us proud, my lovely boy."

She kissed his cheek, stood, narrowed her eyes at the earl, and glided from the room, a lioness leaving her lion and cub to the protection of the pride.

Richard turned to his father, who signaled him to follow. Together they walked to the earl's study. Two men stood when they entered. The earl sat behind his desk but left Richard at the door. "Close the door, Richard. I have someone for you to meet."

Richard closed the door as asked and walked toward the desk. Mr. Burton was to his left, but to the right stood a stranger.

The man resembled Mr. Burton in size—height and weight—but

held himself loosely, fluidly, like one of those animals Richard recalled from the Royal Menagerie. The man was not dressed as a gentleman—more like a tradesman. He was clean-shaven. His gray eyes resembled the ice filling the Derwent during the deepest winters. His mouth was a slash—a thin, expressionless line. Richard looked to the earl for an introduction.

"Richard, this is Captain Ivan Markov, your martial arts master. He will prepare you for your future service to the King."

Richard looked at the earl, inquiring of Mr. Burton's presence by tilting his head at the surgeon.

"Mr. Burton is here for the introduction and to take part in your first lessons."

Richard nodded at his father.

"Clarke," called the earl.

"Yes, my lord?"

"Please see these gentlemen to the ballroom."

The earl addressed Mr. Burton. "Continue your reporting with an emphasis on the consequence of these lessons."

"Yes, my lord."

The earl stared at the closed door. *That should put an end to this nonsense. A Fitzwilliam wearing the King's scarlet. Balderdash!*

Chapter 12

Clarke escorted the trio down a hallway and opened a set of double doors. The ballroom, a bright open space, was empty except for new and unfamiliar—to Burton—equipment clustered about the entrance

After the trio entered, Clarke closed the door behind them. Burton could hear his command voice through the door as he addressed a footman. "Jenkins: no one enters unless invited in by Captain Markov or Mr. Burton. There will be no exceptions, including the earl and the countess."

Markov looked about and grunted approvingly. To his left was an upright stand holding wooden clubs of all sizes resembling cutlasses, sabers, and rapiers. Across from this "sword" stand was another, similar rack filled with long staffs, short staffs, and cudgels. Trunks labeled "Pistols," "Whips," "Chains," and "Ropes" lined one wall.

He walked to the nearest stand, and Burton followed. Richard did not.

"Please join us, Cadet Fitzwilliam," Markov directed in a voice touched with a Prussian accent.

Richard complied, and Markov continued. "The earl has retained me to instruct you in the martial arts. This will include physical exercise, strength training, fitness games, weapons training, and survival skills. Do you understand?"

Richard stared at the Prussian; Markov looked at Burton. The surgeon raised his eyebrows but remained silent.

Without warning, the Prussian backhanded the young man across the face. Hard. Richard's chin turned to his shoulder, then righted itself.

Burton leapt forward. He reached for Richard's chin. It was wasted effort on his part.

Richard turned, grabbed a short club, and swung it at the arms master in one motion. It connected with a *thock* as it hit its opposite number in the hands of his new instructor. Rather than stop, Richard pressed his attack, swinging again and again in measured, controlled arcs. The Prussian parried and countered each attack with a return strike to Richard's upper arm and body.

Markov was astonished. *How does he keep fighting after taking all these blows?* The child continued to attack, seemingly impervious to injury. Markov was breathing hard. He decided to end the contest on his terms. A student must respect his instructor.

Markov countered the next attack with an unforgiving strike to his opponent's neck. The child grunted, then growled at him. Markov lost his train of thought but for a second.

The Prussian dropped his guard. Richard stepped forward and savagely brought his club down on the captain's left thigh. The man collapsed. In the blink of an eye, the boy straddled his much larger opponent, knelt on his wrists, and began beating his chest. He rained blows unceasingly until Burton hauled him away.

The surgeon laid him down on an open table. Richard twisted in his grip, brought up his knees, and kicked him in his chest. The medico took several steps back to recover his balance, then squared his shoulders and shouted at his patient.

"TRIAGE, NOW!"

Richard laid back and closed his eyes. Confirming his patient had begun his triage protocol, Burton knelt beside Markov. He passed an open bottle of smelling salts beneath the unconscious man's nose several times. The Prussian sputtered. Burton sat him up, at which the man groaned and hugged his ribs. As Burton helped him, he finally stood with much effort, hunched over, his elbows tight against his sides. Burton kneaded his ribs.

"You shall be quite uncomfortable for a fortnight, I daresay."

Markov nodded—his face a portrait of pain.

Burton hurried over to Richard. "Any degree two or three swellings?"

Richard shook his head.

"Respect the protocol. Verbal, please."

"No."

"Sit up."

Richard sat up by himself. He needed no assistance.

"Neck turns, five each, please."

Richard looked right as far as he could turn his chin. He repeated the same in the other direction, which did not match the previous effort.

"I am calling an end to this day's training. Master Richard, please report to the infirmary and ask the nurse to prepare ice packs."

Richard smiled, although it was a touch higher on the right.

His eyes widened as he whispered, "May I also request ices with the packs?"

Burton grinned. "Of course, you may. Specifically, ask for brandy flavoring. Off you go. Slowly. Bump nothing on your way there." Burton knew his warning was unnecessary. Master Richard was the most agile young man he had ever encountered.

Once off the table, Richard held up his hand, looked at the Prussian, and spoke between clenched teeth. "I will overlook your ignorance this time. But, should you ever touch me again without permission, I will kill you as I would a common footpad."

Captain Markov took a step back. His face was the definition of shock, disbelief, and fear. The Prussian, to his credit, stood as straight as he could, winced, and bowed deeply. "Please accept my apologies. An error of this type will not be repeated. I beg your pardon."

Richard nodded.

"We shall begin anew at *my* discretion," warned Burton, his tone brooking no argument. The medico marched to the ballroom door and banged on it with his fist. "Open the door, Jenkins."

April 1791

London Gazette, social pages—

Announcing the nuptials of Thomas Robert Bennet, Esq. of Longbourn House to Francine Agnes Gardiner of Meryton, the couple both hailing from Hertfordshire...

Chapter 13

Pemberley, March 1792

Young Fitzwilliam Darcy, known as William by his family, paced back and forth in the schoolroom, waiting to hear anything regarding his mother. Lady Anne Darcy's labor pains began twelve hours earlier, and the boy—scared, excited, confused, and subject to a myriad of other feelings he could not sort out—was as a ship at sea without a rudder. Too old for a nurse, he was yet to be assigned a valet. He spent much of his free time with Pemberley's housekeeper, Mrs. Reynolds—his mother's health having been inconsistent for many years. She doted on him as much as a surrogate mother could.

His father, George Darcy, was his hero. Intelligent and soft-spoken, he earned the respect of whomever he encountered. An emotionally reticent man, the elder Darcy worshiped the Lord, cared for his estate and its tenants, and loved his wife with all his heart. As his mother's health fluctuated, William saw the repressed panic on his father's face. He did not yet understand his father's fear of losing his beloved. Had he read the Darcy ancestral Bible earlier rather than later, he would see that his father and he were the last of the Darcy lineage, all other direct blood relatives dead or gone.

His mother was everything to the lad. Loving and nurturing, she represented everything beautiful and peaceful in his world.

A knock on the door and Mrs. Reynolds stood in the doorway, her stress displayed on her face.

"Your father awaits you in his study, Master William."

Panic set in. He stood up straight, swallowed, and walked to the housekeeper, who pulled out a handkerchief and wiped his eyes. He nodded his thanks and followed her into the hallway, down two sets of stairs to his father's study door. He knocked, waited to be acknowledged, and entered.

His father, George Darcy, usually immaculate in every way, slumped in a chair in front of his desk, a drink in his hand. The crystal bottle on the side table next to his chair was less than half full.

William assumed the chair opposite his father. He sat back, folded his hands in his lap, and waited.

"Fitzwilliam, I asked you here so that neither you nor I would be alone."

"How is Mother?" the youngster cried, his eyes filling.

George Darcy's frowning stare bore down upon his son. His narrowed eyes forced William to sit straighter, swallow, and swipe at his tears. The seven-old struggled but succeeded in regaining his composure, remounting the Darcy Mask. He was the heir and *"Darcys always set the example."* His father approved of his son's exercise in regulation.

George Darcy pitied his son. His existence would be a lonely road as he would know the weight of ensuring Pemberley's posterity: it would be William's responsibility to further the Darcy bloodline. He, George Darcy, would never remarry to beget another child, that much sought-after "spare." He could never fall so far as to turn a successor wife into a broodmare, not when his and Anne's marriage bed had been the cradle for so much love. Before he could continue, the last disagreement he had had with his wife assailed him.

"You worry about that which you cannot control, but only contribute, husband. And contribute you will."

"I cannot but question your love for me when all the medical experts we have consulted are unanimous in their opinions, wife. You have suffered too much heartbreak from that which the Almighty seeks not to allow to fruition. Am I, and our son, not enough for you to love? I am not asking for another child. What compels you so?"

Anne Darcy, standing at the window of their shared sitting room, staring out the window over the grounds of her paradise, saw the fear on her husband's face in the window pane's reflection. Without turning, she stated, "Men, supposing themselves as the Lord's representation, calling themselves physicians, however high in the instep, offer mortal opinions. Surely, there is no need for me to remind you of this. Dare I continue?"

Her husband gazed at her, unable to speak. He nodded.

Anne Darcy unleashed one of her weapons that tethered her rather dour husband to her will again and again when he was in one of his frequent moods. She laughed.

Her enchantment filled his ears—she knew he could never deny her that which she demanded; he knew she did that and was unable to prevent himself from performing to her desires. Both smiled and the stress in the room seeped away.

"My dearest, surely *you* of all people would avoid any reason for our Lord to perceive hubris in a George Darcy decision."

George Darcy surrendered the argument. He buried his reservations. With tearful regret, he walked to his wife and embraced her, pulling her against his person while she continued to gaze over the rolling fields of the estate.

Her last response to him was a quip wrapped in an unseen death sentence.

"What plans you men make, only to have our Lord rearrange them to his purpose."

"Your mother's health is in the Lord's hands. Find comfort, for she is serving His will by bringing you a brother or sister."

"Yes, Father."

The child watched his father take a sip from the drink in his hand, not missing the minute shaking. *Is father as afraid as I am?*

When his father said no more, William rose, bowed, and sat at the corner table placed for his use when allowed into the study. Staring at *Robinson Crusoe,* he read not a word as he prayed again and again for his mother to overcome her current indisposition. Unknowingly, he laid his forehead on the book, hands clasped together in his lap under the table. He continued to pray until he drifted off to sleep.

He woke to a dark and silent room, the fireplace embers throwing the light of fireflies against the lower portion of the opposite curtain. That memory inspired William to recall a picnic on the great lawn stretching below the fountain, a day that lasted until dusk, hence the fireflies…

"Mother, why does Aunt Catherine say I am to be her son in the future? I am your son, am I not? Will you give me up? Do you not love me?"

"My lovely boy, you are my heart and soul. I am your mother, and no one can ever change that, as the Lord has deemed it so. I shall always be with you."

William lay in the grass, his head in his mother's lap. She caressed his hair and, from time to time, tenderly scratched her nails against his scalp. He sighed in contentment. "Must I marry my cousin? Is that what my future holds?"

Lady Anne chuckled, letting her son know he did not. "You must do as your father did and measure those who would look to you for your monetary worth and dismiss them. Seek those who see your character's worth and marry for passion."

The study door opened, and John the footman cleared his throat, breaking his reverie. "Master William, they expect you in the family wing."

The stripling stood, holding back from running in a panic to his mother's chamber. He joined his father in the master's sitting room. Together, silently, they waited for the Lord's verdict.

Ten hours later, he was at the side of his mother's bed, her cold pale hand encased in both of his.

"Sing with me, William," she weakly whispered.

He nodded, careful not to let her feel his tears upon her skin. In a low voice, he sang the one song he could think of, such was his distress.

Come live with me and be my Love,[7]
And we will all the pleasures prove
That hills and valleys, dale and field,
And all the craggy mountains yield.

And we will sit upon the rocks,
Seeing the shepherds feed their flocks
By shallow rivers, to whose falls
Melodious birds sing madrigals.

And I will make thee beds of roses
And a thousand fragrant posies;
A cap of flowers, and a kirtle
Embroidered all with leaves of myrtle;

---

7 Listen to a folk tune that works with the poem: https://www.contemplator.com/england/livewme.html

A gown made of the finest wool
Which from our pretty lambs we pull;
Fair-lined slippers for the cold,
With buckles of the purest gold;

A belt of straw and ivy-buds,
With coral clasps and amber-studs:
And if these pleasures may thee move,
Come live with me, and be my love.

The shepherd-swains shall dance and sing
For thy delight each May-morning:
If these delights thy mind may move,
Then live with me and be my love.

His mother's voice, in harmony with his, seemed to gain strength as the song ended. William closed his eyes and kissed the hand he held, even after it went limp. He held it against his cheek as if he could provide warmth to forestall the inevitable. Opening his eyes, he stared at the cold still beauty at the center of his universe.

"You promised you would not give me up," whispered William, numb. His heart, his mother, Lady Anne Darcy—his heart, was gone.

On the darkest, bleakest November day in Derbyshire's recent memory, Fitzwilliam Darcy, together with his father, buried his mother. She held his stillborn sister, named Georgiana, in her arms.

Chapter 14

Pemberley, June, 1792

Mrs. Reynolds led the young man up to the schoolroom. After delivering the requisite double-knock on the door, the good lady walked in without waiting for an answer, knowing her boy would immerse himself in a book and not hear a sound.

Correct again, she mused. Young Fitzwilliam Darcy sat reading on the floor of the schoolroom, his back supported by a wall, a book open in his lap, and his face tilted down, noticing nothing of his surroundings.

She could not hide the small smile on her face. She adored the child; his kindness to the staff was already a happy topic below stairs. "Master Darcy!"

William stood, looking a bit flustered. "I do beg your pardon, Mrs. Reynolds."

They who are good-natured when children are good-natured when they grow up. My Master William is the sweetest-tempered, most generous-hearted boy in the world.

"May I present your cousin, Master Richard Fitzwilliam."

Mrs. Reynolds held out her arm, gesturing to the inside of the schoolroom. Darcy's cousin stepped inside and remained still.

"I believe you two should get on right proper. Master Richard is staying for the summer. No mischief, mind you."

The door closed, and the two cousins were alone.

Darcy looked at his cousin, nothing coming to mind of their past together. Odd that Cousin Richard did not move. *Maybe an offer?*

"Would you like to ride? The stable master will fit you for a mount."

Richard shook his head, walked to the window, and looked out at the grounds.

"We could go outside and race around the lanes. Would that not be fun?"

Again, Richard shook his head, keeping his back to the room.

William pondered his dark-haired cousin, now remembering from their few previous encounters that, although Richard spoke little, he appeared to watch everyone.

"Would you like to read a book with me?"

Richard nodded. Darcy held up the book in his hand.

"Robinson Crusoe?"

Richard nodded again.

William walked over to the reading table. He looked over to Richard, who shook his head and pointed to the floor. Darcy shrugged and joined him.

"Chairs?"

Richard shook his head. He sat on the floor, his feet flat, his arms wrapped around his knees.

"Do I sit next to you?"

Darcy, already understood that to communicate with his silent cousin, he needed to tailor his questions. Richard shook his head.

"Do I sit in front of you?"

Richard pointed his thumb to the area behind his back.

Darcy nodded and sat down behind his cousin, resting his back against him. Richard leaned back against Darcy, each perfectly balancing the other.

Darcy began reading aloud. *"I was born in the Year 1632, in the City of York, of a good Family, tho' not of that Country, my Father being a Foreigner of Bremen..."*

Over the next several weeks, the boys rode together, played together, climbed trees together, and swam together. They ate every meal together, both in the dining room and from trays in the schoolroom. Not one waking hour of one summer day found the pair separated. Amid the fifth week of their adventure, Mrs. Reynolds interrupted them. "Gentlemen, the master requests you both join him in the study."

William turned and looked at his cousin, who mirrored him perfectly. As if choreographed, they both turned back to her.

Mrs. Reynolds shook her head, turned, walked out of the schoolroom, and did not stop until she reached the master's study. She knocked.

"Enter." George Darcy watched his son and nephew approach. "Sit. We have matters to discuss."

"'Matters,' Father?"

"Yes...matters."

"*We*, Father?"

"Yes, William—*we*."

The two boys sat before his desk.

"I have received a letter from the earl, Richard. It is provident in its timing."

George Darcy looked at his nephew who remained motionless. He turned back to his son.

"William, you are at an age to have your own man. Richard, it is time for you to accept society's expectations. You are a future gentleman. Gentlemen have valets. Your father has asked for my assistance to guide you in this matter, and I will not be gainsaid. Thus, a group of applicants has been put together from which you both may choose."

"Father, we are comfortable assisting each other. We have done so these past fortnights. Until summer ends, may we not continue as such?"

"William, I understand your point. However, both you and Richard are no longer in leading strings. You are of an age to make your own choice, that of your most personal servant. It is our wish, the earl and myself, for the two of you to settle this task together."

The two youngsters turned to each other. A few facial and eye gestures passed between them. They both turned back to him.

"When will we begin this endeavor, Father?"

George Darcy shook his head. It was as if someone had dropped him into a pantomime. *What an extraordinary bond…and so quickly.*

"Mrs. Reynolds will speak with you. It pleases me that you two have found such kinship. You may return to your pursuits."

The boys rose in unison, bowed in unison, and exited, William trailing his cousin.

George Darcy returned to his letters.

The following week, the Pemberley housekeeper caught the two boys sneaking out of the kitchen—hot buns, possibly pilfered, shoved in their mouths and pockets. "Please tell me Cook gave you those treats, my lovelies."

"Yes, Mrs. Reynolds, she did," answered Master William.

Mrs. Reynolds noticed the slight smile on Master Richard's face. "All of them, Master William?"

"No, Mrs. Reynolds, not all."

William turned and looked at his cousin, who silently smirked back at him. The Pemberley heir's eyebrows rose, followed by a giggle. Both turned back to her. "We were hungry and dinner is so far off."

"Thank you for your honesty. Please apologize to Cook. You have a rendezvous in the schoolroom. Off you two go now."

She watched them finish chewing the last of their booty and return to the kitchen. She followed. After they had made their apologies, they dashed upstairs. The valet interviews were to start.

Such fine boys. If only Lady Anne could see them together. Her handkerchief dried her eyes as she walked up the stairs to the schoolroom. She was eager to observe their behavior with the candidates.

"Send in the first prospect," instructed Mrs. Reynolds.

The next hour passed as boys and men of all ages presented themselves, recited their experience, and answered questions. After the eighth hopeful departed, the Pemberley housekeeper turned to the boys. "What do you seek in a valet?"

William leaned toward his cousin. Whispers were exchanged, and Pemberley's heir answered the question. "We are looking for someone we can trust to hold our confidences."

"Excellent, masters. You have defined the need most accurately."

The next possibility was a young man introduced as Bartholomew. His family had a laudable reputation for service from several of the shire families. He was two years older than the younger master and quite cheeky. "Me father served as a man to the Quality. 'E made sure to learn me not to cry rope on no one."

Mrs. Reynolds chimed in. "You are quite fortunate to have had such an upbringing, Mr. Bartholomew."

"Barty, mum."

"Excuse me?"

"It be Barty, mum. Me full name be the mouthful. Takes too much time."

William said nothing but assessed Barty for half a minute. Then he nodded. "I believe Barty will do just fine, Mrs. Reynolds."

"Will he, Master William?"

"He will, mum."

Mrs. Reynolds smiled as Richard snickered.

"Barty, welcome to Pemberley."

"Thank you, mum."

"We now wait on you, Master Richard."

Six prospects later a peculiar-looking young man entered the schoolroom.

Michael Villiers was the fourth son of an impoverished estate owner from Stoke-on-Trent. Having had to leave Eton early and too young and uneducated to be a tutor, Villiers was seeking a position as a valet for a young gentleman or a batman for an officer. The Kympton rector had sent a favorable letter regarding his family. He was fifteen years old but appeared older and more imposing. His arms were unnaturally long.

A raspy voice asked, "Fight much?"

Mrs. Reynolds, surprised, turned to look at Richard.

"Yes, sir, I did."

"Win much?"

The young man grimaced. "Sir, no one profits from a fight."

What a wise young man, thought Mrs. Reynolds. She turned back to Master Richard, who nodded his acceptance. "Michael, welcome to Pemberley and Matlock."

Barty and Villiers spent the first part of the summer as Pemberley second footmen. They trained under the master's valet in the latter half, learning overall service before taking on the personal needs of their charges.

Sunny weather, cloudy weather, windy days, hot humid days, clement weather, inclement weather—after exhausting themselves with outdoor pursuits, the boys were to be found back-to-back, hour upon hour in the schoolroom reading. Darcy read aloud while Richard listened.

Darcy read treatises, histories, and philosophies; he excluded no subject. He expanded their repertoire of languages, starting with French. From French they moved on to Greek and Latin. It was then that Richard interrupted his cousin's reading for the first time.

Darcy was reading Latin phrases from an old textbook he had found on the top shelf in the library where many of his father's and grandfather's university books were shelved. The aged spine crackled as he opened it.

"*Veni, Vidi, Vici*—I came, I saw, I conquered. *Alea iacta est*—the die has been cast. *Carpe diem*—seize the day. *Cogito, ergo sum*—I think, therefore I am. *Acta non verba*—actions, not words. *Non est dubium*—doubt not."

"Yes," whispered Richard.

Darcy raised his eyebrows. "*Non est dubium*," he repeated.

"Yes," said Richard hoarsely but a bit louder.

"Doubt not."

"—Cousin."

Darcy turned to stare at Richard, who stared back at him.

"Doubt not, Cousin," proclaimed Richard, his black eyes resolute.

Darcy stared back at his best friend. "I never shall."

Chapter 15

Ashdale, May 1794

The Earl of Matlock was a worried man. His heir's latest trials seemed cruelty laid atop foul misfortune. "Well, Mr. Burton, you have examined my eldest?"

"The viscount is resting comfortably, my lord. We have stanched the bleeding, but the danger remains."

"If my brother permits, please tell me what happened and how you have helped my nephew," requested George Darcy, turning away from the mantel where he had been stationed.

Burton looked at the earl, who nodded. "The viscount brushed a fence post while riding. A nail from a fallen cross-timber punctured his left calf and resulted in a laceration—more of a deep scratch and not a gash. The viscount wrapped his leg with his cravat, believing this action would stop the bleeding. He continued riding but faltered. Fortunately, the groom accompanying his lordship was attentive and raised the alarm. Lord Hopton was brought home without delay and cared for by Cook, who put the viscount into a reclining position with his leg raised above his heart, thus reducing the further loss of blood."

The surgeon paused, allowing the facts to be digested by the earl and Mr. Darcy.

"Clarke."

The door to the study opened. "Yes, my lord?"

"Please have Cook and all other servants involved in the viscount's care gathered downstairs to receive gratitude from her ladyship and me."

The servant nodded and withdrew.

"Continue, Mr. Burton."

Burton paused as he noticed Mr. Darcy turn to the earl. "I am curious as to the remaining danger to the viscount."

Upon the earl's grim nod, the medico continued. "There is no escaping the obvious conclusion: the viscount suffers from a bleeding disorder. These are well documented in the royal houses of several countries—ancient and modern—including France, Russia, and Egypt. It is more prominent in royal circles because of the high rate of marriage between first-degree family members. It is less prevalent in the first circles, but not unheard of."

The two men absorbed the obvious. Darcy snorted. "Fate strikes another blow against Catherine's insistence that your heir wed her daughter."

Burton remained impassive as he absorbed this bit of Fitzwilliam family business. He waited for questions from either man. Hearing none, he carried on. "The viscount must remain supine with the injury in a raised position at all times. This must continue until the wound closes. Not heals—that will take considerable time—but closes. This will prevent further seepage. Once scar tissue forms, we may return the viscount to town under strict conditions."

"How long do you estimate the viscount will be supine?"

"At least a se'nnight, possibly ten days, Mr. Darcy."

George Darcy winced at the answer.

"What is eluding my understanding, Darcy?" The earl turned and raised his eyebrows in question as he looked at his brother.

"Mr. Burton, correct me if I am in error, but the viscount will require hourly attention and nurses to take care of his bodily functions. For him to remain immobile, may he require restraints?"

Burton nodded. "You are correct in the generalities, sir. The specifics are more complex and involved."

"What do you need to bring my heir back to health?"

"I shall draw up a list including supplies, staffing requirements, and scheduling."

"Will this impact his current treatment regime?"

"Yes."

Both the earl and his brother appeared surprised by the short, abrupt answer.

"We had hoped that increased physical activity would provide enough stimulation to overcome his emotional challenges—"

"What are you not saying, Mr. Burton?" interrupted the earl.

"Successful medical treatment of the viscount will most likely result in an excessively costly victory for the earldom."

George Darcy cleared his throat. The earl nodded to his friend and, now, family advisor. "Please elaborate."

"For the patient to recover, he must remain still. This will, at times—as you alluded to, Mr. Darcy—require restraints. His current distrust of all but the familiar will impel him to physically resist such treatment. The only true, long-range medical course is to calm him with laudanum." The surgeon stopped talking and waited on the two gentlemen.

Mr. Darcy sourly summarized the surgeon's words. "The viscount faces bleeding to death, mental collapse, or the lotus-eater's disease—one or more poisons from which to choose. That is the young man's fate?"

Burton ignored what he thought was censure. "You must prepare for losing all previous progress; for whichever course of treatment we attempt, we should anticipate even greater mental repercussions."

The earl held up his hand, cutting off further conversation. "Clarke."

The Ashdale butler reentered the study.

"See to Mr. Burton's requests, and ensure he faces no impediments."

Clarke opened the study door further and stood at attention. Burton bowed to both men and exited the study. The Ashdale butler closed the door.

The earl addressed his brother. "Now, you know what no one else knows, Darcy. Tell me what you believe to be the [illegible] in my son's treatment details."

George Darcy understood the impact of the surgeon's diagnosis. It was a disaster for the entire Fitzwilliam family. The heir to one of the largest earldoms in the country had just received what amounted to a death sentence.

"Henry, let us allow cooler heads to prevail for the moment. Mr. Burton is competent and compassionate. His focus will need to be on your heir. Allow Richard to spend more time at Pemberley with his cousin."

The earl, his nose and chin resting on his fist, nodded his compliance. "I shall inform his mother this evening as Langston must repair to town as early as possible. Thank you, Darcy. While Richard says little, he does speak well of William."

The earl rose to his feet. "We shall keep our perspective. Let us garner her ladyship's opinion when we gather for dinner."

October 1794

Richard, Villiers behind him, entered the ballroom, hopeful for combat training. He enjoyed physical contact and looked forward to tussling. As he expected to see the Prussian and no others, Mr. Burton's presence pleased him.

Engagement day today. What will the Prussian surprise me with this time?

Richard nodded at Mr. Burton, looked at the Prussian, and smiled. The arms master's eyes widened. He looked over to Richard's long-time medical retainer.

Villiers watched his captain—the rank to which his young master answered—walk toward his instructor. Captain Fitzwilliam was a lithe, fit boy, hardened by constant physical training. He moved like a cat, his shoulders undulating with his gait and each of his steps silent as he rolled from his heels to his toes—predatory and dangerous.

I would not want to be his foe. Villiers shuddered.

The Prussian began at the surgeon's nod. "Cadet Fitzwilliam, we train in hand-to-hand combat today. We must expect situations where no weapons are available, and still we must vanquish our enemy. Is today's objective clear?"

"Yes."

"I shall have to assist you with the required protective garments. May I proceed?"

The young man set his arms out like wings with his feet shoulder-width apart. He looked over his shoulder at the surgeon, one eyebrow raised. Markov stepped back.

Mr. Burton's reply was succinct. "I am here because this is a trauma engagement."

Without warning, Captain Fitzwilliam twisted his upper body, his opponent's fist glancing off his shoulder. A lean man in military garb assumed a stance like a pugilist. Villiers had seen him hiding behind the weapon's rack but did not shout a warning.

The two fighters circled each other. The man reached forward and grabbed his opponent's arm with ease. The young lord spun around, trapping his opponent's arm. He threw himself up into the man's chest and wrapped his arms and his legs around his opponent's neck and torso. The sound of cracking bone filled the air. Villiers saw that the man's arm and wrist were trapped between his own body and his opponent's. The man cried out.

Fitzwilliam hooked his ankles behind his opponent's thighs, then threw his weight up and forward. The injured man's feet flew up in the air as he fell flat on his back, a giant *woof* forced from his lungs as he crashed to the padded floor. His young opponent rode him to the ground.

The man tried to strike his opponent with his uninjured arm. The effort failed as Richard blocked the attempt and then smashed his forehead against his opponent's nose.

Broken, thought Villiers.

The same attack was repeated once, twice, and thrice more. The captain finally appeared to rest, sitting upon his opponent like he was riding a horse—knees bent, shins parallel to the ground. Blood stained his forehead. He tilted his face up to the ceiling, eyes closed, and roared, his hands clenched upon his thighs.

Mr. Burton grasped Captain Markov's forearm. Neither moved. The air was pungent with perspiration, the sound of pain, the smell of blood, and fear. Villiers himself had rocks in his stomach; he panted in disbelief.

"Cadet, explain yourself."

Captain Fitzwilliam opened his eyes and pointed at the man on the ground.

"Enemy."

"Why did you continue to attack him?"

"You said vanquish, not defeat," he growled.

Villiers gasped.

The young master turned and peered at his adversary. He leaned down to a point where they were nose-to-nose.

The man opened his one unswollen eye.

"You…are…vanquished."

"Yer a [illegible], ye!"

Richard pressed the man's lips shut with his hand. He shook his head.

No, thought Villiers. *He is Raguel, the angel of justice.*

Letter from David Burton to Thomas Bennet, Esq.—

My friend, today I witnessed that which words cannot express, as the entire event is without description.

The Prussian scheduled a weapons-free combat engagement with an armorer of the Seventh Foot. I need not remind you of the prowess of such men, as you are tended by Sergeant Reeves—a more capable man of such a group one has yet to meet.

Know I have all my faculties in place and I do not exaggerate. RF, at twelve years of age, dismantled the man in mere seconds. Nothing more need be said. The man's injuries will keep him from his duties for months. Months!

I am aware members of this august family do not voluntarily serve the King, but mark my words...if given the opportunity, the kingdom's security would benefit should he be allowed to do so. The battlefield, as you and I well know, would appeal to one of his caliber: he who hides a natural brutality that he controls so well.

Pass my regards to Reeves and Hill.

—David Burton

Chapter 16

Lambton, June 1795

A thirteen-year-old Richard Fitzwilliam slowed his mount, allowing his batman to catch up to him. He snorted to himself. The earl's outrage at his refusal to join the Ashdale estate survey still amused him. His mother's pleading was less so. He did not consider himself heartless; rather, he knew what he wanted, and he would not accept anyone who would think to dictate to him. Spending the summer at Pemberley was a welcome respite.

His cousin William was spending the day with his father and Pemberley's new steward, Mr. Wickham. They were to ride the estate and make tenant visits. Richard had met the man and found him admirable—his son, less so. Darcy acknowledged that his father held Mr. Wickham, his former solicitor, in high regard and offered the man the Pemberley estate stewardship, which included patronage for his motherless son. George Wickham would join them at Cambridge. *We shall see how that goes.*

"Fancy a bite, Captain?"

Richard nodded. "Let us ride to the Crown."

The inn bustled with travelers. They settled at a small table in the rear and sat in silence. Richard noticed that Villiers seemed intent upon a point in the room and looked in the same direction. "What?"

Villiers's face darkened. "That group looks like trouble. Reminds me of the crowd I fought at school—cowards one and all. They flock together."

Richard saw them whispering amongst themselves, heads close together. They were watching the inn's side door. A pretty brunette walked in that direction carrying a basket.

"Nothing good ever happens to one leaving by the back door of the inn, Captain."

Richard nodded, his anger now a bitter copper taste in his mouth. He ground his teeth.

The young woman closed the door behind her. The four young men at the table rose and followed.

Villiers turned to warn his master. He discovered naught but an empty chair.

She again was that young girl cowering beneath a coach bench. Fear choked her as her gorge rose. Her mother wore a blank look, and blood gushed from her neck.

No! Not again!

Holding the basket up, Maddy tried to fend off her adolescent attackers. Their hands were everywhere. Hideous words filled her ears. The basket was knocked from her hand. She looked up, then turned her head and grimaced as a tongue licked her cheek. Without looking, she clawed at the face of the miscreant who abused her. She heard a yelp, then her cheek exploded in pain and her head bounced against something hard. Everything went dark.

Villiers shouldered his way through the lunchtime throng and burst through the door no less than ten seconds after he found his master's chair empty. Once outside, he breathed easier. The captain, one arm wrapped about a boy's neck, held the attacker's arm high up his back. A quick scan showed three others—two motionless, the other holding his groin and gagging into the dirt. The young lady remained still on the ground.

"Gather her things." Richard lifted the boy's arm higher.

"You are breaking my arm!"

Richard spun the offender around. He squeezed the miscreant's throat; with his other hand, he pressed a thumb into the boy's eye. Deeply. Wickham gagged.

"Leave or die."

Richard released him. Wickham ran off.

"Remove them."

Richard walked over and sat next to the unconscious girl. Villiers pulled up the first insensate boy by his lapels and slapped him in the face until he sputtered.

"Take your friends and leave."

The ruffian stumbled to his other friend, lifted him, and walked him to the third, who still held his groin. Together, they limped away.

"Go inside. Get a room and a chaperone."

Villiers entered the inn, went to the kitchen, and caught the attention of an older woman wearing an apron. "Mum, pardon me. I need your help."

"Yes, luv?"

"We need a room and a chaperone. A young lady has had an accident."

"Oh, my. Of course. I shall be at the stairs."

"Thank you, mum."

Villiers went back out the door and nodded to his master. Richard scooped up the girl and walked through the door. "Bring the basket."

Maddy heard murmurings, followed by words. Her head ached, and she was loath to open her eyes.

"She is coming around, Captain."

The pressure in Maddy's chest vanished. He had returned! "Captain Bennet, you came back," she whispered.

"Who is Captain Bennet?"

Maddy opened her eyes. It was not Captain Bennet.

Richard Fitzwilliam's mouth went dry. Langston women alone had been blessed with violet eyes. This young woman had to be an aunt or cousin, but one he had never met. He recalled his mother speaking to his father about their missing relations. Observation and information combined into a conclusion. "You are Madeleine Lambert. You are my cousin."

The young woman shook her head, her face etched with fear.

Common sense overruled Richard's normally direct nature. "My name is Richard Fitzwilliam. I am the second son of the Earl of Matlock. My mother was a Langston—like your mother. You are Madeleine Lambert, my cousin. We have been looking for you and your parents for a very long time."

The young woman continued to shake her head. Her eyes filled.

"I will not hurt you. I am here to protect you."

The young woman stared at him. A moment later, she blinked away her tears and sat up.

"How old are you?" she asked.

Richard smiled, tilting his head. "I am thirteen. How old are you?"

His cousin's eyes wide, she replied, "I am twenty."

Richard nodded. "Would you like to go home?"

"My *home* is nearby."

Richard understood her meaning. He would protect her secret. "Where is *home*?"

"The bookstore."

"May I escort you?"

"You may."

Maddy accepted Richard's arm. Together, they walked down the street toward the bookstore. The long-armed young man followed them with her basket.

Maddy looked at her savior. "Did those boys strike you?"

"No."

"Your mouth is bleeding."

Richard grinned. He made a mental note to complete a detailed triage with his batman later. His mind course-corrected to the important revelation of the day. "Who is Captain Bennet?"

"He is the one who saved me when my parents were killed."

Richard nodded.

"Do you know of him?" she asked.

"Not yet."

She looked at Richard, confusion on her face.

"But I soon shall."

Matlock House, September 1795

Hurst exited the earl's study and walked toward the front door. An arm waving from the door of a small parlor distracted him. Intrigued, he pivoted and entered the room. The door closed behind him.

"With whom am I to speak?"

"Me."

Hurst turned to his rear. Richard Fitzwilliam stood in front of the closed door. He motioned to a pair of wingback chairs. Hurst, never one to pass on an opportunity to gather information, took the far chair, crossed his legs, and settled in. Minutes passed while the silence remained unbroken.

Well, by Jove, he is patient. "How may I assist you, Captain?"

Richard grinned.

"Yes, I listen," admitted Hurst.

"You do, sir."

Hurst smiled. The lad was top-notch. "What would you like to discuss?"

"I spend my summers at Pemberley."

"I am aware."

"My batman and I ride the shire."

"You must experience many new sites and make great discoveries."

"Yes, I do. I have."

"Pray tell, what is the greatest discovery from this past summer?"

Richard's face turned to stone. Hurst involuntarily swallowed. "The Lambton Bookstore."

Hurst slowly nodded. "What else have you discovered?"

"Wrong question, Mr. Hurst."

Hurst decided not to toy with this young man. He did not fear for his life, but prudence was a principle. "What have you learned, Captain?"

"That is the correct rank, Mr. Hurst."

"Hurst. We are speaking as equals. Call me Hurst."

"What do you know of Captain Bennet, Hurst?"

"You have spoken with her?"

"I have."

"She identified him?"

"She did."

"In what manner, may I inquire?"

"As her savior."

Hurst leaned back and expelled a breath. "Thank you for the confirmation. He does not deserve to be harmed."

"He must give testimony."

"Yes, Captain. When the opportunity presents itself."

Richard nodded.

Chapter 17

Matlock House, August 1796

The earl perused the cover note in his left hand, the script quite familiar. He was unsure whether it was a gift or a curse. He read again the letter on his desk.

My Lady,
The banns have been read for the first time in Lambton and St. Mary's in Watford, just outside of town. With my uncle's passing at the end of this last winter, once I wed, I shall leave here forever. I have sold the shop to an enterprising young man who comes well recommended. I owe you my gratitude for having kept my secret and for your promise to be available if needed. That responsibility will now pass to my soon-to-be husband, Mr. Edward Gardiner.
Madeleine Wells

Returning to the cover note, the earl shook his head.

Henry.
It is she.
Thea

"Smythe!"
"Yes, my lord?"
"Fetch Hurst."

Watford, September 1796

Thomas Bennet stepped out of his carriage in Watford, followed by his brother Philips and Philips's wife, Hattie. They had traveled together to attend Edward's wedding at St. Mary's. Thomas was alone because Franny, heavy with their fifth, and Lord willing, male child, could not travel. *This blasted entail is making a mockery of family felicity!*

All understood that Thomas could attend the ceremony but had to return quickly to his wife, so Hattie would travel to London with the newly married couple. Gardiner had requested Philips stand in as the father of the bride; she had lost her only uncle after a prolonged illness. Her three months of mourning had ended; the bride was eager to leave her uncle's village, and the young bridegroom was eager to wed.

Gardiner was sitting in the pew closest to the altar. His left knee jittered. He saw Thomas and smiled. Thomas pointed at his leg.

"My bride is not ready yet. I hope she is not changing her mind."

"You worry too much, Brother. Although I have not met her, I am sure she knows that you are a good man, full of love. I doubt whether she knows the word 'jilt.'"

Gardiner chuckled and smiled his appreciation. "Thank you, Brother."

"Not at all. Not at all. So, if we have time, tell me a little more about…?"

"Maddy. Maddy Wells."

A knot twisted Thomas's stomach. Though "Wells" was not a common surname, it was not so uncommon. It was no "Smith," "Jones," or "Baxter," but it was neither a "Yeatman" nor a "Snodgrass." It could be equal to say...Bennet or Gardiner. *Irony, thy name becomes you.*

"From where does your bride hail?"

"She hails from Lambton, in Derbyshire."

Thomas's stomach relaxed a bit.

Gardiner continued a bit dreamily as all young men did in the first throes of love. "Her uncle owned the bookstore and managed the circulating library. I made her acquaintance when I spent time in the shop during a business trip in the region. Afterward, I managed to find a way to put the town on my circuit! She is a voracious reader, one whom I believe Lizzy will emulate as she ages. She is kind, compassionate, gracious...I could extol her virtues all day and never tire!"

Thomas tried to smile. It pleased him that Edward was so happy, but he was unsettled. His brother continued as footsteps sounded in the aisle.

"Maddy is so beautiful. Lovely brunette tresses framing the face of a princess, a face containing eyes so unique, so striking, the color of..." He paused as the parson made his way across the chapel's front. Then Gardiner rose and turned. "Sorry, sorry, Bennet, please forgive me for leaving you on your own. The rector signals that all is in readiness."

After Gardiner moved away toward his future, Bennet settled in a pew near the center of the church. He was inclined to sit by himself. The situation did not remain so, as someone approached him and sat to his right, adjacent to the aisle.

Whom he saw astonished him. "Hurst?"

"Bennet."

Bennet's former colleague nodded and then faced the altar. Bennet stared at him.

Without having met Gardiner's fiancée, Bennet, seeing Hurst, understood that the future Mrs. Edward Gardiner née Wells would have *"...eyes so unique, so striking, the color of...violet."*

The bride appeared on Philips's arm. Thomas kept his head down, hiding behind Hurst.

Hurst never looked away from the ceremony. "Bennet, you are a secretive man. Your service to the King required this. Today is not a day to exhibit such dedication."

"Hurst?"

"Take advantage of your presence in this church today to absolve that which you hold in error."

"Hurst!"

"Speak freely. Do not incur the Lord's wrath nor that of his messenger on today of all days." Hurst stood and joined the couple, placing himself beside the groom.

Thomas failed to understand the Lord's sense of humor. Nor the earl's. Nor Hurst's. Ultimately, he surrendered to the inevitable.

That came twenty minutes after the vows. The bride surrendered a maiden name saturated with secrecy and gained another primed with potential. Gardiner escorted his wife up the aisle.

Speechless, nauseous, and unsure of himself for maybe the first time in his life, Thomas Bennet gawked at the grown-up version of a child he had last seen in a tired rectory.

Madeleine Gardiner gazed back at Captain Thomas Bennet, aged far beyond what one would expect in the fifteen years since their last meeting. "I have waited a lifetime to see you again, sir."

Thomas shook his head in denial, unable to form words, his jaw tight. His eyes filled with tears and regret. He found it difficult to breathe properly. He gagged out. "I lost you."

"Maddy?" queried her new husband.

The new Mrs. Gardiner held up a delicate hand. "I realized that and forgave you for your tardiness. You have been in my prayers every night." She rose onto her toes and kissed Bennet's cheek, cupping the other side of his face with her hand. "Thank you so very, very much," she whispered.

Thomas cared not that his tears spilled over. Madeleine Lambert Gardiner's majestic violet eyes embraced him. She knew his innocence and absolved him of his guilt. Would that he could do the same for himself. Yet, he could not.

She laced her arm through her husband's, turned to leave, and took one last look over her shoulder at him, a Vermeer painting handsomely come to life.

Thomas left the church, eschewing the wedding breakfast and avoiding Hurst. Had he been less affected, he would have been more attuned to the danger Hurst's attendance represented.

Thomas climbed into his carriage and sat on the front-facing seat, ignorant of his immediate environment. He reached up to rap the ceiling and failed, his walking stick parried. He looked across and stared into Death's face. Bennet's angel of judgment sat stock still in the guise of an adolescent. Thomas recognized his executioner from David Burton's letters.

Richard Fitzwilliam pulled a short knife from the inside of his boot.

"Are you going to kill me?"

Richard rolled the knife in his hand. His black eyes were resolute.

Thomas sighed in resignation. "My final wish would be for my friend Hugh to see his daughter's happiness."

The young killer replaced the knife into his boot. He sat back.

Thomas leaned back to think. He looked across at Richard.

"Why are you here?"

"Cousin Maddy."

Thomas's mind cleared. He now understood all of it: Hurst appearing at his wartime preparations, the earl's request for Bennet's participation in smoking out disgruntled servants, and the hunt for the forger backed by an aristocrat. His expertise never had been required for the assignments. *He* was the assignment. The Earl of Matlock had learned something of his participation in the young Miss Madeleine Lambert's relocation. Now they wanted to claim justice for the years of forced separation.

Or is it my silence they desire? "Allow me to share with you a sorrowful tragedy." Bennet's voice was low and lacked inflection.

The wolf in sheep's clothing leaned forward to listen, ready to reconcile Bennet with the Almighty, one way or another. His eyes narrowed, wary but receptive.

"Entrusting my friend's daughter to a priest to keep her safe, uncertain of your family's intentions, is my greatest regret. I placed caution—not for myself, but for your cousin—over care. Having realized my faulty judgment, I immediately returned, only to find my friend's fresh grave and no sign of Maddy. I had lost her. Know that I have, to this day, rued my most miserable actions."

Thomas Bennet looked down at his hands, surprised they did not shake. Looking back up, he recounted every detail, nearly every name, and every location related to that horrible week.

"A Matlock Fitzwilliam figures in this horrible affair. I have never known which one, although your connection with Hurst suggests it is not your branch."

"Send Hurst the letters you recovered from the murderers."

Bennet nodded. He did not ask questions. As was his wont, he withheld the name of the surgeon, protecting Mr. Burton from possible recriminations.

The interview carried on for some minutes until the wraith was satisfied that all had been spoken. He slipped from the coach but not before he had leaned across to rest his hand atop Bennet's knee. "Thank you for being a friend and doing that which her father was unable to accomplish. My family—I—shall remember your service."

The carriage transported a depleted Thomas Bennet to Hertfordshire. His ride back to Longbourn lasted too long and was not long enough. Bennet would have traded places with Odysseus given the opportunity. It was the one time in his life he despised Homer.

Thomas arrived home well after sunset. He entered the house

through the kitchen door, walked up the stairs, and entered the sitting room he shared with Franny. He expected to sit alone in front of the fire and dwell upon his failures. His wife surprised him, awake and waiting. Thomas sat, not knowing what to expect.

"Mr. Bennet, we must have a conversation."

He nodded dumbly.

Franny adjusted her dressing gown over her abundant abdomen. She stared at him without speaking for a few moments. Thomas knew not how to feel, his discomfort palpable. His wife cleared her throat, capturing his attention. "We cannot go on in this manner, Thomas."

"What manner is that, Franny?"

"This distraction of yours, that which pulls your attention away from your family."

Thomas raised his fist to his mouth and bit his knuckle. His breathing quickened, so he bit down harder. The pain felt real; all else was a haze. His stomach lurched. He pressed his other hand into his abdomen. He looked for a basket, a vessel, a pitcher, anything!

"Breathe, Thomas."

He looked to the ceiling, his head and body leaning back against the sofa. A wet cloth cooled his forehead. Tears leaked from his eyes. He did not deserve the forgiveness of another woman whose life, he now realized, he had not improved upon.

He took a few stabilizing breaths and sat up. Taking his wife's hand, he looked her in the eye.

"May I tell you of a sorrowful tragedy…?" his voice cracking upon the last word.

He recited the entire horror and his related failures. His shame compelled him to fixate upon his hands as he did so. The tale finished, and he looked up.

Franny sat next to him, a sad smile on her face. She opened her arms wide in invitation. Smothering a whimper, Thomas fell into her embrace and back into his family.

Chapter 18

Pemberley, May 1799

Inside the stable, two young men close in age and of long-standing but deteriorating friendship were arguing while a third looked on from the shadows, unseen.

"You force me to repeat myself, Wickham. You are abusing the trust of our family," insisted Fitzwilliam Darcy. "It is your father who holds a position here at Pemberley. That gives *you* little right to trade on his good name and none to trade on ours."

"As much as your father sponsors my education, my father and I are servants, paid as servants, treated as servants, and, therefore, respected as servants," argued George Wickham. Older than Darcy, Wickham believed his opinion should carry the day. He had become accustomed to being the leader in his circle of ruffians, bullying them to accept his point of view. "If my father is so important, we should have more money!"

"This is not something you or I can approach our fathers over, so why are we speaking of it?"

Wickham again repeated, "I need more money. I should be able to sit at the table with you and your friends. I should have finer clothes."

Wickham watched Darcy level a haughty glare at him. "It is hard to address your concerns when you trade on the Darcy name in less than reputable activities and locales."

"I was wondering when His Highness would speak his true opinion. Do you plan to inform your father? Ruin my prospects?"

Darcy shook his head in the negative. "You will scuttle your own ship, Wickham. When that occurs, do not approach me for assistance. I know who and what you are, and it is nothing like the charismatic young man my father believes you to be. You are on notice."

Darcy turned and walked to his horse, his back to Wickham. Seeing Darcy's back, Wickham seethed. The injustice. The unfairness. He told himself over and over that he deserved the wealth as much as Fitzwilliam Darcy. Yet George Wickham, deep down, was a coward. Seeing his opportunity for some revenge, Wickham bent down and picked up a palm-sized stone. But as he went to throw it, his arm was caught in an iron grip.

He looked backward and found it hard to breathe. His wrist was squeezed so hard, he dropped the rock. He swung his other fist and hit his assailant's forehead, missing the targeted nose as Darcy's silent cousin lowered his face out of the way.

Richard Fitzwilliam looked up and smiled, his upper incisors hooked upon his lower lip. Wickham's bladder voided. "No, no, no…" was as far as he got before something rock-hard connected with his chest. He collapsed to the ground. He could not draw air and repeatedly wheezed. Richard dropped to his knees and straddled him.

Wickham could not stop himself. He whimpered.

Richard looked up as Darcy called out, "Oy, cuz?"

"Threw a rub in the way."[8]

8 Spoiled one's plans

Darcy must have made some kind of hand gesture. Wickham did not hear a question.

"Teach him a lesson," whispered Richard, flicking his chin toward the stable door.

Darcy handed his cousin a broken shovel handle as he walked past. Wickham's eyes teared up. Three strikes to his chest pushed him into unconsciousness.

Richard Fitzwilliam methodically battered every inch of Wickham's body that would be hidden from view. He never touched his victim's face or lower arms, but he marked his legs, buttocks, back, and chest. No doubt, George Wickham would be incapable of riding a horse for several weeks, and he would never, ever forget the moment he betrayed the Darcy family. How the wretch would explain his injuries mattered not. Let the time his recovery from these injuries required leave a lasting impression upon his disloyalty.

Richard dropped the cudgel when his cousin alerted him and kicked loose hay over Wickham's inert form. A quick look confirmed no blood had been spilled. Richard tapped Darcy on the shoulder, finger to his lips. Darcy nodded. Richard walked forward to intercept the footman before anyone could enter through the stable door.

The footman stopped and spoke. "It be me—John, sir." He looked down at his hands holding a paper. "I 'as a message for ye."

Richard held out his hand. Taking the note, he nodded. John the footman knuckled his forehead and ran off. Richard waited, and a moment later, Darcy appeared over his shoulder.

Richard handed the message up to Darcy without looking at it, and Darcy summarized it aloud, as this was their way. Darcy read. Darcy spoke. Darcy wrote. Richard planned. Richard acted. Richard resolved. They allowed none to influence them; they permitted none to breach their bond. It was a formidable pairing of two teen boys. As men, they would be a force to reckon with.

"You are to go to Matlock House immediately. The carriage is waiting with your bags stowed. Your batman is efficient." Darcy looked at his cousin. "Your brother must have had another accident. Hopefully, he still lives."

Richard nodded, looked down, and sighed loudly. He did not object to being pulled into an embrace. Words seemed to fail Darcy, but his heart spoke this time. "Do not allow them to change your plans."

Richard snorted his derision at such a notion. He signed their credo. *"Non est dubium."*

Darcy signed it back. Richard peered at him as if measuring his mettle. Darcy stared back, refusing to flinch. Richard nodded.

"Race you," rasped Richard, gesturing toward the main house with his chin.

Both young men launched, sprinting at full speed toward the Pemberley kitchens, laughing and grappling, each looking for an advantage over the other for a victory. Neither gave a second thought to the unconscious George Wickham buried in the hay on the stable floor.

Intermezzo:
1803–1806

Chapter 19

Longbourn Village, Hertfordshire, October 1803

Reeves, Longbourn's first footman, trailed a respectful distance behind the two eldest Bennet daughters. He was ever vigilant against threats, tasked by his commander to ensure their well-being. However, the doughty soldier could not insulate them from what he could not see.

Jane and Elizabeth Bennet carried baskets as they walked through the woods on their regular tenant visits.

"I hope these dresses are not too large for Dottie. Perhaps we ought to consider other girls."

Reeves smiled. Miss Lizzy was once again three steps ahead of everyone in case they were too optimistic.

"Let's complete our visit to the West family before we reclothe the entire female tenantry, shall we?"

Lizzy laughed and grasped her sister's free hand. "What would I do without your beautiful practicality, Jane?"

She smiled a Jane smile—sweet, loving—but her teeth remained hidden.

Reeves continued to trail the pair as the West cottage became visible through the tree line.

Dottie West walked along the Meryton road on her way back home from picking flowers. Her scruffy dress was worn and patched. Hopelessly overlarge, the frock hung low on her shoulders. Not minding the mud from the road, she swung the ragged basket full of wildflowers back and forth as she concentrated on taking large, brave steps like her hero, Miss Lizzy. Dottie did not see the peddler and his cart until she all but crashed into both.

"Ho there now, li'l missy."

Dottie gasped, then lowered her chin.

"Pard'n me."

"Lovely flowers there, li'l missy. Takin' 'em to your mum?"

"Ayuh." She looked up and saw it was a peddler. She hesitated.

"I be on me way to Meryton…will I see your mum in one of 'em shops?"

"Uh-uh," shaking her head, "we farm the Bennet land."

He bent, sniffed her bouquet, and let loose a tremendous sneeze. He pulled a grubby rag from a pocket and scrubbed at his dripping nose. "Ah be sensitive to wildflowers. Ah'll be on me way."

The peddler grabbed his cart and walked off. Dottie continued on her way and gave her mother the basket the moment she arrived home. This happy surprise led to loving hugs and kisses. More hugs were exchanged when the Bennet sisters handed her mother their basket. The best part of Dottie's day was when her hero, Miss Lizzy, picked her up and twirled her like a weathervane.

That next evening, the Bennet women sat together in the family parlor. Mrs. Bennet had settled herself in the chair closest to the hearth, her "ducklings" arranged around her. Six-year-old Lydia and Kitty, aged eight, sat to her left and whispered amongst themselves. Jane and Lizzy, on their mother's right, focused on their needlework. Miss Sarah Abernathy, their governess, sat in the opposite corner with a book. She looked up from time to time to monitor the youngest girl's behavior, as they were rarely allowed below stairs. Musical scales bled through the wall as eleven-year-old Mary worked to perfect her pianoforte playing.

Lydia pouted. "I wish Mary would practice something else."

Mrs. Bennet smiled at her youngest. "No one ever improved without constant practice. Mark my words, I assure you that you will hear this from others."

Before she could continue, Kitty sneezed. "Mama, I do not feel well."

Mrs. Bennet got up and put her lips to her daughter's forehead. "Hill…Hill! Bring the medicinals!"

She turned a partial pirouette, fluttering her handkerchief in the air.

In unison, all four girls groaned. Miss Abernathy bowed her head. She knew what the *medicinals* meant for the girls. Mary made it unanimous, her groan heard through the wall.

Kitty cringed as her nose filled with the vapors that emanated from slathered wrists, neck, and forehead. She coughed in defiance.

Jane and Lizzy lined up in front of their mother as Mary came into the parlor from the music room and queued up. All waited their turn for their mother's lips.

Mrs. Bennet gasped. "Jane…you are also warm."

Jane maintained her placidity as her mother coated her wrists, neck, and forehead with her "miracle salve."

"Jane…go to your room. Lizzy…you are fine. Of course, you are. You never get sick, traipsing all over the countryside. Well, your sisters must join you, I daresay. Mary…you too are fine. Humph. To be safe, though, both of you will sleep together until Jane and Kitty improve."

Mrs. Bennet put the back of her wrist to her forehead, signifying the beginnings of a plan. "Mary, take Kitty to your room. Go…go." She fluttered her handkerchief toward the stairs.

"Come here, Lydia. Do not think you have gone unnoticed."

Lydia stood in front of her mother, a frown on her face as her mother's lips touched her forehead. Her large smile matched her mother's as she was granted clemency from the medicinal punishment she loathed.

Mrs. Bennet slept very poorly that evening, worry for her ducklings foremost in her thoughts.

Upon her husband's desk, William Shakespeare's *The Life and Death of King Richard the Second* lay open. Had the master of Longbourn looked closely, he would have despaired over the displayed *Act III, Scene II:*

> *"Woe, destruction, ruin, and decay;*
> *The worst is death, and death will have his day."*

Chapter 20

Longbourn, November 1803

Jane opened her eyes although her vision remained blurry. Her head ached. Violently. Blinking several times cleared the haze but not her megrim. She peered left. Grandmama Bennet sat in a chair, reading. As Grammy had passed years ago, Jane knew it was a dream. She closed her eyes.

Jane watched Grammy. Her father's mother read from the book she held. It was very strange. Her lips moved but Jane heard no words. The pain in her head exhausted her. She closed her eyes.

Jane heard a throat clear. She opened her eyes. Grammy held up her book. Jane blinked. Grammy was still there. "What are you reading, Grammy?" Dream or not, Jane craved conversation.

"The Castle of Otranto."

Jane had never enjoyed her grandmother's taste in the Gothic and reminded her Grammy of that fact.

"How will you learn to escape the heir if I do not educate you?"

"Whatever do you mean, Grammy?"

"Beware of Conrad, the coming heir, for he will avoid the falling helmet if you do not direct the path."

Jane was bewildered. She closed her eyes. The name Conrad compounded the ever-present headache she felt would never diminish. She drifted off to sleep.

Jane woke and winced in discomfort. She desired to massage her temples but stopped, the effort to move exhausting. A throat cleared. She slowly, slowly turned toward the sound.

Mrs. Hill sat in a chair at her bedside with a washbasin and wet tea towel in her hand. She wiped Jane's forehead.

"Mrs. Hill?" she whispered.

"You 'ave been ill these three weeks, Miss Jane."

"And Lizzy?"

"You be seein' 'er in due course. Let us get you well. Time to sit you up."

Jane placed her hands flat on the bed at her sides to push herself up, to no avail. Mrs. Hill tutted and lifted Jane into a sitting position.

Mr. Hill came through the door carrying a bowl; the aroma indicated chicken broth. Jane's stomach rumbled.

"Forgive me, Mrs. Hill."

"Never you mind, luv. Try a spoonful."

Jane swallowed. Her stomach rebelled. She turned and vomited into the chamber pot Mr. Hill held by her head. Mrs. Hill held her through her continued dry heaving. Jane hugged herself in pain. She felt her ribs through her chemise.

Jane's convulsions slowed and then stopped. Mrs. Hill wiped her mouth, and then laid her back on the pillow. Jane turned her head away, covered her face, and wept.

A se'nnight later, the housekeeper helped Jane down the stairs to the back parlor. Lizzy was grimly dressed. She sat at the writing table, staring at the wall, spinning a quill pen atop her fingertips like a weathervane swirling with the wind. *I must learn how she does that one day.*

Jane shivered as Mrs. Hill guided her across the parlor. Lizzy jumped up and draped her with one of their mother's shawls. Then, relieving Mrs. Hill of her precious cargo, she tenderly looped her arm through Jane's and led her to Mrs. Bennet's favorite wingback chair closest to the hearth. Jane sank down, grateful for the warmth. "I am glad you have recovered, dearest."

Her sister's eyes widened.

She must still be as weak as I. "Lizzy, where is everyone? Have they gone calling?"

Her sister's eyes filled with tears.

Lizzy never cries!

Jane tried to reach for Lizzy's hand but lacked the energy. She retreated. The small parlor lacked the everyday chaos of over-spilled work baskets, ribbons draped over the furniture, and music sheets on every table. Jane turned to her sister.

"Lizzy, why are you wearing black?"

Lizzy shook her head back and forth. A faint mewl escaped her lips.

Fatigued, Jane withdrew into herself and closed her eyes. Her senses picked up where her tired eyes had left off. Nothing seemed familiar.

A ruckus from the rear servant stairs alerted her that the others were home, although the amount of noise and raised voices was extraordinary. Finding herself alone, she staggered to the window that overlooked the garden and the small stable. It was there she witnessed the devastation the epidemic had visited upon her family.

A group of men hurried across the yard. Her father and Reeves were in front. Each grasped a corner of a sheet. Mr. Hill and Mr. Jones were in the rear, the remaining sheet corners clutched in theirs. In the center of the makeshift stretcher was Kitty, clad only in her chemise. She undulated back and forth. Froth bubbled about her mouth.

Jane watched the men plunge her sister into a horse trough filled with water and snow. She gasped. Her father pushed Kitty below the water's surface. Jane's eyes rolled up into her head. *I cannot…I cannot breathe!*

Mrs. Hill's arms kept Jane from collapsing into a boneless pile.

Kitty awakened from a dreamless sleep. Her throat ached. Her body ached. She closed her eyes to listen. The normal din of the house was absent. *It must be late.* She tried to kick the counterpane down, but the left side failed to move. Kitty peered in that direction. Lizzy was hunched over in a chair, her arm on the bed, her forehead upon her arm. Her other hand held a closed book, her thumb a bookmark. Kitty poked Lizzy's shoulder.

Her elder sister lifted her head. She looked at Kitty. Her eyes widened. She burst into tears.

"What happened?" asked Kitty. Her throat was on fire. "Uh. Was I sick?"

Lizzy put a finger to her own lips.

"Where is Jane?" If one sister was ill, Jane nursed them back to health. Jane measured out the herbs for teas. Jane hugged. Jane murmured sweet tidings. *Where is Jane?*

Kitty saw Lizzy's lips move, but no sound came out.

"Speak louder, I cannot hear you," cried Kitty in a panic. Lizzy winced. "What happened to me?"

Kitty panted in her distress. Lizzy crawled under the blankets and embraced her.

"No." She pushed at her sister. "What happened to me?" She felt faint. She ceased struggling. Lizzy held her. Her breathing eased. Soon she wept, as did her sister.

Both girls wailed for the unknowns in their lives.

Kitty cried for the fear of not hearing, not knowing why Lizzy cried, not knowing where Jane was.

Lizzy cried for not being Jane, not knowing how to explain Kitty's trials, and not knowing how to tell Kitty of the losses their family had endured.

The se'nnight that Kitty remained abed, she cried. Lydia, her best friend, was gone. Mary was gone. God was gone. She whispered prayers but could not hear herself. Disheartened, she screamed. Frustrated, she screamed again, then stopped as a tiny vibration near her left ear on her jawline made itself known. Wondering whether she could make it happen again, she screamed long and loud. She felt the tremor again—more pronounced now that she knew what to expect.

Lizzy ran into her room and Jane trailed behind. Waving her hands, Kitty mimed writing, and Elizabeth pushed a paper and pencil into her trembling hands.

Simple words told her elder sisters of a wonder: not that Kitty's hearing was returning, but rather that her world was not as closed as it had seemed just minutes before, and her recovery began in earnest.

Jane sat with Kitty, embraced her, and whispered love into her left ear. Kitty heard none of it, but she experimented by moving the left side of her face in all directions against Jane's lips. Jane giggled at Kitty's antics, as she did not understand her younger sister's intent. Kitty pointed her finger at her jaw, buzzed her lips, and wriggled her fingers. Eventually, she made herself understood. Together they tested Kitty's hypothesis until Jane identified the exact place where she felt the most vibration.

Finally able to climb toward the new light before her, Kitty rejoined her family. Her first dinner saw her making amends. Kitty wrote her apologies for her noisome behavior—not just during her illness, but before. Her mother accepted her regrets silently with a nonchalant flicking of her hand, not in dismissal but rather in sympathy for her daughter's condition. This led Kitty to tell of her discovery. She pointed to where she felt the sound's vibration. Jane demonstrated with her lips on Kitty's left jaw.

Her father narrowed his eyes and frowned at Kitty and Jane. He did not speak. The girls fidgeted. Thomas took Kitty's plain book, and in large letters, wrote: *Any man aware of this had better ask for your hand!*

Four faces turned to him, wide-eyed. Thomas smiled and winked.

Mr. and Mrs. Hill were having tea and cake with Reeves in the kitchen when they jumped at hearing, for the first time since the funerals, laughter in the dining room.

Chapter 21

Longbourn, February 1804

Miss Ophelia Ecclestone came to the Bennets on the recommendation of an archdeacon at St. Albans Cathedral. Miss Ecclestone twice had educated gentlewomen from girlhood to betrothal. Having learned of Longbourn's tragedy, she accepted her first *multiple-child* assignment. She was a tall, stocky woman who wore unadorned dresses with high collars, her hair pulled tight in a matron's bun. Her mantra was consistency; her visage was everything proper.

Little was required for the Bennet youngsters to behave properly and attend to their lessons promptly. A subtle throat clearing would settle Lizzy back into feminine behavior. Kitty continued to work through her hearing loss and adjusting to her new reality. Jane was…Jane.

"Decorum, decorum, decorum," repeated Miss Ecclestone to her pupils. Her girls. Her beautiful ladies. When alone, sitting in her reading chair, eyes closed and hands folded together, Ophelia rejoiced in her current circumstances.

Her first young lady, now so long ago, had been a client to her—nothing more, nothing less. She had educated her. She had outlined proper behavior. She had mentored. After the young lady came out, Miss Ecclestone continued as a companion. She had guided her charge through courtship and betrothal. She had accepted the young woman's gratitude. She had not been invited to the wedding.

Ophelia did not repine for she had already moved on. She would adhere to the script she had developed. Guide another insipid young lady from maiden to wife without scandal—all without investing anything of herself, of her heart. That all changed with the Bennet family. Ophelia Ecclestone, the spinster governess, had found something unexpected: purpose, passion, and family!

Now, nine weeks into her tenure, she was leading the girls in learning how to be in company, particularly that of gentlemen. Today's lesson was coordinated curtsies. The purpose was to demonstrate a dignified display and project respect with elegance and grace.

"Zoologists must be mistaken as they have written that the male peacock performs to attract his mate," quipped Lizzy. "Yet here we are learning to do just that."

"Miss Elizabeth, may we revisit that impertinent tongue of yours at a later hour? We have much to do if we are to remain on schedule," scolded Miss Ecclestone.

Jane rapped Lizzy with her fan and rolled her eyes.

"Miss Bennet, I am shocked to see *you* roll your eyes. My, my, what a morning we are having." She turned to Kitty, pulled a small notebook from her day dress pocket, flipped through some pages, and held it up for Kitty to see.

Et tu, Brute? Was written in large block letters. Kitty shook her head.

"Delightful. Let us continue."

Chagrined, the girls stood shoulder to shoulder. Jane first, next was Lizzy, Kitty to her left.

Before the governess could begin anew, Lizzy lifted her chin, miming the instructor. "The elegance is found in the *synchronicity*."

Miss Ecclestone shot Lizzy a dry look. "Yes, Miss Elizabeth, a word of over four syllables. They do exist, and I do know them." All three girls smirked. Kitty emulated her sisters. She would laugh later when they explained the governess's quip to her.

"Normally, the eldest would use a pursing of the lips to signal the 'dip,' as you refer to it, Miss Elizabeth. However, our situation warrants another, more overt approach."

Jane, Lizzy, and Kitty adored Miss Ecclestone for that single declaration alone. It had taken them no time to see through her gruff exterior and discover her huge heart. A heart that belonged to them, as they had given theirs to her freely. Their indispositions were *our* indispositions. Their lessons were *our* lessons. Their failures were *our* failures. Their governess embraced *our* limitations and rejoiced in her girls' successes.

"Miss Bennet, let us try a small head bob. You are much taller than Miss Catherine. She should be able to see your signal quite easily, I daresay."

The girls milled about the parlor as if at an assembly. Their governess then waved her hands to signify a pending introduction. The youngsters lined up as instructed. Kitty watched Jane from the corner of her eye. Jane nodded minutely, and in unison, the girls curtsied to the same depth and returned to a standing position.

"Well done, ladies. Again." The *again* was emphasized with a swirl of her arms.

The girls all checked their positions. Jane nodded. The girls curtsied.

"Well done. Let us practice until we—meaning *I*—tire of the exercise."

Jane and Lizzy had a delayed reaction, wide-eyed as they stared at their governess. Kitty sensed Miss Ecclestone had made a jest.

Everyone broke into laughter. Most unladylike, but oh, so diverting. The lesson continued.

The girls would practice their coordinated curtsies before sitting for a meal and again afterward. It took no time for Lizzy and Kitty to revert to mischief. They began curtseying every time Jane nodded her head, a habit common amongst all Bennets. The eldest quickly tired of being mocked by her younger sisters. Jane took her unexpected revenge in a most un-Jane-like manner. It happened while the Lucas ladies paid a call.

Jane, knowing of the anticipated visit from her mother, sent a short note to their friend Charlotte. In it, she implored her to ask direct Yes or No questions, as Jane would have both her sisters with her sharing the settee. The stage set, Jane embraced Ben Jonson's *The Silent Woman.*

"O Revenge, how sweet art thou!"

"Mama, is Maria joining Lady Lucas and Charlotte this afternoon?" inquired Lizzy, voicing both her and Kitty's question.

"I do not believe so." Franny looked to Jane. "Are you well enough for company, my dear?"

"I feel a bit fatigued, Mama. Rather than retire, may I remain seated? Lady Lucas would hopefully not take offense." Jane, with wide eyes, looked to her next younger sister.

"You must remain seated, Jane. We will act in your stead," replied Lizzy.

"Thank you, dearest." Jane lowered her eyes to her lap, better to conceal the slight smile she allowed herself.

Several minutes later, Hill announced their guests. "Lady Lucas and Miss Charlotte Lucas."

The Bennet ladies—sans Jane—rose and curtsied. Lady Lucas and Charlotte returned the compliment, then sat.

"Are you well, dearest Jane?" inquired Lady Lucas.

"My fatigue has returned earlier today than usual."

"I hope it has not curtailed your lessons?" queried Charlotte, a pointed look upon her face.

"No, dear Charlotte. My sisters adhere to all our decorum lessons as they are easily able to see my direction. Is that not true, sisters?" Jane shot a piercing look at her younger sisters.

Lizzy's eyes opened wide. She fiercely gripped Kitty's forearm, who looked up in surprise at her elder sister.

"Jane?" voiced a perplexed Lizzy.

"Yes?" replied Jane, then bobbing her head at her sisters.

Lizzy yanked Kitty up from the settee and squared her shoulders. Together, the two youngest Bennets curtsied.

"How delightful!" declared Lady Lucas.

"Yes, Miss Ecclestone indicates that elegance is found in the synchronicity," stated Franny proudly.

"Jane, did it take long to coordinate among the three of you?" asked Charlotte.

Jane bobbed her head. "It took little time." Jane peered at her sisters.

Lizzy and Kitty stood and curtsied.

"Without sounding indecorous, I imagine your three differing health situations provided a small challenge?" continued Charlotte.

"You imagine correctly." Jane nodded.

Lizzy and Kitty stood again and curtsied.

Franny and Lady Lucas shared a questioning look but allowed their eldest daughters to carry the conversation.

"I have so many questions, Jane."

"I am sure you do, Charlotte."

The girls' mothers heard a faint whimper from the younger Bennet daughters.

The next morning, an unsurprised Franny and Thomas entered the dining room to see Jane alone, her sisters yet to come down.

"Mrs. Hill!" bellowed Thomas, in good humor.

"Yes, Mr. Bennet?"

"Please go upstairs and remind our two younger *children* that the Bennet family dines together. The kitchen shall tender no trays. Take Reeves if you require assistance."

Mr. and Mrs. Bennet stared at Jane, who was breaking her fast in a most exaggerated ladylike fashion. Father and mother watched their eldest, first in wonder, then with a more piercing gaze upon their—until now—perfect daughter. Receiving no notice, they returned to their plates.

Moments later, Jane cleared her throat and looked her father in the eye.

"Irony takes nothing away from pathos."

Franny's eyes went as wide as a tea tray. Thomas, who had been drinking from his water glass, inhaled a mouthful. He leapt out of his chair and folded over the table, coughing violently.

Reeves, Hill, and moments later, the two younger girls, in a tizzy, ran to render him aid. They pounded his back and raised his arms. Anything to ease his distress. Thomas recovered himself and the family again sat. Lizzy and Kitty avoided looking directly at Jane. When their eldest sister stood, the girls cringed. Thomas made sure his water glass was on the table. Franny looked lost. Jane's lovely soprano wafted across the room as she exited with a quote from the Book of Common Prayer:

"Here endeth the lesson."

The epidemic also changed the way the Bennets dealt with their children. Thomas and Franny chose to actively participate in their daughters' education.

Franny taught ladies' pursuits— household budgeting, menu planning, and needlework. Lizzy usually ended up with Mrs. Ecclestone for deportment lessons as she could not sit still, nor had she the patience to produce displayable garments. Kitty and Jane both enjoyed sewing and stitching. Jane's patience was legendary, and Kitty strived to emulate her. Jane's formidable skill with an embroidery needle was widely praised by the twenty-four families who dined in after the Bennets' mourning had moved from black to gray.

Thomas covered history, classics, philosophy, and languages. He thrived on spending time with his daughters, either as a group or separately. Their individuality amazed him. He found Jane to be highly intelligent though she hid it well, her reasons personal to herself. He did not worry about her character because Jane was...Jane, although she had her moments: the Day of the Thousand Curtsies was always good for a chuckle. Thomas was pleased, for he now knew Jane for who she was.

He allowed Lizzy her choices from his library. Over several weeks, she borrowed many books. Notably, more than half were on treatises of mathematical theorems, dusty from disuse. Thinking to tease her about overreaching, he asked her opinion of an obscure equation in one of his older texts. Much to his surprise, she rectified his mistaken reference and cited the correct formula verbatim. Seeking to nurture her apparent passion, he gave her leave to work independently if she summarized her work to him. He worried her self-confidence would bring out unpleasant character traits. He listened attentively and counseled her to dilute the pomposity in her explanations. Eventually, she found a balance between expertise and arrogance.

Thomas marveled at how Kitty immersed herself while she read. Her concentration remained uninterrupted as sounds did not distract her. She would curl up in the chair by the fire, head down in concentration. She traced the words in her book with her right forefinger as her left hand curled the ends of her tresses around her fingers. It was a perfect picture that Thomas knew he would cherish until his final breath.

Thomas, at his leisure one afternoon, shared a decanter with his brother Philips, who was Meryton's lone solicitor. Sitting in the two chairs in front of a low-burning fire, they sipped port and let the conversation meander. It ended with the metaphorical Sword of Damocles hanging over the Bennet ladies' future security.

"Bennet, if I might offer an observation?"

"Yes?"

"Franny and Hattie had a bit of a row, a wee tiff, and Hattie is not satisfied with Franny's bland reaction to her concerns—big sisters and all that, you know."

"What was the subject of contention?"

"Bennet, I find I must side with Hattie's point—not with its delivery, mind you."

"Of course, Philips." Thomas waited, his patience at a healthy peak after his second glass of port.

"Would you mind relating to me what you know of the estate entail?"

"Only what my father told me: that Longbourn is entailed away from the female line and only a Bennet male—or in my case, a Collins—may inherit."

"Your father was a good man, but he had a mind shaped to be a gentleman farmer and not a man of business—or a solicitor. I have often asked myself whether there was more to the entail than you know.

"Hattie must have overheard my musings and wrestled with Franny over the nuances of what none of us knows."

Thomas paused to consider his brother's revelation. It surprised him that he had left any stones unturned. He had always accepted his father's pronouncements at face value. He admired his brother's perspicacity.

"I now realize I have been remiss, Philips. What do you propose?"

During the next fortnight, Philips reviewed the Longbourn copy of the entail documents. He rode post into town and purchased a certified copy of the entail documents as registered and filed with the Courts of Chancery. He suspected the Longbourn copy might be incomplete. His intuition proved correct. Deep in the ponderous document was salvation for the Bennet women.

John Bennet, Thomas's father, had never mentioned that three codicils were attached to the end of the entailment document, as he had not needed to reference them. His wife had borne him an heir, a spare, and a trey.

The first codicil covered the prohibition to sell, lease, or indemnify the lands of the manor or the home farm. A Bennet descendant of the direct bloodline or an indirect descendant, whether by blood or marriage, named Bennet, must occupy the manor, manage the home farm, or allow Longbourn to revert to the Crown. A detailed description of the definition of "occupy" was included. It was a standard document albeit written in lofty legalese.

The second dealt with the inheritance by a male heir not born of the Bennet surname. Should a Bennet male sire all daughters and no sons, the closest blood-relative male heritor must adopt the surname Bennet or forfeit the estate. The rest of the document explained in minute detail the ramifications of the inheritor failing to take the Bennet name, taking the Bennet name temporarily and reverting to his original surname, and all other types of subterfuge.

Philips knew Thomas Bennet had had an older cousin. A near-illiterate, miserly, vicious pastor named William Collins, Senior. He held the world at fault for his diminished circumstances. He hated Thomas Bennet for having inherited Longbourn after the death of his uncle, Thomas's father. William Collins, Senior had a clerk write a letter to Thomas Bennet every month demanding compensation for fraud. After reading the first three letters, which cursed his existence and demanded retribution from the Almighty, Thomas consigned each new one, unopened, to the fire.

The last document glittered like Spanish gold. The third codicil, like the second, covered the inheritance should a Bennet male sire all daughters and no sons but offered a solution to maintain the natural Bennet bloodline on the Longbourn property.

Philips's shock was compounded when he saw that this codicil had been added only twenty-five years ago. *John Bennet would have added this provision after he realized his monstrosity of a cousin may inherit.*

He continued reading. Should a daughter marry and bear a son while the incumbent, direct-blood descendant Bennet estate owner yet lived, the male child would be *inheritor-designee* until his twentieth year, at which time he would adopt the Bennet surname and assume the Longbourn estate inheritance. If Thomas Bennet did not survive to see his grandson reach his majority, the child's mother would serve as *regent-inheritor-in trust* with all the legal safeguards mandated by the Courts of Chancery.

Philips smiled and organized all the documents back into their original order. He wrote a quick note, called his junior clerk, and sent the young man to fetch his friend. It was Philip's pleasure to inform his brother of some good news.

Chapter 22

Longbourn Village, March 1804

Robert Stephens took his time riding to Hertfordshire. He planned to begin his tenure as the steward of Longbourn within a se'nnight. Somewhat handsome, young, and sturdy in body, he had studied under his father from the time he could walk. He had accepted employment at Longbourn with the understanding it was a temporary assignment for him to get his feet wet, as it were, before returning north and taking responsibility for a larger portion of Ashdale, the largest Matlock holding in Derbyshire. Stephens attended church every Sunday as expected although, personally, his love of nature and the outdoors confirmed his belief in the beauty of the Lord. As he rode through Meryton, he would have been better equipped to understand his immediate future had he recalled his Bible reading of Psalms 33:10:

"The LORD brings the counsel of the nations to nothing; He makes the plans of the peoples of no effect."

Robert Stephens arrived at Longbourn and, in short order, had all his previous beliefs about the natural order, the gentry, and the fairer sex turned upside down by little Lizzy Bennet.

Bennet indulged his most inquisitive daughter regarding her desire to learn estate management. Her natural talents impressed him. He found she excelled at chess, winning more than a third of the games they played together.

One evening, Thomas called Lizzy to attend to him in the study where he had the estate account ledgers open. He was working to balance them out, but as in every month, he failed to make the entries match. He offered his daughter his chair.

"Read through this ledger and decipher the entries."

Thomas moved closer to the fire and allowed Lizzy to find her way. She would leaf through one page, then revert to the page before. He offered no assistance. After an hour, he informed her that they had completed the lesson time for the evening and would resume tomorrow night. He did not ask his daughter whether she had questions. He could see the spark in her eyes. *Let us wait this out.*

Over the next week, they spent an hour each evening together—he read while she studied.

The first evening after Sunday services, Lizzy showed up with a journal, sat down at her father's desk, and prepared a pencil. Thomas raised an eyebrow but continued to read. For an hour with no break in her focus, she flipped a page, wrote something, flipped another page, wrote more, and continued this pattern until the lesson hour ended. For the next fortnight, she repeated her "journaling" until the evening before morning services. She put down her pencil, cleared her throat, and waited for her father's attention.

Thomas closed his book, his page marked with an exquisite linen-embroidered strip presented to him by Jane. He cherished the realistic apple trees, their shadows cast toward Longbourn Pond. It was a sublime piece of work.

The Longbourn patriarch looked his middle daughter in the eye. *She knows.*

"Papa, the estate's income is reported to be less than it actually is."

"How did you come to that conclusion?"

"This estate ledger shows all the rental income, tenant payments, and bank interest coming in. Those figures are combined with outgoing expenses, household spending, and capital outlays. Once I understood the figures were intermixed, I separated them on opposite sides of a line—income on the left and expenses on the right. I totaled the bottom of each column. Subtracting the right from the left shows the end of period income, which is much more than you have been telling us."

"Show me your work, please."

Lizzy handed over her journal. Written on the left side were all the entry descriptions. A thick line ran from the top of the page to the bottom on the right half of the journal. The corresponding income amount or expense amount leapt off the page on each side of the line, written as gains or losses. It was an incomparable piece of work, as professional as any Drummond's bank clerk could produce. His daughter of thirteen assembled it in less than three weeks. Thomas was speechless. He invited Lizzy to sit opposite him.

"You are my bright, shining star and now have sensitive information about our standing. Your mother and I do not wish for the community to know."

"Why, Papa?"

"We want you and your sisters to enjoy your lives without fear of individuals who would importune us—either for good or evil. The knowledge of our true income would be an open invitation to do so. Please help us protect your sisters."

Thomas knew this last statement would secure his daughter's confidence. It did.

"Yes, Papa. I shall help protect my sisters," she vowed.

"Thank you, child. We shall get new ledgers and start to track our income, investments, and dowries with both methods going forward. Well done, my clever, clever Lizzy."

He kissed her forehead and shooed her out of the study.

"Poor Mr. Stephens," thought Thomas aloud.

Watching their future steward keep up with his brilliant daughter would entertain him at length. Thomas chuckled and continued reading, happy to delegate that which had been distasteful.

Mr. Stephens spent his third and fourth days completing his assessments of Longbourn's twelve tenant farms. He would have been better pleased to include all in his first report, but one tenant family had been unavailable.

He detailed the needed repairs of the tenant homes and barns. The list was lengthy and needed prioritization. He regretted that this would be his first real discussion with his employer as his estimates would require a sizable outlay from the estate budget.

Once Stephens arrived back at his cottage, he sent a note to Mr. Bennet. He received an immediate verbal reply from a young kitchen boy that he was to join them for tea. The steward assumed "them" included Mrs. Bennet, which—while not unheard of—was irregular.

Stephens changed for tea and walked to the main house. He heard himself announced, entered the study, and came to a sudden halt just past the doorway as he saw his employer sitting in a chair in front of a large desk; a noticeably young girl sat in a proprietary manner behind it.

Stephens looked at his employer. He was unable to comprehend the scene in front of him. He looked at the young girl and realized he was out of his depth.

Thomas Bennet chuckled, gesturing to the chair opposite. "You have questions, Stephens?"

The steward gaped at his employer as if he had lost his wits.

"You will find Longbourn is an estate not managed in the classic manner with which you are familiar."

Stephens warily nodded in acknowledgment of his employer's comment. He remembered his lessons with his father. *Think before you act; think twice before you speak.* It was comforting advice to recall as he waited for further explanations.

"Please sit down. My daughter Elizabeth has joined us as she manages the income and expense ledgers. I assume you have monetary requests. She is best positioned to award them."

Stephens blinked as he sat in the opposite chair. A tickle at the back of his consciousness allowed him to recall a brief conversation between his father and the earl that he had been privileged to witness.

"Bennet is more than he appears. He is more capable than many I have relied upon in the past."

With that thought fresh in his mind, he turned to the young lady behind the desk. "May I present my requests?"

"Yes, Mr. Stephens."

"Miss Elizabeth, here is a list of the needed repairs of the tenant homes sorted by priority and gross costs, including materials and labor. Market prices for some supplies may vary, but I feel the overall budget number is accurate."

The steward placed the list on the desk and sat back. He was unsure of what to expect.

Stephens watched Miss Elizabeth pick up the list, read through it quickly, and put it back flat on the desk. With a pencil, she drew circles and added slashes with new figures. In seconds. She flipped to a page toward the back of the open ledger on the desk, compared it to the list, and then closed the ledger, pushing it off to the side. She next turned his list over, made three vertical lines, rewrote the figures in columns, and never once referenced the closed journal or the figures on the front side. She put down her pencil and folded her hands together on the desk. She looked up at him and smiled.

"Thank you for confirming all the repairs for which we budgeted.

Your list is quite thorough."

She handed him his altered list.

"This is the prioritized schedule of capital outlay for the repairs. Please let us know whether there are additional costs not on the list."

Miss Elizabeth smiled.

Robert Stephens considered himself a rational man, maybe even enlightened. Ashdale was a vast estate with no shortage of new experiences involving tenants, crop rotations, farming incidences, and servant and owner interactions. He even believed some of the medical rumors regarding the sons of the earldom. None of that could compare to today's orientation at Longbourn. Taking a deep breath, he absorbed his employer's wide smile and then turned to the young girl with sparkling eyes. Robert Stephens decided he had joined something extraordinary. Gathering his wits, he, too, broke into a smile.

"Tea, Mr. Stephens?" inquired Miss Elizabeth.

Chapter 23

Chatsworth, Derbyshire, May 1805

George Darcy brought his mount to a halt. He looked up into the near horizon and between the Derwent and Wye valleys; his destination came into view.

Chatsworth, comfortably situated in the Derbyshire Dales, stood on the east bank of the Derwent amid parkland backed by wooded hills. The stately home had housed the Cavendish family for over two hundred fifty years. Cavendish. As in the Duke of Devonshire. Yet it was not the duke whom the gentleman from Pemberley sought but, rather, the duke's granddaughter.

George Darcy smiled to himself. He remembered Thea Cavendish as a rarity—a debutante of the first circles, betrothed even before her come out at the young age of seventeen. Others viewed her as political currency. How little they knew.

It was neither her age nor her betrothal to a man decades her senior that was unusual. No—George Darcy recalled her utter indifference to societal rules regarding the behavior of marriageable young ladies from outstanding families of the *ton.* Prospective brides of peers were required to be elegant, graceful, demure—a lady always. They were accomplished in the art of smiling gently, laughing in a tittering manner behind a raised hand, drawing attention with a fan, and enticing with subtlety. Theodosia Cavendish was capable in those surface embellishments but was not characterized by any of those things. She was so much more.

Outspoken and fearless, Thea Cavendish knew where the line was and never once tripped upon it. Had she not been a Cavendish, society would have labeled her a bluestocking. But a Cavendish she was, so a bluestocking she was not. The two pretentious debutantes who tried to challenge her mettle paid dearly for it.

Sarah Rawlings had pompously pointed out her immediate future elevation to the peerage and attempted to slight Thea's betrothal to a man with one foot in the grave. Miss Rawlings had been told that her own betrothed's estate and wealth were derived from animal husbandry and mining. What had not been explained to her was the source of their farming and mineral wealth. The elder Baron Baston had been a pig farmer. His son, Lord Kesteven, had discovered their estate grounds were rich in iron. The mining and refining of the mineral wealth added thousands of pounds to their coffers. The family had become rich producing pig iron.

Lady Theodosia Cavendish, holding court at a post-Epiphany ball in the Derbyshire Dales, happily informed the future Lady Sarah Baston that her surname and her Kesteven estate represented her new status as the *Baroness of Baston,* as in the Lincolnshire Curly-coated Baston Pig. Socially humiliated and therefore ruined, Sarah Rawlings abandoned her betrothal, fled north, and married a Scottish laird, never again to be seen in town.

Lady Catherine Fitzwilliam would have ended up a spinster had her younger sister not agreed to relinquish her dowry. The setdown Thea

Cavendish rained on her at the Earl of Westfield's Twelfth Night ball, even to this day, continued to reverberate about the *ton* that summered in the gentle plains of the Kentish countryside.

Darcy rode up to Chatsworth accompanied by a Cavendish escort, a welcome addition to his final miles. At the staircase leading up to the front door, he dismounted and followed an impeccably dressed footman into Chatsworth.

An immaculate, rather short, lean, gray-haired senior servant asked him for his hat, coat, and gloves. Darcy allowed himself to be assisted, thanking the man whose name was Fats.

"Fats?" asked Darcy, a bit incredulous.

"Yes, sir. Fats," he replied, accustomed to the question. "Please follow me, Mr. Darcy."

Darcy followed Fats to a set of double doors. A loud knock, a muffled voice, and Fats opened the door.

"Mr. George Darcy of Pemberley."

Darcy walked into a room decorated entirely in blue. It took him aback for a moment. He came to his senses when he heard his hostess call out, "Thank you, Fatsssssss," extending the sibilant.

Fats bowed and backed out of the room, his face a credit to the neutral masks of English butlers throughout history. Darcy took in his hostess's appearance. Theodosia Manners-Sutton was immaculate, stately, and still quite beautiful in an absolute, untouchable manner. She gestured to an adjacent chair. He sat and waited for her to begin. She did not.

"I hope the room is not indicative of our pending discourse, madam." He remembered how Anne had stripped the family parlor of every hint of blue. She had despised melancholy.

Thea Sutton's eyes twinkled. Darcy could see the intelligence gleaming there. He would be careful.

"George, thank you for coming. I hope for a splendid time."

"Hope, Thea?"

"Well, unfortunately, I cannot be certain, can I?"

Now George Darcy was on his guard.

"What are you certain of, madam?"

Thea looked at him and laughed. She saw his bewilderment.

"I shall certainly entertain you as a prologue to our upcoming uncertainty," Thea ventured.

Darcy blinked. The repartee was too rapid.

"Do you recall the Season of '75?" asked Thea.

"How could I forget? It was a time of unmatched beauty and elegance, owing itself to you and my dear Anne."

"I agree, sir. This kingdom may never see another of Lady Anne's like. I miss her immensely, and my admiration cannot be but a fraction of yours."

"Thank you. You are too kind."

"Well, I shall have you know the machinations between the Manners and Suttons put my mother quite out regarding my betrothal."

"She could not have known years ago what we all know to be fact now, madam," Darcy said, smiling.

"My grandpapa did," boasted Thea proudly.

"Thea, you alone speak in kindness of the duke. We mortals were but drones to him. You were his Queen Bee."

Thea bristled. "I know you as a gentleman and a true servant of the Lord, so I shall not read into your metaphor, sir."

"You misunderstand me, madam. My metaphor relates to status, I assure you, and nothing else." Darcy would not back down but would make his point clear.

Thea sighed. "Thank you, George. I miss Grandpapa every day. Whether anyone else does concerns me not."

Darcy brought the conversation back in line. "You were speaking of the '75 Season, madam?" he asked.

"Yes." She giggled.

"I must inquire as to the pleasure I unknowingly brought to you," he said rather dryly.

"Gladly, sir. It may surprise you, as I repeat myself, that my mother did not enjoy 'selling' me to the Suttons. She offered me an alternative while we summered in Canterbury before my betrothal."

"That is surprising. I recall no talk of it. May I inquire of the alternative, as you seem to have a desire to inform me?"

"You may."

"And he was?"

"You."

"Me?" replied an incredulous George Darcy.

"Yes—you. George Darcy. You were the alternative my mother offered up." Thea sat back, diverted. George Darcy looked…well, he looked shocked.

A minute of silence passed. Darcy cleared his throat. Thea waited for it. He rewarded her.

"What was your response?"

"I demurred."

"You *demurred*?"

"Yes."

Darcy seemed to chew on that. Thea wondered whether he would let it go or satisfy his vanity. Vanity won out. *Men are so predictable!*

"Enlighten me if you will. That may be a Mrs. Manners-Sutton answer at this moment, but what did the irrepressible Thea Cavendish tell her mother? I implore you to tell me."

Thea Sutton smiled and looked the handsome George Darcy in the eye.

"I dismissed the suggestion entirely. I told my mother that I would never allow myself to be sold to a sheep farmer, even if his flocks numbered in the tens of thousands."

George Darcy's eyes went wide. He threw his head back and laughed. Once he regained himself, he quipped, "Quite a refusal, Thea. So utterly biblical, I daresay. I had not heard I was ever a candidate for your hand."

"No one who witnessed you and Anne dance together could ever think either of you had an alternative, I assure you," she replied tenderly.

Darcy sobered and looked down at his feet, his mask of neutrality reassumed.

Thea reached out and touched his forearm.

"Please do not do that, my old friend. Do not hide your true self from me. Anne was so dear to us both. To your son. Do not hide anymore, George."

"May I…may I defer further conversation, Thea? I am quite spent from the journey."

"Of course you may. Inform Fats of your requirements."

George Darcy bowed to his hostess and retired.

He woke up the next morning without prompting and took care of his needs. Darcy found his riding outfit laid out on the bed; Fats prepared to assist him.

Darcy met the same under-groom at the front door with a stallion from the stable.

"Yer 'orse needs a rest, Mr. Darcy."

"Quite so," he replied. With assistance, he mounted the dapple-gray stallion and adjusted his seat. An escort appeared behind him. Together, they rode off. Darcy took to the stallion with joy.

Darcy later joined Thea in the small dining room to break his fast.

"I do hope you are enjoying yourself, sir."

"Very well indeed, madam."

"Excellent. We must keep this morning's joys in mind when we next speak in the blue parlor."

"Must we?"

"We must," insisted Thea.

The pair spent the remaining hour exchanging pleasant memories. Darcy excused himself as he had a rendezvous with the fencing master.

That afternoon, Darcy joined Thea in the blue parlor.

"Tea will arrive in an hour. I have a pleasant light blend to remove the upcoming distaste of today's conversation," warned Thea.

Darcy ignored the threat. He understood, and it compelled him to listen. There was no fighting the alliance that had enlisted Thea to represent them.

Thea waited no longer to fire the first salvo.

"George, I have a missive from your brother."

She spoke of Lord Henry, as Sir Lewis had passed. "Concerning?"

"It is not something a well-bred lady should speak of to a gentleman."

"We are then lucky we are both above those inane societal concerns," he countered.

"I daresay we are, George."

"Need I venture a guess, or shall you join the countless others who inform me of my protégé's dissipations?" he snapped.

Theodosia Cavendish Manners-Sutton sat up straight. She locked her eyes—blazing fire—on her guest; her face was taut at the offense.

"I have permitted no one *ever* to address me in such an insolent manner. Not my husband, not my father, not the duke! Certainly not *you*. I suggest you reconsider your response."

Darcy lowered his face into his hand. Taking a deep breath, he recognized the oncoming headache. It only happened when the subject of his protégé arose. He looked up.

"Please accept my most fervent apology, Mrs. Sutton. I regret that I have lost perspective regarding the subject at hand."

Thea nodded. "I accept your apology, George."

"Thank you, Thea." he grimaced. "Shall we continue?"

"Need we? You are aware of his proclivities, his profligacy, and his complete disregard for all, including that which stains the Darcy name. Are you ambivalent to the effect this must have on William?"

"I am not," he replied, defensively.

Thea pursed her lips, folded her hands in her lap, and straightened her back again.

"You compel me to inquire of the measures you have taken to mitigate this situation?" she challenged.

"You feel compelled?" asked Darcy, shocked at the tone to which the discourse had devolved.

"Yes."

"May I inquire by whom?" he asked, both offended and fearful.

"Do not be obtuse, Darcy. It becomes you not."

Thea Sutton was not just a wealthy widow. Few in the kingdom, even titled, had connections as lofty and vast as hers. The Cavendish, Manners, Sutton, Fitzwilliam, and Langston surnames were at the top of her sphere of influence, an incalculable power base. Dukes, earls, archbishops, bishops, and barons. The peerage. The Anglican church.

Darcy immediately capitulated. "Once his debts exceeded the value of the living I had intended to gift him, my man of business followed my instructions to cease covering his accounts."

His hostess nodded for him to continue.

"I have amended my final testament. It does not recognize him as receiving a bequest."

"Thank you, George."

Darcy nodded. Exhaustion crept up his legs into his chest.

"Let us forgo tea and take trays in our rooms. We may continue on the morrow." Thea stood to show the afternoon had ended.

Darcy spent the rest of the day in his room, pacing, thinking of his legacy. His son. How Anne's death had left an insurmountable hole in his soul. He was overwhelmed by his oversight of his protégé's perfidy. He blamed himself over and over. It was a long, remorseful evening.

The following morning, Darcy met the under-groom at the door with another horse, not his mount.

"Still resting my horse in the stables, young man?"

"Yes, sir, as you be needin' 'im for yer return on th' morrow."

"I shall?"

"Ayuh, sir. Here be yer escort. G'day, Mr. Darcy."

Darcy rode hard and rode long to the point of exhaustion. He and his horse returned lathered to excess. His escort, a large smile upon his face, saluted his charge. Darcy limped to his room, stripped out of his clothes, and collapsed on the bed. Fats woke him, a set of clothes laid out for the day. A tub of steaming water awaited him.

As Darcy headed to the door, Fats cleared his throat.

"Yes, Fats?" asked Darcy, still feeling a bit ridiculous ending a sentence in such a manner.

"Sir, I would remind you of the need for the silhouettes."

"I have them in my pocket," Darcy replied, his tone testy.

"Very good, sir."

A pensive George Darcy joined Thea Sutton for the morning meal.

"Good morning, George. I understand the stable hands hold you in very high regard."

"The stables, grooms, and escorts are a credit to the estate. I thank you."

"Wonderful. We have a busy day today. We shall continue in the study after we complete our repast."

"Yes, I understand I am to leave on the morrow."

"Pemberley requires your presence. Yorkshire requires mine."

"Might I offer assistance?"

Thea looked at Darcy speculatively. "Maybe in the future, yes, you soon may. Thank you for your kind offer."

"I am at your service, madam."

Darcy followed Thea to the study. Two men stood in the center of the room, uncomfortable and quite nervous. The most intimidating footman Darcy had ever seen loomed behind the men.

Thea sat in the first chair of two, facing the men. Darcy took the other. Darcy noticed a large, scarred hand on each of their shoulders.

Thea's eyes narrowed. One gulped, his face wearing a look of utter defeat. The other had a bit more impertinence, opening his mouth to say…what? Darcy did not learn as the hand on his shoulder flexed and the man's face went white. His teeth clapped shut.

Thea held up an elegant finger. "Gentleman, you know why you are here. At best, the magistrate awaits you. Speak the truth; otherwise… well, it is your choice."

The men, not tradesmen, confessed to heinous, despicable acts of moneylending and trafficking in stolen goods, gambling, prostitution, child abduction, and the sale of helpless girls into sex slavery.

Darcy held up his hand. "What is my part in these confessions?"

Thea ignored him and addressed the men. "I warn you now to answer each question truthfully and be concise."

Seeing that the word "concise" received a blank look, she reiterated with steel, "With truth and in as few…words…as…possible."

Unsatisfied, Thea ensured their compliance with a single word. "Portman."

Both men shrieked. They bobbed their heads up and down repeatedly.

"Who brought you goods stolen from the homes and carriages of genteel families?"

The first man offered, "William Darcy, mum," and bowed his head.

Darcy sat stunned.

"Who brought young girls, stolen from their families, and sold them to brothels?" asked Thea, spitting the last word out of her mouth.

The second man looked at his feet and whispered, "Darcy. Fitzwilliam Darcy."

George Darcy stood up and pointed his finger. "If you had one ounce of honor, I would kill you now. How dare you speak my family name—my son's name! How dare you!" he shouted.

Both men cowered, their footman wall providing no protection.

Thea pulled Darcy back down into his chair. "George."

"Yes?"

"George," she repeated herself.

He turned to his hostess. "Yes?" he repeated himself, not understanding.

Thea narrowed her eyes at him. *So handsome but…so closed.* "George!"

"Yes, Thea. I hear you."

"No, Darcy, I am afraid you do not. So, I shall, unfortunately, insult you and lower myself to the mundane."

"Thea, you are speaking in riddles. Please, what is it I do not comprehend?" begged Darcy, uncaring of his audience.

Thea, exasperated, huffed. "Wickham, Darcy…George…George Wickham!"

Darcy's jaw dropped. It all became clear to him. He reached into his vest pockets with both hands and pulled out the two miniatures. His right hand held his son's, the Archangel Michael, and in his left, his protégé's, Lucifer. The men in front of him stood as representatives from the Book of Revelation. Darcy rose and held the two portraits before the men. Both nodded toward the left. The fallen angels had unmasked their ancient serpent leader.

George Darcy was adrift. Sick. Shocked. Numb. He lost his balance, staggered, and bumped into the chair. He lurched from the room and into the arms of two footmen and Fats, who half-walked, half-carried him to his room. A nurse waited with a wash basin of heated water and rags. Darcy allowed the darkness to cushion his defeat.

He awoke to a warm room with a blazing fire. His banyan was plastered to his chest. He pulled it off and dropped it onto the floor next to the bed. Never doubting the service of Chatsworth, Darcy inquired from within the closed bed curtains.

"Mr. Fats?"

"Fats, sir. Your bath awaits."

Of course it did. Darcy padded to the steaming tub of water, uncaring and exhausted. He sat down in the hot water, leaned back, closed his eyes, and inhaled.

"Menthol, sir," answered Fats. "Very therapeutic, I am told."

Darcy nodded, clearing his mind. "Fats, I shall require time to send expresses if you would inform your mistress as such."

"We prepared the writing desk, for such was the expectation, sir."

"Indeed."

Darcy rose, Fats ready with a heated robe.

"Drink choices are available on the tray next to the writing desk, sir. I regret madam overruled me regarding spirits. None at hand, I fear."

"I would suspend no pleasure of your mistress."

Fats smiled and exited.

George Darcy sat and wrote out several expresses, addressing them to Giles Jeffers, Lord Henry Fitzwilliam, and Fitzwilliam Darcy. He dressed himself and joined his hostess.

After a light dinner, just two courses, the pair sat together in the music room. Thea sat at the piano and played a light Irish pastoral. She tinkled the keys pleasantly.

A footman entered with a tray, atop which was a single exquisite crystal decanter filled with a smoky amber liquid and two matching glasses. Fats poured two fingers of the extract into each glass and presented the first to Darcy. The order of precedence was noticed by the participants.

"Your cognac," Fats announced.

"Anything else, madam?"

"No, thank you, Fatsssssss," she replied, extending his name again.

Fats bowed and left the room.

Darcy took a sip. The smoke and oak erupted upon his palate. He could not help himself. He ran his tongue around the inside of his mouth and between his lips and gums.

Thea chuckled.

"I suppose every one of your guests behaves as improperly, I would hope?"

"I would not know, as you are the first, outside of my family, to partake of this treasure."

Darcy bowed his head in thanks and looked at Thea. She smiled back at him, amused. *Too intelligent for me by far,* he thought. *I would bore her.*

"Why do you stretch out your manservant's name?"

"I miss Quince."

"Quince?"

"Yes, my husband's man. Quinzzzzzzz," she replied fondly. "He was so diverting to tease."

Darcy nodded. "I believe Fats is biding his time."

"I daresay he is. It has been quite the standoff. I should have prevailed had I spent more time here; but alas, I cannot, so he continues to endure through the siege."

Darcy grinned. Thea was captivating.

"Thea, what shall you do with your time once you complete your mission in Yorkshire?"

Thea smiled widely. "I knew you were charming, George. It just takes time and a dram of cognac to draw you out, I shall admit."

Darcy raised his eyebrows. She had yet to answer.

Then Thea unleashed a surprise. "Botany."

"Botany?"

"Botany. I have a deep regard for nature, and now I have the time and the means to pursue my passion. Botany."

Darcy thought about it. Botany. Gardening. Anne and her rose garden. He could not help but smile. He quoted one of Anne's favorite metaphors:

"The world is a rose; smell it and pass it to your friends."

Thea smiled at him. "Yes, exactly."

She stood, and Darcy rose with her. Thea offered her hand. Darcy bowed over it and brushed her knuckles with his lips. She did not blush.

"Ride safely back to Pemberley, George. I wish you well with your immediate endeavors."

"Thank you, Thea."

They never saw each other again in this life.

Chapter 24

Pemberley, June 1805

George Darcy struggled to breathe. He lay in his bed in the master's suite, a punctured lung bringing a rattling rasp that was the Pemberley master's death knell.

He lifted his arm to beckon anyone in the room as his vision failed him, surrounding him in clouds.

"Yes, Mr. Darcy?" answered Giles Jeffers.

Ah, loyal Jeffers, here even now to execute my wishes.

"Lift…me…me…up…"

Propped up, Darcy breathed easier, but that was only an illusion of comfort. The medicos' long faces told the tale. There was extraordinarily little time to seek retribution…or redemption.

His eyes closed; Darcy gestured at Jeffers. His man of business recognized what he needed and pulled out a dog-eared folio to document his employer's orders.

"Ready," he stated for the ten thousandth, but last, time.

As the greatest man he had ever known slid away, Jeffers recorded his employer's final directions. George Darcy, a pious man, left no doubt of the identity of the faithless villain responsible for forcing Pemberley's heir to assume the mantle of responsibility much earlier than he ought. His instructions, should that villain ever broach the Darcy sphere again, were quite clear.

Later that evening, a full moon glowed in a cloudless sky. George Darcy recognized the inevitable. He gazed out his bedroom window and caught the attention of his incandescent wife, Lady Anne, illuminated by starlight. He stood and offered her his hand. She accepted. Together, they stepped toward the center line to dance.

The master of Pemberley died smiling.

Fitzwilliam Darcy leapt off his mount, the animal nearly dead of exhaustion. The rider stumbled, his footing unsure. He started for the front door but stopped and dropped to his knees. The black wreath left him bereft with the knowledge that he was too late.

He had left school immediately upon reading the express. He had been sharing a meal with Charles Bingley, his friend's sister Louisa, and his Cambridge mentor Reginald Hurst. While Darcy had been immobilized with indecision, Hurst answered the express, secured him a mount, and ensured the horse carried enough provisions for both it and its rider for much of the journey. Had his wits been about him, Darcy may have wondered how his mentor managed the situation, but William's thoughts focused on one thing and one thing only—getting home.

Now he was there but *there* had been forever changed.

Unable to swallow, Darcy struggled to breathe. He placed both hands palms down on the ground and lowered his head to regulate himself. He failed. He gave in to the darkness that encroached upon his vision. He woke up the next morning in his room, Barty puttering around setting things to rights.

Darcy sat in the worn but familiar chair in his sitting room. His father's most recent weekly letter had spoken of an obligation to visit their northern relations, the church-affiliated branch of the family by marriage. William tried to recall having met the man who was now the archbishop, but his memory failed him. He did recall the tales of a stunning beauty—the granddaughter of the late Duke of Devonshire—who married into the Sutton family, but her name eluded him.

He would have to review his father's journals to gain insight into the reason the great man would take an unguarded journey north to a distant branch of his family. Until that time came, he focused on his immediate duties: his father and Pemberley.

Four days later

The funeral carriages, having departed from the crypt, went their separate ways—Kympton, Lambton, Derby—at the first crossroads. Alone in his coach as he looked out the window, Darcy noticed nothing.

He descended from the carriage, thanked his team, and proceeded into the house where he was relieved of his hat, gloves, and coat. The great clock in the foyer ticked second after second, his future inviolably moving forward.

In the receiving parlor, Darcy greeted those guests and family who marked his father's passing. No one could find fault in his proper attention to duty, even if the young host chose silence over conversation, as all understood him to be grieving.

He continued his great silence into the following day. His devotions included the reading of George Darcy's last will, which detailed his father's bequests. He silently ground his teeth throughout his Aunt Catherine's harangue regarding her expectations of his betrothal to her daughter. He allowed himself a hint of a smile when his aunt was manhandled from Pemberley and into her carriage. He never brooked conversation, let alone a single word, as offer after offer to assist him made by well-meaning relatives and intimate friends filled his ears, his study, and his house. Eventually, they all went away dissatisfied. Pemberley's wonders remained Darcy's.

His single moment of emotion was his wistful huff as he read a short note from his cousin Richard. He dropped the note onto his desk, summoned his valet, and dressed for a hard ride. Barty, aware of his master's fastidiousness with his correspondence, secured the missive after a glance at its content. It was a mystery to the valet, but it appeared to lift his master's spirits.

"Non est dubium, Cousin."

The following day, Darcy sat in his father's chair. A knock sounded on the study door. Mrs. Reynolds asked whether he would entertain the day's business.

Darcy nodded.

Giles Jeffers entered the study, unsure whether he would continue in his role as Pemberley's—and thus Darcy's—man of business. He stopped in front of the new master and bowed.

"Mr. Darcy, dare I ask how you would like to continue?"

Darcy looked at Jeffers. He knew him to be a competent, honest man who acted in the family's best interest at every step. He answered with the first phrase that entered his mind, a phrase he would repeat again and again over the years. "Press on, Mr. Jeffers."

"Yes, sir," the man of business replied. He would resume their daily meetings after the Sabbath once the new master had rested.

Three weeks later, Mrs. Reynolds knocked on the study door. Darcy bade her enter, motioning Jeffers to remain seated.

"Sir, *he* has come."

"*He* may stand in the foyer until I send word."

"Very good, sir." Mrs. Reynolds closed the door as she departed. Jeffers stood, pulled out a small chatelaine, and gripped a specific key.

"With your permission, Mr. Darcy."

"Of course."

Darcy stood aside as Jeffers pulled open the bottom right drawer of the master's desk and inserted the key into the top of a lockbox. Once open, he removed a leather pouch and placed it on the desk.

"May I explain?" asked Jeffers.

"Please do."

"I shall not repeat what you have already heard of your father's last hours. However, I shall relate his last instructions to me before his final breath."

Darcy nodded. He heard his father's voice echoing in his mind: *"Darcy men set the example."*

"Your father believed everything you related to him about his protégé. In the lockbox to your lower right are the receipts for every debt bought up from the shopkeepers of Lambton, Kympton, Matlock, and Derby."

Darcy nodded. Jeffers continued.

"Once the amount exceeded £1,000, your father changed his will, eliminating George Wickham as a beneficiary. This change remained undisclosed for obvious reasons."

Darcy nodded.

"Your father stopped covering Wickham's debts once the amount exceeded £3,000."

Darcy's eyes widened. Yet, he remained silent and nodded again.

"The earl's man of business learned that London moneylenders had bought Wickham's town debts to collect from the Darcy coffers. He brought the matter to the earl's attention. The earl immediately wrote Mr. Darcy. Your father, however, never received the missive as someone intercepted the express. We suspected George Wickham."

Darcy nodded.

"A firearm discharged before your father's horse reared, causing his fall. His mount never before had spooked, even while on the hunt."

Darcy digested the information; its bilious nature nauseated him.

"The purse on your desk is your father's amended bequest. Wickham must count it in front of you."

Darcy nodded. His father had been a pious man, a God-fearing man, a *righteous* man. Understanding his father's intent, Darcy now relished the meeting about to take place.

"Tell Mrs. Reynolds to have several footmen prepared to escort the individual from the grounds once he and I complete our business."

"Yes, Mr. Darcy." Jeffers turned to leave.

"Mr. Jeffers?"

"Yes, sir?"

"Why do we not make it, Jeffers and Darcy, going forward?"

"Thank you, Darcy."

"Thank *you*, Jeffers."

Jeffers left to inform Mrs. Reynolds of her master's requirements.

Several minutes later, she opened the study door. "George Wickham to see you, Mr. Darcy."

Wickham, wearing fashionable clothing and boots, swaggered into Darcy's study. He sat on the corner of his godfather's desk.

"You believe yourself able to sit in that chair—I think not!" taunted Wickham.

Darcy allowed his disdain free rein. "Why are you here?"

"I have come for my inheritance. My godfather promised me a living. Let us have it, right?" George Wickham held out his hand as if Darcy would place a land deed or a bank draft into it.

"All bequests have been bestowed as per the Courts of Chancery directives. Nothing outstanding remains."

"You lie! You are withholding my due. I will not tolerate this!" Wickham leaped to his feet.

"Impugn my honor again and you are free to name your second. Otherwise, go to London if you feel the need to contest that which is true."

"I spent all my coin to arrive here and acceptably present myself to honor my godfather. You must help me return to London."

Darcy lofted the leather sack from his desk. Wickham caught it and bounced it in his hand. "I knew you would not disappoint, old boy."

"Count it," Darcy growled.

So eager was he to see his reward, Wickham neglected to consider Darcy's tone. He untied the bag and poured it on the desk.

"I know what you did, you blackguard," hissed Darcy.

Wickham stared at thirty pieces of dull silver on the empty desk.

Chapter 25

Grosvenor Square, March 1806

Louisa Bingley sat with her brother, Charles, in the parlor as she read a treatise on the war. Bingley was balancing a portable desk on his lap as he rewrote his letter to Darcy for the seventh time. Louisa peeked over the pamphlet, saw him toss another sheet of paper to the floor, and raised her reading material higher to hide her face and the grin that enlivened it. Her anticipation of the request to come lasted mere seconds.

"Lou, will you lend me your considerable talents?"

Louisa could not help herself and snickered in a most unladylike fashion. She suppressed a full-throated laugh as the parlor door opened and the house's butler, Cartwright, entered with a calling card on a silver salver. He presented it to Charles but distinctively peered at her. Louisa's eyebrows rose, which she knew, of course, was Cartwright's object.

"Cartwright, you wicked, wicked man."

"Yes, Miss Bingley, I believe you would be correct."

"Show him in, Cartwright!" prompted Charles, looking at Louisa.

The butler left the parlor as Charles pulled open a drawer and dropped the card inside, saying nothing more.

Louisa placed the pamphlet on the side table, stood, and brushed out her dress. She perched herself on the edge of the settee, ready to rise and greet their mystery guest. A knock on the door and Cartwright reappeared. "Mr. Reginald Hurst of Suffolk."

Louisa was sure Cartwright winked at her, *the rascal!*

Charles was expansive in his greeting. "Hurst! Join us, join us, please."

"Thank you, Bingley."

Mr. Hurst walked over to Louisa and bowed.

"It is my greatest pleasure to see you again, Miss Bingley."

Louisa's face flushed. She had enjoyed encountering Mr. Hurst in Cambridge when she and Charles dined with Mr. Darcy. She frowned as she remembered the express their friend received and his chaotic departure.

"I, too, continue to grieve for our friend."

It did not surprise Louisa that Mr. Hurst knew her thoughts. She was sure his character had hidden depths.

Charles interrupted her musing. "Hurst, what brings you to call? Not that *you* need a reason, of course."

"Bingley, I'd like for you to join me for a theatre night if your schedule permits," he said as he looked at Louisa.

Charles looked at Mr. Hurst, who Louisa saw looked at her. Louisa stared back, a bit amused, a bit intrigued, a bit...*flustered? Am I?*

Charles broke the silence. "For goodness' sake, Lou, answer the man. I realize, as did Cartwright, to whom Hurst addressed the invitation. He is only being scrupulously proper. My—and here I thought you were the clever one!"

Charles sat back in his favorite chair, crossed his legs, and brushed off the nonexistent lint from his trousers in quite the exaggerated manner. He looked up and flashed as many teeth as he could in his celebrated Bingley smile.

All three began laughing. A chuckle from outside the parlor seeped through the door.

The following evening, Hurst joined Charles and his sister outside a new theatre on Adams Street. Louisa asked about the unknown venue.

"Welcome to the new Adelphi Theatre, built by merchants John Scott and Abraham Aronson, not yet open to the public."

"Really?"

"Yes, Bingley, my friend. We are to attend a private showing as Mr. Aronson is my particular friend."

"Well done, Hurst. I am sure it will be a jolly good evening. Lead the way."

"Regretfully, there is a cost, Bingley."

"Oh?"

"Yes, I must claim an entry fee as the production is not pro bono."

Charles looked confused. Louisa, diverted, put her brother to rights. "For goodness' sake, Charles, understand the man. I realize, as did he, to whom he addressed the inducement. My—and I thought you were the clever one!" Charles had the grace to look abashed.

Mr. Hurst guffawed and offered Louisa his arm.

"I see which way the wind blows now," scoffed Charles.

"Your particular friend?" she whispered.

Mr. Hurst winked.

Together, the three walked to the new theatre's front door where a footman in a tailored livery nodded to Mr. Hurst. He opened the door and welcomed them to the Adelphi.

Mr. Hurst escorted Louisa up to the private boxes. Bingley followed close behind, absorbing the feel of the crowd as he walked. Music flowed around them as the pit orchestra warmed up. A footman pulled back a drape and gestured for them to enter.

The box had twelve seats, four of which were already occupied. The two older couples, well-to-do by their clothing, stood and welcomed the trio. For those used to the British predilection for introductions, the lack of that ritual was noticeable but not mentioned. The conversation followed the usual mundane topics, but Louisa detected a pattern early on. The older of the gentlemen frequently spoke in alliteration, beyond what Louisa had ever heard. She tempered her participation to listen more.

The repeated consonants used in the speech device spelled out words without vowels. She stole a glance at the speaker and was startled to see him staring back at her. She nodded. He answered with a smile.

Louisa turned back to Mr. Hurst's conversation with the other gentleman while Bingley spoke with their wives. Her host recaptured her attention. "Miss Bingley, you must desire some refreshment. Allow me to leave you with our new acquaintance while I fetch some wine."

Mr. Hurst handed her to the older gentleman. He gracefully rested her hand on his arm and escorted her to the furthest corner of the box. "Miss Bingley, I am honored to make your acquaintance."

"Thank you, Sir John."

He chuckled. "You are a sharp one, my dear. I am pleased to see my impressions confirmed."

"This has been a most irregular introduction. What more lies in store, sir?"

"The real voyage of discovery consists not in seeking new landscapes, but in seeing the old ones with new eyes."

"Well, I am intrigued, sir, but I shall leave the *intrigue* for the gentlemen and remain intrigued by this evening's entertainment."

"Brava, Miss Bingley."

Mr. Hurst returned with three glasses of wine.

"Hurst, this has been an illuminating evening. Enjoy the show."

"Thank you, C."

Sir John and his friend departed with their wives.

Bingley bounded back to the couple. "Wonderful ladies, Hurst.

Sister, how was the gentleman's conversation?"

"Brother, we lamented the Lord's lost labor," quipped Louisa. She threw a raised eyebrow at Mr. Hurst. He returned it with a nod of approval.

Throughout the balance of the Season, Mr. Hurst called every two to three days. He spent requisite time with Charles but, for the most part, paid court to Louisa. Together, they toured the Kew Gardens. Louisa spent the day on Mr. Hurst's arm, and he attended to her every observation. Several days later, he escorted brother and sister to King's College where they entered a large ballroom filled with partially unpacked crates, wooden stands, and half-full tables.

"What delights do you hide within, sir?"

"Ah, Miss Bingley. Welcome to the future Anatomy Museum of King's College."

"Shocking!"

They walked from case to table to stand where they saw skulls, shoes with skeletal feet both within and without, and a plethora of phalanges. They discussed each of their discoveries with wonder and humor. They ended up in front of a nondescript door on a street in the back of Mayfair. Mr. Hurst knocked on the door with his walking stick, three rather sharp raps, followed by two more. The door was opened by a tall servant who peered down his nose at them both.

Mr. Hurst was ready to answer his silent inquiry. "Darby and Joan, my good man."

The door swung open, and Mr. Hurst ushered Louisa and Charles inside. Well-dressed couples mingled with one another while liveried servants slithered through the crowd carrying small trays filled with glassware—some empty, most not.

Louisa was introduced to several of Mr. Hurst's colleagues; each man was pleasant, well-spoken, and highly educated. As they rode in the carriage back to her brother's house, Louisa regretted the evening's end.

She appraised Mr. Hurst. How dear he had become to her. He valued her conversation, admired her mind, and nurtured her inquisitiveness.

Louisa realized that her heart was engaged. Yet now the lady wondered at the gentleman's regard.

She resolved to beard the lion. *He is a pleasant friend and an intelligent dinner companion. I believe we could rub along quite well. Yes, there it is. I shall make my case and let the cards fall where they may.*

That following evening, the Bingley butler detained Hurst. Cartwright cleared his throat while he helped remove the gentleman's coat. Hurst looked over his shoulder. "Yes, Cartwright?"

"Sir, I must report a bit of angst."

"Must you?"

"I must," confirmed Cartwright. He nodded gravely.

"Thank you, Cartwright. You must know, you now have less time to make your decision regarding your future."

Cartwright's lips twitched. "Sir, the *lady* deserves the very best."

"Jolly good, Cartwright."

Hurst made his way to the study. "Bingley, old boy, just a quick word."

"By all means, Hurst. What service may I provide you?"

"You, nothing, though I shall reserve the right to reclaim that which I have denied at a later date."

"Ever the planner, Hurst."

"I daresay, yes. I plan to ask your sister for her hand if she will have me."

"Capital, just capital, Hurst. Do not let me keep you. I shall have Cartwright pop a cork when the door opens. Off you go, my friend, and good luck."

Hurst saluted Bingley and walked to the parlor. Cartwright announced him.

Louisa had waited impatiently for Mr. Hurst to be presented. Now that she had bolstered her balloon of courage, it seemed to deflate as time passed.

Hurst entered the parlor at a time that Louisa had worked herself into a fret. She spun on him and blurted, "Enough of these silly games, sir."

Hurst paled. "How do you know Thomas Bennet?"

Louisa looked confused. "Who is Thomas Bennet?"

Hurst covered his mouth. Lowering his hand, he cleared his throat, took her hand, and led her to the sofa. "My dear, I misinterpreted what you said. May we begin anew?"

Louisa's face relaxed in relief. "We may."

"Miss Bingley...Louisa...I was going to ask you to consider whether I was worthy of your most generous, beguiling hand."

Louisa sat raptly.

"After just one brief contretemps, I realize that, without you, my life is ash."

Her widened eyes urged him to continue. "Please allow our future misunderstandings to occur while we share the same surname, as I want to be confident that you will forever be by my side through every misstep, every discovery, and every victory."

Louisa nodded. *Get on with it, you frustrating, darling man!*

"Louisa Bingley, my one and always, would you do me the greatest of honors and allow me to worship you for the rest of our lives? Will you marry me?"

"YES, YES, A THOUSAND TIMES YES!"

The parlor doors crashed open. Bingley, Cartwright, and the other service staff joined the betrothed couple with champagne flutes and hearty congratulations.

Longbourn, May 1806

Kitty dropped the piece of charcoal on the easel's little shelf, then picked up a towel and wiped the dust from her hands. She was pleased with her progress. She had two more days to complete her still life before her art master, Mr. Styles, returned. It was still early enough in the day to join Jane and keep her company in the stillroom.

Jane was Kitty's refuge. She calmed when she was with Jane, anger and self-pity diminished. Although Jane tried to appease her like her parents did, she was sweeter and more loving. Jane smelled like fresh herbs, which Kitty found to be quite soothing. Jane emotionally embraced her; Lizzy did not. Lizzy was not Jane. Lizzy pushed.

Lizzy never stopped pressing Kitty to communicate, regardless of her mood. It was all so tiring. Over time, Kitty understood she would have to share herself or join a nunnery, which made her giggle. She imagined whispering the same thought to Lydia and waiting for her brash younger sister to bray with laughter, uncaring that others thought she sounded like a mule. Kitty became tearful thinking of Lydia and realized she wanted to talk to someone. Talk about her feelings. Share her grief. Thus, she understood Lizzy's intent for her. Her wisdom. In a short time, with Lizzy near, she felt protected. *Outsiders* were sometimes unpleasant with their pointing and whispering things she could not understand. Lizzy stopped them before they became rude or mean. Sweet, fearless Lizzy!

"Yet, Kitty, you will learn. You will understand. Today, you do not. Tomorrow, you may. So, those rude people say things you do not understand...yet."

Kitty was learning to read lips but was not quite proficient. She vowed to practice more. A memory curled up like a smoke tendril, a remembrance before *it* happened. She recalled her mother smiling at Lydia and saying,

"No one ever improved upon an accomplishment without constant practice. Mark my words, as you will not only hear this from me."

Yes, Mama. Now I hear it from ME!

Kitty giggled. She was coming to acknowledge her silence, accepting her deafness.

She walked through the parlor toward the kitchen to get to the stillroom. Her passage was arrested when she found Jane in the parlor, sitting with their mother. They were working on an embroidery project. The work basket at their feet overflowed with half-finished pieces in stitching circles and ribbon scraps of all colors and sizes. Both looked up as she entered the room. Not seeing Lizzy, Kitty assumed she was with Mr. Stephens. *Poor Mr. Stephens.*

Jane put down her work, picked up a journal, and wrote, *"How fares your art project?"*

Kitty nodded and smiled. Accepting her sister's expression as indicating satisfaction, Jane patted the cushion beside her.

Kitty sat and laid her head on her sister's shoulder to breathe in Jane's rosemary and thyme scent. She closed her eyes and snuggled into the lamb's-wool shawl across Jane's shoulders. Jane kissed her forehead.

Mrs. Bennet looked at the lovely picture her girls made. Her eyes filled, but she blinked to keep her tears within. Not wanting to be perceived as maudlin, she focused on the task at hand and left the girls to themselves. She would share the moment with Thomas later in the evening.

Kettleburgh House, Suffolk, June 1806

Hurst's parents had already left the church, his mother eager to ensure the wedding breakfast was perfect. The bride and groom followed behind, having taken a few moments to sign the registry. A knowing look from her, her elegant eyebrow raised, and the groom leaned in and kissed her. Soundly. She wrapped her arms around the groom and gave him her special *attention.* A well-timed throat clearing brought the couple back to reality where they thanked the minister, and Hurst made a generous donation to the parsonage.

An unabashed Louisa Hurst reached up and grasped her new husband's handsome chin.

"Yes, my dear?"

"Darby and Joan?" she asked.

Hurst chuckled. He crooned:

Old Darby, with Joan by his side
You've often regarded with wonder.
He's dropsical, she is sore-eyed
Yet they're ever uneasy asunder.

Louisa could not help herself. She kissed her one and only, as he had her, most soundly.

Act Two:
Walls and Windows, 1807–1812

Chapter 26

Sutton House, Mayfair, May 1807

"Your correspondence, Mistressssssss," offered Mays, the dowager duchess's butler.

Thea Manners-Sutton tried to look stern and succeeded, mostly. She nodded her head. Mays waited to be dismissed.

Clearing her throat, Thea regained her composure. "Thank you, Maysssssss."

Mays nodded, turned, and departed, ensuring his mistress did not see his grin. He relished adding another tick to the wall calendar in his office, marking today's victory.

Thea waited for Mays to close the door before scowling, angry at herself for falling further behind in their game of composure. She turned her attention to her letters.

Thea read the names and sorted them into piles: read now, read later, and read if bored. The latter pile, fortunately, was the largest.

The single letter that caught her notice was from the junior Mr. Cecil

Humphries. Apparently, Mr. Humphries was a young gentleman from Yorkshire. He asserted that he was a magistrate in that northern shire, having assumed the position from his father, former magistrate Cecil Humphries, Sr. The young man was fulfilling a posthumous commission from his father, who had left a journal to his son. He insisted that his son contact her, the Dowager Duchess of Rutland, only after his demise. The son requested her presence in Yorkshire to review his father's findings. He relayed a brief but captivating passage:

"...after extensive investigation and exhaustive, repetitive interviews... conclusion the duel...not fabricated on a drunken whim...nefarious plot...conceited intent to destroy a family...reckless disregard for the law... senseless waste of lives..."

Thea folded the Humphries note. Pursing her lips, her resolve set in. She rang the bell for the butler.

"Yes, madam?"

"I require two express couriers, Mays."

Mays knew his mistress. The matter must be quite serious if she spoke his name without sibilance. "Madam, what else may we offer to provide you comfort?"

Thea smiled. "You have already succeeded. Thank you." She turned to her writing desk. Two messages were completed in minutes and dispatched.

Several hours later, Mays returned with an express. It bore the Matlock seal.

...Captain Thomas Bennet was our cousin Hugh's second at Chalk Farm...

Thea nodded to herself. Pleased that her initial judgment of the Bennet patriarch was accurate, she waited for an answer from the remaining courier.

Sir John Beckett answered her express in the guise of a Crown agent.

"Mr. Reginald Hurst," announced Mays.

Thea rose to welcome the agent. A well-dressed man of neutral features executed a perfect bow and remained standing.

"It is a pleasure to make your acquaintance, Mr. Hurst."

"The honor is mine, your ladyship."

"Please be seated."

They both sat. Mays entered, followed by a maid with a tea tray, and the housekeeper.

Hurst gave his tea preferences. The service staff departed; Mays closed the door.

Thea assessed the young man. He gave every appearance of being at his ease.

"I understand you have assisted Lord Henry for quite some time, Mr. Hurst."

Hurst smiled. "How may I assist you, milady?"

Thea matched his smile. "Brevity is the soul of wit, Mr. Hurst."

"More matter with less art, milady," he replied.

"Well countered, Mr. Hurst."

"Hurst, milady."

"Hurst?"

"Yes, milady. Hurst."

"Very well, Hurst. What answers does Sir John provide?"

Hurst pulled out a letter. He recited without looking at the page. *"Thomas Bennet was the army officer who defended Hugh Lambert, rescued Madeleine, and saw to her welfare after the slaying of her parents."* Hurst looked up. "This information has been confirmed by three parties—two who were present at the incident."

Thea's eyebrows shot skyward.

"Yes, milady. We were aware of Miss Madeleine's whereabouts before her nuptials. Your promise to the young lady was honored. As she kept her word to your request, she remained protected."

Thea shook her head. Involuntarily, she voiced her thoughts. "Who provided her protection?"

Hurst met her questioning gaze. "A young man of unmatched skill and devotion."

Thea's interest was piqued. "May I inquire as to the identity of this young man."

"You may, milady."

Thea waited. Hurst waited. Thea smiled.

"Come now, Hurst. Let us not sully such a splendid start."

Hurst smiled widely, apparently savoring the wordplay.

"The young man is well-known to you milady. He is his lordship's second son."

Thea's eyes opened wide. "You cannot mean…"

"Yes, milady. Madeleine Lambert's most avid protector was Richard Fitzwilliam."

After Hurst departed, Thea locked the correspondence in her writing desk. Her resolve was set. She would go to Yorkshire on her next trip to Chatsworth. There was no hurry as the principal article of interest was a written document in the hands of a known person.

At present, she would travel to Meryton, join the Bennet family for tea, and offer to mentor Miss Jane Bennet. The previous week, Thea Sutton had made the acquaintance of Mrs. Bennet and Miss Bennet in Meryton during a regular market day before she had decided to let her Hertfordshire estate, Netherfield Park. It was a happy coincidence that the three ladies admired the same horticulture display. After a pleasant discussion centering on herbals, Thea had accepted an invitation to join the ladies that day for tea at Longbourn.

She had spent several hours with the four Bennet ladies, their governess, and the housekeeper. She had enjoyed the absence of affected town manners and the open, gracious hospitality of the family. Thomas Bennet had joined their happy party and contributed his dry sense of humor. Thea saw through his genial mask, though, to a hidden intelligence. She had been both entertained and intrigued. Now her inquiries had borne fruit, pleasant and sweet. Her visits to Meryton now would take on a dual purpose.

Pemberley, September 1807

Fitzwilliam Darcy had spent two years ceaselessly working. He made mistakes. He corrected them. Nothing was too inconsequential to gain his attention. He kept in mind a phrase he overheard between the steward and the under-steward of his uncle's horse-breeding estate one day during a visit: *think before you act; think twice before you speak.*

Following this maxim, Darcy made no rash decisions. He remained circumspect. Reticent by nature, he now bordered on aloof. He remained polite with his tenants, servants, and employees, and he respected those who supported the estate without underlying motive.

His tenants praised his active personal involvement.

"Mr. Darcy be the most considerate master."

His servants smiled as they worked. They felt safe, secure, and valued.

"The master asked after me family."

"The master sent a basket to me mum, she bein' not able to work."

"The master sent two men to tend me da's farm 'til 'is leg 'eals."

The town shopkeepers and tradesmen lauded his loyalty.

"Pemberley buy out me canning reserves."

"Mrs. Reynolds doubled 'er flour order."

"Mr. Darcy 'imself come in and fitted up fer boots."

Derbyshire revered Fitzwilliam Darcy as a generous, polite, honest, true country gentleman.

What no one knew—what Jeffers sensed but did not broach—was Darcy's enormous fear of failing.

Darcy took his meals in his study. He feared showing his staff any glimpse of his insecurity: failure of the estate to prosper, failure to live up to his father's example. He preferred to work alone, dine alone, and live alone. He would have continued this way had not the *ton's* expectations required his attention. Bowing before society, Fitzwilliam Darcy girded his loins.

Lizzy prepared a stillroom expense budget and an income forecast for the future soaps, oils, lotions, and other herbal products Jane planned for the estate to produce. Their uncle Gardiner warned her to be careful not to be tainted by transacting in trade. In that vein, Edward Gardiner Imports signed an agreement with Mr. Robert Stephens to be Longbourn's commercial agent to avoid challenging Jane's reputation as the daughter of a gentleman. Her father employed his expertise in deception and misdirection to protect Jane by focusing attention on Stephens. Soon, the Meryton gossip mill feasted on the tales of the handsome young steward's ingenuity to improve the poor output of Longbourn's lands. Franny wrote regularly to her brother about Jane's progress. Edward asked about anything salable that Longbourn produced once he received a sample of the stillroom herbals. It did not surprise Bennet that Gardiner took at face value what had been intended to be a token contract.

Soon Gardiner & Co. products appeared in local shops from Hertford to St. Albans.

Chapter 27

Longbourn now hosted another schoolmaster.

Friar Peregrine Ambrose Abbott resembled Sir William Lucas in many ways. He, too, was a stout, jovial man in appearance. His eyes were genial and pleasant with the outer edges drooping in the slightest. He took joy in meeting new people, but unlike Sir William, he expressed himself concisely.

When standing, Brother Peregrine tended to rock back and forth on his feet, from heel to toe. This was the same nervous habit that Miss Ecclestone had spent seven years failing to break Miss Elizabeth from exhibiting when nervous.

Before he appeared at Longbourn's front door, the Bennets expected a monk in a well-worn wardrobe. Friar Perry, as he insisted he be named, appeared like a member of the high clergy. He sported a well-tailored topcoat of the best superfine, a light-colored waistcoat over a white lawn shirt, and pantaloons. Several weeks, two family dinners, and quite a few drinks in Bennet's library led to the discovery that the congenial friar had the backing of several powerful members of the peerage, including the Earl of Matlock. This, though, only confirmed what Bennet already knew.

Friar Perry had had students in the northern shires but had moved his practice to London. He took on two to three candidates per month and enjoyed awakening the minds of those living in silence. His pleasure came in the brightening of eyes formerly used to living in the dark shadows of frustration and failure. Little could he have imagined that his understanding, his structured life, and his latent faith in the Lord would change forevermore with the wondrous tumult brought into his life by the brilliant and beautiful Miss Kitty Bennet.

Ashdale, Derbyshire

The refurbished family parlor at Ashdale was, in a word, hideous. The overall color palette was pink. Varying shades of pink floated on the walls, a seemingly embarrassing tribute to summer days at Gunther's slurping ices coated with colored sugar where entreaties to behave in a more gentleman-like manner were ignored. The chairs and reclining sofas were covered in alternating colors of pinks and creams. Footmen in pristine white liveries stood midpoint at each wall. Richard entered the room without hesitation.

Viscount Hopton, Langston Fitzwilliam—Richard's twin brother—sat in a comfortable wingback chair of pink-and-cream stripes, one leg casually thrown over the arm. He looked up from the book he had been reading and saw Richard. His jaw tightened, and he took a few deep breaths.

"Please join me, Richard. Pardon my poor manners, but should I attempt to stand, these gentlemen will most rudely force me to remain seated."

Richard nodded. "I am pleased to see you in good health, Brother."

Langston's fears rose when Richard nodded but again receded upon hearing his brother's voice. "Thank you, Richard. I understand speaking is a chore for you, but I appreciate your consideration of my condition."

"Of course."

Langston gestured to a similar pink-and-cream-covered chair several feet away, directly across from him. Richard sat and threw a leg over the wing chair arm.

Langston laughed. "We may be twins, though we look naught alike, but anyone observing our posture could surely not doubt our relationship!" Langston pointed at Richard's leg, followed by his own, also resting upon the armchair arm.

Richard grunted, which for him counted as a laugh. "How do you fare?"

Langston tossed his hand about, much like an orchestra conductor. "I am kept comfortable and safe."

Richard looked around the parlor, his distaste evident.

Langston chuckled. "I see you do not care for the calming effect of pink. It is all the rage this season. Peers who suffer from maladies of the brain, bowels, and buttocks, convalesce in a room resembling the womb. Quite uterine, I must say. One no longer wonders why we men spend so much of our time endeavoring to return by any means available."

Langston appreciated his brother's happy reaction. Richard laughed until tears trickled from his eyes. He scrubbed away the mirth on his face revealing the back of his hand.

"Richard, please accept my apologies for the scars you bear. I am truly regretful."

Richard waved off his brother's entreaty. "It is nothing."

The viscount continued. "Mr. Burton informed me you choose not to speak at length. Did you pen your thoughts to facilitate our limited time?"

Richard removed a folded document from his inside pocket and held it up. A footman stepped from the wall, accepted the offering, bowed, walked to the viscount, bowed again, and presented the missive. The viscount took the letter and shooed the footman away.

"One would think I was Mad King George. Well, maybe the 'mad' designation applies, but not by desire, I assure you."

Richard said nothing.

"Let us begin, Brother."

Langston opened the letter and began reading it, stopping to cast a dubious look at Richard. Then he resumed reading, closed the missive, and looked up at the papier-mâché framing of the parlor ceiling. He re-opened the letter, repeated reading it, and again looked at Richard, now suspicious. Finished, he cleared his throat.

"Richard, you are aware the footmen will not leave us alone."

"Yes."

"So, the earl and the countess may learn of our…meeting and its contents."

"Yes."

Langston dropped his foot to the floor and sat square in his chair. Richard followed suit. This was business, serious business—the future of the earldom hung on their conversation.

"I am not ignorant of your abilities, Brother. Mr. Burton shares much with me."

"I am aware."

"All that you do not feel could cause your demise. Much of what I do feel, what does come in contact with me, can do the same. You and I, as twins, are two sides of the same coin."

"That we are."

"I no longer fear you. I do fear what you have become. Yet, I believe our status quo would do well to remain in place."

"Indeed."

"Do you seek to replace me?"

"No."

"You write you will declaim any right to usurp me as viscount."

"Yes."

"Why?"

"You are the heir. I have other interests." After this lengthy speech, Richard opened his mouth and pointed to his tongue.

"Ahh…I shall try to move to *Yes* and *No* questions. Forgive me if, from time to time, I revert to my fears."

Richard nodded.

"You believe the earl will purchase you a commission?"

"Yes."

"You feel a calling to shed blood?"

"No."

"What drives you then to pursue this path?"

Richard pointed at him. "To protect mine."

Langston nodded. He understood. "To protect our family."

"Yes."

"Cousin Maddy's trials were horrific."

"Yes."

"Shall you seek out those villains?"

Richard's face turned malevolent. "Every…last…one."

Langston shuddered. He closed his eyes and regulated his breathing. "You shall never be free from the line of inheritance even though I am protected in such a manner." Langston waved his hands about the room. "You shall be required to remain—how shall we phrase it—available."

Richard held up a finger. Langston nodded his acknowledgment. Richard leaned back and closed his eyes. A minute later, he narrowed his eyes at his elder brother. "Make me unavailable."

Langston tilted his head. "What compels you to make such a request?"

Richard smirked. "I am not ignorant of your abilities either, Brother. Hurst shares much with me."

Langston grinned. He knew just the family to sacrifice for his brother's wishes: worthless social climbers who needed a comeuppance. *Would Richard accept temporary discomfort to their darling sisters? Well, nothing ventured, nothing gained.*

"I believe I can assist you, Brother. I know of a family of pretenders to instigate a necessary retaliation. Unfortunately, our beloved sisters will face temporary distress. Will you accept this condition? We both know you are quite the protective beast."

"What is your definition of 'distress'?"

Langston did not dismiss the threat in Richard's tone.

"It will be nothing but parlor gossip."

Richard, eyes narrow, glared daggers at his brother.

Langston swallowed. *Mr. Burton downplayed the threat. I shall tread lightly.*

"Richard, I assure you. On my honor."

"Be...sure!" The threatening tone in his voice was unmistakable.

Langston nodded. "Do you understand your part?"

"Not yet."

Langston lifted an eyebrow.

"But I soon will."

Langston revealed his plan. "You, Brother, will have no choice but to escape to the Continent."

Richard tilted his head. Langston recognized the gesture to continue. His fears again rose, but he quashed them quickly.

"You will show the *ton* what tying one's garter in public,[9] without remorse, can amount to."

Richard smiled, his frightful feral grin on display. Opposite him, Langston wore an identical fearsome expression. The footmen in the room labored to hide their discomfort. They failed, and Langston noticed.

The viscount spoke to the ceiling. "My brother will leave now. He will stand. If you enjoy spending your leisure time with all of your appendages attached to your person, do not approach him."

Richard stood. Langston looked up.

"Thank you, Langston."

---

9 Doing something extremely shocking

Langston flipped his hand away from his forehead.

"Happy hunting, Brother."

Richard left the salon and the estate.

Langston watched his brother depart. He regretted Shakespeare's words were out of their reach:

"We came into the world like brother and brother; And now let's go hand in hand, not one before another."

Matlock House, November 1807

Ladies Eleanor and Phoebe Fitzwilliam shared a piano bench as they practiced their scales with no regard to their performance. To say that something distracted them would be an understatement. They played poorly as they could not stop glancing at each other, dismayed about the argument they had overheard while eavesdropping on their older relatives' last conversation.

They stopped, dropped their hands, and turned to each other. Similar bottom lips quivered, and identical blue eyes filled. As if choreographed, they embraced and wept.

Ellie and Phoebe were typical Fitzwilliams: light hair, light eyes, light figures. They did not share their mother's extraordinary eyes nor her beauty. Sadly, they took after their father. What they lacked in appearance, the female fraternal Matlock twins made up in loving care and compassion. Many of the older generation compared them to another Fitzwilliam, Lady Anne Darcy. Said compassion was a strength when recognized by family, friends, and servants. That same compassion was a weakness targeted by the spiteful mothers and scheming fathers of debt-ridden sons of the Upper Ten Thousand.

The young ladies had had a successful come out. Their curtsy to the Queen was error-free, and they exhibited well at the ball thrown in their honor. As with all debutantes, rumors circulated amongst the parents and families of their competition regarding their pedigree—outstanding, their dowries—ample, and their accomplishments—usual.

That they were daughters of the senior Fitzwilliam branch ensured all but the most malicious withheld their animus. The Earl of Matlock was a formidable foe.

One reckless family, the Waltons, ignored conventional wisdom and threw caution to the wind. Their daughter, Winnifred, needed every advantage to secure a desirable match. The Walton estate was burdened by multiple mortgages taken to cover the sins of indifferent management and gluttonous indulgence. Why should they consider the ramifications of a few poisonous pills dropped at parlor visits if it gave their daughter a slight edge in the marriage mart? They could deal with a teary-eyed family, regardless of rank, and render their profuse apologies after a settlement of marriage had both patrons' signatures. So that is what they did.

They achieved their desired result. The Fitzwilliam twins returned home one day from a morning call near tears as they struggled to maintain their dignity. They failed. Had they fallen into the arms of their parents, Lord Henry or Lady Audrey would have resolved the situation. The offenders would have rendered apologies, paid penance, and accepted a temporary social cut by a powerful family.

Unfortunately for Winnie Walton's two elder brothers, Ellie and Phoebe latched onto Richard, who was unexpectedly home that day, and the following chain of events, set in motion as promised by the viscount, resulted in the younger Matlock son successfully defying his father and going off to wage war.

Chapter 28

Boodles, London, November 1807

Darcy entered the club for a quiet lunch, having had a desire for a change of scenery but wishing to avoid being importuned. A private room would meet his needs: food, drink, and solitude. A note delivered from a Darcy footman to the club secretary guaranteed such privacy was waiting. The butler welcomed him by name. Darcy handed off his coat, hat, and walking stick, and followed the man across the lobby, ignoring the denizens who sought his attention. A boisterous crowd around the betting book drew his notice.

His guide opened the door to a small private room. Darcy saw his meal neatly laid out. "Would you have information regarding that distasteful display at the book's table?"

"Sir, a most extraordinary entry has appeared. It has the membership all in a hoo."

Darcy waited for more information.

"It is a pugilistic entry, sir."

"How is this different from the past?"

"Sir, the wager is for a three-on-one event."

Darcy closed his eyes and pursed his lips. He could taste his unease. He stepped into the room and looked back at the servant. "Bring me the names of the fight's participants. Quietly."

"Yes, Mr. Darcy."

Darcy ignored the plate of food under his nose. A light tap on the closed door broke into his reverie.

"Enter."

The butler leaned toward him, a bit too close for Darcy's comfort. There was no need for the display; Darcy was sitting straight, and the servant was not tall. The man whispered theatrically. "Sir, I have the information you requested."

Darcy sighed, reached into his pocket, and produced a coin. The bearer of the news made it disappear and continued. "The provocateurs are the Walton brothers, Messieurs Wallace and Walter."

"I distinctly heard you state three, not two, provocateurs."

The servant failed to notice the sarcasm in Darcy's reply. Rather, the man continued; his voice laced with awe. "Yes, Mr. Darcy. The third participant—not a challenger—is by proxy: the infamous Bristol Bruiser, Tom Cribb."

Darcy held up his hand, demanding silence to digest the information he had received. Three men, one a champion pugilist, were all in the ring against a single opponent. An opponent who could not avoid punishment from three separate directions—an opponent who would have to absorb injury without losing his focus and his energy. Darcy sighed. He knew the identity of the aggrieved and could do nothing. To try and stop him would be an exercise in futility.

"You may leave."

The butler found it puzzling that Mr. Darcy did not ask to confirm that his cousin, Richard Fitzwilliam, was the challenger.

Matlock House

The earl was at his wit's end. He demanded that Darcy and Mr. Burton attend him to try to talk sense into Richard. The earl had an inkling that his second son had manipulated the situation to his ends, but this type of subterfuge was not in his character. It screamed of his elder brother. *Have Richard and Langston been communicating with one another, conniving together?* This would not be the first time Richard had defied the earl's edicts. Unfortunately, the event had been too well touted far and wide for his son to delope. The family name could never entertain such a stain of disgrace.

Captain Markov had confirmed that Richard was in no danger from three "civilians" in a closed ring. At the mention of the absence of weapons, the arms master scoffed, fighting to hold back his incredulity. The earl replayed the Prussian's words in his mind.

"Mein cadet? In danger from three unarmed men? Surely you jest, mein Herr!"

Matlock looked up as Richard entered the study. Darcy followed, and Mr. Burton closed the door. The earl moved out from behind his desk. He relinquished his place of power to sit amongst the participants, hoping that his son would view the gesture with equanimity.

Stillness surrounded Richard. Now that he was sitting next to his cousin, the silence hardened into a wall. The earl found it daunting. Trying to remain unintimidated, he made a diplomatic opening.

"Well, how do you two young men plan to mitigate this scandal?"

Darcy and Richard turned to each other. Lord Matlock clenched his jaw to keep from shouting.

Darcy spoke. "It is only a scandal if Richard does not execute, Uncle."

The earl gaped at his nephew. He could not help himself. His composure cracked.

"Execute? Execute? What in the blazes is *EXECUTE?*"

Darcy glanced at Richard. Richard nodded. The earl felt as if he were part of a pantomime.

Richard rasped, "You spoke to the Prussian?"

The earl nodded, keeping his face neutral, seeking to be more like his son. He saw Richard smile at him. *Maybe there is hope?*

Richard signed something. The earl looked to Darcy.

"*Non est dubium*," Darcy translated. "Doubt not."

The earl leaned back in his chair, rested his cheek onto the top of his fist, and sighed. He swung his eyes over to Mr. Burton.

"My lord, I am in complete agreement with the young gentlemen."

The earl sighed again, blinked, and remained silent. Surrendering to the inevitable, he tried one last appeal. "What am I going to say to your mother?" he pleaded. He was referring to Richard's inevitable departure to the Regulars, now unavoidable if his son inflicted even a minimum amount of damage on his opponents.

Richard held his hand out, palm forward. "Allow me. Mother will favor a visit."

He pointed at Darcy and exited. Darcy now had both gentlemen's undivided attention.

"I shall not break a confidence," he offered gravely.

"Go on, Nephew," urged his uncle. He looked for some type of reprieve and hoped he would not be sorely disappointed.

"That these people chose to disparage two of the sweetest young ladies I have ever known is unconscionable. If Richard had not issued his challenge, I assure you that I would have defended my cousins' honor."

"*You* are not your cousin, Nephew," countered his uncle. Both understood the implication.

Darcy nodded his agreement. "Greed is an ugly thing, but it is not the ugliest of things. The decayed and denigrated state of morality, the social assassination of innocents, apparently acceptable to our social circle, is as unpalatable as it is disgusting. This quagmire masking itself as the London Season is evil."

The earl could not stop himself from shaking his head.

Darcy continued. "For evil to flourish, it only requires good men to do nothing."

"What in the Lord's name does that mean?" asked the earl, turning his palms up.

Darcy stood and walked toward the door.

"You shall see, Uncle."

Richard sat in his sisters' sitting room. The twins occupied a place under each of his arms; two blonde heads lay upon his chest. His sisters hummed a pleasant Irish pastoral in two-part harmony. They knew of Richard's favorites from Siobhan; she had told them before she accepted a generous pension and retired back to her homeland.

Ellie reached up and turned his chin so that he would look at her. "You do not have to do this."

"I do," he whispered.

Phoebe reached over, grabbed his chin, and turned it so he looked at her. This game of theirs he could play for hours. When they were toddlers, he did.

"We overheard you and Cousin William. We are not upset anymore," she offered.

"You eavesdropped. I remain so," he answered her back. He shrugged his shoulders. Their time together had ended. The twins pulled themselves up and assumed proper ladylike postures. He stood and faced them to hear their final entreaty. They turned, each twin taking a moment to look the other in the eye, and next focused on him.

Here comes the harmony!

"We are not so handsome, that you must champion us so," they spoke in unison.

"You are to me."

Figg's Amphitheatre

Figg's was London's first sporting house if one desired to watch fisticuffs in an organized manner. It was here that men flocked by the dozens to witness a thrashing—and a rather good one at that. The son of a peer—a second son, albeit—challenged not one but two brothers and allowed them their choice of a third by proxy! Unheard of! It was all London could talk about. It was all that Lord and Lady Matlock did *not* want to hear.

Darcy stood next to Richard—he inside the ring, Darcy outside of it. Twelve feet away stood three men: two cream puffs and an experienced brawler. The Waltons were making a show of it as they bounced up and down on their toes and threw punches in the air. The veteran fighter stood stock still, a very worried look on his face.

Tom Cribb ignored the children dancing next to him, intent as he was on the dark-haired, lean, cat-like young man across the ring. His adversary removed his shirt and handed it to the tall Corinthian at his side. Cribb's opponent shrugged his shoulders and rolled his head around on his neck; sinewy, well-defined muscles rippled in the dim light. It took but a second for all the hair on the back of the fighter's neck to rise. When his opponent turned and locked eyes with him, Cribb knew he was staring into the abyss. His survival instinct screamed for him to run. To his credit, he listened.

Darcy looked up in time to watch the veteran fighter climb out of the ring, push a few men to the side, and stomp away.

"That makes this rather one-sided now, I daresay." Darcy smiled, knowing he had amused Richard, who snorted.

The Walton brothers stepped toward Richard with their fists clenched. Richard squared up to face them.

Darcy counted down from ten. He made it to three before the fight was over. However, the punishment Richard visited upon the unfortunates lasted another thirty minutes. The shameless display of his unadulterated brutality followed the future Captain Fitzwilliam to his assignment in the Regulars and escorted him to the Continent.

Wallace, the elder Walton, stepped forward and threw a looping punch. Richard nonchalantly grabbed his opponent's wrist, folded it back upon itself, and broke it. The bones popping silenced the crowd. He spun his opponent around into the moving fist of his younger brother.

Richard kicked Walter's legs out from under him, the hapless young man landing flat on his back. The snapping of his ribs and the simultaneous impact of his head hitting the hard floor created a sickening anatomical harmony. Darcy swallowed, his mouth tasting of bile. A brutal forehead to Wallace's face and the eldest Walton joined his brother on the floor, blood from his broken nose puddling around his head.

Darcy seized the moment. "Mr. Fitzwilliam, is your family's honor satisfied?"

The crowd murmured its agreement.

"NO!" Richard disagreed.

The murmuring stopped. The younger Fitzwilliam son prowled about his victims like a great cat of the African veldt preparing to feast on his prey. Richard squatted over the younger Walton and began breaking the fingers of his hands, one by one.

Someone in the crowd vomited. Richard looked up and glared in that general direction, his coal-black eyes afire, his face emotionless. He hissed at the crowd; the closest men immediately stepped back. Richard turned back to his victim and dislocated the young man's shoulder.

Chapter 29

Mayfair, January 1808

The Wentworth's Twelfth Night ball was a crush. Windows were opened wide, despite the cold weather, to cool the ballroom. Ladies wore their best; silks, turbans, ribbons, and feathers of every shape, size, and color were on display. The broadsheets would memorialize the Season of 1808 as the Winter of the Waistcoat—every gentleman trying to outdo the next with the most outrageous of colors, patterns, and button counts. The Royal Menagerie paled by comparison!

Darcy, at Lady Audrey's request, escorted Ellie and Phoebe. He agreed to dance the second with Ellie, Phoebe the third.

Phoebe watched her tall and stately cousin lead her sister to the center line. She enjoyed watching Ellie dance. She was a bit surprised at Cousin William's skill as he moved her sister through the set. Her attention on the couple, she failed to sense someone coming up from behind. She looked over her shoulder at the sound of the unwelcome voice.

"I am unsurprised to see you are without a partner," drawled a thin, over-dressed peacock wearing a dull yellow waistcoat crowded with elephants. Pachyderms!

"I suggest you take your leave before my family returns. We are a protective lot, I daresay."

"Yet, here you stand, all alone, as one would expect of a woman like you. I shall set the example as I am quite in humor at present to give consequence to young ladies slighted by other men."

"You are revolting."

The unnamed peacock grabbed her hand. "You will dance with me, my lady. I insist."

Phoebe returned her focus to the dance floor. "I warn you now. Release my hand or lose yours."

She tried to pull her hand free. He squeezed until she gritted her teeth. Then the music ended. A murmur began; it increased into a buzzing of mutterings. Several dancers stepped backward, gracelessly. Phoebe smiled in relief as a cavalry officer, saber at his side, stood in the middle of the dance floor at the head of the line. He was a statue except for his eyes: black marbles roving from side to side.

"Who let that animal in here?" hissed the mustard-coated popinjay, her hand still trapped in his.

Phoebe turned her head and glared at her unwanted partner. She sensed her brother Richard at her side. She knew so when his hand gripped hers, as well as the dastard's. "That…animal…is Captain Richard Fitzwilliam, my *brother*."

The fop opened and closed his mouth several times, performing an excellent impression of a trout. His fingers opened and freed the young woman. Richard tilted his head and stared at the quivering buffoon. Phoebe could see he was not amused.

"Any problems, Cousin?" said Darcy, as he and Ellie completed the circle of five. The man from Derbyshire stilled, matching Richard.

"Problem?" whispered Richard to the peacock, whose hand he crushed. Phoebe stepped back, no longer encumbered, and nestled into her sister's side. Darcy pressed up against the bully from behind. Spectators crowded around.

The coxcomb jerkily shook his head. He tried to step back but encountered the Darcy wall.

Richard released all but the fop's forefinger. Richard snapped his fist counterclockwise. The young man squeaked.

"Problem?" repeated Richard.

The peacock again shook his head back and forth, tears in his eyes.

Richard snapped his fist clockwise. Phoebe heard bones crackle.

"Problem?" growled Richard, loudly, menacing, a third time.

"No, sir," he whimpered.

Richard released him. The man moaned and staggered away; his damaged hand pressed to his breast.

"Problem?" mimicked Darcy, sporting a genuine smile with teeth.

Goodness me, Cousin William should smile more. Dimples! Phoebe fanned herself.

Richard saw his sister blush and shook his head, raised eyebrows accompanying a small smile.

Darcy held his hand out to Phoebe; they moved toward the dance floor.

Richard walked Ellie to the line and waited for the music to start. Standing apart from the dancers, more women found relief in their fluttering fans. Men measured themselves against the fearsome captain and found themselves wanting.

The four cousins danced alone that set as no others joined nor neighbored their quadrille.

Darcy House, October 1808

Fitzwilliam Darcy, now twenty-four, was the premier untitled, unmarried gentleman in the kingdom.

After Pemberley's harvest was completed, Jeffers suggested that Darcy open his town home to enjoy some diversion and spend time with family and friends. Darcy reluctantly agreed because he felt he had to fulfill society's expectations. Barty and Jeffers rode together in the advance carriage. Darcy traveled alone.

London was a cesspool. Darcy loathed the emptiness, the pettiness, and the faithlessness of the Season. He was a commodity, a prize to be won, no matter how dishonorable or compromising the circumstances warranted, and that disgusted him. He was not looking for a wife nor did he require a hostess.

He quickly tired of the *ton's* pretentious behavior and had the knocker removed from the door. Darcy withdrew behind the limestone façade and burrowed into his study and book room. The post, except for matters of business, remained unopened, at least by Darcy.

"Enter."

"Darcy, may I have a moment?"

"Certainly, Jeffers."

The solicitor sat down, pulled out a journal, and flipped to a marked page.

"Sir, although you have been clear regarding your instructions about social invitations, I must point out the repercussions to your entire family should you not respond to a single one."

"What do you propose?"

"A social secretary, sir."

"Some fop looking to improve his standing by bandying my calendar about? I think not."

Jeffers raised an eyebrow at his employer.

"Go on, Jeffers. You will give me no peace until you have had your say."

Jeffers smiled at the younger man. "This conversation reminds me of one I had with your father."

Darcy gave him a lopsided grin beneath raised eyebrows.

"We hired a social secretary to answer your unasked question."

Darcy prodded. "And…?"

"The candidate, a keen young man, handed in his resignation after two weeks."

"Why?"

"He complained that the position advertised was for a 'social secretary,' not an 'unsocial secretary,' and he said he spent all his time sending regrets."

Darcy threw his head back and laughed. Jeffers joined in the merriment.

"May we rehire him as he was apparently quite competent?"

Jeffers continued to laugh even louder after he spotted a twinkle in his employer's eye.

Jeffers, at the recommendation of Lady Matlock, hired a Mrs. Tremaine, an impoverished war widow, who had previously been a gentleman's daughter. That good lady sorted invitations into three piles: Imperative, Useful, and Meaningless.

The first were connections of such import—one of the royals or Mr. Pitt, for instance—that they demanded that Darcy either attend or pen a personal regret. "Useful" tended to be from acquaintances who either could benefit Darcy's business interests or might eventually be promoted into an Imperative connection. Darcy could, if he chose not to burden Cook with preparing a meal-for-one, join in, eat his hosts' viands, and plead an early morning. "Meaningless" were just that. Mrs. Tremaine would send a brief note of thanks for remembering Mr. Darcy in recognition that a flock of outraged sparrows could rival an eagle with their cries of social outrage.

After a few weeks, Darcy remarked on how the piles of missives had vanished from his desk. "Jeffers, I see Mrs. Tremaine remains employed."

"Yes, Darcy, your 'unsocial scribe' fares quite well."

"Press on, Jeffers."

Chapter 30

Longbourn, April 1809

Bennet peered through the parlor door to watch the dance lesson. His midriff was roiled by an uneasy premonition. His daughters' lack of volubility regarding this part of their education had caught his, as well as their mother's, attention. His wife had come to him, and he gave her his undivided attention. Franny was an excellent mother with unmatched intuition; her instincts were not to be dismissed.

He had asked Franny to open the subject at yesterday's dinner table to lessen the focus on his interest in the matter. He recalled his daughters' facial expressions and body language more than the conversation.

"How did the dance lesson fare today?" Franny asked of the table at large.

Unlike the usual replies about their lessons, which were immediate and enthusiastic, the girls were silent for a few seconds. They fidgeted before they answered.

Jane flatly offered, "We are still learning the quadrille forms, as we must change partners frequently." She then looked down at her plate. Lizzy's face was tight. Kitty looked off, allowing her deafness to separate her from an uncomfortable subject. That no one wrote or signed spoke volumes.

Franny dropped the topic. "Jane, dearest, tell us about your newest grafting experiment."

Jane perked up and spoke at length about the new strain of apple under observation. Lizzy and Kitty joined in with their contributions. Pencils in journals raced and fingers flew.

Thomas brought himself back to the present. The dance master, Mr. Mallus, tapped a stick on the back of the reclining settee in an exaggerated manner while loudly counting the beat. The girls stepped correctly through the forms. The tapping motion slowed, which caused Kitty to miss a step. She turned into her sister Jane, who hugged her, and both giggled. Mr. Mallus moved behind Kitty, put each of his hands on her shoulders, and guided her back into the line. Kitty winced at his touch. Jane ceased giggling. Lizzy's face was stone. Thomas's anger ignited, but he waited.

The dance master began again as before. And as before, the tapping motion slowed. Kitty again turned into her sister Jane. Thomas had seen enough. He stepped away from the doorway and entered the kitchen.

"Mrs. Hill, please chaperone the girl's dance lesson for the remainder of the day."

Mrs. Hill looked up from the table where she had been preparing the girl's tea. Once she saw Mr. Bennet's face, she understood. She shook off her apron and carted the ready repast to the parlor. Tea today would come earlier than usual.

Captain Bennet walked into the library, closed the door, and locked it. From a middle bookshelf, he emptied the books onto his desk and used his fingernails to pry open a hidden compartment. He removed a rolled oilskin and set it all back to rights. He unlocked the door, pulled the bell cord, and waited.

Hill entered the room, saw the roll on the desk, and left.

Captain Bennet unrolled the oilskin to reveal a detailed artillery map of the shire. He planned his evening. Sergeant Reeves joined him.

The following week, Hill announced Sir William Lucas. Bennet rose to greet his friend.

He gestured for his neighbor to sit. "Good afternoon, Sir William. To what do I owe this unexpected pleasure?"

"Thank you, Bennet. It is not that I need a reason to visit, do I? Of course not. I do not. We have been friends and neighbors these past fifteen years. Who but you and I go back as far? No one I know of, though I daresay I do not know everyone you know, do I? Well, that is neither here nor there. Back to my reason for visiting—again, not that I needed one, though I believe we covered that earlier now, did we not?"

Thomas waited for Sir William to come around to the point. He expected the investiture at St. James's would arise, but Sir William cut his preamble short.

"Bennet, my friend, I am, unfortunately, here in my official capacity as magistrate. I inquire regarding a victim of an assault in our shire."

"Please enlighten me, as I have not heard of any ill tidings of late."

"I have visited the Longs and next will visit the Gouldings should my inquiry here not bear fruit."

"Please proceed."

"As it transpired in our shire, I inquire whether you or Franny know a Mr. Octavius Mallus of Clapham?"

"Lucas, I shall save you a trip to the Gouldings' where you may now make better use of your time."

"Will you?"

"I shall," confirmed Thomas, much diverted by his friend's surprise.

"How will you do that?"

"The gentleman in question is our dance master."

Sir William's hairy eyebrows wiggled several times. "Extraordinary."

Thomas tried not to smile. Sir William was an expressive man; his facial gestures held much to entertain.

"I am sorry to inform you that your dance master will not be returning. Apparently, ruffians beat him severely several days ago."

Thomas half-listened as Sir William provided all the details of the injuries. Broken bones. Lacerations. He stopped listening and stood.

"Lucas, what other assistance may I offer?"

"None, Bennet. You have solved my mystery of why Mr. Mallus was in our shire. I shall send a letter to the assizes. It is now in the hands of the Crown Court." Sir William wished his friend good tidings. Thomas saw him to the door, returned to the library, and smiled.

The next morning, while everyone broke their fast, Thomas informed the family he had found a new dance master, a Mrs. Shields. Four beautiful female faces turned to him, and four identical left eyebrows rose inquiringly. Thomas, amused, fought against his natural inclination to tease. His good sense conquered.

"Unfortunately, your previous dance master met with ruffians while leaving the shire. Had he been a fencing master, he may have fared better," Thomas stated dryly, unable to resist.

Bennet looked down to cut his ham slice. He watched his daughters with his peripheral vision. Three simultaneous breaths were expelled, a signal of their approval.

Thomas put a forkful of ham into his mouth, looked up at Franny across the table, caught her eye, and winked.

The widow Sutton, the botanical master working with Jane, amended her earlier travel arrangements and joined Friar Abbot in his weekly carriage ride from London to Longbourn and back. As Mrs. Sutton was a widow and he was a man of the cloth, they were free to travel without chaperones, allowing them to foster a cordial traveling companionship.

Having never been incautious in public, Peregrine and Theodosia, in private referring to each other as Pear and Thea, enjoyed a friendship fueled by stimulating discourse and mutual recognition of intelligence. They enjoyed discussing their passions and the talents of their Bennet students; Perry lauded Miss Catherine's extraordinary progress in embracing her disability and turning it into a unique strength, while Thea countered with Miss Bennet's natural talents with horticulture complemented by a well-hidden dry wit.

Jane adjusted her apron, which kept drifting down her slim hips while she awaited her master's evaluation. Mrs. Sutton held a dish of coffee beans in her hand as she bent over the collection of mortars containing Jane's latest herbal mixtures.

She closed her eyes and inhaled the waiting fragrances. She stood straight, exhaled, and swallowed, keeping her mouth closed. She then ran her tongue across her teeth and gums, giving her a comical puckered appearance. Jane giggled, then demurely blushed. Thea opened her eyes, laughed, and placed her hand on Jane's delicate shoulder.

Mrs. Sutton smiled at her gifted, fragile student. "Never you mind, dear. We are here to learn, have enjoyment, and create the next great herbal to bankrupt town dandies and peacocks.

"I sense a rose base with hints of fennel, thyme, and something quite inert." She passed the jar of coffee beans under her nose, inhaled, bent over again, and intending to sniff from the same mortar, stopped and peered at the mixture. She reached in and picked up a piece of a leaf—blue with hints of yellow. Holding it between her fingers, she asked rhetorically, "Bluebells? Yes. How original and thought-provoking." Looking at Jane, she asked, "Whatever prompted you to mix wildflowers with herbs and staples?"

Jane defended her choice with passion. "I see smaller woodland creatures frolicking amongst the bluebells. I believe that which is attractive to the most vulnerable of the Lord's creatures surely must attract the boldest."

Mrs. Sutton nodded vigorously. "Well done, well done indeed, my dear. You have grasped the most important of principles when working with botanicals: that which ensnares those of the fairer constitution attracts those of the hardier."

Jane blushed under her mentor's praise. Her master tutted; a gentle hand gripped Jane's upper arm. "Jane, my brilliant child, you must, MUST, attend to yourself. Do not deflect my concerns. Those who love and esteem you, even those unknown to *you*, have your best interests at heart. Promise me you will heed my words. I expect to see your apron better fitted on our next visit where I shall inspect it to ensure you have not altered it, for I know of your skill with a needle! Eat child, eat. You must take a second serving of syllabub tonight and every night until I can pinch you and not feel bone."

Jane assayed a look of mock horror and lifted one perfectly arched eyebrow. "I would by no means suspend any pleasure of yours, my dear Mrs. Sutton," Thea chuckled as Jane's sense of humor, so rarely seen, surprised her yet again.

Together, they removed their aprons, brushed their day dresses clean of lingering debris, and arm in arm joined the others in the parlor for tea, cakes, and the latest news from town.

Friar Perry arrived at Longbourn earlier than usual as Mrs. Sutton had sent word she would not visit the Bennets this week.

He observed Miss Catherine in the music room through the door as she "listened" in her own way to Miss Elizabeth practice on the pianoforte. Delighted by the setting's conviviality, Friar Perry closed his eyes and absorbed the precise way the middle daughter played scales. Although he was not a master, he considered himself an aficionado. He attended concerts in season whenever he was invited to enjoy them from a private box. He was not one for the milling crowds of the main floor. Elizabeth Bennet's performance was as enjoyable as those of more accomplished pianists he had heard. While she was technically proficient, her performance evoked within him profound emotion colored with deep passion.

Miss Catherine stood to the right of her sister, resting one hand on Miss Elizabeth's shoulder with the other atop the piano. Friar Perry surmised that Catherine Bennet was *feeling* the music instead of hearing it. He diverted himself wondering whether the high notes felt different to Miss Catherine's fingers than did those in the lower register.

Peregrine next noticed a music stand to his student's right, and perched upon it was the workbook for a silent language he had given to her. *Interesting,* he thought to himself in delight. He waited and held his breath in anticipation.

Miss Catherine tapped her sister on the shoulder with her left forefinger. Miss Elizabeth began playing Handel's "Quando spieghi tuoi tormenti," her tempo light and sprightly. The young lady shifted her hands; her left dropped to the piano cover, her right lifted and, Peregrine understood, began to "sing" in her special way. She spelled the libretto as her right hand wove through the air, her fingers forming shapes and letters, pointing back and forth from herself to her surroundings. The song ended, and Friar Perry had to stop himself from applauding. Thank goodness, he had not interrupted this idyll, for Miss Catherine nodded to her sister, and they began anew.

Miss Elizabeth replayed the Handel, but louder, striking the keys with more force. Miss Catherine leaned into the instrument, molding her body to its angles and curves. She raised her left hand and, joining with her right, began spelling the lyrics, but in a different manner. This time, her hands combined to paint shapes in the shimmering air. Birds, butterflies, the sun, rain, clouds. It was a cornucopia of symbols, all accompanied by music. The piece ended with a small flourish. Friar Perry waited, hoping against hope. Rewarded he was.

Unprompted, Lizzy played the same piece again. Much louder and with much more force, ferocious like the third movement of Beethoven's "Piano Sonata No. 14." The sound filled the room. Kitty now stepped away from the instrument and complemented her sister's offering with incomparable finger signs—shape-forming her hands and arms but adding subtle body movements to her display. Her hands danced, pointed, and flowed; her head and neck nodded, turned, and bobbed; her torso angled, arced, and twisted. Her performance was music, dance, pantomime, and composition—a most unique communication at its finest!

Miss Elizabeth rested her hands on her lap. Miss Catherine relaxed; her hands fell to her sides. She graced her elder sister with a grateful smile. Friar Perry could not help himself. He entered the room, passed into his student's vision, and applauded, long, loud, and with vigor. "Sophos! Sophos! I am overcome. The beauty. The beauty of it all. What a blessing!"

Elizabeth stood, grasped Kitty's hand, and turned her to see the adulation on the friar's face. Kitty's smile reached her eyes as she held out her left hand. The friar grasped it, stepped closer, and touched it with his lips.

"My dear, dear Miss Catherine, the Lord is wonderful, is He not?"

Chapter 31

Badajoz, Spain, April 1812

The Earl of Wellington, Arthur Wellesley, commander of Great Britain's ground forces in the Peninsular Campaign, tasked the Twenty-Fifth Cavalry for the upcoming mission. Wellington relied on Lieutenant Colonel Richard Fitzwilliam for personal bravery, strategic vision, and precise tactical execution. What remained unsaid, but agreed upon, was the recognition of the extraordinary officer's unparalleled brutality. Upon entering the fray, Lieutenant Colonel Fitzwilliam engaged the adversary systematically, relentlessly, and without mercy until the last enemy combatant fell. He razed the battlefield and left nothing but ash. He never took prisoners. None.

If asked, Fitzwilliam would have informed his inquisitor that he chose not to fight the same man twice. Such a response would have been understood as a jest from any man but Richard Fitzwilliam. Although he was rumored to have no sense of humor, no one wished to test him to see whether he did.

His men, blooded veterans of multiple battles, obeyed him without question. The regiment moved quietly and communicated without words. With every fight won, every enemy force flanked, every encounter turned into a rout, the earl's staff reported the Lieutenant Colonel's accomplishments to the War Office with similar adjectives: savage, ferocious, fierce, and ruthless. Fitzwilliam never lost.

The cavalry commander engaged no noncombatants; he disallowed harm to women and children. He acted honorably away from the battlefield, but on it, he was the kingdom's most prolific, professional killer. None had neared the cavalry officer's skill except his own men. Had Fitzwilliam lived two millennia earlier, he would be the recipient of the Grass Crown, the Roman Army's highest accolade for military achievement.

Wellesley, unlike most of London's braggarts, had been ringside at Figg's Amphitheatre the evening Fitzwilliam, at the time a young man, brutalized a pair of blowhards who had insulted his younger twin sisters. The commander of the peninsular forces did not see a sadistic bully who maimed two young men whose uncharitable comments were, at worst, misunderstood by a powerful family—or so the social climbers within the bon ton would have London society believe.

The Earl of Wellington viewed the evening in a much different light—one that involved the security of the kingdom. He saw, inarguably, a demonstration of the mindset required to win a war. These were the exact words he used in his overture to the Earl of Matlock. Captain Fitzwilliam received orders to report to the Twenty-Fifth Cavalry the next morning.

Now, having spearheaded Wellington's breakout from Torres Vedras through the mountains to the Spanish fortress, Lieutenant Colonel Fitzwilliam was ordered to reconnoiter the territory around the town of Badajoz. His mission was to confirm that the French troop levels were as low as earlier reported or whether reinforcements had arrived to bolster the enemy position. Further instructions were to hinder the enemy's ability to secure lines of communication to Portugal. The last instruction, penned by hand, directed him to eliminate any small pockets of resistance.

The mission failed from the first foray. The French commander intercepted Fitzwilliam's men with two dozen cavalrymen and over a thousand infantry. The Twenty-Fifth Cavalry commander rallied his men and, with a small troop, led the French attacking force away from his regiment's main body. Without warning, he turned his men back upon the chasing unit. The French cavalry was shocked into confused inaction. Fitzwilliam and his men tore through the enemy, a trail of bodies left in their wake. They next turned their mounts to engage the enemy infantry. Lieutenant Colonel Fitzwilliam's counterattack succeeded. His quick thinking and decisive actions allowed his men to escape capture and allowed the remaining English forces freedom to maneuver.

Unfortunately, he was not aware of his success. The percussion wave from a cannon shot had blown him from his horse.

Fitzwilliam regained consciousness chained to a stone wall. He was naked. A bored French subaltern was sitting in a chair watching the prisoner. Richard's vision wavered as he sat in his own waste.

Time passed. How much, Richard could not determine as he lost consciousness frequently. At some point, a French officer joined the party. Richard stared at both. He knew his duty. Delay, delay, delay. The older officer spoke.

"*Comment vous appelez-vous*?"[10]

Richard stared at them blankly.

"*Qui es toi?*"[11]

Richard continued to stare. The men looked at each other, turned, and left the cell.

10 What is your name?
11 Who are you?

Before every skirmish, Lieutenant Colonel Fitzwilliam required his men to remove their rank insignia and pins. There was no advantage to be had if the enemy understood who attacked them. He led by example.

They do not know who I am.

Richard dropped his chin and dozed. He awakened to heat on his chest. One of his tormentors, wearing a leather apron, held a glowing red poker. Richard stared at him. He would have spit, but his mouth lacked saliva. Richard never flinched when the instrument contacted his person, nor did he make a sound when he smelled his seared flesh.

Richard whispered in French. The man leaned in.

Not near enough.

Richard whispered of English troop strengths. His persecutor laid the poker on the ground and leaned in closer.

Richard clamped his teeth on the side of his neck. He bit through skin and muscle. An apex predator locked onto his prey, he flung his head back and forth repeatedly, until a portion of the man's neck draped from his mouth and down his chin. The man's body, lying across his lap, twitched in its death throes. The officer, terrified, turned, and dashed from the cellar, forgetting to latch the door behind him.

Richard spit out the offending rasher. He self-assessed as much as the chains allowed him, estimating he had less than two days to live. He did not know how long he had been a prisoner.

The Lord had decided that the world still needed the second Matlock son. Less than an hour later, berserk English soldiers rampaged through the camp. They liberated him while they leveled the French canton and killed all who did not flee. Fitzwilliam was too delirious to notice.

The discovery of Lieutenant Colonel Richard Fitzwilliam was a triumph for peninsular command. His regiment eagerly spread his story, adding to his already legendary status. His rescuers spoke in awe of the dead soldier, missing most of his neck, lying across the legs of their commander while he was chained, tortured, and burned. The litter transporting the officer through the British camp to the medical tent passed between files of grateful soldiers. Richard, unconscious, did not hear the awe or see the reverence, the bestowal of "Imperator, Imperator," spoken by each man as he was carried past.

The general's surgeons worked ceaselessly to clean and close his wounds—over thirty lacerations of all sizes and depths as well as dozens of various burns all over his arms, chest, and legs. Mercifully, his face remained untouched. The cannon blast, which had left his horse unscathed, discombobulated Fitzwilliam and saw him drifting in and out of consciousness for two weeks. Once he was ambulatory, his commander informed him the French had tortured him over the three days of his captivity. General Wellesley promoted Fitzwilliam to colonel and awarded him six months of convalescent leave.

All his honors outside of the promotion were kept secret at Matlock's request. The countess did not want their son heralded as a hero by the tabloids. *How will he be allowed to recover from his wounds in peace and unencumbered by unwanted attention?*

Darcy House, August 1812

The isolation in which Darcy wrapped himself eroded the good principles he had been taught as a child. The fawning, insipid adoration he pretended to ignore filled him with conceit as no one dared offer correction lest they alienate him. His single respite from the social whirl's tedium was the rare outing with his cousin, although those were silent and sometimes dangerous affairs. Wearing his hauteur for display, Darcy became suspicious of anyone not of his trusted circle. In trying to live up to the example of his excellent father, he discarded the exemplar of his gracious mother.

Fitzwilliam Darcy had now lived twice-over more years without his mother than he had lived with her. His father was a pious man, a good man, an excellent man, but he made propriety paramount. *"Darcy men set the example."*

Fitzwilliam Darcy had buried "Little William" with Lady

Anne—albeit months later, but bury him he did. Little William Darcy had thrived upon his mother's tenderness, her love, her hugs, her *aspect*. He had adored her soft caresses through his hair while lying in the grass enjoying a picnic during the temperate Derbyshire summers. The post-funeral Fitzwilliam Darcy evolved into a rational, competent, educated English gentleman who bottled up every hurt, every slight, and every misdeed he perceived but never acted upon.

In his loneliness, the one woman in his circle who possessed an active intelligence did not have the time to educate him. Louisa Hurst had familial and social obligations. Thus, Darcy never encountered sensible ladies. He missed out on the period where a young man, through trial and error, became versed in the ways of young women who are more interested in the world than in lace.

Darcy's separation, and his willingness to hide behind his mask, left him ill-equipped to act spontaneously. He receded further into himself and constructed walls that contained his emotional pain. He became unable to express his feelings. When Charles Bingley presented an opportunity to escape London, Darcy latched on to it—a drowning man's last desperate act to save himself.

This powder keg of repression—an educated, intelligent, wealthy exterior hiding a shy, lonely, needy, motherless boy—traveled to Hertfordshire. As with all explosives, just a spark was needed to ignite the conflagration.

Act Three:
Spires and Chimney Pieces, The Present

Chapter 32

Netherfield Park, September 1812

Three mounted gentlemen trotted through Meryton—two in town dress, one in work-a-day regimentals. Each man's horse told a different story.

Charles Bingley rode a dapple-gray Andalusian mare. The beautiful beast, pale gray with random white spots, stepped sprightly. She appeared to be delighted with the environment and the bustle of people. Fitzwilliam Darcy sat tall upon his black Arabian stallion. Head forward, expression schooled, the great beast gave no notice to the goings-on about them. Both rider and horse represented the epitome of English wealth. The party's third member, Colonel Richard Fitzwilliam, rode atop his warhorse, a black Friesian—a unique beast that interested none of the lay population but never failed to garner great notice. Experts in horseflesh and breeding stables were always drawn to the *Belgian Black*. Only the most observant would notice that the soldier's knees gripped his mount tightly in contrast to his compatriot's more loose-jointed style.

The trio arrived at Netherfield Park, one of the larger estates in the neighborhood, or so Bingley had told his companions. The young man, hoping to be a son who realized his father's dream, had settled on the manor as a prime candidate for a lease that would allow him to learn the ropes. To that end, he had begged Darcy to join him. He found it impossible to deny his friend's request that the colonel join them. The second son of Matlock terrified the genial Bingley.

A well-dressed man awaited them in front of the steps. "Might you be the Bingley party?"

"We are," replied Bingley. "I am Charles Bingley. With me are Colonel Richard Fitzwilliam and Fitzwilliam Darcy, cousins to each other and my dear friends and advisors." All was said with such an amiable smile, the man could not help but smile back.

"I am pleased to make your acquaintance, sir. I am Marion Philips, your lessor's solicitor. Should you choose to proceed after the inspection, I shall be your point of contact regarding all estate matters outside the lessee's responsibility."

Darcy frowned. "Is not your principal on hand to take part in the endeavor?"

Richard closed his eyes. His cousin—once again without meaning to—gave offense by voicing his observation rather than holding his peace.

Mr. Philips gave a sardonic smile. "Sir, I am sure a gentleman such as yourself—with what I suspect are sizable responsibilities—has not the time nor the inclination to involve himself in every minor financial matter within his investment portfolio."

Richard snickered, and Bingley chuckled. Darcy's eyes widened a bit. He swallowed, looked at the solicitor, but remained silent. Richard sighed to himself.

The quartet spent the day touring the house, the parkland, and the tenant farms. Darcy perused Netherfield's ledgers and reported them well kept. He would later show Bingley two or three improvements that would boost the property's income. Richard approved of the stable block. He remarked on their unfortunate emptiness because, while Darcy loved discussing drainage and crop rotation, Fitzwilliam enjoyed sizing up unfamiliar horseflesh. The grooms were amiable and professional, which pleased the rehabilitating war veteran. Bingley, having grown up in a tradesman's house, was not shy as he inspected the kitchens, scullery, and servants' quarters. He spoke with the housekeeper, cook, maids, and footmen. He deemed all acceptable.

They regrouped in the study, which was well appointed. Darcy, Bingley, and Mr. Philips gathered to review the leasing documents, make addenda, and complete bank draft requirements. Neither Darcy nor Bingley inquired about the identity of the estate owner. Richard walked around the study, self-triaging some stiffness, and glanced at the wall displays and objects d'art. Unseen by his friends, he stopped, focused, closed his eyes, and ran through his remembrances from his teen years up north and his lessons under his cousin Charles, now the archbishop of Canterbury. His aunt Catherine and the rumors regarding her match to Sir Lewis popped into his head. He put two and two together and sighed with satisfaction as another, but not the last, piece of a troubling puzzle dropped into place.

Bingley, Darcy, and Fitzwilliam were enjoying the unexpected pleasure of a good meal in a private room at the Red Bull Inn in Meryton. They were quite the odd trio when one looked from the outside in, as that was the thought that passed through the mind of Mr. Melville, the inn's owner. Melville, long the tavern's landlord, saw them as exemplars of the upper crusts of English society: a rising wealthy tradesman, the master of a landed estate, and the younger son of the aristocracy. Given that, the owner saw to their needs personally, and not one of them could render a complaint. The food was light, seasoned well, and presented in adequate quantity. The ale had substance. The orderliness of the room, tableware, and server's clothing was impeccable.

Bingley, amiable to a fault, invited Mr. Melville to join them for an after-dinner drink. Melville warily glanced at Mr. Darcy, who dipped his head in a nod of acquiescence. Fitzwilliam was pleased with Bingley's unknowing initiative. Innkeepers were founts of information; they gossiped as much as soldiers did. Melville did not disappoint, although it took far too long as Bingley had to have his share in the conversation. Fitzwilliam occupied himself by performing his triage exercises under the table until the conversation pulled his attention back among the diners.

"Pardon me, I was woolgathering," he rasped.

"We have just the thing for that sore throat, Colonel. Produced by the estate of the finest family in the shire."

Fitzwilliam put his hand on his cousin's forearm to still his reply. He nodded to his host, encouraging him to continue.

"Longbourn produces an array of draughts, salves, and cremes lauded by Mr. Jones, our apothecary. Everyone uses them. Our blacksmith swears by the estate's lotions to treat his burns. And you might be interested, Colonel, as I seen your mount. The livery uses many of the salves to treat their boarders."

"Who is this paragon of a family?" drawled Darcy.

The colonel elbowed him. Darcy coughed. Bingley chuckled.

"Why, they be the Bennets. The patriarch, Mr. Bennet, his wife Mrs. Bennet, and their daughters. Never a finer family produced anywhere in the kingdom. Proper, proper ladies all."

It took less than a second for Bingley to be Bingley. "Are these ladies out?"

Darcy huffed, and his cousin smiled. Bingley blushed but continued to look hopeful as he awaited Melville's reply.

"They are, they are. And if I am not too forward, the assembly hall down the street hosts a seasonal dance the first Tuesday evening of each quarter. That would be in a fortnight." Mr. Melville stood as he said this. "I shall see that your rooms are refreshed before your evening ends, sirs." He bowed and departed.

Bingley also rose, wished his friends a pleasant sleep, and took his brandy with him calling out over his shoulder. "What a pleasant fellow. So welcoming. And charming. Yes, a welcoming, charming fellow, as is the town. What do you say, Darcy? Shall we return for the assembly? I say, we shall."

Darcy peered at his cousin, who solemnly peered back before offering a lopsided smirk. Both burst out laughing. Richard wished his cousin would allow others to see him thus. They tempered their drinking but extended their time together deep into the night, Darcy happy that Richard had joined their party.

Fitzwilliam had surprised Darcy and Bingley with his acceptance, nay insistence, that he join them when they traveled to Hertfordshire. He did not inform them of his ulterior motive, inspired once he heard Bingley elaborate on his potential lease of Netherfield Park near the market town of Meryton. The name of the shire caught his ear before he dismissed everything from Bingley's ramblings; the name of the town sharpened his focus. Now he had confirmed a surname that echoed down the corridors of his mind.

The following morning, their large, well-sprung carriage rolled through the streets of Meryton on its return to town. The party expected a quiet, incident-free ride. Armed postillions and outriders—Darcy's regular protection bubble—had not accompanied their master. A lone British Army colonel was more than enough to put down any road rabble stupid enough to challenge the coach.

Passing along the High Street, Bingley spied three exquisite young women meet up with Mr. Philips and a liveried footman outside a milliner's shop.

Bingley banged the carriage roof.

"Bingley. You cannot demand an introduction in the middle of the street," warned Darcy, forgetting to temper his voice.

Bingley stepped down from the carriage. "Come, my good man, come." Darcy followed, and he looked back at his cousin. Richard seemed focused on the footman behind the ladies. Darcy hurried after his friend.

Bingley stepped up to the party of five, his eyes growing larger as they both took in the absolute beauty of the trio of ladies who had stopped to watch his approach. Darcy decided he may need to rescue his friend from a social disaster. A wraith hovering overhead and knowing the future would have chuckled at the irony.

Bingley bowed to the group; the ladies looked wide-eyed at him.

The solicitor granted Bingley a measure of mercy by opening the conversation. "Mr. Bingley, good morning, sir."

"Mr. Philips, good morning to you too, sir. Might I request an introduction to your party?"

Mr. Philips, fully aware that Bingley was of lower social standing, turned to the women. "Shall I make the introductions?"

The tallest looked to the shorter of the remaining two, as did what appeared to be the youngest.

"You may, Uncle."

"I have the great honor to introduce my nieces Miss Jane Bennet, Miss Elizabeth Bennet, and Miss Catherine Bennet, all of Longbourn here in Hertfordshire." The ladies curtsied together.

"My dears, allow me to introduce to your acquaintance Mr. Fitzwilliam Darcy of Pemberley in Derbyshire and Mr. Charles Bingley of London." Both men bowed.

By way of acknowledgment, Bingley helpfully added, "In the carriage is my friend and Darcy's cousin, Colonel Richard Fitzwilliam of Ashdale." Neither noticed the footman's eyes widen at the mention of the third member of their party.

The men could not take their eyes off the ladies. Mr. Bingley was riveted on Miss Bennet. Mr. Darcy fared no better; his eyes could not be torn from Miss Elizabeth. Ex-sergeant Reeves, amused, was eager to return to Longbourn and entertain his commander with another tale of the way his daughters' beauty had once again rendered another pair of gentlemen speechless.

"What brings you to Meryton, gentlemen?" asked Miss Elizabeth. Miss Kitty looked sideways at her sister.

Mr. Bingley smiled and launched into their coming to Meryton, his lease of Netherfield Park, the amiability of the inn, and his anticipation at getting to know his new neighbors at the next assembly.

"Do you enjoy dancing, Mr. Bingley?" asked Miss Jane.

"There is nothing I like better than a country dance, I must say," announced Mr. Bingley, generating smiles all around.

"Well, we should hope to see you at the next assembly. You too, Mr. Darcy, if you enjoy dancing as well. Do you?" inquired Miss Elizabeth.

Darcy was intoxicated. Her eyes—her voice—her *everything* moved him as he had never been moved. He felt stupid. He was lost. He was drowning. He panicked, reached for refuge, and spewed the first thing that came to mind. "Any savage can dance."

Miss Bennet's and Miss Catherine's eyes went wide. The footman's eyes narrowed. Both Mr. Philips and Bingley's mouths dropped open.

"Well, we should be happy to witness your superior skills in that arena, sir," Miss Elizabeth replied. Her words dripped with disdain.

Here the footman intervened. "Mr. Philips, we ought t' return t' Longbourn. Th' master will want t' hear o' 'is new neighbors."

"I agree, Reeves. Nieces."

The Bennet ladies all curtsied; the gentlemen, understanding the warning Reeves issued, bowed in return. The women turned and walked off. Their trailing footman glanced over his shoulder and sent Darcy a piercing look.

Bingley waited a few moments and turned to his friend. "Have you lost your wits?"

Darcy looked at him, befuddled. He opened his hands in supplication and shook his head. He climbed back into the carriage. Bingley followed, closed the door, and pounded on the roof.

No one spoke. Words were unnecessary.

Bingley daydreamed of the blonde sylph he had just met. He hoped to secure a dance or two at the upcoming assembly. Richard closed his eyes and committed the Bennet information and Reeves's face to memory. He was positive that the footman, in some fashion, had served the Crown. Something about him brought back a memory of his own impertinent, cheeky armorer. Darcy would have self-recriminated over his blunder had he been able to gather his wits. The short, brunette siren's flashing, angry, brown eyes with hazel flecks rendered him doltish. It was a long, silent ride back to London.

Chapter 33

Matlock House, October 1812

Hurst walked toward the earl's study, only to be distracted by an arm beckoning him to the small parlor. Experiencing a sense of déjà vu, he pivoted and entered the room. The door closed behind him. "With whom am I to speak?"

"Me."

Hurst turned around. Colonel Fitzwilliam was standing in front of the closed door, motioning to a pair of chairs. Hurst settled in and crossed his legs. "How may I assist you, Captain?"

The colonel smiled.

"Yes, I remember you well," quipped Hurst.

"You do, sir."

Hurst smiled. The colonel had no equal. "What would you like to discuss?"

"I spent the last two weeks in Yorkshire."

"I was unaware."

"My batman and I traveled there."

"You must have experienced many new sights and made great discoveries."

"Yes, I did. I have."

"Pray tell, what is the greatest discovery from this summer?"

The colonel leaned forward. Hurst uncrossed his legs and did the same.

"Tang Hall."

Hurst nodded. "As did I."

The colonel's eyes narrowed. "I am aware, but that was twenty years ago."

Hurst leaned back and expelled a breath. "What did I not see?"

"It was what was there then but remained unseen. We found one girl dead. In chains."

Hurst shook his head. The colonel nodded.

"And the servants?"

"Wrong question, Hurst."

Hurst's eyes widened. He knew of the colonel's tactics. "You cannot mean…? You did not…?"

"The earldom will bear the cost to rebuild."

Hurst exhaled, his eyes rolling in his head. Shaking his head and blinking, his thoughts came together. *What else did I not see?* "Forgive me for what you offer is evidence of the most heinous of crimes. Where else did you visit?"

"Broadmoor."

Hurst sat up straight. "Were you engaged in similar research?"

"We rescued one, still just a child."

Hurst clenched his teeth tightly. He reached up and massaged his cheeks. "The duke?"

The colonel shook his head.

Hurst next whispered, "The marquess?"

The colonel handed him a journal. "Their confessions and those of their minions are found here. Everything else you seek is in the mews. In a carriage. Speak with Bill."

Fitzwilliam's face turned to stone. Hurst audibly swallowed.

"Doubt not that I have dealt with this matter."

"Colonel, those peers must testify despite their crimes."

"Hurst, the matter is closed."

The colonel stood. Hurst looked up, speechless.

"The earl is expecting you."

The colonel exited the parlor. Hurst did not notice Smythe in the doorway. He quickly turned page after page as he read to himself.

"Mr. Reginald Hurst."

The earl put down the broadsheet, looked up, and gestured to an adjacent chair. Hurst sat, a journal in his hands.

"An enormous amount of information appeared in my mews earlier. Would you know of this?"

"I would, your lordship."

"Would you care to summarize it for me?"

"The Duke of Grafton and his son, Marquess Bradford, conspired through forgery and fraud to take ownership of Tang Hall for its established income and mineral potential."

"Is there more?"

"Yes, my lord."

"And?"

"We are still gathering evidence regarding a second related matter."

"We?"

"Yes, my lord."

"Who is 'we'?"

Hurst looked at the earl without speaking. The earl grimaced and spoke through clenched teeth. "What is this silence? First Richard, next Darcy, and now you. This tendency to withhold wears on my patience."

"Oh yes, your lordship. On that point, I must agree."

"Ha! So, you agree that this interminable silence is unbearable."

"No, your lordship. I do agree it wears on many a man's patience."

The earl sat back, closed his eyes, and chuckled. "Hurst, your acquaintance, I must say, has added much to my entertainment."

"I am your humble servant, my lord. But I must make a request of you."

"How may I be of service?"

"I shall require correspondence from your connections."

"For what purpose?"

"To examine their handwriting. I am sure you understand my meaning."

The earl's next breath was labored. Hurst was serious. Someone in his circle was involved in these nefarious actions. "Which connections are you requesting, Hurst?"

Hurst's face turned to stone. "All of them, Lord Matlock. The countess's as well."

The Royal Exchange

"HURST, MY OLD FRIEND, WELCOME, WELCOME!"

"Good afternoon, Aronson."

"Sit, sit. What can I ring for?"

"Tea will suit. Thank you."

Aronson pulled a cord and called for a tea tray. The two friends exchanged pleasantries. Aronson asked of Hurst's wife, Louisa. Hurst congratulated Aronson on his daughter, Rivkah Goldberg née Aronson, becoming a mother. The arrival of refreshments signaled an end to small talk.

"How may I help you, Hurst?"

"I need the handwriting of several documents compared to many others."

"Why do you seek this, my friend?"

"I believe a peer is guilty of many crimes—both against man and God. Rather heinous."

Aronson, a deeply religious man, sucked his lips between his teeth for he well understood Hurst's meaning. "I have just the man although his English is sadly lacking."

"I would think that a benefit, Aronson."

"Yes, Hurst! Yes! You, of all people, understand nuance like no other."

"Thank you, Aronson. I shall require haste, and I must be informed daily as I fear our bird may fly if our efforts become known."

"As you wish."

"I would also ask another favor of you, my friend. A carriage loaded with an unfortunate cargo will arrive here in an hour. I need to have the shipment disposed of in an undiscoverable manner. My masters and I cannot relate to it in any way. The bottom of a Welsh tin mine might serve.

"Oh, and do not be disconcerted by my factotum. He is a rather kind sort once you move past his rough exterior."

"Of course, my friend. What is his name?"

"Bill."

Chapter 34

Meryton, October 1812

The Meryton assembly hall was abuzz with excitement. Musicians tuned their instruments on the upper balcony. Members of all the leading families clustered in small groups, chatting and socializing. Other Meryton residents—shopkeepers and solicitors alike—escorted wives across the floor. The din, though, was not as loud as one would expect at such an event. The epidemic of 1803 had left its permanent mark on many clans. Parts of several generations had been swept away to leave chairs unfilled and gaps in the sets that would form on the dance floor. Although years had gone by, such visible reminders augmented memories of those who had been lost in that dire age.

Eligible young Goulding, Long, and Harrington women were spread around the dance floor's perimeter, clad in their finest and waiting for dances to be requested or claimed. The Lucas ladies clustered hopefully near the refreshment table. The Bennet daughters stood near their mother and father and acknowledged friends' greetings. Kitty stood a bit behind Lizzy, observant but divorced from the proceedings. The dearth of young men in the area, an effect of the war atop the scourge, left many a well-dressed young lady in want of a partner. It was not unusual to see two young ladies dancing together because what graceful young swan does not love to display to an audience, even if to family and friends of twenty years standing.

While all agreed that it was a good thing to greet one's neighbors, another event, now a fortnight old, continued to excite all and sundry. A wealthy young man from the north, a Mr. Bingley, had leased Netherfield Park. Acknowledged to be handsome, amiable, and rich, he was the target of every mother and unmarried daughter in the hall that night. He was supposed to be entertaining a large party of other single men and ladies from town, but those rumors concerning the number of men were as varying as town on-dits.

Sir William Lucas walked to the center of the floor and welcomed everyone to the gathering. He proclaimed his pleasure to see such a happy turnout for the evening, wished everyone well, and urged all to enjoy themselves. He looked at the musicians and, with a flourish, signaled them to begin.

Harmonious warming notes announced the beginning of the first set. Couples paired up and walked to the center of the floor. Mr. Goulding, still in his early twenties, paired with Charlotte Lucas, his betrothed. Her younger brother escorted a Harrington girl, and so on and so on. None of the Miss Bennets had been asked to dance. They remained next to their parents. This, though, was by their design and not due to their neighbors' disregard.

Mr. Bennet cleared his throat. Mrs. Bennet turned toward her husband, as did Jane. Lizzy touched Kitty's arm, and both turned to their father. As a family, they thanked the Lord for allowing them to be together and asked for peace to be given to the lost but loved Mary and Lydia. Kitty mouthed what the others whispered. Their prayer completed, they all turned to the dance floor, which told the hall of their availability for dancing. The town residents respected the Bennets' first-set ritual. Jane and Lizzy did not have to wait long. Kitty acknowledged her father's dance request.

As the second set concluded, the doors signaled the Netherfield party's arrival. Four newcomers, three men and one woman in fine town dress, stepped in, stopped, and watched the proceedings. Sir William Lucas hurried over to greet the newcomers as the second dance finished and the musicians took an unscheduled break. They, too, were interested to see whether the rumors were true.

"Welcome to Meryton. How good of you to join our little assembly!" intoned Sir William loudly.

A light-haired, handsome young man smiled and greeted Sir William enthusiastically. "You are well met, Sir William. Thank you for the kind greeting. Please allow me to introduce my friends." The attenders heard of Mr. Reginald Hurst and his wife Louisa from Suffolk, and Bingley's tall, dark, and handsome friend, Mr. Fitzwilliam Darcy of Pemberley in Derbyshire. All appeared eager to join in the festivities.

Sir William offered to introduce the Netherfield group to the leading families, which Mr. Bingley accepted with enthusiasm. Lucas introduced his eldest daughter, Charlotte, to the group, and Bingley secured her next set. Sir William moved on to the Longs, the Harringtons, and his remaining family first. By the third introduction, the whispers had begun. Rumors of the gentlemen's income were interspersed with compliments — Mr. Bingley's manners and his £5,000 received positive recognition. Mr. Darcy's aloofness and disdain were noticed but not condemned, for his £10,000 a year forgave much. The Hursts seemed pleasant and genteel, but little was bruited about of their worth.

The Bennets watched the ritual with humor. Mrs. Bennet opined to her husband, as she recalled Reeves's retelling of the market encounter, "I wonder about this Mr. Darcy. He is either insufferably proud of the ground over which he floats or intolerably stupid of his dour society.

Who comes to an assembly in a new town having insulted the neighborhood? Who are his people?"

"I agree, my dear. Who are his people?"

Thomas Bennet knew Mr. Darcy's uncle, but that was information he kept to himself. Seeing Hurst again surprised him, yet as he thought about it, he found himself happy for his old colleague's married state.

The musicians picked up their instruments and signaled the next set. Mr. Bingley took Charlotte Lucas to the floor. Others joined them. The Bennets watched and listened to the gossip floating through the hall.

"Poor Mr. Bingley. The mothers of the village will quite besiege him," quipped Franny Bennet. She fanned herself, drawing her husband's attention as well as admiring looks from nearby gentlemen who envied the master of Longbourn. Franny Bennet was a striking woman.

"Well, his friend need not worry about being hunted as no one wants to snare that which is unpalatable," Lizzy quipped back, feeling no remorse at displaying her sharp wit.

Thomas smirked at his daughter. Jane tapped Lizzy on the shoulder with her fan. Kitty ignored them all. She watched the newcomers react to endless introductions.

Unbeknownst to the Bennet clan, others overheard Elizabeth's slashing quip. As the Bennets were the area's first family and rarely participated in a public event, any cuts by them were noteworthy. Lizzy's riposte rippled through the hall. The gossip finally made it to the card room and Hurst's ever-ready ears. He shook his head, foreseeing difficulty for his house party in the weeks ahead. He mused whether that would interfere with his instructions and concluded it would not. He continued his play, mindful of the surname of the quip's originator.

As the evening progressed, Mr. Bingley continued to glance at Jane from across the hall while she fiddled with her gloves. From time to time, she looked back through her eyelashes. Eventually, Bingley took heart and resolved his uncertainty. He approached.

"Miss Bennet, may I claim your next open set?"

"I would be honored, Mr. Bingley." He remained, and the group spent a pleasant time together, though much of his attention was on Miss Bennet.

The fourth set ended. Bingley escorted Miss Bennet to their place in line. The music began again, and the dancing recommenced. After half an hour, the set ended, and Bingley escorted his partner back to her parents. She seemed fatigued. Bingley requested and received permission to dance with Miss Catherine. Mr. Bennet engaged Miss Elizabeth for the same set as she had elbowed him, and they lined up next to Bingley and Kitty. They were nearly beneath the musicians.

Darcy, hidden against the wall, watched Miss Elizabeth dance with her father. Her grace in the forms, her beauty in the movement, her lithesome figure rotating, and her silk evening dress swishing around her hips and ankles left him breathless. Her eyes, wide with laughter, sparkled in the candlelight. Her garnet-studded, gold heart locket bounced back and forth across her bosom. Mesmerizing!

So intent was he that he failed to notice Hurst's wife approach until she grasped his sleeve.

"I can guess the subject of your reverie," ventured Louisa.

"I should imagine not."

"You are considering, however insupportable your principles may consider it, how delightful it would be to pass many evenings in this manner—in such society; and indeed, I am quite of your opinion. I never have been more pleased! The gentility, and the quality of the music—the amiability, and yet the lack of self-importance, so refreshing after town!" She spoke quietly, careful of those in her immediate vicinity, which included Mrs. and Miss Bennet.

"Your conjecture is wrong, I assure you. My mind was more agreeably engaged."

Louisa fixed her eyes on his face and gripped his arm more tightly.

"Do tell, sir." Diverted but a moment, she wondered whether some femme fatale had finally broken through his reserve.

"I have been meditating on the great pleasure which a pair of fine eyes in the face of a pretty woman can bestow."

As she was a woman happy within her own romance, Louisa's thoughts flitted from regard to marriage in the blink of an eye. She laughed at herself. *I have become one of those dreaded mothers of the ton.* She noted the direction of his focus. *Who would have imagined the stoic Fitzwilliam Darcy losing his heart to an incandescent country miss?*

"Miss Elizabeth Bennet?" whispered Louisa. "I am all astonishment. How long has she been such a favorite? And pray, when am I to wish you joy?" Seeing the painful look on Darcy's face, she patted his upper arm. "Faith, my friend." She glanced over, noting the Bennet patriarch. *So that is Thomas Bennet…hmm.*

The set ended, and both couples returned. She noticed her brother lead his previous dance partner back to the line for a second time, then received a pleasant surprise as Darcy asked her to dance.

"Try to pay attention to your partner, dear friend," she quipped.

Darcy looked nonplussed. He could not hide that his heart was on his sleeve for all to see. Louisa worked to engage him in conversation but to no avail. He was a man lost. She tutted as the dance finished.

Charles again escorted Miss Bennet back to her parents and remained, as he continued his amiable chatter. Louisa returned with Darcy to the wall behind the Bennet group.

Charles looked up and spied Darcy with his sister. He walked over and secured his friend's arm to pull him away. Darcy dug in his heels, and they both came to a stop.

"Darcy, I must have you dance with our new neighbors. I hate to see you standing about by yourself in this stupid manner. You ought to dance."

"I certainly shall not. You know how I detest it unless I am particularly acquainted with my partner. At such an assembly as this, it would be insupportable."

"I would not be as fastidious as you are," cried Bingley. "Upon my honor, I have never met with so many pleasant girls in all my life as I have this evening, and several of them are uncommonly pretty."

"*You* consider every woman handsome, a term applied too liberally," countered Darcy.

"The family is entirely handsome and, I dare say, quite agreeable. Let me reacquaint you."

It was during the gentlemen's tête-à-tête that Kitty, unaware of who might see her, narrated Mr. Darcy's second insult to her sister Lizzy. Her finger signs drew attention.

The music had ended, and Darcy chanced a quick look at the Bennet group. He spotted Kitty gesticulating and asked without thinking, "Is the young lady having a fit?"

Jane turned and gasped. Kitty's eyes opened as wide as saucers, for she had read his lips. Lizzy's eyes narrowed. She stepped in front of Kitty and brushed her younger sister behind her with a sweep of her arm. Thomas glared daggers at the threesome. Franny took her husband's arm, her hope to keep him from reacting. But hope was futile in this case.

Thomas Bennet took in the arrogant countenance of the gentleman from Derbyshire. Mr. Darcy tried to look down on the squire in front of him, but to no avail.

"I invite you to meet me at Longbourn tomorrow morning to discuss terms, sir."

Gasps filled the hall, but no one commented. Bingley turned from gaping at his friend to gape at Mr. Bennet.

Thomas continued. "No one insults one of mine and fails to make amends. You may call at half past the hour of nine, with or without your second."

The thrum of murmurings, redolent with accusation, galloped

through the attenders. Several repeated Mrs. Bennet's earlier observation but with more rancor. "Who comes to a new town and insults the neighborhood?" The din of accusations grew louder.

The Bennets left the hall, heads held high.

Sir William walked up, his face grave. "I believe ending the evening early would be a reasonable decision, sirs. Your coach has already been called and is awaiting your party." Sir William walked away with no adieu.

Hurst joined Bingley. He had witnessed the entire exchange. Hurst understood the direction of Bennet's manipulation—admired it even—but feared the crowd would choose to defend one of its own. "Let us get our friend into the carriage quickly before anything else befalls us." He grabbed his wife and hurried her out the door, Bingley behind him. Darcy noted the animosity radiating from every eye in the hall. He bowed and exited.

Chapter 35

Once home, the Bennets gathered in the small parlor. Jane wrapped herself in a thick shawl and sat by the fireplace. Her thoughts were of Mr. Bingley and whether she should further his acquaintance after the night's debacle. He appeared to be unlike his friend in manners, but his character remained unexplored.

Elizabeth dropped into a chair, her neck stiff in anger. She could not care less of the scornful gentleman's opinion of *her*, but no one—NO ONE—had leave to injure a most beloved sister! For the first time in her life, Lizzy wished she were a man so she could call out the blackguard who had insulted one she loved.

Mr. and Mrs. Bennet sat together on a sofa and watched as Kitty voiced her temper through her signing. Her anger radiated from her being, causing her hair to stand on end like a furious feline.

"We have spent years dealing with the ignorant prejudice of those outside our community. Even if I am constantly surprised at the depth of ignorance of those with wealth and rank, it has no bearing on placing our family harmony in jeopardy. I cannot bear to see you allow your pride to

sacrifice our family's well-being over a slight that will be repeated over and over throughout my lifetime."

Kitty, spent, sat and laid her head on Lizzy's shoulder. Lizzy exhaled in a great gust. She hugged Kitty. Fierce, protective Lizzy. Kitty looked at her mother, tilted her head a bit, and asked her condition with an expressive widening of her eyes.

Franny blew her a kiss. "I am fine, sweetling. All is well. We shall sort this out to everyone's satisfaction. Now, shall we retire and rise with a fresh new attitude tomorrow morning? Lizzy, please limit your morning walk to the garden, and have Reeves accompany you, my darling."

"Of course, Mama." Lizzy stood, took Kitty by the hand, and walked to Jane. "Come, let us be to bed."

Franny kissed her husband. "You will resolve this tomorrow with no danger to our family."

"Yes, my heart," Bennet assured her.

Outside of Meryton

Colonel Fitzwilliam pulled up on the reins as a signpost marking a fork in the road rose out of the gloom. Sergeant Villiers did the same.

The colonel pointed his chin to the left. "Netherfield. Eat. Get some sleep."

"Yes, sir."

Sergeant Villiers rode off as Fitzwilliam gazed into the darkness. The moon was high, and the road visible, so he cantered on. Spotting the Red Bull Inn, he rode over, dismounted, and tossed a coin to the waiting stable boy.

"Walk him. Rub him down."

The stable boy knuckled his forehead.

"Is Melville about?"

"Inside, guv'nor. Quite a to-do t'is evenin'."

Richard walked into the common room. The noise he had heard outside grew from a murmur to an outright roar.

"Colonel. Colonel, sir. How good of you to come!"

"Melville, good evening."

"Colonel, please find a seat. I shall have a tray brought to you in a moment."

Richard moved to the back wall where a long table had some free space. He sat, leaned back, and listened to the goings-on while he performed his triage exercises. He slowed as he picked up on the thread of a conversation.

"No reason to insult a family, hobbled or not."

"Who is he to come into a new neighborhood and expect to act that way without paying for it?"

"Never seen a gentleman so high in the instep."

"If I were Bennet, I'd horsewhip him."

Richard closed his eyes to focus, the name "Bennet" catching his attention.

"I be worried the girls become homeless should the dastard kill him."

"Philips will challenge the entail. He challenges everything. Top-of-the-trees[12] in his circle, he is."

Melville appeared. Richard waved him closer, and Melville leaned in.

"Private room?"

"Of course, Colonel."

"Join me?"

Melville seemed surprised. "It would be my honor, sir."

Melville led him to their earlier meeting place. Richard sat down and waited. A young girl wearing a clean apron entered with a tray of food and drink. For two.

"Thank you…?"

"Agnes, Colonel."

"Thank you, Agnes."

12 Someone of high esteem

Melville entered. "I see you have met my daughter, Colonel."

"Agnes is a credit to you."

Melville beamed. "Her mother and I are very proud."

Richard pulled out a chair into which his host lowered himself.

"Colonel, you do not mince words, so I shall not insult an intelligent man."

Richard smiled. Meryton was suiting him quite well.

"Your cousin is in the basket."[13]

Richard nodded.

"He has forced Mr. Bennet to call him out. Just as I love my Agnes, Longbourn's master would crawl bare naked over broken glass for his wife and girls."

Richard held up his hand. "From the beginning, please."

Richard listened more than he ate. At the end of the meal, he stood, thanked his host, and reached into his pocket.

"No, Colonel, your coin is no good here."

"How may I be of service?"

"Stop this nonsense, sir. No one wins in such a nasty business."

Richard bowed. Melville returned the gesture, surprised.

"So, I have been told."

Netherfield Park

The ride back to Netherfield Park was silent except for the unceasing, pleasing observations Louisa provided. Hurst offered a word here and there to support her, aware of her goal in trying to diffuse the tense atmosphere weighing down the coach.

Darcy and Bingley sat on the rear-facing bench as far apart as two individuals could be seated and still be in the same conveyance. Darcy was white-faced and silent. Bingley was red-faced and getting redder. Darcy leaned his head back on the squabs. Bingley looked out the window and fumed.

---

13 To be in lots of trouble

The short ride back ended with Hurst exiting the carriage to hand out his wife. He cleared his throat to warn the two younger men to mind their manners. They entered the foyer and divested themselves of their outerwear to the waiting butler and footmen.

"Express for you, Mr. Hurst."

"Thank you." Hurst pocketed the missive.

"Darcy," Bingley growled, "my study, now, if you please." He stormed away.

Darcy stared after his friend. Trying not to be offended, he trailed behind. Hurst pulled his wife to his side and whispered, "They may need me." He left her at the parlor door.

Darcy entered the study. Bingley's cheerful, affable aspect was absent. In its place was a rigid, angry man. *He reminds me of me.*

Bingley glared at him. "Tell me why I should not ask you to leave, Darcy."

Darcy gaped at his friend.

"I never thought to accuse you of *cruelty.*" Bingley spat out the last word. "Arrogance, yes. Excessive fastidiousness, yes. Disdain for the feeling of others? Not your friends, but God help the rest of the world. But tonight's behavior? Insulting those of standing in the community? You pledged to assist me in stepping up into the gentry. Was this your example of being a gentleman?"

Darcy dropped into the nearest chair. "I have no excuse, my friend—if you are still my friend."

He glanced at Hurst who was occupied perusing a painting.

Bingley walked past Darcy and out the study door. "Let us allow for cooler heads to further address our current situation."

Darcy turned to answer Bingley but saw an empty doorway. Hurst appeared not to notice either man as he was captivated by a small hanging on the study's wall. It was the same piece of art—the same coat of arms—that had captured the attention of another a month before.

In their sitting room, while his wife slept, Hurst opened the express.

...first four names on the list exonerated. A.A.

Darcy entered the dining room just after dawn. He was in no mood to converse. He had tossed and turned all night in recrimination.

He had already prepared himself a cup of coffee from the sideboard before he saw he was not alone. "I never doubted you would come."

Colonel Richard Fitzwilliam sat in a chair on the opposite side of the table, an empty plate and a half-full cup of coffee in front of him. Darcy saw the smile on his face.

Fitzwilliam's eyes crinkled with merriment. "You have been busy. Badly done, Cousin."

Darcy sat down across from him. "I do not need your help."

"I beg to differ."

"Do you need to hear my side of it?"

Richard shook his head. "Bingley?"

"They still keep to town hours."

The colonel rapped his knuckles on the table. Darcy looked up. *"Outside,"* the military man gestured with his finger.

"How are your wounds healing?" Not *"how do you feel?"* If you were a confidante of the colonel, you inquired of the physical, never the emotional.

"Coming along." The colonel's whisper dissipated in the light breeze that wafted over the formal hedges.

They walked out into the gardens without speaking, comfortable in their shared silence. It was a Pemberley summer. Good times. The best of times.

"You have a problem. Thomas Bennet is not an ordinary country squire. He is a decorated officer from the King's Secret Service. Few know."

Darcy, uncharacteristically, doubted his cousin. The Mr. Bennet he saw at the dance did not strike him as intimidating. He looked at his cousin, his lip curling in disdain. "Rather hard to believe."

"He will choose not to duel if offered recompense."

Darcy thought of his achievements—advanced rating in fencing, excellent target shot, impressive pugilism score.

He broke out of his reverie when Richard raised his voice. "Would you like to duel *me*, Cousin?"

"Of course not," answered Darcy quietly, his eyes down. He did not fear confrontation, but he was not a professional soldier. Richard, on the other hand, had no equal.

"Think of why you would not." The colonel walked away.

Darcy knew his cousin would serve as his second. His confidence in his own abilities never wavered. He had never had to duel as his great height and physique forced his possible opponents to recant. Mr. Bennet did not impress him as a potential adversary. Darcy believed that he, like all the others, would yammer a bit, flatter him, make excuses, and bow out with grace. Yet, Richard cautioned him regarding the Longbourn patriarch.

Darcy disregarded his cousin's warning, his self-confidence in place. He continued in the same attitude as Barty dressed him for the upcoming conversation. His cousin did not speak with him; the ride to Longbourn was made in silence. As Darcy dismounted and handed the reins to a waiting stable boy, he decided, when offered, to accept Mr. Bennet's appeal to negotiate.

Chapter 36

Longbourn's front door opened before they were able to knock. The colonel placed his card atop Darcy's on the butler's silver salver.

"I shall see whether the master is available."

"Thank you…?"

"Hill, Mr. Darcy."

"Thank you, Hill."

They removed their coats and hats and handed them to the waiting footman, Reeves. Darcy thanked the man, turned away, and examined a landscape hanging on the wall. Richard appraised the footman from head to toe and back up. Reeves grinned back and acknowledged the colonel's examination with a slight nod.

Reeves leaned in to whisper, "His nibs is lookin' for'erd to seein' ye agin."

Richard sighed. Another cheeky armorer. The kingdom was much smaller than one believed.

Mr. Hill returned. "This way, please."

"The Honorable Colonel Richard Fitzwilliam, second son of the Earl of Matlock, and Mr. Fitzwilliam Darcy of Pemberley in Derbyshire, to see you, Mr. Bennet."

"Thank you, Hill."

Mr. Darcy bowed his way into the study. "Good morning, Mr. Bennet. Thank you for receiving us."

Colonel Fitzwilliam looked at him out of the corner of his eye and frowned.

Bennet was not alone. A handsome woman rose from her chair, smoothed out nonexistent wrinkles from her morning dress, and curtsied.

"Good morning, gentlemen. Welcome to Longbourn. I am Mrs. Francine Bennet, mistress of the estate."

Both men bowed again.

"I shall order tea and refreshments, if you will partake?"

Darcy seemed to have rediscovered gentle behavior overnight. "That would be lovely, Mrs. Bennet. My cousin and I thank you for the consideration."

Thomas nodded. Franny grasped his forearm and pulled him toward her.

"Remember your promise," she whispered into his ear. She kissed his cheek. Thomas smiled and watched her leave the study. "Let us sit, gentlemen."

Bennet gestured to four chairs arranged in a circle. He had moved his reading table, leaving a rather obvious omission. Darcy looked at the carpet, frowned, then looked about. The displaced furniture was now on the opposite side of the room. Atop were two ornate wooden cases—one was long and rectangular, the other perfectly square.

Darcy paled.

The three men settled in for a lengthy visit. No one spoke. The case clock in the corner marked the passage of minutes. This conference was to determine whether and how one would kill the other, yet nobody said a word. Bennet's past dealings with the present gentlemen's elder relatives did not prevent him from being diverted. *Irony at its finest!*

He looked at young Darcy, thinking that the apple must have rolled far from the Fitzwilliam tree. The haughtiness the young man seemed unable to shed little offended him. *Let us assess this…Darcy.*

"The colonel is your second?"

Darcy froze. Bennet could see the young man forcing himself not to look at his cousin.

"Yes, he is."

The captain waited, evaluating his adversary and ignoring the colonel. Darcy stared back. He was unaware he fidgeted.

"I have heard of your prowess with weapons, Mr. Darcy. Your grouse hunts, where you display your accuracy, are laudable."

He saw Darcy take a calm breath and noticed a tiny smile begin on the young man's face. *Arrogance, thy name is youth!*

Bennet continued to probe. "Friends have written to me of your success at Angelo's. You have quite the following and few willing opponents."

Now he saw that Darcy could not stop the grin. *So typical of the wealthy. First, flattery, followed by excuses. The lad has never been brought up short for his behavior.*

Longbourn's master narrowed his eyes and audibly exhaled. The young man's face adopted the mask of hauteur.

With a voice as cold as a Russian winter, Captain Thomas Bennet glanced at the displaced table, turned back to Darcy, and stated harshly, "Choose your weapon."

A third voice rasped through the heavy air. "This is not Chalk Farm, sir!"

Thomas Bennet turned to the colonel; the negotiation field surrendered. Little did it matter.

On the one hand, Fitzwilliam Darcy was a child in a man's body. He was filled with insecurities camouflaged by wealth, hereditary prestige, and familial connections. The obvious lack of a mother figure throughout his life left his arrogance unchecked.

On the other hand, Richard Fitzwilliam was more than a man. The colonel, when acting in his family's interests and those he loved, bore the flaming sword of the archangel Raguel—a ruthless executioner for any he labeled enemy.

Bennet would never forget that day, exactly sixteen years ago, in Watford. He never expected to leave his carriage alive, grateful that his abject confession granted him a reprieve from the charge of being complicit in Madeleine Lambert's disappearance, thereby preserving his own life.

Bennet closely attended the cautioning inflection in Fitzwilliam's voice.

"How does Lord Matlock fare?" Thomas asked, offering an olive branch.

Colonel Fitzwilliam exhaled. "Why did you not preface his name with 'my friend and your father,' sir?"

Darcy, his arrogant mask shattered, displayed his confusion. Thomas's lips broke into a smile. "Call me Bennet, if you will, young Richard."

"Thank you, sir. The gentleman, unaware of the danger before him, is my *younger* cousin."

"I shall take that under consideration."

"Benneeeeeet," parried Richard, drawing out the last vowel, a faux, painful expression on his face. "I would consider it a favor if you would not kill him."

"I never planned to. Today is a negotiation—one that will lead to a lesson in manners."

Richard nodded. Darcy's head whipped back and forth between his cousin and his host—if one could call a challenger that. "I am in the room," he interjected dryly.

Richard and Thomas both chuckled. Bennet reached over and patted Darcy's knee twice. "Let us delay explanations for another day, Mr. Darcy. If given the opportunity, what course would you wish to take?"

The discourse had confused Darcy with its speed-disguising nuance. Thus, he sat in silence. In the meantime, Bennet stood and walked to the sideboard, poured a small amount of brandy into three separate glasses, and served his guests. He was unsurprised to see Darcy drain his. Bennet refilled it.

Darcy came to his senses, accepted defeat, and offered his concession. "If you would permit me, sir, I should like to apologize to your daughter for my behavior at the assembly. My assumptions about *her* behavior were impolite and ungentlemanly. Voicing them aloud only compounded my offense."

Bennet assayed a serious look. "My youngest daughter takes after her eldest sister in many ways. Kitty has a forgiving and tolerant soul. She is used to the comments of the ignorant and the unknowing."

Darcy looked abashed at Bennet's barb.

"However, young man, you may have earned the lifelong enmity of my tigress-like middle child. She has been known to remove the hide of a fool who disparages either of her sisters, but she reserves special measures for any who attack Kitty. You will have to work diligently to win over Elizabeth."

Darcy now sipped his second brandy of the morning. "Then it is good that I plan to assist Bingley in learning estate management for a month or more. Hopefully, I can repair the poor first impression I made at the assembly, and taking your advice, sir, I shall exert a special effort with Miss Elizabeth."

Thomas nodded in approval. "Let us discuss this with Franny. She has the ear of the community. Shall we join the ladies for tea so that you may make your confession and beg for forgiveness? By the way, I have a sense that we shall be in close concert over the next months.

Call me Bennet if I may name you Darcy."

That gesture made and accepted, Bennet asked Mr. Hill to inform the mistress that their visitors would join them for tea and refreshments.

As they stood, Darcy extended his hand. "Thank you, Bennet, for your forbearance. By way of explanation, and not to excuse my iniquities, I shall admit I am not comfortable in a large crush like an assembly. Four ladies in a parlor will not be that. I much prefer small gatherings with close friends, as my cousin will attest."

Bennet smiled. "Well, let us add to that small group of friends, shall we?"

He anticipated quite the display from Lizzy when she espied their guest.

JANE, LIZZY, AND KITTY ENTERTAINED EACH OTHER IN THE PARLOR. Jane, wrapped in her signature shawl, embroidered a handkerchief. She stopped, leaned her head back, and closed her eyes, so enchanted was she by Lizzy's reading of Wordsworth. Her contralto was smooth and quite alluring. She looked up regularly to allow a standing Kitty to read her lips.

I wandered lonely as a cloud
That floats on high o'er vales and hills,
When all at once I saw a crowd,
A host, of golden daffodils;
Beside the lake, beneath the trees,
Fluttering and dancing in the breeze.

Continuous as the stars that shine
And twinkle on the milky way,
They stretched in never-ending line
Along the margin of a bay:
Ten thousand saw I at a glance,
Tossing their heads in sprightly dance.

The waves beside them danced; but they
Out-did the sparkling waves in glee:
A poet could not but be gay,
In such a jocund company:
I gazed—and gazed—but little thought
What wealth the show to me had brought:
For oft, when on my couch I lie

In vacant or in pensive mood,
They flash upon that inward eye
Which is the bliss of solitude;
And then my heart with pleasure fills,
And dances with the daffodils.

Kitty signed the words as Lizzy read, her hands and arms forming elegant shapes in the air. Unconsciously, she sinuously swayed back and forth as her body bent to the words' meaning. Her sea-blue muslin morning dress ebbed and flowed around her ankles like a walk along the beach at the ocean's edge on a fine summer day in Brighton. Both Darcy and Fitzwilliam gawked, captivated.

Darcy was lost in the performer's dulcet tones. His tongue went dry as he again feasted his eyes on the enchantress who had haunted his dreams for the past fortnight. *I am in the same room as she!* His self-control slipped; his panic blossomed. He tried to control his breathing and failed. Sweat stippled his brow and upper lip. His feet were leaden, mired in mud. Looking for a refuge, he turned to his cousin. *What? Is Richard triaging? In public? And is he…? Good Lord, he is perspiring!*

Richard recalled the youngest Bennet daughter from their initial encounter. Light spots flickered in his vision. *She danced, did she not?* He thought she was finger signing, but he had never seen the like in his long history with Perry and other scholars of silent communication. He shook his head, but the light sparkles remained. The young lady was Jophiel, the Dionysian archangel. He felt warm in a very pleasant way. He was sure he had not injured himself. His extremities felt normal. *Wait! Am I triaging? In public?* Unsure how to sort out his emotions, he turned to his cousin. *Good Lord, the man is sweating!*

Thomas, behind the gentlemen, nudged Darcy slightly, breaking the spell.

"Pardon me, gentlemen," he said, grinning.

Franny walked in. Mrs. Hill followed behind carrying a tray loaded with tea, cakes, and sandwiches. She stopped and looked from her daughters to the men.

"Oh dear."

Thomas stepped forward to make the introductions. "Ladies, with your permission, please allow me *formally* to introduce our visitors."

Jane nodded.

"Jane, Elizabeth, Kitty, please allow me to present the Honorable Colonel Richard Fitzwilliam, second son of the Earl of Matlock, and his cousin Fitzwilliam Darcy of Pemberley in Derbyshire, our newest *friends*. Gentlemen, my daughters, Miss Bennet, Miss Elizabeth, and Miss Catherine."

Mrs. Bennet urged everyone to sit and took the serving honors upon herself. Once everyone had tea and refreshments, perfunctory conversation ensued. The road conditions: dry; the quality of the shooting: first outing next week; and the weather in town: not as pleasant as in the country. Exhausting the mundane, the parlor strained from the sounds of silence.

Everyone felt the amiable atmosphere's fallacy. Thomas noticed

Lizzy laboring to keep her composure. Kitty seemed distracted. Jane was…Jane. Bennet cleared his throat and peered from his peripheral vision at their visitors. Darcy placed his cup and saucer on the nearest side table and rose. A tall man, he involuntarily forced the ladies to look up to maintain politeness.

"Mr. Bennet, Mrs. Bennet, and the Miss Bennets: please consider my apology for my boorish behavior last evening at the assembly. I have no excuse other than personal discomfort in large gatherings, which is not acceptable for a gentleman to own or display."

He continued with true regret in his voice. "I am not a man who intentionally insults others"—Richard's snort interrupted him, but only for a moment—"for any reason and must reassure you that my discourteous remarks were regrettable, untrue, and ungentlemanly. With that said, I do beg your forgiveness."

Darcy swiped at his forehead and dipped his head.

All looked at Kitty, for she had been the target of the most insensitive of his remarks. She signed to Lizzy that she accepted Darcy's apology without reservation. Before Elizabeth could translate, Richard leaned forward and spelled a formal and elegant, *"Thank you for your graciousness."*

Jane gasped and put a delicate hand over her mouth. Lizzy froze. Kitty's smile reached her eyes and made them shine like summer sunlight dappling upon a pond. The colonel was mesmerized. Thomas was thoroughly diverted.

Franny looked at her youngest child and repeated, "Oh dear."

Darcy rode back to Netherfield Park, confused. An enthralled Richard kept pace, exhibiting emotions Darcy had never before seen.

"Cousin, she is too young for you. Your parents would never accept her, notwithstanding her infirmity. Her situation is not agreeable. She is far beneath you."

Richard growled. "I will *make* it agreeable, Cousin." His warning glance left no room for further conversation on the subject.

Richard gave Perseus his head, drove his rowels into the beast's flanks, and galloped off. Darcy reined in his horse, and both circled several times. Now was not the time to return splattered with mud. He wisely understood that his cousin was not challenging him. Richard, always a solitary creature, clearly needed time alone with newfound feelings. As Richard disappeared over the next hill's crest, Darcy prodded Goliath forward.

His mother's memory whispered at the edges of his consciousness—indistinct but for a flavor of happiness promised. His father's voice thundered in and smothered his mother's soft message. *"Darcy men set the example."*

Darcy pushed his horse to a canter and tried not to replay Miss Elizabeth's appealing recitation of Wordsworth. He failed. He asked himself whether he was being a faithless son. *I wonder whether she sings?*

Chapter 37

Netherfield Park

Colonel Fitzwilliam entered his sitting room and sat down in an armchair. He signaled his batman.

Sergeant Villiers took a moment to readjust his glove. Though a year had passed, he was still acclimating to his amputation—the two smallest fingers on his left hand. He lost them at Ciudad Rodrigo when he had deflected a French infantryman's bayonet thrust away from the colonel's back.

The colonel raised a boot. Villiers turned his backside to the colonel and grabbed the heel between his legs. The colonel put his other foot on Villiers' rear and pushed as Villiers pulled. One more cycle saw Fitzwilliam unshod in an exercise repeated several times a day for the past twenty years.

The colonel cleared his throat. "Go to town. Learn of the Bennets."

"Anywhere specific, sir?"

"Forge, stables, apothecary."

Villiers nodded. "Anything else, sir?"

The colonel shook his head and signaled with his eyes. *"No, you have your orders. Go"* Villiers departed.

The colonel flowed bootless across the room to his portable writing slope and pulled out paper and ink. He closed his eyes and pictured the luminous young lady from Longbourn. His first letter began, *"Your ladyship…"*

Sergeant Villiers quick-marched—the duke's vaunted 108 beats per minute—into the little market town. To Villiers's experienced eye, a militia must have had an advance team somewhere nearby given the carts and equipment outside the smithy. *A good place to start.* He walked toward the sound of hammering.

The blacksmith was a large man. His shirtless arms and massive chest glistened in the heat. He worked horseshoes between the forge, a water trough, and an anvil. Efficient and strong, he knew his craft.

Villiers nodded in greeting and shed his uniform coat. He grabbed a spare leather apron off the wall hook and worked side-by-side with Mr. Smith. Villiers pegged "Smitty" to be the same age as the colonel, which would place him between the Bennet parents and children. The sergeant listened as Smitty praised the graciousness and the compassion of the Bennet daughters—their charity to their tenants as well as the town. Villiers noted that he mentioned their beauty as an afterthought.

Three hours, twelve horseshoes, and an exchange of thanks later, Villiers left with a headful of the Bennet ladies' history. He headed over to the livery.

Villiers spent two hours mucking stalls as he listened to Mr. Piles. He estimated him to be a few years older than the Bennet patriarch. Piles added to his Bennet knowledge with anecdotes of the girls' love of horses—except for Miss Lizzy. She had suffered a broken arm at a young age from an untrained draft horse. At the time, the injury in no way prevented her from scolding the horse immediately afterward!

Villiers laughed with Piles. Story after story followed. All cast the Bennet family in a positive light. He accepted Piles's thanks but deferred a drink invitation. Villiers headed to the apothecary, Mr. Jones.

Villiers struck gold at Jones's residence above the shop. The apothecary was out tending to a broken leg on one of Haye Park's farms. He was not expected home before nightfall. Mrs. Jones, a friendly woman who kept her finger on Meryton's pulse, provided tea, cakes, and an unending monologue. Her news had merit without gossip's malice. In teary, heartfelt dismay, she relayed the tragedy of the epidemic that scarred the Bennets. Villiers, himself moved to emotion, handed her his handkerchief.

He learned of the changing chapters in the Bennet's marriage: their hasty, lust-driven wedding followed by the couple's near estrangement from his distraction and her failure to produce a son. Now, their model relationship of respect, esteem, and love. Such a shame they had to lose two daughters to find what every couple desired! Mrs. Jones was staunch in her veneration of the family. She admired their "family-first" focus and praised the townsfolk for their acceptance and support of the Bennets, a respected name in the shire for hundreds of years.

As the hour grew late, Villiers had to make his regrets. *What a wonderful lady*, he thought as he pulled on his greatcoat. So, he told her that very thought, and received a sweet smile and pat on the cheek, akin to what his grand-*mère* Villiers used to do. As he walked back to Netherfield Park, he hummed a near-forgotten French lullaby while, in his head, he organized the lengthy history and tragic story of the Bennets.

Another note from Aronson—

...first eight names on the list cleared. A.A.

Longbourn

Two days later, the Netherfield party called at Longbourn. Once announced, Mr. Darcy stood post near a window and looked upon the front garden, his back to the room even though a seat near Elizabeth was unoccupied. He was unaware that the ladies interpreted his actions as further contempt of their station.

The colonel, unmoved by the antipathy aimed at Darcy, bowed to Mrs. Bennet and asked to sit with Miss Catherine. He signed as he spoke. Mrs. Bennet looked over at Kitty who blushed cherry red and looked down at her hands, clasped tightly together.

"You may, Colonel."

Although the couple spoke with their hands, their understanding of the manual language differed. Kitty's forms radiated poetry when she expressed herself. Fitzwilliam's efforts indicated his profession: his gestures were direct and efficient. They shared thoughts in a journal when required. Thomas Bennet was fascinated by the interplay. Kitty glowed in the attention of a suitor. Franny glowed with hope for her unique daughter.

Darcy remained at the window. He covertly listened as Bingley engaged the ladies in conversation. Mrs. Hurst and Miss Elizabeth exchanged comments with a speed such as Darcy had never experienced in town. The subject did not matter—Shakespeare, chess, tenantry, the parson's sermon the past Sunday—nothing escaped Miss Elizabeth's keen observations and decidedly witty opinions.

At one point, fixed upon her discourse, Darcy had an inkling that the lady argued a side he was sure she never would have supported. *Is she trying to draw my attention?* Later, Miss Elizabeth extemporized on how physics applied to dancing. She simplified Newton's Third Law to the opposing movements of a quadrille—each dancer's lesser partner reacting equally and opposingly to their matched lead partner. He noticed that even Mr. Bennet and Hurst stopped talking to listen. Darcy turned from the window to attend to her unique and mind-boggling postulations.

Bennet later chatted with Hurst on topics typical of the gentry: shooting, riding to the hounds, and estate management. Neither acknowledged their previous acquaintance.

The entire gathering had lost track of time until Mrs. Hurst stood to signify the end of the call. Colonel Fitzwilliam had other ideas. He looked out the window and observed the weather was pleasant for a November day. Elizabeth took his hint and recommended a stroll through the garden despite the fact that she would have to entertain the colonel's rude cousin. Kitty looked at her mother, who nodded her approval.

A small group emerged from Longbourn's front door, circled the building, and took to the garden paths. Colonel Fitzwilliam walked with Kitty. Elizabeth and Mr. Darcy made up a second couple. Inside the manor house, Hurst followed Thomas into the library while Mrs. Bennet and Mrs. Hurst sat with Bingley and Miss Bennet.

Elizabeth maintained her composure as a silent Mr. Darcy walked beside her, his hands clasped behind his back. She was unsure whether his apology was sincere. Mr. Darcy rubbed his forehead and breathed deeply. His disturbed features told of his unease.

His manner reminded Lizzy of the previous day, his apology, and what she had assumed was his haughty disdain. Had she been wrong? Rather than being disdainful, had he been embarrassed? Might he have been truthful regarding his discomfort in large groups, which led to his habit of *involuntarily* insulting others? She abandoned her current thoughts as she looked ahead, happy Kitty had met a man considerate of her unique challenges.

Richard and Kitty walked together in companionable silence. Richard broke the ice with a hand gesture to gain her attention.

"We have a common friend," he signed.

"Perry."

"How did you know? Of course. My style of signing."

Kitty nodded. Fitzwilliam chuckled.

"Does Perry still work with you?" he mouthed.

"When he can share a carriage with Mrs. Sutton."

Richard's next step faltered a bit. *Well, that is QUITE the development.*

"Mrs. Sutton is…?"

"Jane's botany master."

"Of course."

Richard was elated. He mouthed words without intonation, yet still communicated clearly. It was quite heady. He almost missed his companion's query.

"Do you have much discomfort from your wounds?" Kitty blushed.

"Fret not. I am well recovered."

Kitty hesitated, deep in thought. Richard waited. She nodded, permitting herself to take the next step, and lifted her left hand. Richard, without thinking, extended his right hand, palm down.

Kitty placed her hand upon his forearm, causing both to blush.

"I would be honored," Richard offered, having recovered his wit. He was blinded by her…everything! *Why, she is luminous!*

They continued to walk in shared silence, the inevitable now a certainty.

From the library window, two pairs of eyes watched the courtship begin.

"You know what he is, do you not, Bennet?"

"I am quite familiar both with *who* he is and *what* he is, as you well know." Bennet countered.

"I do not interfere nor pass judgment. I only ask you to be aware of all that accompanies him, both sides of the coin, as it were."

Thomas nodded as he kept the colonel and Kitty in sight. They were a striking couple.

"Are you aware of what he *will* be, not what he may be?" queried Hurst.

"Are you *that* certain of your declaration?"

"I am."

"Who else knows?"

"None outside the immediate family."

"But you do."

"You know what I do, my work currency."

"As if I could avoid it," Bennet ruefully replied.

He absorbed Hurst's grin. They raised their glasses and toasted the future of Matlock.

"I caution you, old friend. The question is not whether your daughter is up to the challenge of who he is; for that, I do not doubt, and I congratulate you with warmth. The question is whether she is up to the challenge of his destiny. I leave that in your capable hands, sir."

Hurst bowed and held out his hand. By reflex, Bennet grasped it. Hurst left Longbourn's master at the window. As he watched his daughter and future son, he massaged the message in his hand.

Silly games, he mused.

Thomas gazed, unseeing, out the window. His mind now occupied; he sought out Reeves. He would leave it to his armorer to prepare for the next day's meeting at dawn.

Mrs. Bennet and Mrs. Hurst sat apart from Jane and Mr. Bingley in the parlor, keeping a loose chaperonage on the pair. The colonel's obvious infatuation raised Franny's maternal hopes and fears. She did her best to rein in her pounding heart and promised that she would not cry.

Louisa gently asked, "Would you mind relating how Miss Catherine lost her hearing if it does not bring you too much pain?"

Louisa laid her hand on her new friend's arm. Franny looked over at her. "Influenza took two of her sisters, my Mary and my Lydia. It took much of Jane's strength and Kitty's hearing. That plague also took much of my heart."

Franny dabbed at her eyes with her handkerchief. Louisa did as well.

"Well, I intended to distract you. In that, I have failed. What a wretched friend you have in me," Louisa teased with a watery smile.

"Yes, wretched indeed," Franny teased back with a matching expression.

"We lost my mother and my younger sister, Caroline, in a carriage robbery. They were returning home from her seminary."

Louisa looked to make sure Charles was not close enough to overhear. She leaned closer. "I learned their deaths were violent. The brigands fouled them most dreadfully. I have prayed the Lord took them before they realized their end. Our father has since confined himself to our family's business interests, living apart from Charles and me."

A stricken Franny refreshed their teacups.

An hour later, the Netherfield party rendered their farewells. Louisa promised to send a card for tea at Netherfield. Bingley beamed.

At dinner that evening, Mr. Bennet smiled at Kitty repeatedly, even employing his eyebrows in his quest for diversion. Impossible for her not to notice, she looked to her mother for guidance. Franny laid her hand on her youngest's arm, speared her husband with a mock glare, and let her family know how proud a mother she was to have such beautiful, talented girls. Mr. Bennet, chagrined, stood and made sure he had everyone's attention. He raised his glass to the young ladies at the table and toasted Franny: a beautiful wife and caring mother, unequaled in the kingdom.

Three miles away, Bingley queried his elder sister through her husband. "Hurst, may I make a request of your wife?" Hurst smiled. The "my sister" that usually followed such requests was absent. He nodded his approval, as his mouth was filled with an amazing ragout. "Lou, would you mind taking on the arduous task of planning a ball?"

Louisa excused herself after dinner. The men rose to see her out of the dining room, then regrouped in Bingley's study. Once everyone had their drinks, Bingley cleared his throat.

"Well, Hurst. Why are you not with my sister? She appears to be in an interesting condition."

"I am well aware; however, I wait for her to inform me. You will learn soon enough, little brother. A mother hen is fiercest when she contemplates her nesting box."

The men acknowledged Hurst's wisdom. Their toasts to his impending fatherhood were hale and hearty. Darcy chose to retire early. Bingley ensured his friend had gone up the stairs before he closed the door and flopped into his armchair.

"Hurst, what other pearls of wisdom have you to entertain our lot this evening? Dour Darcy no longer dampens the discourse!"

Bingley reached up and patted himself on the shoulder. Richard guffawed, as did Hurst; both were delighted with the alliteration.

Hurst took up the challenge. "I would enlighten every one of us that the elegant Miss Elizabeth mayhap erases Fitzwilliam's focus most emphatically, expeditiously, and efficiently!"

The colonel and Bingley raised their glasses to Hurst and offered a well-deserved "Huzzah."

"Signing would surely secure success."

Hurst and Bingley hooted at the irony. Fitzwilliam was incredibly pleased with himself.

They dove deeply into the sideboard brandy, Darcy's obvious inner struggle over Miss Elizabeth abandoned as a conversation subject.

Two expresses awaited Hurst—one from the earl, the other from Aronson. He opened the earl's: the black edges the only necessary message. He read it twice, then dropped it into the fire and watched it burn.

He opened Aronson's express.

...all names on the list exculpated. What next? A.A.

Hurst stared at the note. The absence of some critical fact vexed him. The earl's note added to his distraction. He walked to the sofa and sat.

"Hurst darling, what has put that unseemly look upon your face?"

"Sit with me, love."

Louisa dropped into his lap. She wrapped her arms around his neck.

"Riddle me this, my dear: What does one do when one's known connections are exhausted?"

Louisa smiled at him.

"Well, Darby. One must look at those who were connections but no longer are!"

Hurst's heart swelled. *What a magnificent, intelligent woman is my wife!*

"My dearest Joan, you—*kiss*—are—*kiss*—a wonder." *Kiss.*

"Do tell, Darby! And do not stop!"

Chapter 38

Longbourn

Lizzy sat on the edge of her bed and reviewed the day. Her hands, by their own volition, lifted to her heart as she tried not to cry for Kitty's potential happiness. Colonel Fitzwilliam, in her opinion, was everything one would want in a brother and more. Handsome, fit, older, and worldly-wise. No longer would she have to worry for Kitty's safety. The colonel was a veteran of Badajoz. His heroism was real and not that manufactured by the broadsheets. She would encourage Kitty's affection, if she asked, as too many stupid men had dismissed her beautiful sister with nothing more than a glance.

Thinking of glances, she mused, *If I had a farthing for every glare the colonel's rude cousin threw my way, I could buy Uncle Edward another ship!*

"Be charitable, Lizzy." Her dear aunt's loving voice filled her ears.

"Yes, Aunt Maddy," she intoned as she looked up at the ceiling.

Lizzy crossed her legs, put her hands together, and lowered her head so her steepled fingers nested in the space between her lower lip and chin. She closed her eyes and ran through every interaction between Mr. Darcy and her family: the insult in Meryton, the insult at the assembly, his apology, and today's walk.

Elizabeth's talents did not end with her affinity for numbers. Her mathematical facility resulted from being able to see the patterns flowing through the numerical sea. She burrowed down and replayed their first interaction in the Meryton market, his slight at the assembly, the silent looks in the Longbourn parlor, and his movements while they chaperoned Kitty and the colonel.

She listened for the tone floating above the content. At one point, she mumbled to herself, "He appears to find us too low to converse with," but carried on. She envisioned a newborn colt with Mr. Darcy's face, legs all wobbly, knees splayed out as he tried to stand upright for the first time. She giggled.

In her mind's eye, she saw Mr. Darcy wipe dampness off his forehead before he dried his palms on his coat front. What struck her most was the look on his face after he made a rude remark. He was aghast! He was regretful. Was he embarrassed?

He was nervous in my presence! I am never overset by someone who is beneath my notice. If so, does that mean Mr. Darcy has feelings for me? Is Mr. Darcy enamored of me? Surely not!

Netherfield Park

Sergeant Villiers answered the knock on the colonel's sitting-room door. A footman held a silver salver with letters upon it.

"Expresses come for the colonel, sir."

"I am no 'sir,' Peter. I am a sergeant. I would thank you to remember that, but also, I do thank you for delivering the mail."

"The rider be expecting an answer, Sergeant Sir," Peter cheekily replied.

Villiers chuckled. "Send him to the kitchen for a meal. He can wait there for his return instructions."

Villiers knocked on the colonel's bedroom door, then entered without waiting.

Fitzwilliam, shirtless, looked up from his ablutions, his burn scars pink and scaly. The larger lacerations remained red and purple, punctuated by suture marks. He continued washing his torso with a rough towel. The army did not recognize personal privacy. The colonel understood the sentiment.

Villiers signaled with the letters in his hand and waited. Richard, towel around his neck, flicked his chin toward the sitting-room door. Villiers placed the letters on the side table by the chair the colonel favored and sat opposite. He waited to see whether he would be required to read the letters aloud or resume his other duties.

In a state of dishabille, Richard entered, sat in his favored place, and threw his leg over the chair arm. He considered the expresses—one from the earl, and the other a War Office communiqué. His mother's letter was franked rather than having been sent express. Richard experienced a sense of foreboding. Deciding to read the earl's last, he placed it beneath his mother's. He broke the seal on the letter from Horse Guards and read it quickly.

He handed it to Sergeant Villiers. "Reply 'Received.'"

The colonel's attention was already on his next letter. Villiers sat back and read the first.

To The Honorable Colonel Richard Fitzwilliam,

By Order of His Royal Majesty, King George III, awarded under his right as sovereign, and His Royal Highness, Prince Frederick Augustus, Duke of York, under his right as Commander-In-Chief of His Majesty's Army...

Richard Henry Fitzwilliam is named Knight Companion of the Order of the Bath and all the accolades, rights, and privileges contained there within. Investiture will be at the Court of St. James's upon the pleasure of the Grand Commander.

Signed,
Arthur Wellesley, Marquess of Wellington,
Commanding General of
His Majesty's Peninsular forces

—Addenda follows—

It is determined that Colonel Richard Fitzwilliam be forthwith retired with honor, his rank awarded in perpetuity, action effective upon the date of receipt.

Signed,
Major General Sir Andrew Hull Foote

Villiers left to instruct the express rider. Richard opened his mother's letter, which did not fail to draw a smile.

My dearest Richard,

Knowing I may still refer to you as such gladdens my heart, you must know. I shall not fill these pages with the ramblings of a mother beseeching her child to attend her as I know of you, I need ask it but once.

I received your last missive and could not stop myself from crying out with joy, drawing attention to myself from our loyal servants, wide looks from your dearest sisters, and false censure from your father.

We shall accept no more invitations nor commit to social fêtes. You may plan to attend to your father and me before the new moon.

Give our blessings to the good Captain Bennet's lady wife. I look forward to befriending my future counterpart and giving my regards personally.

Your loving mother,
Lady Audrey

Richard tapped his mother's letter against his lips. The countess gave her unreserved approval. It was time to see what the earl had to say for himself. Richard broke the seal on his father's letter and removed the outer paper. Within was a sealed letter, its edges besmirched in sepulchral hue and sealed with the Fitzwilliam thistle pressed into black wax.

Richard lowered the letter to his lap and glanced at the faded scars on his right hand before raising them to his lips to bestow a fraternal kiss. He concentrated on his breathing. *Nothing is ever easy,* he ruminated.

May the good Lord bless Langston, take him to his bosom, and give him the peace he was so denied in this life.

Chapter 39

Darcy opened his eyes. The sunlight filtered through the bed drapes as a swooshing sound reached his ears. *Barty has opened the window curtains.*

Darcy's thoughts, once again, began with Elizabeth Bennet. Her father's connections were unknown. To Darcy's experienced eye, Longbourn's income was reported to be less than actual, which would make the threat of an entail seem insignificant if the master were salting away the surplus to secure his daughters' futures. How many more layers to the Bennet onion existed? Why was he interested in piecing together this puzzle? Why could he not get the brunette with the fierce eyes, sharp tongue, and seductive voice out of his thoughts?

"Barty, a cold bath this morning, if you please."

"Right away, sir."

As Darcy bathed, or rather cringed, his cousin entered. Richard grabbed a chair, swung it through the air, and dropped it next to the tub.

"Having fun?"

"No."

"Deny your attraction," Richard challenged with a laugh.

The tips of Darcy's ears reddened, despite the chilled water cooling his shanks. "Barty, my robe, if you please."

The valet walked over with his master's robe open. Darcy nearly leapt out of the cold water, dove into the woolen wrap, and took the opposite chair. He picked up the waiting hot cup of coffee and saluted Barty.

"When were you last near Kent?"

Darcy stared at Richard. "You said near Kent, not near Rosings, did you not?"

The colonel nodded.

"Near Kent, as in Canterbury?"

Richard nodded again. Darcy tasted bile.

"What, not who, is Mr. Bennet?"

Richard remained mute.

Darcy forged ahead. "How are the Matlock earldom and the Devonshire dukedom connected to an insignificant estate holder in Hertfordshire?"

"What did I warn you of upon our first morning here?"

"You warned me that Thomas Bennet was not an ordinary country squire."

Richard departed. Darcy dressed and went for a long, hard ride.

Matlock House

"Enter."

"An express, your lordship."

"Thank you, Smythe. How is the new man-of-all-work faring?"

"I believe he is enjoying his role, although quite mindful of Bill."

The earl smiled. Bill maintained the finest mews in town.

The earl opened the express and felt his world tilt.

None of the earl and countess's known connections are involved. Who were family connections before, and are not now? H.

"Smythe!"

"Yes, my lord?"

"Ensure the rider is well-rested. He has several legs to complete, and I shall tolerate no delay."

"Yes, my lord."

Lord Matlock cursed to himself. He pulled a key, long unused, from the center drawer in his desk, leaned to his right, unlocked a panel, and extracted a scroll full of nonsensical claims.

"Sister, if you are culpable in this business, I *will* throw you into the Tower myself!"

Longbourn Village

Reeves knocked and stepped back, his right hand on the pistol in his belt, the left holding a cocked pistol behind his back.

The door opened. A voice from behind the panel bid them to enter. Reeves entered, both pistols pointed forward. Hurst peeked. Reeves lowered his weapons.

"I see you have not become lackadaisical in your retirement."

"Any more than you, I imagine," Captain Bennet dryly replied as he entered the chamber. He turned to his armorer.

"Thank you, Sergeant Reeves. Leave those cannons with me. You may return to your duties. I am sure your fearsome appearance will keep evildoers at bay."

"Aye, aye, commander. Back to hard duty…er…to the Miss Bennets."

"Cheeky devil," laughed Bennet. Reeves departed, leaving the current and former intelligence agents to conduct their business.

"Why do you put up with him?"

"Rhetorical question, Hurst?"

Hurst snickered, walked over to the table near the wall, and sat in one of the two chairs. Bennet joined him.

"Bennet, you are the most secretive man with whom I have ever worked—yet know that the good colonel is in your league."

"Yet, none are in yours, I daresay."

Hurst let that pass. Thomas continued. "Colonel Fitzwilliam is now viscount?"

Hurst peered at Thomas with one eyebrow raised and evaluated his colleague's level of interest. Satisfied, he answered.

"I had it on good authority that Viscount Hopton's treatment program had measured success. That changed with his medical diagnosis. His regression became a concern of safety over security."

Bennet nodded.

"The late viscount ended his suffering two days ago. He pilfered a spoon from his meal tray. He sharpened it on the floor and used it on his wrists. It was careless of the staff, but it was done, and nothing can change it. I understand he passed quickly."

Thomas said nothing.

"The family respects and esteems you. Your brother's marriage connects you."

Bennet stirred. "I suspected it might, but thank you for confirming the fact."

"Thank the Fitzwilliams. They wanted you to know that they knew."

Bennet paused. "Hurst, Franny tells me you and your wife expect a happy event soon."

Hurst nodded. "It appears so."

"The blessing of a child brings with it the absolute terror of the loss. The love you find is as hearty as it is fragile. I wish you and Mrs. Hurst every joy."

Hurst blinked several times.

"Thank you, Bennet. I imagine you are cognizant of another attraction growing between our households.

"Know that Lord Matlock is under the countess's thumb concerning the good colonel's choices."

Thomas Bennet laughed. "Of that, I have no doubt."

Chapter 40

Darcy reined in Goliath, dropped to the meadow, and caught his breath. Turning round in a circle, he looked about to get his bearings. A rise off to the east—a shoulder of the Chiltern Uplift—captured his attention with its slope checked by a regular rule of walls and hedges. Then he smelled *her* fragrance—lavender. He was bathed in her delectable aroma.

Perspiration-soaked, he dared not take off his coat now that he knew he was not alone. Should he mount and ride away? That would be boorish of him. Yet, the impropriety of staring at her froze him in place. Giving way to indecision, he turned and faced his horse.

Darcy heard her coming closer. He hugged Goliath, who rubbed his face against his master's. That cheeky move forced Darcy's head far enough around to see Elizabeth Bennet assessing him. He glared at Goliath. His now ex-favorite mount snorted. *How dare he laugh at me!*

Darcy's heart leapt at Miss Elizabeth's laughter. Her rich tones filled the grove. He lowered his head a bit and let his shoulders slump. He turned around and greeted her. Standing in front of his horse, hair wet and tousled, Darcy was unaware he was crushing his beaver. His bow, though, was heartfelt.

Miss Elizabeth curtsied, delight on her face.

Darcy smiled. *Could I make myself appear more absurd? I think not!*

Miss Elizabeth closed the distance between them, coming to a stop short of his mount. Noticing her wariness, he moved his reins to his far hand, turned his body, and shielded her from the great beast.

"Mr. Darcy, I am on my way up Oakham Mount to take in the glory of our valley. Would you care to join me?"

Darcy looked past her to see a Bennet footman. He nodded approvingly.

"It would be my pleasure, Miss Elizabeth. Let me secure Goliath so you may walk in comfort."

As Darcy went to tie Goliath to a tree, the Bennet footman, his powerful shoulders far wider than his waist, silkily approached and offered to mind his horse. "I'll watch him fer ye, Mr. Darcy."

"Thank you, Mr. Reeves."

Darcy was perplexed at the look of surprise on both their faces. *What did I do to cause that reaction?*

Darcy looked to Miss Elizabeth for guidance. She turned and began walking up the path. Darcy followed, his long legs keeping him abreast. At the top, Miss Elizabeth spread her arms wide and spun in two complete circles. She counted out in a loud voice, "One" and "Two."

Darcy watched her spin, delighted in her buoyant enjoyment of life.

"That was for my sisters."

"Miss Bennet and Miss Catherine?"

"No, for Mary and Lydia. We miss them so."

Lizzy walked over and sat on a large tree stump.

"Your sisters who passed."

"Yes, Mr. Darcy. Do you have siblings?"

Lizzy waited for his answer.

"No."

Confused by the coldness of his voice, Lizzy took instant offense. She scowled at him. He looked down at his feet.

"It is now your turn to say something, Mr. Darcy. I talked about my sisters. Now you ought to remark on the like." She disliked the bite in her tone but could not help herself.

Darcy's mind went blank. She was angry at him. Even after twenty years, the subject of his mother and her death, the sensation of her cold hand in his, made it difficult to breathe. At the time, he did not understand the meaning of the tiny bundle she held. Now he did, and the sadness unmanned him. The most enchanting woman he had ever encountered was demanding more of his soul than he could give. He chose silence.

Elizabeth glared at him for a few seconds more, then turned and faced the valley. She unleashed what sounded like Haydn. Her contralto broke through his defenses and made him feel vulnerable. Darcy took two long steps and lowered himself onto the stump, making sure to maintain a bit of separation.

O much lov'd Maid, whilst life remains,
To thee I'll consecrate my Strains,
For thee I'll tune my Lyre.
And echoing with my sweetest lays,
The vocal Hills shall speak the Praise
Of Friendship's sacred fire

Elizabeth sensed Mr. Darcy as he sat next to her. She finished singing and waited in silence.

"My mother would sing with me."

She heard him swallow.

"I loved picnics, hearing my mother sing."

His voice cracked a bit on the last two words. He turned his face away from her. She reached out and placed her hand on his forearm.

"That must have been lovely," she whispered.

"She was…I mean, it was."

They sat in silence. The early morning calm was palliative. A whistle from below intruded upon their reverie.

Lizzy stood, brushed off her walking dress, and bid Mr. Darcy adieu.

Reeves saw she was in good stead. The man from Netherfield remained atop the mount to allow her to complete her ramble without raising questions.

The sergeant walked by her side. Miss Bennet appreciated his counsel. She also enjoyed his audience to her observations of life's absurdities.

She blew out a frustrated breath. "I do not understand how that man can be so rude and so pleasant within the same conversation. The two cannot coexist."

"Miss Lizzy, t' hear tell, your young man is well regarded in his terr'try. *Very* well regarded."

Lizzy narrowed her eyes at him. "He is *not* my young man, sir!"

From the distant height, a shouted echoed. "One. Two."

Her eyes clouded. After a few steadying breaths, Elizabeth straightened her back and strode off. The distance between her and Reeves grew.

"So says you, me ducklin'."

An express was received at Netherfield Park.

…the crow is your viper. A.A.

Peter attended Mrs. Hurst in the Netherfield parlor while she penned her invitations. She glanced at the clock and suddenly startled.

Her hand lowered and caressed her abdomen. She looked down and smiled.

"Peter, a moment."

Peter hastened to assist Mrs. Hurst. "Yes, mum?"

"Please see this invitation delivered to the mistress of Longbourn. It would be a kindness."

"Of course, mum."

Peter waited. He did not want to seem impertinent, but lately, Mrs. Hurst would call him back as soon as he took three or four steps toward the door. He wanted to anticipate her needs as the first footman had trained him to do.

Mrs. Hurst looked up at him. "Was there something else, Peter?"

Peter cleared his throat. "Was there anything else, mum?"

Mrs. Hurst smiled. "Thank you, Peter. Carry on."

"Yes, mum."

He turned and counted to himself silently. When he reached four, his hand on the door latch, he heard his name called.

"Peter, have you seen Mr. Hurst today?"

Peter made sure his footman's face was in place, turned, and answered his hostess.

"They say 'e was out o' the manor early this morning, mum."

"Thank you, Peter. Carry on."

"Thank you, mum."

Peter whistled once he was outside the manor as he walked to the stables. He would tell his fellow footmen of the day's entertainment, but only in a most respectful manner.

The servants had heard stories of the nouveau riche who leased estates and played "Laird o' th' Manor" to the detriment of all—slapping maids, firing footmen, and throwing tableware. Not this house party. Proper ladies and gentlemen all!

The colonel's sergeant was a bit of a fright, him with his long, giant arms and missing fingers, but what hero was not? War was a bad business.

They had all overheard as Mr. Darcy cautioned the maids to knock and make themselves known before entering the colonel's suite. A right proper gentleman, that Mr. Darcy.

His valet, Mr. Barty, was tight-lipped but warned one and all not to walk behind the colonel, out of respect for his rank. Odd request that, but the staff did their best to do so. Sally still whined when someone would mention the famous officer. She had surprised him once in his suite while he was napping, him shirtless in his chair in front of the fire. The housekeeper, Mrs. Nichols, had reassigned her to the kitchen quick-like, everyone above stairs concerned with her wanting to minister to his injuries. *He na' be yer brother, y' silly cow!*

It was by common consensus to satisfy this family party, as they were nothing but considerate. *And a handsome hostess,* thought Peter.

The next day, Louisa enthusiastically welcomed Franny and Lizzy. She led them into the parlor where a picturesque tea spread awaited.

At Louisa's raised eyebrow at the diminished party, Franny said, "You must forgive Jane and Kitty's absence, for it is not a slight of any kind."

"The thought never crossed my mind, Franny."

"Jane is in the stillroom with Kitty as her test subject; we dared not interrupt," Elizabeth explained.

They spent the next hour in as fine an attitude as three intelligent, proper English women could. Lizzy reminded Louisa about a treatise she had mentioned in their last conversation and received permission to fetch it from the library. Louisa asked Peter to escort their guest.

Lizzy entered the library after thanking Peter, who left the door open but did not inform his guest the room had an occupant.

I 'ope th' colonel knows what 'e's about.

Darcy sat in a chair in the corner, out of direct sight from the door. He found it fortunate Miss Elizabeth had turned to her left. His mouth went dry as his temptress danced and swayed as she searched the shelves.

She stopped at the fourth section and called over her shoulder, her voice tinged with annoyance. "Mr. Darcy, you should know that I am conscious that my figure appears to its greatest advantage in front of these bookshelves while I am on my toes, but I find your motives quite suspect."

Miss Elizabeth turned around and laughed unabashedly. Darcy put his book down, stood, and motioned to the chair next to him.

"Please join me if you dare." He tried to tease and smiled when she replied.

"Dare, I do. My courage rises with every attempt to intimidate me."

Darcy narrowed his eyes. She raised her eyebrows. They both laughed. Miss Elizabeth walked over and sat down.

"You must allow me to apologize for my behavior on the mount. I cannot forgive myself for the impropriety in your presence and must beg your forgiveness."

"I cannot accept your apology nor forgive you, sir."

Darcy's heart missed a beat.

"As there was no impropriety, there is no need for an apology nor the need for granting forgiveness."

Darcy audibly exhaled.

"However, I shall ask that you consider a penance for your rudeness, not that you are under any obligation to do so."

"I would by no means suspend any pleasure of yours, madam."

Miss Elizabeth tilted her head and smiled. Darcy was enchanted.

"Please, if it does not bring you pain, for I would never seek to do so, tell me of your mother."

Mr. Darcy stilled in his chair. Lizzy knew she asked much of this complex man whose true character still eluded her. She believed she would get glimpses here and there, but an inexplicable aloofness would then rise and eradicate any progress she made.

"My mother..." whispered Mr. Darcy.

Lizzy waited.

"My mother..." he repeated, clearing his throat.

Lizzy continued to wait.

"My mother left me long ago, twenty-one years, to be exact."

Lizzy was speechless. One did not offer condolences for such a painful admission. She knew not what to say. She looked down at her tightly clutched hands. She was ashamed. In trying to push Mr. Darcy out of his stoicism, she ended up being unforgivably insensitive. Her two sisters had been gone for half that time and she still got angry at anyone but her family raising the subject. *How heartless am I? What an unfeeling person I have shown myself to be!*

She looked up. Mr. Darcy stared at her. A throat being cleared allowed her to turn away. "Mum, your party is lookin' fer ye'."

"Thank you, Peter."

Lizzy stood up and curtsied. "Mr. Darcy, good day, sir."

Darcy stood and bowed. Miss Elizabeth exited the library, a shadow of herself from when she entered.

What just happened?

Chapter 41

Longbourn

After dinner, Thomas Bennet asked for everyone's attention. He pulled out a letter, handed a corresponding copy to Kitty, and read it aloud to the family.

Dear Sir,

The disagreement subsisting between yourself and my late honored father always gave me much uneasiness, and since I have had the misfortune to lose him, I have frequently wished to heal the breach but, for some time, kept back by my doubts, fearing it might seem disrespectful to his memory for me to be on good terms with anyone with whom it had always pleased him to be at variance.

My mind, however, is now made up on the subject for, having received ordination at Easter, I have been so fortunate as to be distinguished by the patronage of the Right Honorable Lady Catherine de Bourgh, widow of Sir Lewis de Bourgh, whose bounty and beneficence has preferred me to the valuable rectory of this parish where it shall be my earnest endeavor to demean myself with grateful respect toward her ladyship, and be ever ready to perform those rites and ceremonies which are instituted by the Church of England. As a clergyman, I feel it is my duty to promote and establish the blessing of peace in all families within the reach of my influence; and on these grounds, I flatter myself that my present overtures are highly commendable, and that the circumstance of my being next in line by the entail of Longbourn estate be overlooked by your side, and not lead you to reject the offered olive branch.

I cannot be otherwise than concerned at being the means of injuring your amiable daughters and beg leave to apologize for it, as well as to assure you of my readiness to make them every amend. If you should have no objection to receive me into your house, I propose myself the satisfaction of waiting on you and your family Monday, November 9th by four o'clock and shall probably trespass on your hospitality till the Saturday se'nnight following, which I can do with no inconvenience, as Lady Catherine is far from objecting to my occasional absence on a Sunday, provided that the neighboring curate is engaged to do the duty of the day.

I remain, dear sir, with respectful compliments to your lady and daughters, your well-wisher and friend,

William Collins

Lizzy covered her mouth. She could not hide the mirth in her eyes, though, and looked to her father to share the folly. Jane sat silent, deep in thought. Kitty read the letter again, puzzled. Mr. Bennet motioned to Reeves, who closed the parlor doors. "My dears, you have reached an age where it is time to tell you of pertinent inheritance information we have avoided discussing. I must have your word. You will not speak of this without the utmost caution."

"Yes, Papa." Thomas glanced at Kitty. *"Yes, Papa."*

"Thank you, as it pertains to the entail. I shall not sit here and ask what you know. Instead, I shall inform you of what your uncle Philips and I have learned from the actual entail documents on file at the Courts of Chancery. The Longbourn entail is to heirs male as you are aware. However, the estate will remain in the primary Bennet hereditary line provided that, while I am alive, one of my daughters gives birth to a son who would become the *inheritor* in deed."

Mr. Bennet narrowed his eyes at Lizzy to quell the question he already knew she was forming. Lizzy blushed and looked down at her lap. Thomas continued.

"Should none of you marry and produce a son before my death, my distant cousin, Mr. Collins, the author of this comedy, will inherit Longbourn."

Thomas nodded to Franny who picked up where her husband left off. "We are explaining this to you because we want to be clear about our expectations regarding your future.

"Longbourn is a fine estate and has provided us with a generous living, status, and some hidden wealth."

All three girls nodded, as they knew the true income of the estate.

"It is a *home* because we, as a family, live here together. Otherwise, it is an entailed property for whoever inherits to manage. Am I understood?"

Jane and Lizzy remained silent. Kitty answered first. *"You do not expect us to sacrifice our happiness to maintain the estate."*

Mrs. Bennet smiled. "That is correct, dearest; between our savings, your dowries, and the investments with your uncle Gardiner, you are free to choose your husbands."

Elizabeth, no longer worried that one would be forced to accept the foolish cousin, relaxed. "Mr. Collins appears to be misinformed regarding the true status of his inheritance, Papa."

"That is correct, Lizzy. But I would like to exercise prudence regarding this specimen. His father was vicious and nearly illiterate. I do not know with what fiction he filled his son's head. Let us entertain our cousin with caution until we better learn his intent.

"We are allowing the visit to take his measure. I have reached out to a friend to learn about his situation, his living, and the character of his patroness. Extra footmen will join us for the duration of his stay."

"Why is that, Papa?"

Bennet ignored the "why" in Jane's question and gave his orders. "For now, during and after Mr. Collins's visit, none of you are to venture outside the house without male protection."

Jane's eyes opened wide. Kitty shook her head. Lizzy exploded to her feet. "You cannot do this, Papa. You are curtailing our liberties instead of informing this *cousin* that his inheritance is not as inevitable as he believes. It is unfair—"

She paused, realizing how like a spoiled child she was acting. She hastily sat down, grasped her hands in her lap, and apologized for her outburst.

Franny looked at her husband. "Miss Ecclestone continues to earn her stipend."

They both chuckled.

Captain Thomas Bennet of His Majesty's Royal Secret Service now addressed his family. His voice was steel and dispassionate. "You will entertain NO variation to my instruction."

"Yes, Papa," they signed simultaneously, startled speechless.

"Good."

Lizzy joined Kitty in Jane's room for their nightly discussion of sisterly affairs. Kitty immensely enjoyed these evenings, and she often paired with Jane to overrule Lizzy's impetuous judgments. This evening was no different than previous ones.

Jane began. "Lizzy, you cannot be ignorant of Papa's change in demeanor."

Lizzy raised her chin in defiance. "You cannot lay his despotic declaration at my doorstep."

"Do you truly not see Papa's fear for our safety underlying his command?"

Kitty gripped Lizzy's hand. Her eyes beseeched her elder sister to see reason.

Lizzy blew out a breath. "Yes, dearest. You are quite right. Quite right." She enfolded Kitty in a loving embrace and calmed her anxiety. With a quick kiss on her forehead, Lizzy looked at Jane. Their eldest sister looked toward the window, apparently distracted.

"Jane?"

Jane shook her head. "Yes?"

"What has your attention? You are not smiling."

Jane looked at Lizzy, then Kitty. She cleared her throat.

"I must tell you of something I have kept to myself. From when we were ill."

Lizzy's eyes widened. Kitty nodded. *"Your dreams?"*

Jane nodded. "Yes, dearest. My dreams. My horrible, horrible dreams."

Kitty joined Lizzy embracing their eldest sibling.

"Let us provide you comfort, as you have taken care of us all these years."

Jane regulated her breathing. Her eyes filled.

"Grammy sat with me. She read to me." Jane hiccoughed. "She scared me so."

Jane covered her eyes and wept.

"Jane! What did she say?" Lizzy handed Jane a handkerchief.

Jane sniffled as she regained her self-control. She looked up.

"Grammy warned me of the heir."

Lizzy's jaw tightened. Kitty felt the shock of Jane's admission. Jane's fingers wove through Kitty's. Lizzy hugged her. Kitty was unaware she was shaking.

The three Bennet daughters remained in each other's embrace.

"What shall we do?"

Lizzy, her eyes flashing fire, laid down her gauntlet.

"We shall speak with Mama."

Three simultaneous exhales marked their agreement. They donned their dressing robes and, together, knocked on their mother's sitting room door.

Chapter 42

Longbourn, November 9, 1812

Late that afternoon, a gig pulled by a single horse inched its way up the drive. As the weather was clement, the Bennets waited outside to greet their cousin. At first glance, the gentleman dressed in black appeared well-outfitted if a touch on the heavy side. His wide-brimmed black hat matched his coat; his neck was confined by a set of Geneva bands. He waved before standing, which put him in a bit of a dither, as this gesture nearly catapulted him out of the carriage.

Thomas Bennet trapped his lips between his teeth.

Mr. Collins dismounted from the carriage in what was a gymnastic production of indecision. He turned left, right, left, round and round; he ended by presenting his back end to his hosts as he clambered down from the carriage.

The Bennet ladies maintained their pleasant smiles.

Stumbling toward the Bennets, Mr. Collins bowed low to the ground, his arm high up behind him as his head nearly reached his shoes. He rose, wobbled, then greeted the waiting entourage.

"William Conrad Collins, at your service." Another bow.

Jane paled. Bennet ignored his visitor and moved to her side. "Jane?"

Jane could not conceal her panic. She covered her eyes with one hand and leaned into her father as Grammy's ghostly words bounced behind her eyes. "D-did he s-say C-C…Conrad?"

Bennet was at a loss. He looked at Franny, who minutely shook her head. He resolved to learn more later and turned back to their guest.

"Mr. Collins, I am your cousin Thomas Bennet. This is my wife, Francine. Next to her are our daughters Jane, Elizabeth, and Catherine."

At the mention of their names, each of the ladies curtsied. Jane's graceless effort drew their guest's attention.

"It is my pleasure to meet you all. I hope this next se'nnight will allow us to grow closer and strengthen our familial bond."

Bennet thought it was a congenial and conciliatory speech and was prepared to say as much until he caught Collins's leer directed at Jane. Thomas stepped forward in front of Franny, took his cousin's arm, and walked him away from his daughters.

Franny wrapped her arm around Jane's shoulder. "The family parlor has a lovely fire going. Let us regain our equilibrium. Shall we?"

Inside Longbourn, Thomas turned his cousin over to Mr. Hill, who escorted him to the far end of the guest wing. He informed the gentleman that wash water would arrive shortly. Tea was on the half-hour.

"Why am I not in the family wing?"

"That is a question for the master, sir."

Collins ignored the water. He had already formed ambitions toward the tall, blonde beauty downstairs. His mind engaged in salacious fantasies as her reaction to him outside had gained his special notice. He moved to the parlor.

Thomas Bennet did not retreat to his study. He was quite concerned with Collins's manner. His cousin was a younger version of his father: uncultured, untrustworthy, lecherous, and dangerous. Thomas waited with his ladies for their guest to join them.

Franny asked how he liked his tea. Four spoons of sugar later, she handed him his drink. The girls sipped their tea and waited for the conversation to start. Instead, the parson loaded up a plate with cakes. He did not hesitate to stuff his mouth with Cook's sweet treats. Without waiting to swallow, he thanked Franny for the tea, spraying her with crumbs. All the girls sat back to put as much distance as possible between the parson and their persons.

Bennet waited for his cousin to swallow before asking how the roads fared. Collins put down his tea and empty plate and launched into a practiced monologue. He spoke incessantly of his living, his patroness, his parsonage, his patroness, his garden, his patroness, the road between his parsonage and Rosings Park, his patroness's manor, and repeated himself of his patroness. When he took a breath, Franny cued the girls to return to work that remained unfinished and excused them to their tasks.

Collins's lecherous eyes followed Jane toward the kitchen. Bennet glared at his cousin until he caught the clergyman's attention. His cousin smiled back with cake crumbs bedecking his yellow teeth. He beckoned Collins to join him in his library.

Once in the bookroom, the parson continued to spew disconnected thoughts. Bennet ignored the man until he sensed a natural decrease in Collins's verbosity.

"Collins."

"Yes, Cousin?"

"By your lack of mention, I must assume that the thoroughfares between here and Kent are in good order."

Mr. Collins looked confused.

Bennet forged ahead. "Tell me again why you are here."

Collins repeated the content of his letter. "As a rector, I feel it is my duty to promote and establish the blessing of peace in our family, and on these grounds, I flatter myself that my present overtures are highly commendable and that the circumstance of my being next in the entail of Longbourn estate will eliminate prejudice on your side and not lead you to reject the offered olive branch concerning your eldest daughter—"

"You are interested in my eldest daughter?"

Anger rose and fell on the parson's face. His hands were fists.

Thomas blinked. *Did he mumble a five-count?*

"My reasons for marrying are, first, that I think it a right thing for every priest in easy circumstances, like myself, to set the example of matrimony in his parish. Second, that I am convinced it will add to my happiness; and third, which perhaps I ought to have mentioned earlier, that it is the particular advice and recommendation of the very noble lady whom I have the honor of calling patroness."

Collins continued his rambling. "She bade me, 'Mr. Collins, you must marry. Choose properly, choose a gentlewoman for *my* sake; for your *own*, let her be an active, useful sort of person, not brought up high, but able to make a small income go a good way. This is my advice. Find such a woman as soon as you can bring her to Hunsford, and I will visit her.'

"Allow me to observe that I do not reckon the notice and kindness of Lady Catherine de Bourgh as among the least of the advantages in my power to offer. Her manners are beyond anything I can describe, and your eldest must be acceptable to her, especially when tempered with the silence and respect her rank will inevitably excite."

Thomas pulled the bell cord. Mr. Hill appeared immediately.

"You must be tired from your journey. Hill will show you to your room."

Bennet rose from his chair. Collins did not. "Cousin, I must protest my sleeping arrangements. As the future master of the estate and your closest living male relative, I must insist on being housed in the family wing."

"Yes, yes, it is late. Let us revisit your request at a more convenient time."

Thomas walked around the desk and propelled his cousin toward the door into Mr. Hill's waiting arms.

"Ron and Kale," he whispered to his man.

Thomas sat behind his desk and waited. Two large footmen entered the library and listened to their master's instructions.

That night, as Reeves stood post at the head of the stairs that connected the corridor leading to the family wing, he heard a door open. His candle held high, he peered down the guest wing. He saw no one.

"Mr. Reeves."

He recognized Miss Jane's voice as Miss Lizzy's tone was lower and deeper, and Miss Kitty would knock on the wall. He stepped toward her door.

"How may I assist you, Miss Bennet?"

Jane closed her eyes and shivered. Reeves waited.

"He scares me." Her voice quivered as her eyes filled. Reeves nodded.

"Your father knows. Ron an' Kale know."

He paused and looked directly into her eyes.

"*I* know."

Jane backed into her room and closed the door. She climbed into her bed and pulled the covers up over her head. She hoped to hide from the world and the danger. She dreamed of Mr. Reeves wearing a helmet, and with his sword, he smote a vile reptile wearing Mr. Collins's face. She awoke with a small cry, shivered, and dropped back to sleep.

Chapter 43

Bunyan's Gambling Hell, London, November 10, 1812

George Wickham was down to his last two pounds. Standing in front of a gambling hell, sober because the house would not spot him any credit for drink, he simmered. The fat, purple-stained man had denied him his last payment. He had accused Wickham of bringing slags rather than roses. Well, enough of trying to please those who fail to acknowledge the effort! He returned to his present misery and the one responsible for his straightened circumstances. Darcy. Bloody Darcy. Selfish, disdainful, holier-than-thou Darcy.

Like every denizen centered upon his pleasures, Wickham believed that Providence had blessed him and the world owed him. *I could not be this handsome for no reason, now could I?* Blessed he was, for out the door in front of him walked Michael Denny, an old acquaintance who had worshiped Wickham's facile manners that led bar girls and serving wenches to tumble into his bed.

"Wickham, my old friend, is that you?"

"Denny, my good man, come and join me."

Wickham assumed his Cambridge voice to impress his victim.

"Thank you. I shall."

Wickham re-entered the building and held up coins for drinks. Ale arrived, and the bar girl whisked away the coppers. Both men took a swallow.

"What brings you to Bunyan's, Denny?"

"Recruiting."

"For what?"

"The _____shire Militia."

Wickham remained silent, concealing his eagerness.

"You could do worse than join the militia. With your university education, you could purchase an officer's rank—ensign or lieutenant. Join me."

"Why would I chain myself to the King?" asked Wickham, warming to the idea. He did need to distance himself from town for a time. His vowels weighed upon him as much as the moneylender's collectors.

"The pay is enough for a single man. The country towns entertain us where we are the best form of social diversion for the ladies: balls, assemblies, card parties. They host dinners at the estates. For the summer, the encampment moves to Brighton in the spring: sea air, strolling the Pavilion, and ladies in bathing machines. You would have a jolly good time."

Wickham pretended to be cautious. "What about getting called to fight?"

Deep down, Wickham acknowledged his cowardice. He was the first to run from a mill. A wisp of a memory, the smell of hay, made him shudder.

Denny looked askance at him. "If you read the law, you would know the militia cannot post outside the kingdom. We are a defensive force. And, before we'd fight Napoleon, we'd be ordered to put down rebellious factory workers or field hands."

Wickham liked what he heard. "I *am* educated with good prospects. I will *not* enlist. I have a gentleman's education, old boy."

"Has the ale already gone to your head? Need I remind you that you are a university man like me? A lieutenant rank is less than twice that of an ensign. If I remember your prowess at the gambling tables correctly, you must have that in hand."

"Do you get compensated for recruiting me, Denny?"

"I do. Why?"

"Fine, here is what I shall agree to. You put up the money you receive for recruiting me, as it is not yours. I shall split the rest of a lieutenancy with you."

An incredulous look appeared on Denny's face. "You want me to pay part of your fee to join the militia? Why would I ever consider that?"

"With me by your side, you will never lack female companionship. You know me well."

Wickham gave Denny his most charming smile. Denny faltered. "Fine. Shake hands, and I shall see you in two days at the posting inn down the street. We can ride the mail coach to Meryton."

"Done."

Two days later…

George Wickham signed his enlistment contract for the rank of lieutenant. Denny offered to celebrate with a drink. If Denny was willing to pay, Wickham was ready to drink. He had already identified several target merchants bound to fall for his gentleman's act. He was imagining new boots, clothes, and jewelry.

As the two men walked toward the market square, they spotted two footmen behind a group of three ladies and a tall, heavy-looking parson. Meryton was looking even better to George Wickham. "Did you know that beauties were living in this speck of a town?"

"Those are the Miss Bennets. I neither know the man nor why the footmen are following."

"Acquaint me."

"I cannot. I have not had an introduction."

"Follow me, my good man. Follow me."

Wickham strolled toward the group. As he got closer, he heard mention of a place he had not thought of in a decade.

"...my parsonage has Rosings Park as its neighbor..."

Wickham interrupted the monologue. "Pardon me, sir."

The parson narrowed his eyes at him.

"Are you also acquainted with the de Bourgh family?" asked Wickham, his intonation Cambridge.

The two footmen inserted themselves in front of the Bennet sisters before he finished his sentence.

"Step back, fools. This man speaks of my patroness. Step back, I say," demanded the rotund rector.

The footmen turned to the tall blonde, who looked to the short brunette. The clergyman's eyes narrowed.

"You will look to me for instruction after we wed," he hissed. The tallest of the ladies swayed.

The shortest of the three wrapped her arm around the waist of her companion. "Excuse us, I must see to my sister." The three ladies hastened away, a footman on each side.

The parson remained with the unintroduced militia officers. He did not notice a rough-looking fellow dressed in workman's clothing hanging back and paying close attention to the milliner's display window.

Collins sputtered but did not follow. His desire to hear of the glory of his patroness from others overrode polite manners. He introduced himself without prompt.

"Reverend William Conrad Collins, at your service."

"Lieutenants Denny and Wickham, pleased to make your acquaintance," countered Denny.

"What do you know of my patroness, sir?"

George Wickham informed his new acquaintance of his life at Pemberley, his years in the Darcy household, and his Cambridge-funded education. Collins responded with praise of his own making where he compared the charity of the Darcys to that of the de Bourghs.

Wickham agreed. "My dear Mr. Collins, it pleases me to confirm your astute proclamation of the generosity of the former master of Pemberley. Mr. George Darcy was one of the best men who ever breathed and the truest friend I ever had; I can never be in company with his son without being grieved to the soul by a thousand tender recollections."

Collins nodded, so Wickham continued. "The current Mr. Darcy's behavior to myself has been scandalous; but I verily believe I could forgive him anything and everything rather than his disappointing the hopes and disgracing the memory of his father."

Mr. Collins stared, a blank look on his face.

"A military life is not what I had intended, but circumstances have now made it eligible. The church *ought* to have been my profession—like you, sir, they brought me up for the church. You, sir, and I would be colleagues in all things spiritual and *should* be, had I received my bequest—a living that should be mine by rights, had the gentleman we were speaking of just now honored his father's wishes."

The parson found his voice. "Sir, I demand you explain yourself! No connection to the house of de Bourgh, or a relation of the benevolent Lady Catherine, would ever lower themselves to behave in such a disreputable, dishonorable manner. No, sir. You must explain yourself."

Wickham did. "You have heard that Lady Catherine and her sister Lady Anne agreed upon Fitzwilliam Darcy's betrothal to his cousin Miss de Bourgh at birth?"

"Yes, the flower of Kent is the means to join two great houses..." Collins carried on, repeating himself several times.

Wickham broke in at the next pause. "So, you are therefore uninformed; the current Mr. Darcy not only broke that agreement in as ungentlemanly a manner possible, but he also exposed his intended to the censure of the world for caprice and instability and its derision for disappointed hopes, involving them both in a scandal of the acutest kind."

"That cannot be true!" cried the parson.

"So, you had no knowledge he not only refused to do his duty, to honor his betrothal and show his gratitude, he had his aunt, *your patroness,* manhandled off the Pemberley grounds."

Collins turned pale—so much so, that Denny grasped his arm. Collins's breathing was shallow and rapid. Denny walked them to the Horse & Cocke.

"You need refreshment, sir." The trio took a table.

"Three," waved Wickham.

When the drinks arrived, Denny pointed at Collins. The parson, his head spinning, dropped his purse on the table. Wickham turned to Denny and grinned.

COLLINS'S MIND REELED. HE TRIED TO PROCESS ALL THE AFFRONTS to Lady Catherine that he had experienced. Owning neither gentle decorum nor manners and deeply into his second mug of tavern ale, he spoke in a loud and unguarded voice of the Bennets' cavalier treatment of him and, by extension, his patroness.

"Almost as soon as I entered my future estate, I identified the eldest Miss Bennet as the companion of my future life."

Wickham and Denny nodded thoughtfully.

"My reasons for marrying were, first, that I think it a right thing for every clergyman to set the example of matrimony in his parish."

Collins took a breath and noisily sucked at his ale. He smacked his lips.

He pictured Jane Bennet, hand on her heart, swooning with emotion. "Second, I am convinced that it will add to my happiness..."

"Miss Bennet—she is the blonde lady we met, am I correct—appears to be all that is lovely and good. How did the family offend you?" Denny interrupted Collins's musings.

Collins growled at him and counted to five. His two drinking partners looked at each other—for what reason, he could not fathom. "My cousin refused to entertain me in the family wing although I am his closest living male relative and a man of God!"

He wiped his mouth as he had sprayed ale across the table. "My betrothed, permitted by her father, retired with her sisters and mother to a back parlor. She neglected to attend to me, the heir and future master. She did not solicit my approbation. Such sinful, disrespectful behavior. Scandalous, I say!"

Wickham and Denny raised their hands in surrender. Collins ignored them. "I came to heal the breach between the master of Longbourn and my father. Now that I have deciphered the venal nature of my cousin, I can only conclude that he must have swindled the true heir of the estate, my father. My olive branch was not accepted. No, it was cast aside. Seeking familial felicity, I instead found a nest of sinful inhabitants seeking to further injure my patroness's family—daughter and nephew—with their immoral arts and allurements. I can bear this no further!"

Collins stood and swayed. "I must dispatch this information to my patroness immediately. The redress of this travesty of all that is proper cannot be delayed."

Denny and Wickham watched Collins wobble through the door, his purse still on the table.

"Let us drink to the nonsensical fools of Kent, my good man, as it is their folly funding our good fortune," toasted Wickham. Denny joined him in good cheer. The men dove deep into their cups. They did not notice Reeves at the corner table behind them. Mr. Bennet's armorer had altered his mission when his charges retreated to Longbourn.

Chapter 44

Longbourn, November 13, 1812

The following morning, the entire Netherfield party came to call. With five Bennets, Collins, the Hursts, Bingley, Darcy, and the colonel, the parlor was at capacity. Mrs. Bennet decided that a separation of the sexes was in order and led the ladies to the back parlor.

Franny called for tea, and when it arrived, Jane inquired of Mrs. Hurst's preferences. After advising Miss Bennet that two sugars and no milk would set her up properly, Louisa turned to Mrs. Bennet.

"Franny, might I ask for some assistance?"

Franny squeezed Louisa's arm. "Have you yet been ill in the mornings?"

Louisa gasped. "How did you know?"

"Please, my dear. After bringing five chicks into the world, I can recognize a nesting hen. Do you have anyone to talk to?"

Louisa shook her head, her eyes dimmed. "No."

"Oh, none of that now. We shall take care of you, shall we not, girls?"

Thus, Louisa Hurst became an honorary Bennet. She regained the sisterhood denied her by tragedy. Forgetting her second reason for the morning call, she reached into her reticule for a handkerchief to touch her eyes dry. Her hand encountered a card. "Oh, my word, how distracted I have become."

Franny gave her a good-natured look. Smiling back, Louisa handed her the billet. "This is an invitation to our ball in two weeks. My brother wants to thank the neighborhood for their gracious welcome. I hope you will join me in the planning, Franny, as I have never organized such festivities for the gentry."

Franny looked at her benevolently, recalling her first ball for the twenty-four families. At the time, Thomas's mother, another Elizabeth Bennet, was luckily still alive to help her daughter-from-trade. Now she could pay that debt of love. "As you are in a delicate condition, I shall be happy to assist you."

Franny Bennet loved nothing more than a ball. Kitty sketched the gown designs the women described. They sipped tea and discussed fashions.

The men were not having as fine a time as the ladies. Bennet and Hurst paired off once again to discuss the upcoming shooting and their favorite menus. The colonel assumed Darcy's traditional stance: staring out a window, one hand fisted in the small of his back.

Bingley, who sat next to Darcy, was pinioned by a verbal deluge as Bennet's cousin continued to talk incessantly about his situation in life, his parsonage, and Darcy's aunt.

Darcy let the parson's blather flow over him. He ignored Collins's frequent frowns directed toward him during the obsequious monologue. Yet, the inflated glorification of his cousin Anne's fictional accomplishments roused him from his phlegmatic muse. He directed a smoldering glower at his aunt's toady.

How dare this slug think he could mention my cousin's name in the same breath as that of her execrable mother?

Collins faltered but regrouped and carried on. Darcy's mind drifted back to the day after the reading of his father's will. He tried not to smile as he remembered his aunt's explosive expulsion from Pemberley.

When did I last receive a letter from Anne?

At the end of the hour, the ladies reappeared. Bingley looked to his sister, who nodded. He hurried over to Miss Bennet and guided her off to the side. They exchanged a few whispers. Bingley bowed over her hand.

Darcy leaned toward Bingley as they refreshed their drinks. "Well?"

"I asked her to grant me the first and the supper sets. She accepted for the fifth. The family is disinclined to dance the first in honor of their missing sisters, and she desires to sit with her family for supper."

Darcy envied his friend's boldness. He hesitated, unsure about Miss Elizabeth's opinion of him. He said nothing.

Collins paled when he saw his future wife, *his property,* grant favors to another.

He knew his express to his patroness had been the correct path. He was standing in a den of vipers! Disreputable men, ungrateful nephews, and immoral daughters. Lady Catherine, in all her glory, would come hither and set everyone to rights!

Chapter 45

The following morning, after another meal had been ruined by their cousin's revolting table manners, the Bennets spent time in the receiving parlor awaiting callers. Jane was noticeably absent as she was with Mrs. Sutton in the stillroom working on some new herbals her uncle Gardiner was eager to receive.

Reeves perched himself on a spartan chair before the stillroom door. He was prepared for a confrontation. The cousin's attentions to Miss Bennet were now near a state of intense excitement and agitation. Her indignation at being doused in tea and crumbs during his feeble attempts at courting her favor had forced her to flee the table in tears.

The parson walked through the kitchen and stood in front of Reeves. "Move your person!"

Reeves looked up, interlaced his fingers, spun his wrists outward, and cracked his knuckles in a noisy, threatening manner. He locked eyes with the rodent before him.

"I...I...gave you an ord...order."

Reeves leaned a bit forward, causing the front chair legs to drop to the floor with a heavy *thud*. He stood and cracked his knuckles again, this time one by one. He pulled each appendage with the opposite fist. He showed his teeth.

The clatter of a carriage entering the drive cut short the confrontation. Reeves's eyes narrowed as the parson smiled slyly before he scurried off in that direction. The sergeant held his position; he had his orders from the captain.

Inside the still room, Mrs. Sutton cradled a trembling Miss Bennet as she struggled to regain her composure.

"Oh, my dearest, dry your tears as this will not do! But I do not understand. Your father would never allow that man to harm you. What have you not said, my dear?"

Jane hiccoughed and inhaled with a hitch. She frowned but said nothing, her eyes cast downward.

"None of that now. I put many a man in his place many a time. You cannot tell me this country parson has the same consequence as the archbishop of Canterbury?"

Jane gasped. "Truly, Mrs. Sutton?"

Thea laughed as she summoned her youthful impetuousness. "Let us venture forth and vanquish our enemies from without!"

She knocked on the door, which opened without hesitation. "Follow me, Sergeant Reeves."

Reeves stepped in front of Miss Bennet and followed.

Lady Catherine de Bourgh cursed aloud as her carriage came to an abrupt halt, pitching her forward toward the rear-facing seat. She was only able to avoid injury by grasping the strap with both hands. Her distaste for the coarse locale erupted upon her sagging face.

She did not care that her parson's relations mistreated him. It was the news of her nephew—*the* Fitzwilliam Darcy of Pemberley in

Derbyshire—that forced her to rectify the situation to her satisfaction. She had spent years forging letters in her daughter's handwriting to maintain the connection that would become, by her desire, a match. With her daughter securely locked away, Lady Catherine waited impatiently for Darcy to confirm his intentions. Instead, he traipsed about the country and ignored his obligations. Now, the funds she required could be for naught as he called upon a family of harlots—whores who would employ their arts and allurements to lure him from her desired path.

Well, that will be set to rights today!

Collins scuttled out of Longbourn's front door to a large, worn, overly ornate barouche. His bows of submission were so close to the ground that Bennet wondered whether his cousin would crack his head on the lowered carriage step.

Bennet turned away from the window and spoke to his wife. "My love, take the girls to the family parlor. I shall deal with the upcoming unpleasantness."

Franny led the ladies out. Before the door closed, Thomas spied her meeting up with the stillroom party emerging from the kitchen hall. Reeves guided Jane to join her mother. Mrs. Sutton moved to Bennet's side.

Lady Catherine grimaced as she grasped her parson's greasy hand, as he assisted her. Her balance suspect, she teetered when descending steps and breathed easier when both her feet were firmly planted upon solid ground.

She silenced her sycophantic preacher with a wave of her hand. As she absorbed the surroundings, distaste for the utter nothingness of the estate emphasized her disdain.

"Let us put things to right, Mr. Collins. Do not speak."

The manor door opened, and a gentleman stepped into the park. She dismissed him in an instant as inconsequential. A moment later, her eyes deceived her as her greeter's companion made herself known.

"Cathy Fitzwilliam. What in the world would lever you out of Rosings Keep? Coming to terrorize the rational population like a troll? I daresay I thought you had better sense than to expose your brand of insanity to the public eye!"

Lady Catherine de Bourgh looked liable to cast her contents. "What are you doing here, Thea?"

"What am *I* doing here? The question of the hour is what are *you* doing here? Are the coffers of Rosings dry again? Are your famed accomplishments—*'had you ever learned, you'd be a great proficient'*—bankrupting the Berg holdings again?"

Thea could see that Lady Catherine had not aged well—in body or in mind. Behind her verbal target, Colonel Fitzwilliam walked his mount around the back of her carriage. He held his finger to his lips.

"It is 'de Bourgh,' you Jezebel! You know not to whom you speak. I *will* have your head!"

"Oh dear, Catherine the Great rises again. I do not believe your rank ever exceeded mine. The daughter of an earl trying to compare herself with the granddaughter of a duke and the widow of another duke's son? Do you not remember our delightful tête-à-têtes in Canterbury? What was it the broadsheets printed? Oh, yes!

"*'Miss CF's frumpiness never once encroached upon Miss TC's elegance.'*

"Do I remember that on dit correctly, *Catty*?"

Lady Catherine faltered. "You lie! I *will* have you for slander."

"How will you settle Anne? I doubt Rosings, whose windmills have dwindled to a nutshell,[14] will attract anyone suitable."

"Anne would be well settled had my brother not spurned the alliance with the viscount!"

Thea feared she may have pushed too hard but saw the colonel tilt his head, peering at his angry aunt.

"The Matlock heir betrothed by your design? You are mad."

14 To lose one's money

Richard walked up behind his aunt, leaned in, whispered in her ear, then stepped back.

Lady Catherine's eyes grew wide. Her hands went to her chest, and she promptly swooned. Her driver barely caught her. Collins remained frozen in place.

Bennet stepped into the fray. "Reeves, assist the lady and my cousin into her carriage. See that the driver has a basket and that the party leaves Longbourn's property at once."

The carriage driver prodded the parson to grab her ladyship's other arm, and after much difficulty, they heaved her into the carriage.

Thea followed the others back into the house. Looking over her shoulder, she saw the colonel and Mr. Bennet with their heads together.

Reeves returned from the kitchen with a basket and handed it up to the coachman, who bent over from his seat and reached down to assist his benefactor. The sleeves of his livery rode up his arms a bit, the faded ink on his wrist on display. The armorer recognized a kindred war dog, although saltier than Reeves, now retired from his time ripping at His Majesty's enemies' entrails.

"Dunno whether 'eres 'nuff in th' basket fer ye journey."

"We be stoppin' at Watford fer an 'orse change."

"Right yer' be, Davy," countered Reeves, teasing the former navy man.

The carriage driver laughed and mock saluted.

"Armorers. Yer all cheeky."

Mr. Bennet walked up to Reeves. "Change of plan. Take the lady to Netherfield."

"Anything else, Cap'n?"

"See that my cousin understands he is no longer welcome in the shire. Hill will gather his things."

The Longbourn parlor was again filled.

"That was quite the performance, Mrs. Sutton," observed Mr. Bennet.

"It had the feel of a third or fourth act in a continuing theatrical."

"Yes, Mr. Bennet. It is surprising the players one finds making their entrances when and where you least expect them." Mrs. Sutton threw a pointed look at Mrs. Hurst.

Louisa understood the underlying message in Lady Theodosia Cavendish Manners-Sutton's reply. She was the only one.

Franny introduced Louisa to Mrs. Sutton. A single raised eyebrow from her ladyship convinced Louisa to save her breath to cool her porridge. It was not her place to inform the Bennets of Mrs. Sutton's consequence, especially if they had not been made aware.

Mrs. Sutton drew Louisa to the parlor window.

"*Louisa*, might I ask for a small favor?"

Louisa leaned in. "How may I be of service, my lady?" whispered Louisa.

Mrs. Sutton smiled. "Thank you. And do thank Hurst, my dear."

Thea Sutton rode in the Bingley carriage back to Netherfield Park as a special guest of Louisa. Mrs. Hurst ensured her presence remained unannounced; Mrs. Sutton did not join the main party for the evening meal.

At dinner, Bingley focused on the upcoming ball and enthused about how the preparations were progressing. Darcy reminded everyone of the next day's planned shooting excursion. This inspired everyone's input, especially Louisa's, who acquitted herself well. She was quite an avid fan of the sport. As she was the lone female, the men forwent the separation of the sexes. Bingley joined Louisa and Hurst for drinks in the parlor. Richard accompanied Darcy upstairs before they turned to their respective rooms.

Chapter 46

Darcy walked to his favorite chair without regard to his surroundings. A few candles did little to relieve the chamber's dimness. Darcy sat before he realized he had a guest.

He stood and bowed; his good manners were innate. "Good evening, Mrs. Sutton."

Across from him, Thea Sutton sat as properly as one could while improperly ensconced uninvited in a single man's sitting room. "Good evening, Mr. Darcy."

Barty entered with a tray upon which he expertly balanced two tumblers of whiskey. Darcy narrowed his eyes at his valet. Barty ignored the empty threat and served both.

Darcy picked up his goblet, acknowledged his guest, and took a sip. With his eyes closed, he savored the smoky flavor. Eventually, he opened his eyes. Mrs. Sutton sipped hers with an amused smile.

"What brings you here, Mrs. Sutton?"

"I find that the past repeats itself, generation by generation."

Darcy raised his eyebrows.

"I shall repeat to you, verbatim, what I said to your father seven and a half years ago."

Darcy leaned forward.

"Do not be obtuse, Darcy. It becomes you not."

He put down his glass. "*Why* are you here, Thea?"

"Why am I *here,* Darcy?"

Darcy lifted his empty hand, palm up.

Just like his father—handsome but also lacking a certain measure of imagination. "Like you, I take a decided interest in my estate and my family," she answered.

Thea stared at William for a long time. He was much like her grandfather; God rest his soul. She would not allow this young man to spiral down through unhappiness as had the Duke of Devonshire: to live alone, to dine alone, and finally, to die alone. Thinking on her grandfather, Thea now understood how the time stolen from George Darcy had led to his son's cruelly unredeemed state. Darcy's protective emotional walls emulated her beloved grandfather's. She still thought of the duke, missed his presence, his counsel, his hugs, and the smells of Chatsworth.

As she laid her cards on the table, she emphasized his childhood name. "*William*, you cannot continue this way."

Darcy looked at his distant cousin as if she were daft. "I do not comprehend your insinuation, madam."

Thea frowned. "I shall reiterate to you what I advised the lovely Miss Bennet." Seeing Darcy flinch, she clarified. "Miss Jane Bennet."

She paused, desirous to see his further reaction.

"Do you care to hear me?"

Darcy seemed to relax upon hearing the name of Miss Jane. He nodded.

William has feelings for Miss Elizabeth! There may be a difference from George after all. There is hope.

"I advised her thus: *You*, my brilliant child, you must, MUST, attend to yourself. Do not deflect my concerns. Those who love and esteem you, of whom there are countless and unknown to *you*, have only your best interests in their hearts. Promise me you will heed my words."

Darcy's face betrayed his agitation.

"William, my lovely boy. Your family has appealed to me. Your uncle and the archbishop have written to me. My true reason for being here is the promise your mother, my dearest Anne, extracted from me to ensure you understood you are not alone as you move through life. Dear boy: you are not alone."

Darcy's world spun. His small boat rocked. Heat rose from his belly into his chest. His face warmed. His vision clouded. All he saw was a haze filled with black pinpricks. He was angry, intensely angry. He flew to his feet, fists clenched, and glared without sight at his tormentor. Short, shallow breaths made his chest rise and fall. He closed his eyes to regulate his emotions. He controlled his anger, but a surge of self-pity flooded his brain.

"You know nothing," he seethed. "I *am* alone. Completely alone."

"I am an…an orphan," he spat out, the last word in spite.

Thea gasped. "You are not alone. Your family loves you."

Darcy's vision went red. Out of control, his hands fisted again. "MY PARENTS LEFT ME! THEY LEFT ME…DECEIVED ME AND…LEFT ME…LEFT…ME! THEY DIED!"

He collapsed back into his chair. His shaking hand gripped his forehead as he fought to regain his self-control.

Thea rushed to him and embraced him. "My dear, dear boy…oh…oh, what torment you have been fighting. How deep is your pain? Sh…sh…sh. Your parents loved you and would have done anything to stay in this world. But know this: they watch over you even now. I know this."

Darcy wept. Thea nurtured his release until he exhausted himself. They remained in that attitude deep into the evening.

Leg thrown over the chair arm, Fitzwilliam heeded the sounds coming from Darcy's sitting room on the small chance he might be required to intervene. No need to have the archbishop and the earl at odds, although Darcy's well-being would be a worthy compensating factor.

Upon hearing the raised voices coming from Darcy's rooms, Sergeant Villiers burst into the colonel's sitting room, a cudgel in hand. A pair of raised eyebrows and a slight pulling back of his head had his batman tuck the weapon back into a hidden pocket. With a sheepish look on his face, the sergeant returned to his duties.

Comfortable in the silence, Fitzwilliam sipped his ale and waited.

Watford, NW of London

Reeves, Ron, and Kale pulled up to the inn in Watford, relieved to rest and swap the horses. As instructed, Ron and Kale wore their Matlock livery; Reeves was dressed in ragged tenant clothing.

Reeves spoke to them quietly.

"Put the cart t' th' stable. Swap the 'orses. Tie 'em off after ye' wat'r 'em."

Ron and Kale nodded their understanding.

"Meet me at th' kitchen door."

Ron and Kale went off with the horse cart. Once they turned the corner, Reeves walked to the inn window and peered inside. Collins was hunched over a mug.

This one is for Miss Bennet.

Reeves met Ron and Kale at the kitchen door. He peered around to confirm that they were alone. "Ron, go in and bring th' parson 'is things. Off ye' go, and if he give ye guff, draw 'is cork." Reeves touched his nose. Ron went off.

"Kale, get the parson's room number from th' book, if'n he got one."

Kale nodded.

"Go 'elp Ron and 'old 'im for a knock, if'n 'e needs one."

"Aye, sergeant."

"An', 'ave me a bucket o' water in th' cart."

Reeves used the two to conceal himself. He heard the parson had a room. He went up to find the empty room dark, the parson too parsimonious to part with a penny for a candle. Reeves tucked himself under the bed and probed the mattress above him with his fingers. He found it quite thin and the bed slats quite far apart. He settled in and waited.

Ron ignored the parson as the man vented his spleen. Without warning, the heavier man stood. He seemed tipsy as he wobbled in place. He righted himself, then pointed his finger in Kale's face. Ron flicked his hand forward against the man's throat. The fat man sat down hard. His breathing was labored.

"We ought 'elp 'im to th' stairs."

They grasped the parson's arms and lifted him out of his chair.

Ron assisted him as he struggled up the stairs. Kale followed with his carpetbag. They heaved him into the dark room. The small bit of light coming from the hall candles allowed Kale to drop the carpetbag inside the door. He went down the stairs to the innkeeper.

"Yer parson be drunk. Go make sure he be lyin' up or 'is death be on ye."

Ron loomed over Kale's shoulder.

The innkeeper dropped his pen and ran up the stairs. The sound of a door hitting a wall carried down. Less than a minute later, the innkeeper returned.

"Yer parson is well."

Kale pushed a large finger into the innkeeper's chest.

"He na' be our parson," he said, ignoring the innkeeper's yelp of pain. "Don' ye fergit it."

Ron glared at the man, then stepped off to follow Kale to the stable. He fetched the horse cart as Kale filled a bucket of water. They walked the cart a mile down the road, pulled over to the trees, and waited for Reeves.

Collins, his brain muddled from ale and his throat on fire from being thumped, laid down in his clothing. He rolled onto his back and whimpered; his patroness had fallen ill and her nephew had sent him away in her carriage. *How would he minister to her from so far away?* His fears of her disapprobation so exhausted him, he succumbed to sleep.

He opened his eyes and painfully drew a breath. He looked up to see a man. *A man is sitting on me!* He opened his mouth; it immediately clapped shut as he winced from the pain in his face. Something hard had hit his nose. Tears streamed out of his eyes. Everything was dark. His eyes would not open. His breathing eased a bit. Something was near his ear.

"Ye will na' return t' Longbourn."

Collins struggled to move. Something hard hit him in the chest. It hurt to breathe again. *Oh, the pain!*

"I 'eard ye in th' public 'ouse."

Collins opened his mouth, only to feel his gorge rise. He tasted bile. *The pain between my legs! Lord help me!* He tried to move. He could not.

"Go anywhere in th' kingdom, 'cept Meryton."

The last thing Collins remembered was the pain in his face.

Reeves put his hand under the parson's nose. He counted to twenty. Expelled air continued to warm his fingers. No one saw Reeves as he flitted through the shadows back to the cart. He nodded his praise to the *twins* for following his instructions and, with a glance, confirmed the bucket of water in the cart.

Reaching beneath the horse blanket, Reeves pulled out an oilskin sack from which he removed his livery. He stripped out of his rags and dipped the shirt he had been wearing into the water. He wiped down his face and chest. Ron stepped over, took the rag, and wiped down his back. Reeves dressed quickly, emptied the bucket, and put all the used clothing into the oilskin.

"Boys, we won' be talkin' o' this to the cap'n, yeh?"

Chapter 47

Netherfield Park, November 15, 1812

Lady Catherine wet her lips. Her head rocked from side to side, followed by her eyes opening and blinking. After a few moments, she looked to her right.

"Who are you?"

"Hurst."

"Hurst?"

"Yes, mum. Hurst."

"Well, sit not like a base-born child.[15] Call my abigail."

"I think not, mum."

"You think not?"

"No, mum."

"Who are you to deny my orders?"

Hurst leaned in. "Lady Catherine, you have brought yourself to a *point non plus*."[16]

15 Illegitimate offspring

16 Situation with no options

"Who are you to speak to me thus?"

"We know *who* you have harmed. We know *when* you have harmed them. We know *how* you have harmed them."

"You know nothing!"

"Allow me to disabuse you of that notion, mum." Hurst sat back and opened a journal. He held up a pair of letters. They were old, the paper tender with age. Hurst read a sentence from the first.

"...a Matlock Fitzwilliam guarantees the scheme...compensation after your agreement for the estate is penned."

Lady Catherine displayed her disbelief on her face.

"There were only three Matlock Fitzwilliams at the time of this missive, mum." Hurst's face turned stony. "I caution you to consider our nation's slander laws before leveling a false accusation upon either of your siblings, living or not."

Lady Catherine remained mute.

Hurst held up a letter familiar to his conversation partner. He held it close enough for her to see her handwriting regarding the betrothal between her brother's heir and hers.

"From whence did you purloin that? I demand you turn it over to me as it is my property!"

Hurst smiled. "Thank you for your corroboration, mum. I have one more letter to present for your consideration. May I?"

Lady Catherine nodded warily.

Hurst held up a letter with matching penmanship. "Dare I ask why you were writing to the countess, posing as her cousin Lady Penelope Lambert?"

Lady Catherine forcibly swallowed.

"Lady Catherine. I shall neither insult your rank nor your intelligence as I am sure you are aware of the ramifications of your actions and their subsequent results. We have informed the Crown."

Lady Catherine gawked at him, her face showing her shock.

Hurst waited. She cleared her throat. "Who are you referring to when you say *we*?"

"The bishop of Leeds, his Reverence, the archbishop of Canterbury, and the Earl of Matlock are but the tip of the iceberg of those knowledgeable of your heinous actions."

A door opened. Hurst looked up and frowned. Colonel Fitzwilliam closed the door and joined the interrogation. He sat on the bed. His aunt recoiled as he leaned in toward her.

"Who is your patron?" he asked, his voice without emotion.

Lady Catherine spat at him. "You. The spare. Now viscount. Are the orchards of Ashdale to be so polluted?"

Fitzwilliam grasped her hand and squeezed. His aunt screeched. "Give me his name."

His aunt looked up in fear. Hurst intervened. "Mum, a name is the difference between transportation and the Tower."

Both men watched the tears roll down the broken woman's face. Her breath hitched several times as she chose the former.

"He lives."

With what little control she retained, she whispered aloud her greatest fears. His name. His hideous claret birthmark. His missing appendage. His staged death.

Longbourn

Reeves knocked on the study door.

"Enter."

Captain Thomas Bennet, steely-eyed, nodded to him. Sergeant Reeves understood whom he was addressing and nodded once. Mr. Bennet sighed, then motioned his first footman to the chairs by the fireplace. Both men sat.

"What kin I do fer ye, Mr. Bennet?"

Thomas Bennet smiled. He would miss his cheeky armorer, but the circle of life took precedence, and his daughters' welfare came first and foremost. "Reeves, fetch Ron and Kale. Our time together is at an end."

"So, the winds are blowin' north, Cap'n?"

"That they are, Reeves. Kitty will join the colonel, either in London or Matlock. Lizzy will eventually get out of her own way and join Darcy in Derbyshire."

Reeves chuckled. "In the land o' th' blind, th' one-eyed man is king."

Thomas nodded his agreement. "Where will Ron and Kale choose to go?"

Reeves put two fingers against his forehead. "Well, Kale got family about Matlock an' all. Ron has taken to mindin' Miss Kitty, them both bein' o' a silent bent."

Thomas nodded his agreement.

"You know my fancy, Cap'n. I be watchin' over Miss Jane 'til she chooses to change 'er Bennet name."

"Quite." Thomas slapped his thighs and stood. "Fetch the *twins* and let us inform them of their soon-to-be happy future."

Reeves rose and turned to his commander. "Sir, what o' th' mistress?"

"Reeves, my boy, it appears the very *troublesome* task of keeping Mrs. Bennet safe will fall to my lot."

Both men looked at each other, lips shut tightly, one waiting for the other to break first. Reeves lost, as expected.

"Ayuhm, 'is nibs knows best," said Reeves with a smirk.

"That I do."

Later that same evening

"Enter."

"You asked to speak with me, Papa?"

"Yes, Jane. Join me."

Jane sat in the chair next to her father and leaned in toward the small fire. Thomas draped a wool shawl across her shoulders.

"Thank you, Papa."

She reached up and grasped her father's hand; he squeezed hers in return, then sat back down in his chair. "My dear, it appears Cupid is lodging at Netherfield. I fear for the number of courtships about the kingdom that remain unresolved as he spends his arrows about our little neighborhood."

Jane lifted an eyebrow. "Surely, Papa, is there nothing more substantial in your library that you could quote? The child of Venus and Mars? Really?"

Thomas smiled. Here was his Jane, giving as much as taking. "And what of Mr. Bingley?"

Jane japed back at her father. "He sees me as sugar and spice and everything nice. I confirm to you he is snips and snails and puppy-dog tails."

"I see. No little boys for you. Pity."

Jane smirked.

"What do you see for yourself, my dear? Meryton has little to offer you."

Jane's smile was lopsided. Thomas spied the slight narrowing of one eye and prepared himself. Jane, in a credible pompous baritone, rewarded him. "To my misfortune, the last good man of my acquaintance is unavailable."

Thomas enjoyed her mockery. "Yes, your mother is a most fortunate woman."

"I have only your opinion on the matter, Papa."

Thomas barked out a laugh.

Netherfield Park, the following day

Darcy made it to the stables without attracting notice. He saddled Goliath, who happily accepted a small lump of sugar. He rubbed his large head against Darcy's aching one. Darcy hugged the great horse's neck until he recovered his equilibrium. Swinging up into the saddle, Darcy rode toward Oakham Mount, slowly warming the stallion until he was eating up the furlongs with ever-increasing strides. Sensing that his horse recognized where they were headed,

Darcy let his mind wander, focusing on nothing. Goliath soon slowed and eventually stopped near the same tree where he had spoken with *her* the previous week.

A sense of urgency roiled his insides, and Darcy hastened up to the hill's crest. Disappointed to see the stump empty, he walked over, glanced at where *she* had before perched herself, and lowered himself onto his previous seat. Closing his eyes, he leaned forward, forearms on his thighs, and slowly breathed in and out. How long he stayed in this position, he did not know.

When she arrived, he sensed her more than heard her through her trademark lavender. "It is quite early, Miss Elizabeth."

"Indeed, it is, Mr. Darcy."

"May I inquire as to your escort arrangements?"

"You may."

Darcy waited, unsure whether his query affronted her. "I ask as a concerned friend."

Miss Elizabeth huffed. "Is that what we are, Mr. Darcy? Are we friends? For if we were to canvass those in our current circle, they might think the contrary. But, in answer to your question, a footman accompanied me."

Darcy opened his eyes. Her hair, although held up by pins, strained to free itself, an unstable dam straining to contain the bevy of chestnut breakers. Her bonnet, suspended by a single wide ribbon, dangled from her hand. And her eyes! So large, so brown, so shiny, so expressive. *So magnificent!*

"*I* have long considered us friends."

Miss Elizabeth did not smile, a quizzical look upon her face. "Mr. Darcy, I hear such different accounts of you, it leaves me puzzled."

His earlier megrim returned with a vengeance. Darcy winced.

"Is there anything I may do to relieve your pain? I shall grant you solitude should you desire it, sir."

Darcy blinked, unsure how the conversation again escaped his control. He stood, careful to avoid concerning his visitor. His temples pulsed. "I see you are wishing me gone. Please allow me to yield your oasis to you and wish you a good morning, madam."

Darcy walked down the hill as his head throbbed. He did not look back.

He quietly wished Mr. Reeves a good morning as he passed him.

Had Darcy turned his head, he would have seen a similar look of confusion on Miss Elizabeth's face. Reeves looked at the ground and shook his head, disappointed he must inform Mr. Bennet his observations of his daughter and her possible suitor were, at best, premature. As brilliant as Miss Lizzy was, she seemed oblivious to what was right in front of her.

Chapter 48

Lucas Lodge

The next evening, Lady Lucas hosted an evening of cards. The young ladies played whist with the militia officers while the gentlemen drank and discussed their estates. Their wives exchanged local gossip, rumors from town, and on-dits that had town tongues wagging.

The Netherfield party, sans Colonel Fitzwilliam and the Hursts, arrived after the Bennet ladies. Charles Bingley, eager to engage the eldest Miss Bennet, entered with Darcy trailing behind him. Bingley found her standing with her mother. Miss Bennet wore a gossamer-thin sky-blue cashmere shawl across her shoulders; it highlighted her extraordinary eyes. He blinked several times before approaching the young lady.

Darcy, with his great height, spotted his Elizabeth sitting on the far sofa with her younger sister. *MY Elizabeth? Where did that come from?* He drifted around the room, the younger Bennet ladies his focus.

George Wickham could see that Darcy had not noticed him, secluded as he was in a corner with a drink in his hand, obscured by other militia officers.

Wickham could not believe his luck. Providence had followed him from London to Meryton! He remained hidden as he studied Darcy's face, the cracks in his mask evident. Following Darcy's eyes, he saw both the young Bennet ladies. Plotting *His Highness's* trajectory, he wondered which was the object of his interest and settled in to watch the upcoming production as one would with tickets to Hay-Market.

Darcy made the conscious decision to show equal attention to both the Bennet ladies. It would not be proper to raise expectations without the possibility of fulfilling them. His father's voice popped into his head, this time a mere whisper. *"Darcy men set the example."*

The ladies stood as Darcy approached, and he bowed as they curtsied. They spoke of the usual mundane topics. Darcy gave more of his attention to Miss Catherine. It would not do to inspire Miss Elizabeth's ire. For once, that lady seemed to enjoy her conversation with him. It was her habit to sign as she spoke. Miss Catherine followed along. Darcy faced the youngest Bennet sister when he spoke. She mouthed her thanks to him for being a gentleman and understanding her situation, her limitations stoutly refuted by Miss Elizabeth. Darcy felt a display of gallantry was required. He took Miss Catherine's hand and bowed over it, thanking her for the positive evaluation.

Wickham could not look away. Darcy esteemed the youngest, lovely, speechless Bennet daughter. *Two silent wallflowers,* he thought to himself. He started planning his revenge, surprised that Darcy preferred the less mature of the pair.

Charlotte Lucas walked over to Elizabeth and challenged her to play for the company. Miss Elizabeth looked to Miss Catherine, who nodded encouragement but signed that she would not join, as there were too many new faces. Charlotte laid her hand on the youngest Bennet sister's arm and, with her other, engaged Darcy's.

"I am sure there are gentlemen about to provide you with excellent company while your sister amazes us," laughed Miss Lucas, giving Darcy a pointed look.

"Of course. Miss Catherine, it would be my distinct pleasure to enjoy your sister's exhibition while keeping you company."

Darcy bowed to Miss Catherine's curtsy and off went the ladies toward the pianoforte. Darcy sat with Miss Catherine, but his eyes remained on her elder sister. Miss Elizabeth opened the instrument, sat down, and began warming up with alternating musical scales. Darcy stared at his siren from across the room. His ears twitched to hear her perform. *I wonder whether she will sing.* The same random thought from the previous week again crossed his mind. From the corner of his eye, he noticed movement. He turned to Miss Catherine, who had her journal out, pencil in her hand.

"May I speak freely, sir?"

"You may."

"You are not as reserved as you believe."

Darcy gulped. After a moment, he held out his hand in a tacit request for the pencil. His partner complied.

"I am trying to be careful not to raise expectations."

Miss Catherine leaned her head back and silently laughed. She put her hand up to cover her mouth.

Darcy, confused, raised his eyebrows as he did with Richard.

"Lizzy is unaware of your interest. You did insult her rather well. Twice! She believes that you, on most occasions, find fault with her."

Darcy looked to the piano as Miss Elizabeth began to play. She played an Italian love song by Sammartini without a score. She played well and with great feeling. It was equal to what one found in London's salons. She did not sing. Darcy found it exceedingly difficult, but he turned back to her sister.

"Thank you for your discretion."

He gripped her hand and placed a chaste kiss on her knuckles. Miss Catherine blushed and looked down.

George Wickham witnessed it all. The silent doxy was his target for riches and a better life.

Netherfield Park

Colonel Fitzwilliam sat in front of the study fireplace in the furthest comfortable chair from the door. The embers struggled to break through the darkness, their effort admirable but receiving no assistance nor reinforcements. His thoughts centered on a young lady three miles away, her image alone—a bonfire of light in his mind.

A shadow appeared in his peripheral vision. Richard had been expecting her company. He cleared his throat, a signal to her that he was aware she had come.

Thea Sutton lowered herself into the chair adjacent to the colonel. She was not afraid, but as a perceptive woman, she appreciated the care he had taken to leave a seat open next to him.

Soothing peace surrounded them as Thea waited for an overture.

"Your Grace," whispered Richard.

Thea smiled. Richard Fitzwilliam was so much more than a mere mortal. He had earned a reprieve; he deserved expiation, a cleansing of his sins.

"Your mother spends much of her time at Gracechurch Street."

Richard exhaled and relaxed back into his chair. "The countess is nothing less than genuine in her love of family."

Thea looked at him. She repeated her first assessment of him, one she had made when he was a young boy. "You are extraordinary."

"*She* is extraordinary." He surprised himself with the emotion he perceived in his voice.

"She?" alluded Thea, her understanding openly acknowledged.

"Yes, she. Miss Catherine Bennet."

Thea reached out and laid her hand on his forearm. In the faint light of the embers, Richard spied the outline of the smile on her face. "The cousins are looking forward to welcoming her."

"You have my undivided loyalty."

She patted his forearm, words unnecessary.

"Is it done?" she inquired.

"There is one more."

Colonel Fitzwilliam and Mrs. Sutton took their time to exchange their gathered intelligence. He outlined his requirements; she confirmed her influence. Together, they would remove a blight in the kingdom revealed by the results of a tragedy that had occurred twenty-five years previously.

The following morning, Mrs. Sutton's carriage left Netherfield Park before the other guests broke their fast. She left a gracious handwritten note for Louisa Hurst on the salver in the foyer.

Chapter 49

Longbourn

The date for the Netherfield ball approached quickly. Franny and Louisa grew ever closer. As they worked together, Louisa listened with interest to Franny's stories about her pregnancies, eating habits, day-to-day activities, and confinement preparations. Mrs. Hill joined the ladies, as did her sister, Mrs. Nichols.

Louisa gathered up her courage to ask that which, in her opinion, should not be asked. "Franny, why do housekeepers, maids, laundresses, midwives, even stable hands know of these things, yet I am but learning them now?"

"It is a quandary. Gently-bred women who act above their station may never acquire this education."

Both Mrs. Hill and Mrs. Nichols nodded in agreement. Franny continued, "Thomas once observed that the Quality seems to die of trivial ailments, whereas their tailors and cobblers recover easily. He attributes it to the difference between retaining physicians over apothecaries and surgeons."

"Please continue, Franny. You cannot deny your audience is hanging on your every word."

"Physicians do not touch their patients. It is beneath them. They attend, listen to the patient's version of their maladies, and recommend treatment in line with the narration offered. Nor do they accept payment for their services. They accept gratuities such that they do not 'trade' on their knowledge."

"How like a gentleman."

"Surgeons and apothecaries examine their patients. They push and probe, thump and listen to their body cavities. They also ask questions to confirm or deny their suppositions. They sometimes treat the patient for something they knew not of having had."

Mrs. Hill nodded to her sister. Mrs. Nichols confirmed her nod. "It 'twas the master's army surgeon who saved me Hill when he were threwn from 'is 'orse."

Louisa shook her head, the disparity between reputations and reality alarming her. Franny changed the subject. "How many days should we allow before starting the white soup, Mrs. Nichols?"

Meryton, later in the day

The Bennet carriage stopped on the corner of the street leading to the Meryton shops. The weather, as pleasant as a November day could be, ensured the tradesman and shop clerks would be busy selling their wares, servicing their clientele, passing rumors, and trading gossip. A perfect day for friends to sit and enjoy each other's company without the burden of entertaining men!

Louisa laughed when Franny told her the reason for the outing. Both ladies reverted to decorum when the carriage door opened, and a large hand reached in to assist them out.

Once both ladies were out of the carriage, Franny turned and looked up at the footman. He was quite large. "Kale, what are your instructions?"

"Ah'm to take th' curr'ge to Smitty for th' once-over, mum." He paused. "Ron sets."

"Thank you, Kale."

Franny turned and looked up at the other footman. He was larger and more intimidating than his partner. "Ron, would you like some refreshments?"

Ron shook his head and pointed to the empty chair outside the shop door.

The delicate curtains seen through the clean, clear windows gave nothing away. Franny took Louisa's arm and entered. Once inside, Louisa gasped in delight as a tearoom worthy of any found in the middle of Bond Street opened before her.

Louisa gazed at the space, all feminine frills, lace, and pastels. The shop was warm, comforting, and soothing. She looked at Franny in wonder.

"Louisa, welcome to Tea Room West. We would have come earlier, but this was the first occasion I could confirm."

Louisa counted six small tables. Five were occupied by well-dressed ladies seated in pairs and trios. The walls were chair-railed—white-washed slats below the border, wide pastel stripes above. A minimal number of different-sized framed pastoral scenes adorned the walls.

A handsome woman walked toward them, her hands out to welcome them. "Mrs. Bennet, how delightful to see you again."

"Millie Stephens, my, my, my, you look lovelier every time I see you. What is your secret?"

The object of the compliment colored and dipped her head. Then she regrouped and guided the two ladies to what appeared to be the best table in the room.

Louisa could not help staring at their hostess's dress.

"Lovely, is it not?"

"Yes, I daresay it is. Where did you get that delightful creation?"

Louisa envied the fashionable apron incorporated to be the actual front of the dress. The utility! The fashion! How expedient to have one about the house.

"This was a gift from Miss Bennet. She is genuinely gifted with a needle. My clientele informs me that London has nothing even close to the skill displayed in these stitches alone."

Franny demurred for Jane's sake. "Let us leave Jane to her passions, for it keeps her quite satisfied."

Franny nodded to Millie, who departed.

"Tell me about this oasis, Franny."

"It is a sad tale. It ends happily, but grief paved the road."

Louisa leaned in and whispered. "Tell me."

Franny smacked Louisa's arm with her fan and laughed. "I said it is sad, not secret, you wicked woman."

Louisa joined her with a giggle.

"Millie West, as she was then, her husband Jim, and their daughter Dottie were Longbourn tenants. They were a wonderful family and loving parents. Their little Dottie was a delightful child."

Louisa swallowed. She already knew where this sad tale would lead but could not bring herself to stop listening.

"Dottie and her father passed from the influenza in the year four. Thomas and I could not help them, buried as we were in our grief."

Louisa took out her handkerchief and dabbed her eyes.

"When we could begin looking after our tenants, Thomas found Millie alone in a lean-to off their cottage. She had nearly starved to death. My husband refuses to describe what he found, but the surviving men went back later as a burial party. They burned the hut."

Louisa gasped and looked about for their hostess.

"We took her in at Longbourn."

Franny shushed her friend. Louisa looked to see Millie bringing a tea tray loaded with biscuits and lady fingers. Louisa could not stop her eyes from filling.

Millie looked at Franny and frowned. "Telling my story again,

Mrs. Bennet?"

"Yes, Millie, I am. Rather proudly, I daresay."

"I did not think it so maudlin as to bring tears."

"Your story is not. Louisa's emotions are not her own."

"How wonderful! Oh, please accept my best wishes."

"Thank you, Millie. This all looks so lovely. Will you not join us?"

Millie sat down. "Just a quick bite. I love the limoncellos."

She picked up a dainty, yellow-tinted roll and took a bite.

Turning to Mrs. Stephens, Louisa asked her about the brew. "Now you, my dear, must explain how your tea is so rich and aromatic."

Millie glanced at Franny. "The Bennets took me in. My health, once restored, allowed me to repay them for their kindness. Of course, they refused, but with Mrs. Hill's assistance, I persevered."

"How so?"

"I worked with Cook in the kitchen, helping here and there. I love baking and creating foods. I started experimenting with tea blends and Miss Bennet helped me with certain pekoes. Soon, all the teas and sweets fell to me. A most happy outcome, as far as I am concerned."

"Is that how Tea Room West came about?"

"Everything you see here is because of the Miss Bennets. Several families praised the Longbourn tea trays while they gathered after church. They were unaware that Miss Kitty read their lips. Miss Lizzy put together an income and expense ledger. Miss Bennet worked with the milliner to produce the linens. Miss Kitty decorated."

"My, your daughters are surely accomplished young ladies, Franny."

Millie continued. "Miss Lizzy asked her father whether he would support me by opening a sanctum for ladies. He agreed and the Tea Room idea took hold of everyone. The enthusiasm was quite overwhelming."

"My brother Philips arranged the purchase, and here we sit!" crowed Franny triumphantly.

Millie left Franny and Louisa to their repast. She stopped at each table to speak with her customers, then disappeared behind the back service door.

Louisa grasped her adorable friend's hand. Ready to thank her for her friendship, she halted when the door opened. The women gasped. A man stood in the doorway. It would have alarmed Louisa had Franny not had a beatific glow on her face. Louisa asked her who the man was, but Franny shushed her.

"Her husband," she whispered.

The man was ruggedly handsome. He had his hat in his left hand, his right behind his back. Millie bustled out from the back and came to an abrupt stop. Her hand rose to rest upon her heart.

"My dear Mrs. Stephens, I could not wait a minute more to see you once I had completed my travels."

The room was hushed, enthralled by the intrigue.

"You have been gone for quite a while, sir. A most intolerable amount of time."

Louisa would swear Millie had a saucy glint in her eye.

"Yes, it is unforgivable, and I know I must do penance. I see that. Can you ever see it in your heart to forgive me?"

"What can you say to compel me to do so, sir?"

The man took a step forward. He was now between the two tables closest to the door. His hand was still behind his back.

"Surely, Mrs. Stephens, surely you must know, if *I* know what love is, it is because of *you*. I would vow I could not love you more than I do right now, and yet…and yet I know I shall tomorrow."

From behind his back, he brought forth a bunch of wildflowers.

Mille walked to him and took the flowers. She kissed his cheek and pushed him out the door. Before closing it, Louisa heard, "That was lovely, Mr. Stephens, just…lovely." Millie closed the door and turned back to work. Six tables, fifteen ladies, and not a dry eye at Tea Room West.

That evening, lying in her husband's arms on the fainting couch in their sitting room, Louisa replayed the Tea Room love scene to Hurst. She saw his eyes open a bit wider at the name of the Tea Room owners. He nodded at the confirmation of the Longbourn steward's name. She asked him what he was thinking.

"It pleases me to see the level of regard in which the shire holds Thomas Bennet. It surprises me how he fails to recognize the earldom's desire to continue repaying their debt to him."

Louisa snuggled a bit closer to her husband and let his bit of clandestine thinking go unquestioned.

Chapter 50

The Netherfield party visited Longbourn every day—Louisa meeting with Franny, the men entertaining their choice of young ladies. Mr. Bennet's cousin was neither missed nor his absence questioned. As he did not make his farewells and departed without fanfare, his actions, although inconsistent with his previous behavior, did not impel anyone to further investigate.

Bingley and Darcy called upon the two elder Miss Bennets, and they made quite the picturesque foursome. Bingley and Lizzy carried the conversational load. Darcy, becoming more familiar with this intimate circle, added depth to the substantial debates. Jane tempered the word trading, when needed, between her intelligent, argumentative sister and the educated gentleman from Derbyshire.

Darcy recognized Miss Elizabeth's intellectual gifts. Her ability to assume either side of the debate—for the sake of the activity and not a personal principle—astonished him. She seemed to want nothing more than enjoyable discourse and pleasant attention.

Throwing caution to the wind, he accepted her terms and provided her with the desired entertainment.

Lizzy's regard for Mr. Darcy continued to grow, now that she understood how he had been forced to fend off distaff fortune hunters. With no demands upon him except for his participation, she saw his increased comfort in her company. In a relaxed setting, he quite amazed her at the depth of his education and his thoughtful discourse.

Jane was pleased to see Lizzy moderating her manner toward Mr. Darcy. The three Bennet sisters had discussed his every behavior and reaction to their most stubborn sibling most evenings up in their rooms. As for her interest in Mr. Bingley, Jane was happy in her current situation and did not see a change in her circumstances soon, if at all.

Franny thought her Lizzy and Mr. Darcy made a handsome couple but held her tongue as she chaperoned them within the manor. This duty fell to her because her husband, with the meager excuse that he wanted to entertain Hurst, took over the chaperoning duties of Kitty and the colonel. *Cruel, unfair man.*

Thomas Bennet had never spent a more fascinating set of hours than those he shared with Hurst chaperoning this most unusual unofficial courtship—a courtship conducted with little to no sound in the small parlor. Without crossing the lines of propriety, the two unacknowledged lovers, separated from the others as their communication style distracted all in proximity, entertained each other by writing in journals, signing, and forming pronounced facial expressions. Once they got past the need for perfection, they relaxed into a casual attitude that was quite tactile without being vulgar.

That evening, Thomas sat with Franny in their sitting room and reviewed the wonders of the afternoon. Franny did not begrudge her husband as he shared all the precious moments gloriously.

"I believe, my dear, I am getting close to being petitioned for my blessing. It is already obvious that the colonel and our youngest are courting."

"Why do you think that, Thomas?"

"At one point, the colonel took Kitty's left hand—and this is very important—in his *right* hand, and brushed his lips across her knuckles."

"We have seen him do that regularly. Why is this time significant?"

"You did not let me finish, my dove. After the lip brushing had been completed, Kitty daringly turned his right hand over as if she were to brush her lips across his knuckles."

"How bold!" Franny exclaimed. "And…?"

"She did not! Rather, she noticed the scars on the back of his hand. Faded as they are, they were probably from a childhood incident. She inquired of the scars' provenance."

"And…? What caused them?"

"The colonel informed our precious girl that said scars resulted from poor table manners involving an errant fork."

"And…?" Franny awaited the coup de grâce.

"Kitty dauntlessly informed Fitzwilliam that at *their* future table, she clearly could not trust him to be around sharp dining implements and would permit him only the use of a spoon. All three if required!" triumphed Thomas, his finger pointing upward.

"Oh, oh, oh, my lovely, lovely, sweet Kitty. In love. So mature, so poised. Oh Thomas, how blessed are we."

Thomas pulled Franny into an embrace, leaned back into the sofa, and agreed.

Fitzwilliam surprised no one when, at his next appearance at Longbourn, he walked over to Kitty and took her left hand with his right. He asked permission from Mrs. Bennet to have the honor of Kitty's supper and last sets. Franny granted her approval. Richard signed that he did not dance because of his injuries, but he would like Kitty to accept his company, as well as join him for dinner.

Kitty accepted. Her face bloomed with her feelings.

Before leaving, the colonel secured Mr. Bennet's blessing for their courtship. He did not let Longbourn's master know that he had already written his parents and received an answer from the countess, notwithstanding the revelations from Mrs. Sutton.

Chapter 51

Netherfield Park, November 19, 1812

A week before the ball, Barty woke Darcy. He was quite frustrated with the lack of progress between his master and, in his mind, his perfect match.

The valet had decided his master required a sunrise ride. Darcy spied his riding clothes laid out unprompted. "Barty, is there a reason I am up at the dawn, as the days come up like thunder?"

"Yes, sir, and I daresay you have captured the reason most poetically."

Darcy shook his head to clear the cobwebs.

"Sir, I understand Oakham Mount presents a most desirable view this early in the morning."

"You understand, do you?" Darcy played along.

"I do."

"From whom did you gain this understanding?"

"Mrs. Hill, sir."

"Mrs. Hill?" repeated Darcy, still muddled.

"Yes, sir. Mrs. Hill."

"Mrs. Hill...at Longbourn?"

"Sir, do you know another Mrs. Hill of our acquaintance at another estate?" Barty asked saucily.

He looked at his valet. There seemed to be something in the air in this shire that brought out the impertinence in others. Darcy wondered at the small smile on his face. He sensed intrigue.

Darcy headed down the servants' stairs toward the stables. He detoured to the kitchens where the staff was already preparing for the day. A scullery maid, a bucket full of water in hand, stopped, put the pail down, and curtsied.

"Good mornin' to ye, Mr. Darcy."

"Good morning, Sally."

Sally did not pass.

"May I help you with something?"

Sally kept her eyes on the floor. "The colonel...he be well?"

Cook bustled over. "Stop yer nonsense, girl. Off wid' ye!"

Sally dashed off.

"Ye be wantin' a bite afore headin' out, Mr. Darcy." It was a statement, not a question. Darcy nodded, unsure why he was being managed by so many. It was pleasant.

"Yes, please, Cook."

"Yer basket's over 'ere—plenny fer ye an' more."

"More, Cook?"

"I sez more now, didn' I."

"You did."

"Off ye go."

She turned back to her cutting table. A large ham hock awaited her attention.

Sally peeked out to make sure no other guests lurked, turned, and smiled at Cook.

"He be pretty and p'lite. Miss Lizzy cud do no better."

"He be th' lucky one, I say."

Thus reignited, the debate intensified. All wanted to be heard and all had an opinion. Favorites varied, but the common thread throughout the gossip had Mr. Darcy and Miss Elizabeth betrothed if not wed by Epiphany.

Darcy entered the stables to find Goliath saddled and ready. Tim, the groom, who had assisted Darcy throughout his stay, politely stepped back. He admired that the gentleman needed no assistance mounting such a great beast. Left foot in the stirrup, Darcy stood up using one leg and swung his right up and over Goliath's back. He settled into the saddle and quickly adjusted his seat. The groom grunted his approval. Darcy winked. Tim chuckled.

"Aye suh, it be a pleasu' serving ye' mornin's."

"Thank you, Tim. Are you accompanying me?"

Tim's surprise showed on his face. He shook his head.

"Sir, the view from Oakh'm Mount be unmatch'd this time o' the mornin'."

"Yes, I daresay that is the case."

Tim nodded his agreement.

"Enjoy your morning, Tim."

As Goliath walked off, Darcy let his mind wander. He recognized he was being pushed toward someone. He did not resist. He just hoped Miss Elizabeth was as open to him as he was to her. Twenty minutes later, he arrived at the base of Oakham Mount. Reeves was sitting on the ground, his back up against a large tree. He carved a branch with a rather short, nasty-looking blade.

Darcy dismounted and wished the footman a pleasant morning. Reeves returned the sentiment.

"Mr. Reeves, I daresay I am not surprised to see you this morning."

"A smart gen'leman like yerself shouldn' be."

"May I proceed up?"

"Aye."

Reeves pointed his weapon toward the northeast path, his eyes narrow.

Darcy acknowledged the subtle warning. He walked upward and stopped when he saw *her*. She was sitting on her stump, her younger sister by her side.

Miss Elizabeth's hair was unpinned, a chestnut waterfall cascading down her back. Miss Catherine was combing it. She noticed him out of the corner of her eye. Elizabeth did not. He bowed but remained silent. His mouth was very, very dry.

Miss Catherine laid aside her comb and put her sister's hair to rights, then hugged her. Miss Elizabeth stroked her younger sister's arm.

Darcy wished he were Kitty. He yearned to experience that closeness, that level of intimacy. He turned his head. A hint of sound—his mother's voice—came as a whisper but a moment later was gone.

Miss Catherine wrapped herself in a light green shawl and walked toward him. He nodded as she approached, and as was her custom, she held out her left hand. He bowed over it. She next surprised him.

She stepped in front of him and put her right hand on his face.

Darcy froze. Richard's frightening rictus gleamed at him from the shadows of his primal brain. His heart pounded in his ears. Connected as she was to his cousin, this was a lady he dared not disappoint. Then she dropped her hand and gestured toward Elizabeth. Her face displayed the same expression as did Richard's when Darcy acted the noddy. She walked off. *Did she just roll her eyes at me?*

He moved closer to Elizabeth. Her *contralto* wafted over her shoulder. "Mr. Darcy, we seem to have established the custom of your encountering me in less than proper attitudes."

Is there no moment she is not witty?

"Madam, no one who truly knows you could ever censure you for acting otherwise than in the greatest propriety."

Elizabeth laughed and patted the vacant space beside her. "My, what a diplomatic sentiment so prettily expressed. Will you not join me and share this beautiful morning?"

Whether her question was figurative or literal, Darcy did not know. Miss Elizabeth always ran verbal circles around him whenever he was in her presence. All he knew was that he *wanted* to join her. And so, he did.

She had yet to open her eyes. He was free to feast upon her beauty. Darcy indulged his ardor. His father's voice rose to fight his joy. He closed his mind to his father's censure—his imagined disapprobation. He wanted to hear *his* Elizabeth. When he opened his eyes, she was staring at him.

Elizabeth's senses were flooded with a man's aroma: horse, leather, perspiration, citrus, and spruce. This threw her out of balance. Kitty had reassured her about Mr. Darcy's regard, but his tendency to withdraw behind his mask and give offense tested her faith.

Even in her doubt, there were glimmers of hope. She enjoyed debating with him more than any other, including Papa. Darcy had a subtle, wry sense of humor that fired her amusement. Once he had become more familiar with those in their party, he ventured his opinions—opinions that were well articulated and supported by fact and literary references. Elizabeth found herself challenged—yes, quite challenged by the man from Derbyshire. This feeling was new. It was very heady.

She gave in, stopped her internal argument, and admitted that she enjoyed his company. She looked forward to his company. She craved his company. She thought he reciprocated her feelings. Then a niggling doubt tore at her confidence. How could he admire her? He was Fitzwilliam Darcy of Pemberley! He was worth ten thousand a year—or more! While they spoke of travel and geographical references, he alluded to what could only be his investment interests: coal mines, mills, quarries, canal locks, patents, breeding farms of every type of livestock supported on arable land. How could he even "see" her much less own affection for her? Elizabeth Bennet of Longbourn was so far beneath the notice of Fitzwilliam Darcy of Pemberley.

Disappointed in her impossible hopes, she opened her eyes. She gazed upon his face. He shook his head as if seeking to clear water from his ears. He stared at her as she stared at him.

Does he see what I see?

Does she see what I see?

From the base of the hill, Goliath whinnied. Darcy stood and offered Miss Elizabeth his hand. She accepted and used his strength to rise. He did not release her hand.

"Miss Elizabeth, may I take this opportunity to solicit your company for a set at Bingley's ball?"

"Mr. Darcy, as pleased as I am to *at last* be worthy of your attention, I regret to inform you that all my dance sets have been spoken for."

Darcy nodded, disappointed. "Yes, of course they are. How condescending of me to assume otherwise. Please forgive me. If you will allow me to beg your leave, I shall descend first."

He bowed and walked off briskly; shoulders slumped in dejection. He cursed himself for his earlier caution. He could not face Mr. Reeves or Miss Catherine in his current state. He nodded to them, leapt upon Goliath, and rode off, his hopes once again dashed.

Lizzy strolled down the path and joined Kitty. She linked her arm with her sister's. Reeves fell back.

Kitty looked at Lizzy, eyebrows in the air.

"Yes, Kitty, he asked. And no, I told him my ball dance sets have been spoken for."

Kitty shook her head. She did not understand her sister's obstinacy toward the sensitive man she now understood Mr. Darcy to be. She picked up her pace. Lizzy matched her. They made it home in a handy manner.

Chapter 52

Longbourn, November 20, 1812

Mrs. Bennet sat across from her husband; both entertained themselves with books. She enjoyed their private time together as they shared in the silence with which couples in love were comfortable. Romantic thoughts colored her thinking as she stole appreciative looks at her very handsome, very fit…*very fit*…husband. Having lost herself again in the moment, she looked up. Thomas was smiling at her. Her blush exploded downward. *Odious man!*

A knock on the closed study door ended the underlying tension that had started to build.

"Let us reconvene on this very subject later, my dear," whispered Thomas in her ear.

Franny fanned her face as Thomas acknowledged Hill and exited the study.

"Oh, my," she said as she expelled a breath, an unknowing, tempting smile on her face. She remained seated, committed to collecting herself.

Bennet, despite being diverted by his wife's loveliness, was unsurprised to see Fitzwilliam and Darcy in the receiving parlor.

"Good morning, gentlemen. To what do we owe the pleasure?"

Richard looked at Darcy, who looked at his cousin. They both turned back to their host. Darcy opened the proceedings. "Good morning, Mr. Bennet. We were hoping to escort the younger Miss Bennets out as the weather is quite agreeable."

Richard nodded in affirmation.

"Excellent. Lizzy and Kitty are visiting tenants. I invite you to join them and delay their return."

"Thank you, sir. May we inquire of their direction?"

"I would surmise they are past Longbourn Pond. Off you go, young men."

Darcy and Richard nodded their thanks and quickly departed. Bennet was momentarily diverted until the morning's interrupted conversation with his wife returned to his attention.

"Hill!"

"Sir?"

"The mistress and I shall be occupied with important business for the afternoon. See that we are not disturbed."

"Very good, sir."

Thomas went to the shared suite between his and his wife's bedroom. He poured two glasses of wine and waited for his love to join him and continue their *wordless* conversation.

Darcy and the colonel spotted a small entourage returning from the woody area east of the manor home. Leading the expedition were Elizabeth and Kitty. Trailing behind were Reeves, Ron, and Kale. All carried baskets, clearly empty by the way they were swung in the November air.

"Good afternoon, Colonel, Mr. Darcy."

Miss Catherine stepped up next to her sister, and both curtsied.

The gentlemen bowed.

"Good afternoon, ladies. How well you look this morning," offered Darcy, surprised to find his tongue working.

"Thank you, sir. We have just completed our round of tenant visits. Would you care to join us? We plan to continue our walk out."

Darcy looked to the colonel, who nodded, then jabbed his chin toward the footmen.

"Miss Elizabeth, we would be happy to accompany you. Your father told us how to find you."

Miss Elizabeth looked to her younger sister and raised an eyebrow in question. Kitty nodded enthusiastically.

"Mr. Reeves, I believe we are in safe hands with these gentlemen, would you not agree?"

Reeves nodded. "Ron, Kale, on me."

Lizzy was taken aback as the twin towers did not move. Both looked to the colonel, seeking permission. *Do they know the colonel?*

Fitzwilliam closed his eyes and minutely nodded. Ron and Kale stepped away and joined Reeves. Elizabeth took Darcy's proffered arm. She was immediately surrounded by familiar, welcome scents. Diverted, the scene evaporated from her thoughts. Looking over her shoulder, she saw the colonel had secured Kitty's hand in the crook of his elbow.

Mr. Darcy walked with Lizzy and remembered her earlier admonition about conversation. "How many tenants did you visit?"

Elizabeth smiled at the thoughtful question. She decided to answer literally.

"One."

"One?"

"Yes, Mr. Darcy. One."

"Five baskets, three footmen, and two lovely ladies comprised a single tenant visit?"

She found his enumeration of their endeavor amusing—a compliment and an enticement. She would play along. The weather was beautiful, and her companion was a pleasant surprise. "We, as do you, take prodigious care of our tenants. You encountered us as we had completed our visit at the Pease Warren."

Mr. Darcy had a delayed reaction. "The Pease Warren?"

"Yes, the Pease Warren," Lizzy said, giggling.

Darcy had been so focused on his partner's lips, he nearly stumbled. *Be a gentleman, you buffoon,* he remonstrated himself. "Not a cottage, but rather a warren?"

"That is correct, Mr. Darcy." She giggled again.

Darcy knew he was missing the point. He decided not to allow a misunderstanding as he had done in the past. "May I inquire why the Pease family lives in a rabbit warren rather than a cottage?"

"You may."

"Well?"

"Well what, sir?"

Darcy knew he was being teased. It was glorious! Throughout his life, he had never been so free with anyone but Richard. He could not help himself. He stopped walking, and Elizabeth stopped as well. He looked down into her face and allowed his joy to radiate all about him.

Elizabeth's breath hitched. Looking up at the most handsome man she had ever seen, she was astonished when he grew even more handsome with the addition of two dimples.

I am no swooning miss! she castigated herself. Unfortunately, the Elizabeth she lectured ignored her.

Trying to recover her equilibrium, she volunteered the answer Darcy sought. "The Pease children number twelve."

Darcy's eyes opened wide. "Oh my."

She beckoned him to lean toward her. He turned his head and lent her his ear.

"The Peases are very devoted to cricket," she whispered.

Darcy stood up straight, looked at her innocent face, and barked a loud laugh. Lizzy joined in, coloring his baritone with her crystalline contralto. Darcy again held out his arm. Together, they walked toward Longbourn.

Further behind them, the other couple was engaged in their own tête-à-tête.

"Do Ron and Kale know you?"

"They were under-footmen at Matlock House before coming to Longbourn," mouthed Richard.

Miss Catherine's face adopted a pensive look. They continued walking.

"And Mr. Stephens?"

"He is the son of the Ashdale steward, Big Harry."

"Big Harry?"

"Or Big H-a-i-r-y," he said, signing each letter carefully and drawing the mirth he desired.

"You must tell me the story."

"Mr. Harry Stephens is his proper name. He is, as you would imagine, a large man, wide in the shoulders and narrow in the hips. The head groom is also called Harry, but he had been a jockey. One earned the moniker 'big' and the other 'little.'

"Once, about fifteen years ago, during the spring thaw, Big Harry was working with a team to repair a dyke on the Derwent. A support plank split beneath him. Big Harry fell in and was trapped when his greatcoat became tangled in weeds and roots. His men had to cut off the coat and his shirts to free him. When he stood, he appeared to be wearing a fur coat, so shredded and mud-filled were his clothes. Thus, the spelling alteration to his name: Big Harry became Big Hairy."

Kitty stopped walking, fiercely gripped Richard's arm, threw her head back, and laughed uproariously, albeit quietly. Fitzwilliam heard nothing. He was mesmerized by her elegant throat. He had to fight every impulse that screamed for him to put his lips on her neck and taste her skin's tenderness. His mouth hung half open.

The lady recovered her composure and wrapped her hands around his biceps. She pressed herself against his side, urging him to walk on.

For the first time in his life, Richard Fitzwilliam believed himself inclined to swoon.

Chapter 53

Netherfield Park, November 21, 1812

Darcy waited for his cousin at the stables. Goliath was saddled and champed at his bit. Perseus, too, was saddled, but much like the colonel, awaited his rider motionlessly and mute. The colonel strode into the stable wearing an open military livery coat in blues and golds. Darcy's surprise clearly showed.

The colonel closed his eyes. Darcy knew he did not want to entertain questions but opted to ignore him. "Interesting choice of uniform, Cousin." He did not try in the least to hide the smirk on his face.

Richard narrowed his eyes, looked off into the distance, and exhaled through his nose. Darcy caught the glimpse of a grin.

"Where are your reds?"

"Laundress."

Richard dissembling? Oh ho!

Darcy mounted Goliath. He heard Richard grunt his approval. "A tall beast requires a taller beast, and you, cousin, and Darcy are both very tall beasts."

Darcy grinned. Richard smiled at his own clever wordplay.

Richard mounted Perseus. The war horse drew alongside Goliath. Looking over his shoulder, Darcy confirmed the Hursts followed in their carriage, ensuring that little in the way of footmen or chaperones would be required for the day's outing.

Darcy continued to glance over at his cousin. His excuse regarding his red coat being delayed at the laundress was a bag of moonshine.[17] Fitzwilliam uncharacteristically fidgeted. Darcy offered a helping hand. "Just tell me, Cousin. The boot is quite on the other foot[18] this time, I daresay."

Richard returned his cousin's glance, his eyes flat and emotionless.

Darcy ignored the threat. He knew Richard was planning the many ways he would deal out some level of punishment without leaving marks. He decided the exercise was worth the risk.

Richard exhaled, shaking his head.

"Kitty favors blue," he said in surrender.

"Indeed."

The picnic goers left Longbourn an hour later, a mixed bunch. Darcy and Richard remounted their horses, respecting Mr. Bennet's *suggestion* they travel as such. The carriage held Hurst and Louisa, Elizabeth, and Kitty. Driving the carriage was Reeves; Ron and Kale followed in a cart carrying chairs, linens, a table, and several baskets of food. A basket contained water and various fruit drinks. Mrs. Bennet had not approved of either wine or ale.

Their destination was the large pond east of Hertford, an hour-long carriage ride away.

After Ron and Kale set up the table and chairs, the footmen took the carriage to a vantage point far enough away to be out of the participants' notice but still have a line of sight per Mr. Bennet's orders.

17 Lot of nonsense

18 The situation is quite the reverse

The two single gentlemen suggested a walk around the pond, an invitation the ladies accepted. The Hursts, cognizant of the romantic setting, sat and partook of the delightful repast.

Darcy escorted Elizabeth along the water's edge, satisfied to simply bask in his siren's scent. Unfortunately, the lady was not of a silent bent.

"We must have conversation, Mr. Darcy."

"Must we?"

"We must."

"I am perfectly happy to oblige. Please advise me of what you would like most to hear."

"That reply will do for the present. What say you of favorites?"

"Favorites? Such as…?"

"Colors, sir."

"Colors? Umm…gold, I believe. Yes, gold. And yours, Miss Elizabeth?"

"Green. What of your morning beverage? Coffee or tea?"

"Coffee. Yours?"

"Tea. Oh dear, we are not in accord. Nevertheless, what of flowers?"

"Flowers, Miss Elizabeth?"

"Yes, flowers, Mr. Darcy. What flowers do you enjoy seeing on your desk? In your parlors?"

Darcy gave it a moment of thought. *His* Elizabeth's favorite was surely lavender. Yet, his mother's rose garden formed from the mists of his memory.

"Roses, mum…m…m," he replied. He hoped his wordplay pleased her. She rewarded him.

"Well done, Mr. Darcy." She squeezed his arm. Darcy wanted to jump up and capture a cloud.

"Had I thought you a flirt, sir, I would have expected you to offer lavender."

"My mother adored roses."

"As do you?"

"As do I."

"Well expressed, sir."

Her fingers kneaded his biceps again.

The couple walked on, chatting and exchanging favorites. They circled back to the food table and the Hursts.

Richard ambled along the water's edge, satisfied with the silence of basking in his muse's aura. Fortunately, Miss *Kitty* was also of a silent bent.

Richard saw a large tree atop a small rise that overlooked the pond. He led Kitty to the tree, and his eyes asked her permission to stop. She nodded. Richard stood still, unsure of how to declare himself. Kitty helped him along by raising her left hand.

Richard took her hand and applied the slightest of pressure guiding her toward himself. Miss Kitty stepped closer. Richard placed her fingers over his heart. He felt vulnerable because he knew that she would feel the scars beneath his linen shirt.

Kitty's eyes glistened. He started to explain but stopped as she shook her head. He waited.

"I am overwhelmed at the honor you do me."

Richard released her hand and passed her his handkerchief. She dried her eyes, smiled at him, and lifted her hand, palm up. Unsure of her gesture, Richard placed his right hand in hers.

Kitty raised his hand to her lips and kissed his scars. She lifted it to her face, turning it so that it cupped her cheek. Richard's breathing went ragged. Her eyes were hooded.

Tightening his fingers the tiniest fraction, he gained her attention. *Does fortune favor the bold?*

"My dear, could you…could you ever love one…one such as I?"

The light from her eyes refracted through her tears into a rainbow of acceptance. Richard saw her swallow, her throat tight.

"I already do," she rasped aloud.

Richard exhaled. His insides vibrated as they did after a battle. He realized he had just been in one, the most desperate in his life. He had lost—and won—the battle for his heart. He kissed her knuckles. He vowed, from that day forward, to bestow the same to this much-beloved appendage daily.

In victorious submission, Colonel Richard Fitzwilliam held out his arm and escorted Miss Catherine Bennet back to the food table, more than happy to allow the Hursts to carry the conversation. Neither of the silent lovers hid their looks of shared longing.

Reeves watched his charges. The younger silently gave in to love. The elder stepped onto it, as up to today, it had eluded her.

Chapter 54

Matlock House, November 23, 1812

"Sir John Beckett."

The earl stood and welcomed his most powerful ally for the next step of the journey. "Sir John, thank you for coming."

"I could do no less, having received Hurst's report."

"I have yet to make the acquaintance of a more outstanding young man."

"Thank you, my lord. He has proven to be all that and more. Thus, my presence here today."

"How may I assist you?"

"We must inform the cousins. You cannot be remiss in this."

"Yes, I daresay we must. The Court of Chancery may be loath to reconsider a previous decision"

Sir John agreed.

"How much time will pass before we shall be granted an audience?"

Sir John smiled. His teeth gleamed.

"The cousins expect us within the hour."

Courts of Chancery, London, November 25, 1812

THE RIGHT HONORABLE CYRIL JOHN SCOTT, FIRST BARON ELDON, the Lord Chancellor and Keeper of the King's conscience, sat high above the six vice-chancellors. He awaited the next case. The court scribe cleared his throat. "Milord, the Chancery has received a special request for exception."

The doors to the court opened, and two well-dressed men—one younger but tending toward distinction, one older and already distinguished—approached.

The scribes and attenders fell silent for a moment, then loud murmurings filled the chamber.

"Order. Order, I say!" shouted the bailiff.

The two men stopped in front of the wall that separated the judges from the petitioners. Lord Cyril put his spectacles on. "Lord Matlock?"

"Good morning, my lord."

"Well, this is quite extraordinary. Is the Earl of Matlock petitioning this court?"

"I am not. My young friend here does. He has business which you will find engaging."

"And who is this gentleman?"

"Baron Eldon, it is my pleasure to introduce to your acquaintance Mr. Reginald Hurst from Suffolk."

The young man bowed. Nodding his acknowledgment, Eldon probed. "Are you petitioning for yourself, Mr. Hurst?"

"No, milord."

"May I inquire for whom you petition?"

"You may, milord."

Lord Eldon narrowed his eyes. *What cheek! Reminds me of those blasted parliament agents.*

The Earl of Matlock smothered a grin behind his fist. The court attenders alternately looked aghast and amused.

Eldon was one of those in the former category. "We do not have all day. For whom are you petitioning? Out with it!"

"Begging your pardon, milord. I am petitioning on behalf of Sir John Beckett."

The baron winced. *Not parliament, but the Crown!*

The courtroom exploded in noise. The bailiff shouted for order repeatedly. The roar lessened.

"Bailiff, read the request from the plaintiffs."

The factotum narrated the previous award of trusteeship of Tang Hall and its related properties to the Grafton dukedom from a previous petition.

"What is the claim in the petition for an exception?"

"Milord, please review this small account before our presenting testimony for public consumption."

The Lord Chancellor skimmed the contents. He looked up at the pair of petitioners, who displayed a most serious mien. Lord Cyril closed his eyes and regulated his breathing.

"Bailiff, clear the court."

"My lord?" replied the bailiff.

"Now!" shouted Lord Cyril, in no mood to brook dissent.

Matlock House

"Well?"

Matlock could not help but feel fortunate that such a formidable woman as his countess had agreed to share her life with him.

"It is done."

Lady Audrey's hands went up to her heart, one clasping the other. "Is it true? This viciousness is at an end?"

"It is. Madeleine Lambert Gardiner is a recognized, lawful heiress."

Opening his arms, he was pleased that his countess—his lady—glided into them. She went up on her toes and kissed his cheek. He felt himself stir.

THAT EVENING, THE SCANDAL RAGS SPREAD SHOCKING NEWS throughout town. Rumors abounded of the dissipation of the Grafton dukedom. It became complete bedlam when a Royal Proclamation, posted in the broadsheets the following morning, declared the Grafton title vacant and all its related lands, holdings, and assets reverted to the Crown.

"...on the evening of the rumored dissolution of the patents previously awarded to the D of G and his son, VB, we witnessed the E of M and the very shadowy C leaving the royal palace..."

Matlock House, the next day

THEA PUT HER CUP AND SAUCER ON THE TABLE, HAVING SPIED AN impish look on her friend Audrey's face.

"Henry, dearest?" asked his wife.

"Yes, my love?"

"Must you take Bill with you everywhere?"

Thea was warmed by the twinkle in Matlock's eye.

"Yes, dear. I must."

"May I inquire why?"

"You may."

Thea laughed. *What a lovely exchange!*

"Well, sir?" repeated the countess.

Henry narrowed an eye at Thea. "Law, without teeth, is a tragedy."

"Huzzah, Henry."

"Thank you, Thea."

"Henry, having encountered Bill, I believe I may add a codicil, by your leave."

"Of course, Thea. Dazzle us with your brilliance."

Thea smiled. She sensed her grandfather, the duke, sitting next to her. "Presence, without fear, is contrary."

Lady Audrey looked at her husband, who raised his teacup to their most distinguished friend. "Indeed."

Chapter 55

Netherfield Park, before the ball
November 26, 1812

Darcy and Richard sat in the former's sitting room. Barty puttered about, seeing to their comforts. Each held a glass of whiskey, but the level dropped slowly as they both had pleasant plans for their evening.

Darcy let lie Richard's sudden affinity for blue. Rather, he opened the conversation with his cousin in his usual abrasive manner. "How long are you going to entertain your delusions regarding the delightful but unsuitable Miss Catherine Bennet?"

Darcy allowed Richard to see a raised, mocking eyebrow. He could tell it entertained his cousin.

Richard did not overlook the tiny bump in Darcy's waistcoat watch pocket. From the lack of a chain, he concluded his cousin had finally resolved his doubts.

"How long are you going to entertain your fantasies regarding the brilliant but unsuitable Miss Elizabeth Bennet?"

"*I* answer to no one."

Richard guffawed. He signed his snappy reply with a flourish. *"You answer to yourself, a most difficult sovereign."*

Darcy ignored him as Barty rather loudly dropped his drink tray upon the side table. *Why is Barty so insistent about the choice of my waistcoat for the ball?*

Richard pulled Darcy's attention back into the room. "Cousin, who is Mrs. Bennet's true brother?"

Darcy shrugged and shook his head.

"Barty?"

"Colonel, I believe it is *the* Mr. Edward Gardiner, a successful tradesman who supports many of the peerage and is rumored to conduct business with the royals."

Darcy glanced at his valet, lifting one eyebrow at the man's voice. "What 'appened t' yer 'shire accent, Barty?"

Barty ignored his employer, smiling at the colonel as if he knew something. Darcy scoffed at him, then turned back to Richard. "But, Cousin, he is still in trade!"

Darcy cared not, but enjoyed emulating Miss Elizabeth who excelled at taking the opposite side of the argument. "And what of Bingley?"

"Bingley is Mrs. Hurst's brother. My acquaintance with him is through her husband. You evade the question."

Richard shook his head. With raised eyebrows he queried his cousin, "Have you met Mr. Gardiner's wife?"

"No, but I have heard her mentioned many times. She is a favorite of the Bennet daughters. She and her husband visit every holiday." Darcy sipped his drink. "We share a geographical connection. She is said to hail from Lambton." Darcy looked pointedly at Richard. "You well know the place."

Richard rasped his next volley. "Her unmarried name was…?"

Darcy again raised his eyebrows, remaining silent.

Richard looked over Darcy's shoulder. "Barty?"

Darcy could see his cousin withholding his mirth.

"I believe I heard her described as Madeleine Gardiner née Wells."

Darcy shrugged his shoulders.

"Pray, continue, Barty," prompted the colonel.

"Her last name of Wells was a misdirection. Her correct name is Madeleine Gardiner née Lambert."

Darcy sat back, stunned. The name "Lambert" more than scratched an old, dormant, mental itch.

He whispered, "The missing cousin?"

Richard nodded, smiling. Darcy leaned in. "Is that what took you to Yorkshire?"

Richard's smile turned feral.

Darcy sat back and closed his eyes. Barty placed a freshly filled glass into his hand, which he nearly drained. *Is Yorkshire completely in ashes?*

Darcy lifted himself out of his chair, grimaced, and sat back down. The dull ache in his right thigh continued to annoy him. He narrowed an eye at his cousin.

"Must you be so childish with your retributions?"

Richard smirked.

Darcy blinked, a random thought entering his mind. "Richard, I have not had a letter from Anne in weeks."

"No fortnightly proposal pleas?"

Darcy shook his head.

"When did she last write?"

Sergeant Villiers, in full battle kit, burst into the room without knocking.

"Sir, your orders?"

The colonel stood, motioned for Darcy to remain seated, and looked his batman in the eye.

Richard nodded. Once.

Sergeant Villiers stood to attention, saluted, turned on his heel, and departed.

"What was that about, if I may so inquire?"

"Wickham."

As Darcy tasted the smoky peat, he murmured, *"Cry havoc and let slip the dogs of war."*

Charles Bingley stood next to his sister, Louisa, and her husband, Hurst. As the head of the receiving line, he welcomed the four and twenty families, as well as select militia, to the first ball in a decade at Netherfield Park. Torches lined the drive. Chandelier crystals scattered diamonds across walls, furniture, floor, and guests. For some attenders, the opulence was all that mattered as proof of their hosts' willingness—and ability—to spare no expense for the pleasure of their neighbors and guests.

Bingley was in his element. He greeted, exchanged pleasantries, and accepted congratulations. He even backslapped an enthusiastic neighbor. Fashionably clad, he presented a pleasant picture of wealth and affability.

Louisa Hurst was wearing a simple but elegant evening gown. She had eschewed gaudy town finery. Her pearls set against a blood-red silk evening gown allowed all the female guests to praise her taste and fashion choice without rancor. Louisa's earnest graciousness was well received. The women of the neighborhood praised her lack of pretension and marveled at her beauty. Many sensed she would soon be a mother and join their ranks. A very welcome new member, indeed!

Hurst beamed in pride as he overheard the various conversations. His enjoyment increased as his wife, in her delicate condition, glowed like a candle—the light of his life that she was. He had never felt more blessed than at that moment.

Darcy and Fitzwilliam remained in the shadows of the receiving hall. Neither was interested in stealing Bingley and Mrs. Hurst's thunder. Darcy wore a dark evening jacket with a white lawn shirt that was paired with a forest green waistcoat and cravat, a color he infrequently wore; it had been thrust upon him by Barty who had entertained NO dissent or alternatives. The colonel wore his full-dress uniform, his chest festooned with medals and lanyards.

When the Bennets arrived, conversation trailed off and heads turned; the impact of the magnificence of the family in looks had no equal. Many a man stood with his mouth somewhat open, insensible to the ridiculous picture he presented. Thomas would have had a marvelous time commenting on the absurdity of his vacuous neighbors but kept losing his train of thought, so enamored was he of his wife's unmatched appearance.

Franny Bennet appeared in a flowing, long, gold, ball gown with an ivory, spider-web-thin overlay draping the skirt bottom. Her elegant arms, from fingers to mid-biceps, were adorned in matching, bone-white, silk gloves. Her golden tresses, with a few hints of silver, were piled high on her head, supported by a perfect neck. She showed few of her forty-one years.

Jane and Kitty's resemblance to Franny was uncanny; they could forgive anyone who approached them from behind for mistaking the girls for their mother. The only difference among the three of them was their height, with Jane being the tallest, followed by Kitty. Mrs. Bennet matched Lizzy in height, but this evening, Elizabeth Bennet was the evening's diamond.

She floated through the entry hall in a forest-green ball gown, and a reverse teardrop-cut bosom was laced with gossamer-thin black threading throughout. Lighter green panels sewn into the bodice sides enhanced her lithe figure. Around her neck hung her prized garnet-studded locket, a gift from her father at her coming out. Her sisters had twisted her dark chestnut hair into an intricate bun atop her head, teasing a few tendrils to float about her temples. Garnet-encrusted hair combs complemented her coiffure. The candlelight reflected off the comb's gemstones and set the hazel flecks in her dusky-brown eyes ablaze. Men gazed upon her in awe—mouths open, bewitched.

Mr. Bennet followed his ladies through the receiving line. An animated Mrs. Hurst welcomed them. Bingley, awestruck, greeted none, staring at the Bennet harem like an Ottoman eunuch. Entertained, Hurst and Bennet chuckled together until some other guests behind them started clearing their throats. The Bennets moved into the main hall where Darcy and Fitzwilliam intercepted them.

Thomas went on the attack. He gestured at Richard's formal wear. "Nice fripperies, Commander."

Bennet had received a private note from Richard regarding his future investiture; Fitzwilliam had been concerned about the gentleman's reaction. Richard had been quite pleased to receive a return note lauding the well-deserved honor. Along with the note had been a girl's play doll, quite aged. He guessed it had belonged to his Miss Kitty. It arrived affixed with a piece of lace on its chest, a coin at the end of the ribbon.

"The dull pray, the geniuses are light mockers," was the message pinned to the doll.

Richard had enjoyed the riposte immensely.

Darcy bowed and stuttered his inquiry of Miss Elizabeth's opinion of the music and dancing arrangements planned for the evening. He knew he was failing in his attempt to hide his disappointment at not having secured a set with her previously. How could he not face disappointment? She completely distracted him!

"Mr. Darcy, might we discuss this later in the evening as you have already claimed my supper set."

Darcy's eyes widened, and he allowed a smile to grace his lips. "Have I? Yes, yes…I…I have."

"I am quite taken with your waistcoat, sir. It is an uncommon color, yet it seems suspiciously familiar. Is it Providence or coincidence?" she asked, her eyes sparkling.

Neither knew of the many messages by Barty and Mrs. Hill that flew between the estates, ensuring the color coordination of their principal's ensembles. The stable boy quite enjoyed himself, accepting sweet rewards from the inquisitive kitchen staff of both estates, whom he kept informed of the goings-on. Everyone within the village limits now cheered for the match.

Surprised, Darcy blurted, "Barty entertained no alternatives to my accessories."

"Barty?"

"Yes, my valet, Bartholomew."

Lizzy burst out laughing, her eyes sparkling with good humor. "You shortened your valet's surname? He has a diminutive? How utterly... utterly...*plebeian* of you!"

Darcy raised his eyebrows. Miss Elizabeth's head tilted, and her eyes softened as she smiled. They both gave in to shared laughter.

The musicians began tuning their instruments. Couples and families headed into the ballroom. Bingley mounted a small platform to a fanfare by the orchestra. The crowd hushed. He thanked the community for their gracious welcome, reached for the wineglass on a tray held by a gloved footman, lifted it, and toasted Louisa for all her labors in arranging what he stated would be a "jolly good time!"

The guests applauded, a few *huzzahs* for the hostess were called, and the couples for the first dance stepped to the line. As was their custom, the Bennets did not join in.

Standing amongst the spectators, Darcy watched Miss Elizabeth dance the second and following sets with other men. When he was not dancing, he acknowledged others as he saw them and spent a few moments conversing with everyone. He felt accepted by a community asking nothing of him. His mother's voice again brushed his mentality. He closed his eyes to send his love into the ether.

The fifth set ended. Darcy, having danced with the eldest Long daughter, escorted her to her mother and exchanged pleasantries. Mrs. Long was visibly pleased with his kind words. His duty completed, Darcy signaled to his cousin. He walked with Richard to where the

Bennets had clustered and offered his hand to his partner.

Darcy escorted Elizabeth to the line.

The music began, and the pair came together, face to face. Lizzy's senses picked up a hint of lemon and a touch of sandalwood. Her focus wavered a bit. *Oh my, what is this headiness?*

Mr. Darcy was staring at her. "Might I inquire of your pleasure, madam?"

"I adore a Boulanger. Is it a favorite of yours, sir?"

"Yes, I must say, it is. Now. It is now."

Elizabeth almost lost her step. She giggled.

"How utterly *cultured* of you, sir."

Darcy paled but held her gaze. "You must allow me to make amends for that dreadful display upon our first introduction."

They separated and then returned to each other.

"Mr. Darcy, you must learn some of my philosophy."

"I must?"

"Yes, you must."

"Pray, continue."

Dimples again? Oh, my!

"Thank you. You must think only of the past as its remembrance gives you pleasure."

Darcy blinked. He was lost. He had been for some time now, fixed in the middle, not knowing when it had begun. His resistance to love—to his of Elizabeth—was futile.

A door to his psyche opened. His mother whispered to him, obliterating his primal loss—that which he had laid bare atop Oakham Mount.

"I shall always be with you."

The dance forms separated them again. His feet recalled the moves, freeing his mind to focus on *her*. His mother's voice again echoed through his mind's corridors. As comforting as a cooling breeze, her words wafted across his consciousness, clear as the summer day when she first spoke of it to him.

"You must do as your father did and marry only for the most passionate love."

Darcy did not hesitate. When he met Elizabeth in the center from a turnabout, he confessed. "You speak of remembrance, of recalling only that which brings us pleasure. By that scale, I am blessed. I have remembered…nay, savored…every moment since our introduction. None, except my ungentlemanly behavior—which I hold onto as a mark of what I must avoid—have been forgotten."

Miss Elizabeth gazed at him, her lips parted, her eyes wide. Darcy stared back. His heart expanded. He sucked his top lip through his teeth and bit it. *Does fortune favor the bold?*

The pair continued dancing in silence and traded furtive looks. Their body language exposed their new unspoken understanding to any with eyes to see.

Franny looked to Thomas, whose eyebrows reached toward his hairline. Kitty, ever aware of the gestures and emotions of those she observed, clasped her hands over her heart, her lashes bejeweled at her sister's future happiness. Jane steepled her fingers and whispered to herself.

"Thank you, Lord…finally, it is done."

The set ended. Elizabeth fell deep into the dark pools of Darcy's eyes. Her hands applauded the musicians without thought.

He stares ardently at me…ardently! I see it now. How blind I have been.

His soft baritone broke through her reverie. "Miss Elizabeth, may I…might I have a private word with you on the terrace?"

Her eyes misted, so she blinked. Her hand raised to fan herself; it fluttered on its ascent. She could not trust her throat to correctly form the words. She nodded.

She put her already raised hand on his offered arm.

The terrace doors were blocked open by a pair of potted plants. Darcy led Elizabeth to the railing. If there had been a vista to enjoy, he would have failed to notice. His focus was solely on the vision lightly touching his forearm. He turned to face her.

"Miss Elizabeth…" Darcy stopped talking as a quartet of fingers graced his lips.

"Allow me a moment, sir."

Darcy nodded lightly, fighting every impulse to taste the tips of her digits.

Lizzy closed her eyes; she cleared her mind. Images of Mr. Darcy flashed across her memory. She studied each of his facial expressions. Discarding the disdain that had colored her previous opinions, she focused on his features with her initial impression of him—the most handsome man of her acquaintance. Inhaling deeply, her senses once again filled with his presence. Lemon, sandalwood, and something she could not name but desired more of. Yes, desire! And with that, Miss Elizabeth Bennet knew she was in love. She freed her heart and looked up. She opened her eyes and with a tender smile, gave permission to the man in front of her to proceed. To his credit, he did.

Darcy once again indulged himself by staring at his forever love. Yes. Forever. He watched her features change. Insecurity moved into a soft question. A soft question slid into a relaxed mien. A relaxed mien brought on a raised eyebrow. Darcy held himself firm although the urge to kiss her brow was nearly overwhelming. Her eyebrow lowered and she inhaled. Deeply. Her lips formed a loving, tender smile, and Darcy knew only then his everlasting soul would be paired in comfort, companionship, and…a quick hitched breath… love. He fought to keep from weeping from relief. He promised himself to honor and cherish this gift—this unique woman—the Lord had bestowed upon him. He grasped her fingers when she opened her eyes.

He lowered himself to a knee. He kissed her hand. Looked up slightly. She smiled and nodded.

"Miss Elizabeth, I beg you to allow me to ask for your hand."

An uplifted eyebrow warned Darcy he was to be teased. "Only my hand, sir? Such an acceptance would bring hardship upon us both." She giggled.

Darcy smiled. *What I would not do for this woman!*

"And if I were to offer my heart? In exchange for your hand?"

Elizabeth's eyes filled. "Yes, Mr. Darcy. But not my hand." She cupped his cheek with her free one. "I could, and would, only accept your heart in equal trade."

"May I be so bold as to suppose your heart is as engaged as is mine?"

"You may."

"May I declare my love for you. All of you."

"You may."

"May I..."

Darcy stopped speaking as her mouth covered his, but briefly. Darcy blinked. He stood.

"Mr. Darcy, had I known a proposal from you would have fractured your silent veneer, I may have urged such from you weeks ago. She smiled.

"Darcy," he replied.

"Darcy?"

"We are betrothed. I am Darcy to you. Today, tomorrow, and forevermore."

Lizzy nodded. She looked up into the dark, beautiful eyes of the man with whom she had chosen to spend eternity. Enough words had been exchanged. They were bound. By their hearts. By their souls. They were bound. Sighing, she concluded the proposal for him.

"I love you, Darcy," she whispered.

Richard, standing beside his Miss Kitty, excused himself. He signaled to her father for a private word. Bennet squeezed his wife's arm and followed the colonel to a secluded corner.

"Bennet, I have received a reply from the countess to my letter."

"Have you now?"

"I have, sir."

"And what, may I inquire, compels you to inform *me* of this familial correspondence, hmm?"

Bennet seemed to enjoy himself with their dialogue. Richard played along.

"The countess plans to inform *Mrs.* Bennet personally."

Richard smiled as Mr. Bennet's eyebrows lifted. *Yes, Captain, the earldom is coming to Hertfordshire.*

"To what degree is your petition for my Catherine, young man?"

"Sir, with your blessing, I intend to petition for her hand in marriage."

"So soon, young man?"

"Her ladyship intends to be the first to personally welcome the future viscountess into the Fitzwilliam family."

Bennet offered his hand. Richard gratefully gripped it. Richard attended to his future father who covered a few "paternal matters," now resigned to the inevitable loss of his youngest daughter. Neither saw Mrs. Bennet grip Kitty's hand tightly as she tried to divert the young lady from lip-reading the tête-à-tête between the men. She failed happily. Her youngest treasure glowed in the anticipation of her future happiness.

Earlier that evening,
The _______shire militia encampment

George Wickham sat in his tent surrounded by his compatriots in crime: Lieutenants Denny, Sanderson, and Carsen. Four sullen failures who sought lives of ease at someone else's expense. Wickham's glib tongue had convinced them of his tales of persecution and outright thievery by the high and mighty Fitzwilliam Darcy of Pemberley. They lamented their social isolation in this rural backwater. This, they learned, had come at the hands of Mr. Bennet, who had taken his role as a leading landowner seriously. His warnings had slammed the twenty-four doors of the Meryton families in their faces. Their pique and privation did not end there.

Credit from merchants and tavern keepers ceased overnight. Colonel Forster had demanded all accounts be called in by the village merchants. He informed the camp that the ______shire reputation would be maintained. Outstanding debts to the populace must be paid promptly. Those in violation would be flogged—private soldiers and officers alike. Publicly. Carsen thought the Bennet squire had petitioned their commander as he had seen the Longbourn master with Forster earlier that day. Denny and Sanderson agreed. Wickham supported Carsen's supposition; he suspected the Longbourn estate yielded more income than rumored as the Miss Bennets were escorted by well-trained, aggressive footmen. The liveried giants had prevented even a cursory introduction.

Compromising the ladies would not yield the riches they desired, despite the momentary pleasures of the flesh. Wickham, as the ringleader, convinced them all to follow the plan. They were caught between a rock and a hard place—a flogging for debts they could not repay, or the hangman's noose when eventually they were apprehended for deserting their posts to avoid punishment. Ransoming the youngest Bennet equaled a future of leisure at the expense of her suitor—the wealthiest man any of them had ever known. The steward's son swayed the doubts of his gang by bragging that Darcy Senior had never failed to cover his debts throughout his university years. Denny had confirmed some of Wickham's arrears being paid with Darcy bank drafts. Wickham added that Darcy had given him £3,000 simply to make him vanish from Derbyshire.

Mrs. Younge, Wickham's ongoing paramour, waited in London

with a room in her brothel prepared for their victim. Wickham had made good coin dropping hapless shop girls into her hands before selling them to the purple-stained man.

Wickham's plan was straightforward. Denny had a carriage waiting on the Meryton road. Sanderson had reserved horses at the livery and would ride them to the carriage once they secured their hostage. An abandoned coach would gather little interest; one with horses would attract nosy neighbors.

Carsen had already hidden a rolled carpet near Netherfield Park's servant's entrance. He would grab Kitty Bennet, as his was the only face Wickham was confident their victim had never seen. The lieutenant would dose the silent girl with laudanum and wine.

Wickham forced them all to vow to avoid drink and then sent them on their way. Carsen hung back in an appeal for reassurance. Those promises made, Wickham settled back to count the hours that would lead to his reward.

Chapter 56

Longbourn, November 27, 1812

Contrary to their practice after a night out, the Bennet family had arisen early to await the Gardiners' arrival. They were surprised when an elegant coach and four pulled to a stop in front of the portico. A polished crest reflected sunlight in all directions. Four outriders stationed themselves in the oaks lining the drive. Noticeable, too, were the footmen on the rear steps. They were large men and they, along with the coachman, were armed.

Reeves, Kale, and Ron walked out the front door and stood behind the family.

"The Gardiners didna' come alone, Captain."

"No Reeves, they certainly did not."

One footman stepped down and opened the carriage door. He reached in and handed out a most familiar face: Mrs. Sutton! Following the botany master were Madeleine and Edward Gardiner. The trio walked to the Bennets, wearing large smiles.

Greetings were exchanged and the crowd entered the house. The ever-efficient Mrs. Hill showed the guests to their rooms to remove the road's dust and prepare for dinner.

Conversation around the table was robust. Thomas sat back and listened to the happiness in the voices and felt the energy of the myriad gestures from the conversant. He did not fail to see surreptitious signals passed between Mrs. Sutton and his sister Gardiner.

At the meal's end, Franny stood. "Ladies, let us retire to the parlor. As we are all family, let us forgo tonight's separation. Gentlemen?"

Bennet looked at Gardiner who shrugged and nodded. They followed everyone into the parlor, and Hill closed the doors behind them.

Franny gestured toward Maddy, who cleared her throat. "Ladies, I am not consciously excluding the two gentlemen in the room. However, they do know what I am about to discuss. Our family's future will change most extraordinarily and rather quickly."

She targeted Lizzy with a look that silenced the inquisitive young lady. "I am not referring to the quite satisfactory matches you have made, my dears."

She looked at Jane and smiled apologetically. "I am well, Aunt. My sisters know that I am elated for them."

Lizzy's curiosity would not be quelled. "To what do you refer, Aunt Maddy?"

"For that answer, Lizzy, I must tell all of you a story if you will hear me out. Will you?"

Three heads nodded.

"You three know I am Madeleine Gardiner née Lambert?"

Three heads nodded again.

"What you do not know is that my mother was a Langston. By her marriage, I am related to the Fitzwilliam family of Matlock. This connection makes me distantly related to the Manners-Suttons and the Cavendish family."

The girls looked to their father who was staring down at his shoes.

They turned to their mother, who wore a look of accepting sadness.

Thea Sutton filled the silence. "Before my marriage, I was Theodosia Cavendish. I did intimate this connection during my little theatrical with your cousin's patroness. You know me as Mrs. Sutton. Forgive me my little subterfuge—a sin of omission. I am Lady Theodosia Cavendish Manners-Sutton."

Jane, her mouth covered by her hand, let out a whimper. "A Cavendish of Devonshire, Mrs. Sutton?"

"Yes, Jane, my father was the marquess but died before he could succeed my grandfather as duke."

"The archbishop of Canterbury is a Manners-Sutton, is he not?"

"Yes. He is my cousin Charles as I alluded to you previously."

"You…you…have royal connections!"

"My dear, as the Bard wrote, *'all the world's a stage, and all the men and women merely players. They have their exits and their entrances; and one man, or woman, in their time plays many parts.'*"

Jane's pique was evident. "Mrs. Sutton, or should I say, Lady Theodosia, no legacy… *'No legacy is so rich as honesty.'*"

Aunt Gardiner leapt to the defense of her protector. "Jane, that is quite enough!"

Thea poured oil on the troubled waters. "Maddy, allow her to vent her spleen. She, more than anyone else, has earned that right."

Jane turned her face into Mrs. Sutton's shoulder. "Please forgive me."

"Without a moment's hesitation, Jane dearest."

Madeleine Gardiner waited a few moments for tempers to cool. "I see I have shocked you. I was surprised to learn of these connections, but I cannot deny the hand of Providence in it. We are family in any number of ways now and even more with Kitty's and Lizzy's pending nuptials."

She paused, then continued. "When I was eight years old, I took an early carriage trip together with my mother and father."

Madeleine looked at Thomas.

"Please, do not," he asked softly, his lips trembling. "I beg you." His eyes began to fill.

"Papa!" cried two Bennet daughters, the third sat silent but understood the drama unfolding before her eyes. All three rose as one and rushed over to hug him fiercely. They remained in that posture until he patted their arms.

"Please do not resent me. I could bear anything but that."

Jane, Lizzy, and Kitty looked around frantically, trying to understand.

"Girls, come. Sit with me." Franny Bennet patted the sofa. Her three girls jumped upon her.

A knock on the door and Mrs. Hill brought a tea tray. Hill leaned in and placed a tumbler of brandy at Bennet's elbow. Then he followed his wife from the room.

Once tea had been served, Madeleine continued. "I shall state again"—with a piercing look at her brother Bennet—"that your father saved my life. He may deny it should he choose, but he is not a reliable judge concerning *my* point of view, and *my* perceptions are the ones that matter to *me*."

She took a breath. "A contrived duel led to the murder of my parents. Your father did his best to save my father. He did save me."

"No, that is not true. I failed."

The granddaughter of a duke pushed back. "Mr. Bennet, it is overweening pride to think that the way we see things is everything there is to see."

"Mrs. Sutton, you were not there. I was."

"No, I was not there. What you do not know is that I have the magistrate's journals of the duel and his subsequent investigation."

Thomas looked at Mrs. Sutton with appreciation.

"May I…may I?"

"You may, Mr. Bennet."

"Brother Bennet, as you know, the Reverend Wells cared for me at his parsonage in Flaxby Knares."

"Yes, Maddy, you know I am aware of that."

"Mr. and Mrs. Eriksen of Lambton joined Mr. Wells for a visit. The weather prevented the couple from leaving. They spent the extra night. Thank the good Lord that they remained."

"Why is that?"

"Mr. Wells died that evening of an apoplexy. The Eriksens took me in without reservation. They named me their niece, and that wonderful couple gave me a home, love, and respect."

"I returned to find the parsonage empty. I found Wells's grave. I could find no trace of you."

Madeleine Lambert reached out for Thomas Bennet's hand. "You saved me, Captain Bennet. You cannot escape that, and I will *not* allow you to deny this fact: you, sir, saved me."

Thomas cleared his throat. "Well, I believe I must bow to your superior knowledge, my dear."

Thomas lifted his sister's hand and bussed her knuckles.

Mrs. Gardiner turned toward her nieces. She asked Lizzy to play something calming on the pianoforte, as frayed nerves required soothing. Elizabeth was dazed. To ease herself, she went to the instrument and began playing the first movement of Beethoven's *Moonlight Sonata*, a soft, pleasant recital piece. Kitty remained in her mother's arms, but Jane returned to sit next to her botany instructor. At the composition's conclusion, Lizzy stood and gathered her sisters. Together, they retired for the evening.

Thomas looked at Maddy. "Why now?"

Thea answered his question. "Anne Darcy and I, through Providence, stumbled upon Maddy in Lambton over twenty years ago. Unfortunately, it took years to sort out whether she was Madeleine Lambert, Hugh and Penelope's daughter."

Thomas Bennet nodded his head and offered a one-word summation. "Hurst."

Edward Gardiner nodded. "By the time Mrs. Sutton approached

Maddy again, we were already courting, and Mr. Eriksen relied upon her in the bookstore."

Madeleine's eyes flashed with steel. "How could I leave my adopted uncle, he who gave me the riches of his heart? Who would protect him if I were to pursue the jackals who hovered over my previous life's carcass, greedily stealing a legacy unearned and undeserved?"

Thea added, "With deep reservations, I agreed to Maddy's demand to leave her in peace, to marry her beloved Edward, and to seek reconciliation with the family on her terms. At least we were able to take up her cause and finally recover her legacy."

Mrs. Bennet beamed. "Maddy, dear, we are so happy for you, Edward, and the children. What a bright, happy future you shall have!"

"Thank you, Franny." Maddy took her husband's hand. "We intend to spend much of our time at Tang Hall, my family's estate, upon the completion of repairs to the house. It will require some years before the estate is habitable."

Bennet jumped in. "I am surprised the executors rescinded the inheritance awarded by the Courts of Chancery. They had you declared dead several years ago."

"Yes, Thomas, it could have been quite the hobble."

"Could have been?" parroted Thomas.

"Yes, but for my cousin."

"Which cousin is that, Maddy?" asked Franny.

"Why, my Fitzwilliam cousin, of course."

"I do not understand you, Maddy. To which Fitzwilliam cousin are you referring? The earl?" asked Bennet.

Madeleine Gardiner smiled at Franny Bennet, then Thomas. Her violet eyes opened wide, caught the candlelight, and sparkled like amethysts. "The colonel, Brother Bennet—the colonel went to Yorkshire and came back with my inheritance."

Chapter 57

Longbourn, the gamekeeper's cottage,
November 28, 1812

George Wickham's senses swam through the dissipating fog. His headache, though intense, quickly helped clear his mind. He sniffed the air: lemon and sandalwood. He muttered through dry lips, "Your Highness."

"I see you have come around."

Wickham flexed and twisted his wrists. His fingers touched smooth material. Was he bound by silk stockings? *How ironic!*

He opened his left eye. The pain was not too great. He could see light off to the side. Concentrating, he saw a candle flickering on a windowsill. He tried to peel open his right and winced. The eye did not open well, but a little discomfort would have to be endured. *I must have my wits about me when Darcy offers me my due.*

Wickham focused on the shadowy figure in front of him, clad in black—much more than was fashionable. "I shall have to ask whether your somberness now makes you the first stare."

Wickham had hoped to get a rise out of his nemesis. He failed.

A rooster crowed. Time passed. "What do you want, Darcy?"

"Where is Miss Catherine Bennet?"

Wickham smiled. *Typical Darcy. Straight to the point.* "Just what is your interest in the young lovely? By now, I am sure she has had more than enough training to satisfy you. I was unaware you liked them so young. I knew we had something in common."

Darcy's voice was like a cold wind blowing through the frozen Peak District. "We are nothing alike."

Wickham knew when not to push. "What is your interest, Darcy?"

"You already know, Wickham."

Wickham laughed. "How will you settle with your conscience when the ruin of the Bennet family is widespread? Tell me that, your Highness? How?"

"Where is she, Wickham?"

"Darcy, I shall only tell you if you answer my questions. What is your interest in her? Do you need her to be recovered so you can set up your carte blanche?"

That would get him in a lather. His reputation for taking the moral high ground was legendary.

Darcy stood and walked off. He lit another taper. More light spread deeper into the room's corners.

Wickham looked around. *Hmm, a hunting cabin. No fire ablaze in the hearth, but some embers must remain because it is not too cold. Darcy's question means Carsen must have gotten the job done, and that will mean my freedom!*

Darcy sat back down in the chair and wrapped himself in his cloak of silence. He seemed perturbed—but about what? *Not getting his way, most likely.*

Time passed anon. Wickham thought of the great clock in the Pemberley foyer. It would *tick-tock* as you stood there waiting for your coat, hat, and gloves to be brought to you. Funny what popped into one's head when one was restrained.

"Darcy, expect nothing from me until you appreciate our mutual position. Release my hands so we can find a way to a compromise."

Wickham looked Darcy in the eyes as he said this. He looked for disdain, anger, anything. What he saw surprised him. Fear? Was that fear?

"Wickham, tell me where we can find her."

His voice was full of remorse. Even though Wickham was bound before him, Darcy did not display his traditional arrogance at having the upper hand. Something had frightened him—changed him. This was a different Darcy. And who was we?

"No, my former schoolmate. Meet my minimum terms or you will get nothing."

Wickham smiled. He knew he had his Highness right where he wanted him. Darcy was desperate for the girl. Wickham had heard the talk. Who did not know of his cutting remark at the assembly? *I bet governesses were using the threat of dancing with him to keep their charges in line!* Yes, George Wickham had the great Fitzwilliam Darcy on his knees.

Darcy stood. "I gave you your chance. This much they allowed me. But you brought what comes next upon yourself, Wickham. You cannot know what you have done, who you have pushed beyond the pale. May the Lord have mercy upon you."

"Wait, wait. What are you—?"

Darcy walked out the door without looking back. Wickham was confused. Darcy never walked away. A bit of déjà vu trickled into his consciousness—the smell of hay, a recollection of fear and pain.

A shadow inched its way through the doorway. Someone was coming. Darcy must be coming back. Of course! Walking away was just a negotiating tactic. *His Highness has added to his arsenal!*

Darcy, though, did not reappear. A long-armed man wearing a cavalry sergeant's uniform did.

Darcy turned his body sideways to allow Sergeant Villiers to pass. Shaking his head, he turned the corner and joined Richard, Hurst, and Bennet at the open window. The sounds of heavy slapping made him wince. He closed his eyes to block out Wickham's subsequent cries of pain.

"Enough, enough, bloody hell!" The whining trailed off. "Who are you? What do you want?"

"Ye've been a naughty un, 'ave ye na', Georgie."

"Who sent you?"

"Tell me wha' I wishes t' know, and we ken all go our sep'rate ways."

"I never thought Darcy would hire out to the Seven Dials. My, how the high and mighty have fallen."

Darcy turned to his cousin. Richard's eyes were black and dead.

"You will wish 'twas th' guv'ner, if'n ya' duz naw't gi' me me answers."

"Everything has its price, my good man. What is this information worth to you?"

"Georgie, ye seems t' be mist'k'n 'bout sump'in'. We be na' payin'—we be takin'."

"That which has value will not be issued without due recompense."

Both Bennet and Hurst shook their heads. Richard's lips tugged upward, and Darcy recognized his cousin's feral smile. Wickham's final hours were nigh.

"My father," hissed Darcy.

Richard acknowledged his demand.

The rhythmic repeated sounds of flesh being forcibly struck, interspersed with a few grunts, turned all but one head toward the open window.

Richard Fitzwilliam walked through the cabin door. He stopped, stood still, and inhaled. The air was redolent of past missions on the Continent—dust, dampness, dung—and the most pungent aroma of all: fear. In the center of the small room was his man, tied to a chair.

The colonel motioned with his chin. Villiers walked to the other side of the room, grabbed a small table, and pulled it adjacent to the prisoner. From a knapsack, he removed a thick cylinder of wool tweed. With a flourish, he snapped it open and unrolled it, clattering, upon the tabletop. The candlelight reflected off the polished surfaces of what some would recognize as surgical instruments. Mr. Burton would have utilized these tools for amputating torn limbs after a battle.

The sergeant sidled over to the fireplace, stirred the embers, and dropped in a handful of twigs and a few larger chunks. He placed two iron pokers into the growing blaze, tips down, to heat up in the forge.

Wickham sensed someone in front of him. He was afraid to open his eyes. He had never been subjected to such physical abuse except for the two times he had run afoul of Darcy's scary cousin. The cavalry officer—silent, unspeaking, with coal-black eyes—was Wickham's worst fear. Luckily for him, the continental war still raged, and soldiers died in every battle. Fitzwilliam was probably skewering frogs for Wellington.

Encouraged to push the terror into the background, Wickham opened his eyes and wished he could unsee what he had. Standing before him was his living nightmare and the certainty that he would soon be in pain for a very long time.

Darcy flinched at the sound of a hand slapping wood. A low woof of an exhale followed. A hammer hit a plank. The sound echoed through the grove. Hurst glanced at Bennet, who dropped his chin to his chest. Then the nightmare began.

The early morning sounds of the forest were shattered by screaming. Pitched wails—long and short, breathless and whimpering—continued incessantly.

Darcy covered his ears.

The screams trailed off for a moment, then resumed at a higher pitch in thinner, reedier tones. A minute passed and the screams dwindled to moans. The shallow moans became forced. They then stopped. Silence once again reigned.

Darcy stepped toward the door, but Bennet seized his wrist, looked his future son in the eye, and shook his head. He put a finger to his lips. Darcy's eyes narrowed.

"Your task has ended, son," whispered Thomas Bennet.

Darcy looked again toward the door.

"Do *not*," ordered Captain Bennet in a harsher tone.

Fitzwilliam waited for Wickham to regain consciousness—an unattractive sight as his mouth opened and he sucked in a large, phlegmatic breath. The prisoner began cursing but stopped when he saw his captor's face.

The colonel grabbed a large pair of hoof nippers. He gripped Wickham's little finger and placed it between the razor-sharp jaws.

"No, no, no, no, no, no, no," begged Wickham.

"No, no, no, no, no, no, no."

Darcy covered his mouth with his fist and turned away from the window.

Shrieks rent the air—twice as loud and desperate as before. Over and over, the screams, the wails, and then devolving cries painted a picture of unimaginable pain on the other side of the windowsill.

The smell of burned flesh turned Hurst's face green.

Bennet leaned to Darcy. "Go. Go anywhere. Just go."

The keening tapered off into quiet sobs. Darcy nodded, his face ashen. He agreed with Bennet but could not move his feet.

Then, through the cabin window, came the voice of Azrael. "I am not my cousin."

Darcy ran toward his horse.

"I am not my cousin."

Wickham nodded up and down several times. "One chance. I promised Darcy. One."

Wickham nodded frantically.

"Where is Kitty Bennet?"

Wickham's eyes, bruised as they were, opened as wide as dinner plates.

Fitzwilliam leaned forward and glowered at Wickham. The prisoner recoiled.

"Where is Kitty?"

Wickham's face froze in a rictus of horror. "You?"

"Yes," hissed the Angel of Death.

George Wickham, trembling, closed his eyes, lowered his head, and surrendered to the fact that his Day of Judgment had passed and he had been found wanting.

Chapter 58

"Nine remaining," warned Fitzwilliam.

"Wait, wait, wait, wait."

"Be specific."

George Wickham confessed everything. How Carsen had drugged Kitty Bennet at the ball. How he had smuggled her out of the manor inside a rolled carpet. How Denny delivered her to Mrs. Younge's Edwards Street brothel via an unmarked carriage. How his paramour kept her imprisoned. How he planned to demand ransom from Darcy.

Richard put Wickham's forefinger between the cutting blades.

"I confessed…I confessed everything, everything!"

"Tell me of the Seven Dials."

Wickham's eyes popped wide open. He looked at his mutilated hand. Wickham began babbling and identified the locale of every servant, shop girl, and barmaid from whom he had forced favors. He identified the gaming hells and moneylenders in the Seven Dials to whom he was indebted. He named the patrons he repaid by performing illegal, distasteful acts at their behest. He gave up the locations of the two bordellos that paid him for stolen goods.

"Tell me of George Darcy."

Wickham admitted to shooting at George Darcy. He had to kill him. He had been desperate for money since his debts had stopped being covered by the old man. He had planned to parlay the promised living into a payout by signing away his claim. He had not known his godfather had changed his will and realized it only upon receiving Judas's shekels.

The colonel pulled a dirk from his boot and put the tip to Wickham's right eye. Wickham tried to pull away, but the colonel nicked the lid and drew blood.

Fitzwilliam gave a breath of space between steel and jelly. "Tell me of the fat man with the purple stain."

Wickham described the debt-ridden peer's home in the back of Mayfair. He confirmed it served as a way station for trafficking kidnapped girls into the white-slave trade abroad. He described the fat man with the purple-stained chin and hands—one hand missing the top half of its pinky finger. Fitzwilliam grimaced as the last piece of the puzzle fell into place. He had heard enough.

Wickham, decrepit and barely awake, did not see that the window was open. He did not know that Hurst had recorded his confession. He did not know Thomas Bennet stood outside the window beside Hurst.

Without a doubt, George Wickham would die. Whether he rotted in Bodmin Gaol or succumbed to his wounds, the blackguard would depart this mortal plane sooner rather than later. He had judged himself with his words. Another entity would have to judge his soul.

Georgie Porgie, thought Richard with chagrin. Wickham and his confederates had never stood a chance of success. That their fall was caused by chance—or the gods seeking to right ancient wrongs—mattered little.

A month ago, Richard had joined the__________shire militia

commander, Colonel Robert Forster, another wounded peninsula campaigner, for dinner. It was a coincidence, or Providence, that the two veteran officers traded half-drunk stories of their rambunctious youth. Forster asked about the infamous fight at Figg's Amphitheatre; Richard, as a preface, related the Rose & Crown mêlée to his militia counterpart. He was surprised to see his dining partner's brow crease in consternation upon hearing Wickham's name. Forster's expression chased away all whiskey fumes and set alarm bells clanging. The following morning, Forster arranged for his colleague to confirm the ne'er-do-well's identity during scheduled practice drills from an obscured location.

"How blessed are we, the saints?" Richard murmured when the signed enlistment contract with George Wickham's name was delivered to him via militia courier. From that moment, Colonel Forster had kept him under watch. Richard received daily updates of Wickham's actions and his confederates. Villiers reported Wickham's interest in the Bennet daughters, particularly the youngest. This hardened the colonel's resolve.

Bennet agreed with Richard's plan to insert Lieutenant Carsen, actually a dragoon Captain Carstens, into the fray. A survivor of Badajoz, he owed his life to Richard Fitzwilliam. Carstens took leave when he received Colonel Fitzwilliam's express. He met the other members of the group at a posting inn between Meryton and St. Albans. There, he accepted his brief and assumed his name and new rank. With Forster's blessing, Carstens infiltrated the militia conspiracy. He fell in with Wickham and, subsidized by the Longbourn coffers, played a willing partner.

After the final meeting in Wickham's tent before the ball, Carsen delayed the ringleader's departure. The goal was to isolate him from the others. Sergeant Villiers incapacitated Wickham once he stepped out of his tent. He threw him over a horse and transported him to the Longbourn gamekeeper's cabin. Once they had secured Wickham, it took but an instant to pull from that incompetent wretch, Denny, the full story of how and where he renewed his acquaintance and subsidized Wickham's rank purchase. Sanderson was a disgraceful ruffian, pure and simple. No one would miss him.

Hurst suggested Darcy and the colonel confirm to Wickham that his gang had been successful in kidnapping and transporting Miss Catherine. This would allow them to flush out any unknown participants. Thomas shouted in anger, "*This* is not a silly game!" Hurst flinched in embarrassment. Richard agreed with Bennet, but he did as Hurst suggested.

Colonel Richard Fitzwilliam walked out of the cabin and met with Hurst and Bennet. Plans needed to be completed. Mayfair was but one mission, but not the final stop.

Mayfair, later that same day

A blood-red door, its paint chipped and filthy, appeared as a murky, morbid monster promising nothing good. Bennet reached out, grasped the door handle, and twisted it clockwise. The door opened with little effort.

The captain walked into a cold, large parlor, dark but for wall sconces. Hurst settled by the doorframe. Colonel Fitzwilliam stalked to a window and threw back the curtains. The room came into focus.

In an overly large sedan chair sat an obese man, his hands and neck showing claret-colored stains. His bare feet soaked in a large, shallow pail. His dressing gown hung agape. His eyes narrowed as they opened. "Close the curtains and get out!"

"I think not, Sir Lewis," replied Hurst.

The obese man raised his head. "Sir Lewis de Bourgh is dead."

Captain Bennet took two long steps, put his pistol barrel against the man's head, and pulled the trigger.

"Indeed, he is." Captain Bennet closed his eyes and murmured a short prayer.

Hurst broke his reverie. "I believe our search is complete."

Captain Bennet nodded.

"What about the body?"

"Hurst, you know as well as I, that one cannot kill that which is already dead."

Hurst followed Captain Bennet out of the room.

Colonel Fitzwilliam closed the window curtains and exited the room. Bennet and Hurst may have finished; he had not.

Chapter 59

Rosings Park, November 29, 1812

The lone rider brought his mount to a halt. He dismounted, walked up the steps, and pounded on the great door. His long arms were battering rams, making solid purchase with each impact.

The door cracked open; a withered face appeared, half-obscured by the edifice.

"Who are you to disturb this great house on the Lord's Day?"

Sergeant Villiers ignored the yelp of pain from the other side of the door as the barrier slammed into the uncooperative man's face, the result of a forceful kick. He stepped inside, closed the door, and assisted the injured man to the near staircase where he settled him on the second step. He returned to the entrance, removed a crowbar from his knapsack, and pried off the locks and bars. Both doors now hung open. He found a chair and waited. The outside air carried the sounds of a convoy approaching.

Sergeant Villiers was not a religious man. For over twenty years, he had followed his commander through hell and back on every type of battlefield one could imagine. The Lord would forgive them this Sabbath, he mused to himself.

Riders, followed by carriages—a veritable serpent of goodwill—threaded their way off the carriage road and through Rosings Park's estate grounds. Leading the convoy was the colonel atop Perseus.

Immediately behind him, two coaches were followed by four riders. The remaining train of equipment, a huge dust cloud behind settling, stopped on the curved drive.

"Secure the doors."

Cavalrymen and outriders dismounted. They all pulled pistols from their belts.

"Hurt no one."

The outriders looked at each other, turned to Bill, and handed him their pistols.

"Colonel, a footman needs care," shouted Villiers.

The colonel turned in his saddle and raised a hand. Mr. Dolan poked his head out of the first carriage window and waved to the carriage behind. The door of the following carriage opened, and Mr. Burton descended, his medical satchel in hand. He walked to Sergeant Villiers with an eyebrow cocked.

"He would not open the door, sir."

Mr. Burton smiled. "Indeed."

Once his men had secured the first floor, Richard went in search of an upstairs maid. In the first bedroom, he searched and found one cowering in a wardrobe. Whimpering from within the chiffonier gave up the location of its occupant. He opened the door.

"Dun kill me! Please dun kill me!"

"Fear not." He raised both hands as a sign of surrender. "I give my word."

Richard grabbed a chair, put it in front of the wardrobe door, and sat.

"What is your name?"

"Harriet, sir."

"Harriet, take me to Miss de Bourgh."

"Oh, sir, I kinna do that."

"Why ever not?"

"The Great Lady forbids visitors."

Richard smiled. This was so much more pleasant than Yorkshire.

"I am not a visitor, Harriet."

"Oh, well...yer 'oo, sir?"

"I am the Earl of Matlock's son."

Harriet burst out of the wardrobe and stood in front of Richard, her arms lifting and falling, repeatedly.

"Yer 'ere to save Miss Anne?"

"Does Miss Anne need to be saved?"

The girl wrung her hands. "Oh, sir...we all feel for Miss Anne."

Richard paused until Harriet looked directly at him.

"Why do we not pay Miss Anne a visit?"

"Yes, sir. Foller me."

Bill followed Mr. Burton, who followed Richard, who followed Harriet up a third set of stairs. They came to a lone door. A young footman in livery blocked the way.

"Miss de Bourgh resides in the attics?" asked the surgeon.

"Harriet, why er yer 'ere?" asked the footman.

"Jimmy, these be Miss Anne's people."

"The Great Lady says no visitors."

Harriet stepped closer, stood up on her toes, and whispered. "Jimmy, he be the earl's son."

Jimmy looked shocked. His mouth hung open. Shaking his head, he narrowed his eyes. He crossed his arms, spread his feet shoulder-width apart, and frowned.

"The Great Lady says no visitors!"

Mr. Burton looked at the colonel who was smiling.

"Enjoying yourself?" asked the surgeon.

"Very much." The colonel laughed.

"Who in this kingdom would have ever imagined the legendary Colonel Fitzwilliam's greatest obstacle would be a repetitious, untried, youthful footman?"

Jimmy gasped. "Ye…ye…ye be *him*? Truly?"

"He be 'im," growled Bill. Jimmy fainted.

Mr. Burton frowned and shook his head.

"What vexes you now?" asked Richard.

"Now I shall never know which carried the day: your reputation or Bill's soliloquy."

Richard's head rose through the garret floor opening as he climbed the stairs. He adroitly threw up his arm to deflect a bed-warming pan. Two more steps and he was face to face with a lady of advanced years. She still held her weapon of choice.

"Madam, please desist."

"Who are you?"

"Who are *you?*"

"I am Mrs. Jenkinson, Miss de Bourgh's companion."

"I am Miss de Bourgh's cousin, son of the Earl of Matlock."

Mrs. Jenkinson dropped her weapon. Her left hand went to her heart as her right hand covered her mouth.

"Are you here to save my sweet girl?"

"I am."

Her left hand joined her right, and she began to cry. "I prayed and prayed, always to deaf ears. I shall never lose faith again!"

Richard walked over and sat next to his cousin who lay sleeping in a rather small bed.

"Mrs. Jenkinson, go downstairs and ask for Mr. Burton."

"Is he a physician?"

"Better."

Mrs. Jenkinson approached the stairs. As she descended, her voice trailed off.

"Another prayer answered..."

The Rosings Park servants filled the great room. They whispered amongst themselves as they waited for news. Mr. Dolan entered, stood in front of the room, and cleared his throat. The murmurings quieted.

"My name is Dolan. I am the Earl of Matlock's man of business. I am here to direct the transition of Rosings Park to the heir."

The multitude of servants wore shocked expressions. No one spoke. The silence was then broken in a most irritating manner. A nasal voice, pitched high, screamed in indignation. "No one trespasses upon the rights of my patroness!"

A parson, if his crow-like garb was any indication, pushed through the crowd. His blackened eyes and distorted nose suggested that this man of God had been involved in some less-than-godlike activities.

"No! No, I tell you! Lady Catherine is the mistress of Rosings Park. Miss de Bourgh is the betrothed of her nephew, Mr. Fitzwilliam Darcy of Pemberley, and their nuptials will join two great houses in the kingdom, an event—"

The rector emitted a shriek as he was lifted a foot in the air. Sergeant Villiers had his left side, and his right was firmly in Bill's grasp. They carried him off, his cries echoing until the doors closed. Across the room, another set of doors opened.

Mrs. Jenkinson and Mr. Burton assisted a smiling Anne de Bourgh into the room. They led her to the Great Chair. She sat, which produced a gasp from the congregating servants. The gasps ceased instantly when the earl's son, clad in his regimentals, entered the room.

Whispers raced through the throng unchecked.

"It be him."

"The Hero of Badajoz."

"No, he be the next earl."

"The viscount he be."

Richard sat next to Anne. She peered up at him. "Are you here to take me to marry my cousin?"

"No."

"Who are you?"

"I am your cousin."

"Which cousin?"

"I am your Fitzwilliam cousin."

"Oh," pouted Anne. "You refused to marry me."

"That was my brother, Langston."

"Who are you?"

"I am Richard."

Anne's face took on a frown, which then dissipated in understanding. "Ah, the spare."

Richard chuckled. "Yes, the spare."

"My mother says you are cannon fodder."

Richard laughed. "That I am."

"I will *not* marry you."

"I accept your terms."

Anne looked around. "Why are you here?"

Richard held out his hand, palm up. Anne gave him hers. "Cousin, I am here to take you to Matlock House."

Anne exhaled. A beatific smile graced her face. "Uncle Henry? Aunt Audrey?"

"Yes."

"Thank you, Cousin Richard. But be assured, I will *not* marry you."

"Cousin Anne, you are the mistress of Rosings Park. You may do as you please."

Chapter 60

Longbourn, two days later

"Mr. Fitzwilliam Darcy."

The ladies rose in unison, faced their guest, and curtsied together. Darcy bowed, a smile on his face.

"Mr. Darcy, I know you rise early, and your morning meal may be several hours old. May we interest you in a light repast?"

"Thank you, Mrs. Bennet. I appreciate your kindness."

Elizabeth smiled at her handsome betrothed. He was much improved in his social skills.

"Will you sit with us, Mr. Darcy?"

"Thank you, Miss Bennet. I shall do just that."

Darcy went to the settee upon which his lady sat. "May I join you, Miss Elizabeth?"

"Yes, Mr. Darcy. You may."

Nearby giggling drew her attention. "Mother, Kitty: I would expect better manners from you in front of our guest." She then covered her face and laughed. "I cannot do this, Darcy. We must have a conversation."

"Must we?"

"We must."

Elizabeth's smile widened to match his expression.

Mrs. Hill entered the parlor with a tea tray laden with Darcy's favorite treats. Mrs. Bennet poured for everyone.

As her father and his cousin were away on business, Elizabeth was sure Darcy had come for more than a visit and tea—although if that had been his purpose, she would have been satisfied.

Darcy cleared his throat. "Mrs. Bennet, I have a letter from my cousin."

Kitty sat up straight, her eyes wide with hope.

Mrs. Bennet laid a calming hand on her daughter's arm. "Well, if the colonel has relayed word of Mr. Bennet, we would be pleased to hear you."

Darcy nodded. "The letter contains several messages, Mrs. Bennet. The first is from Mr. Bennet."

Kitty signed, and Elizabeth translated. "Several?"

"Yes, several. Miss Catherine, the colonel has written, and with Mrs. Bennet's permission, I shall read it."

Kitty looked to her mother, who smiled and nodded. "Very well."

Darcy cleared his throat. "Cousin, by the time you read this letter, we shall have completed our business and shall be on our return to Meryton."

Darcy mumbled through a few sentences, looked up, and apologized. "My cousin's handwriting can rival Bingley's. I needed to translate before I could relate this next passage.

"Please inform Mrs. Bennet that her husband is well and will return ahead of me in a Matlock coach. He suffers nothing more than the fatigue of herding younger, more energetic men prepared to act before evaluating. A burden we shall all, in the future, hopefully bear ourselves."

Darcy looked up and smiled at Mrs. Bennet, who returned his. "Such a dear man, Mr. Bennet."

"Quite, madam."

Darcy returned to the letter, read a few more lines, and blushed down to his collar.

"Darcy?"

"Yes, dearest?"

"Ooh, I believe I can become accustomed to such an address rather quickly."

The Longbourn ladies giggled.

"What has you in such a lather?" queried his future wife.

Darcy cleared his throat and glanced at Mrs. Bennet. His face wore a puppy-dog look.

"Come now, Mr. Darcy, can it be so embarrassing? It is the colonel, after all."

"Quite."

Darcy looked at Lizzy, who tilted her head, the hereditary Bennet eyebrow raised.

Darcy cleared his throat. "My dear…"

Lizzy rolled her eyes. "Darcy, get on with it."

"Of course."

Another throat clearing. "My dear Kitty, please do not let my delay in returning give you angst. I must complete one more task so that I may return, hopeful for us never to be parted again."

Mrs. Bennet, Jane, and Elizabeth sighed. Kitty's eyes misted.

"Does the colonel always write such short and charming letters, Mr. Darcy?" asked Mrs. Bennet.

Darcy blinked. It would be rude to stare at Mrs. Bennet. Hearing his Elizabeth laugh, he realized his goddess was blessed with wit from both of his soon-to-be parents. *Well, two can play at that game!*

"Will you give me leave to defer your raptures 'til I see my cousin again? At present we have not his presence to do them justice."

In the kitchen, Reeves and the Hills smiled amongst themselves as laughter burst from the parlor.

Meryton, a se'nnight later

Colonel Fitzwilliam pulled up on his reins at the fork in the road. Sergeant Villiers did the same.

"Déjà vu, mon colonel."[19]

"Tu connais ton chemin."[20]

"Yes, sir."

Sergeant Villiers rode off down the road that forked left.

Richard rode right and arrived at Longbourn's door.

"Lord Hopton, your guests *all* await you at Netherfield."

"Thank you, Hill." Richard turned to remount. He stopped when a throat cleared.

"Your lordship, may we offer a brief refreshment before you encounter your…*party?*"

Richard smiled. He was sure Hill winked at him.

"Thank you again, Hill. Well met."

An hour and a half later, Richard left Perseus with Tim and entered the estate through the kitchen. The Netherfield parlor doors were open; conversations overflowed into the hall.

He stood in silence in the open doorway. To his left, sitting on a large sofa, were the Earl and Countess of Matlock; his mother beamed. Behind them stood Lady Theodosia Cavendish Manners-Sutton. *Welcome back to your estate, your Grace.*

Next to his parents sat Madeleine and Edward Gardiner. The ladies were side-by-side, holding hands. Their resemblance, despite their age difference, was unmistakable.

How nice they look together.

Mr. Burton stood by the fireplace. Bennet was to his left. Both men were quite comfortable in each other's company.

Ah, the surgeon at the duel. How had I not grasped that one?

Hurst stood off to Bennet's right, their gracious hostess, his wife Louisa, next to him.

19 This seems familiar, Colonel.

20 You know your way.

Such a well-matched pair.

The four Bennet ladies sat across from their visitors. They whispered amongst themselves. Darcy stood behind the seated Miss Elizabeth, his right hand protectively on her left shoulder, her elegant left hand covering his. A ring adorned her finger.

Well done, Cousin. She will be the making of you.

Richard's angel sat to Lizzy's right. The colonel stepped into the parlor.

Kitty dropped her journal, flew from the settee, and threw herself into the ready embrace of her beloved. She could not help herself; she nestled into his chest. A brief squeeze from his arms reminded her of her surroundings.

The colonel placed his hands on her shoulders and extended his arms. She understood and took a small step back. As was their custom, she raised her left hand for him to take, which he did, but with his left, which was *not* their custom. Kitty raised an eyebrow. The colonel reached into his topcoat's tail pocket; a ring box emerged. The women gasped, although Lady Matlock's squeal of delight—accompanied by her quiet, rapid, ladylike clapping of her hands—trumped all. The earl smiled at her subdued, "Yes, yes, yes, yes, yes!"

Kitty focused on the lips of her soon-to-be husband, Colonel Richard Fitzwilliam, decorated Peninsular Campaign hero, revered leader of men, strategist nonpareil, and now Viscount Hopton.

Thomas Bennet watched his most artistic daughter step into her future husband's arms and tilt her head to her right shoulder. Her gesture suggested the first time his family had laughed together after losing Mary and Lydia. He recalled the faux warning he had given Kitty and why.

Richard placed his lips upon Kitty's left jaw, perfectly situated, and proclaimed, "My future is you, my Silent Viscountess."

Epilogue

Grosvenor Square, April 1816

The two couples sitting in the parlor at the Bingley town home allowed their conversations to trail off as a knock on the door signaled the final guests' arrival.

"The Right Honorable the Viscount and Viscountess Hopton," announced Cartwright. The Hurst butler filled his old role while Sir Reginald, KCB, and Lady Hurst squatted at her brother's London home. Charles had moved up north to spend the next few years taking over the business from their ailing father. Darcy and Elizabeth rose to their feet, as did the Hursts.

Darcy bowed; his lack of grace was noticeable to his cousin. Richard suspected Elizabeth had some type of mischief planned. She confirmed his suspicions.

Lizzy squared her shoulders and curtsied. Her derriere touched her heels. She lowered her head and eyes before rising with a loud, "Your ladyship."

Richard's eyes widened in mirth as he fought to keep his lips clamped shut. Kitty glared daggers at her elder sister. She waited to make eye contact.

"Need I call Jane? Once was not enough for you?"

Lizzy's eyes went wide. Kitty had related to Richard the Day of the Thousand Curtsies—an event their father referred to with glee. Lizzy covered her mouth in delight. Kitty joined her.

Everyone sat and made small talk. They chatted and they signed. It was another typical extended Bennet sibling day in the parlor. Louisa nodded to a footman, who opened the door. Cartwright entered. "Yes, milady?"

"Cartwright, you seem to have enjoyed our investiture," observed Lady Hurst.

"Yes, milady. I only strive to maintain that which I informed Sir Reginald of before he made a most wise declaration."

Louisa's eyes widened. The party's interest was piqued. Richard and Darcy looked at Hurst, both with identical eyebrows uplifted.

"Well, Hurst?" asked Darcy, rather dryly. "Your man there alludes to having predicted your recent change in rank."

Lizzy unleashed her fan on her husband's arm. "Behave, sir."

Richard snickered. Kitty shook her head. *"Boys will be boys."*

"Yes, I remember that conversation, Cartwright. You are correct, as your prophecy was most accurate—*most*."

"Do tell, dear," urged Lady Hurst. Her eyes glowed with mirth.

"It started with a warning, did it not, Cartwright?"

"You are correct, Sir Reginald. Informed you were—on that most memorable of evenings—of a bit of angst."

"You did not," moaned Louisa.

Cartwright smiled at his mistress. His eyes confirmed that he did. Louisa dropped her face into her hands. Lizzy and Kitty giggled.

"I believe I queried the *veracity* of said—how did you put it, Cartwright?—*angst*?"

"You did, Sir Reginald."

Richard and Darcy guffawed.

"It was at that time you made the prediction if I recall correctly."

"You are thrice again correct, Sir Reginald."

Everyone's attention was riveted on the repartee. They awaited the coup de grâce.

"Tell us, Cartwright, the exact words you used that evening, as I remember a most memorable, perfect proposal, forever etched in my mind," purred Louisa Hurst. She lifted her hand. Her husband grasped her fingers and kissed her knuckles. Louisa sighed—as did Lizzy, as did Kitty.

"Our dialogue ended with my informing Sir Reginald that the *lady* deserves the very best."

Cartwright bowed. Making sure he had his mistress's eye, he winked and exited.

Kitty's eyes opened wide. Darcy reached over and pushed the bottom of his wife's mouth closed. Hurst chuckled.

Louisa shook her head. "Still a rascal," she mused with fondness.

Dinner was announced and the couples adhered to protocol; Richard escorted Louisa into the dining room, followed by Hurst and Kitty. Darcy escorted Lizzy.

Kitty signed of her progress with the charity works she remained focused on when motherhood and her two children allowed her to do so.

"The charity is sponsoring a knowledge exchange with the American Thomas Gallaudet so that the kingdom may learn varied techniques for teaching deaf people."

Lizzy voiced the narrative.

"The success of the enterprise will secure donations, including a bequest from the crown. We intend to establish the Cornwall Asylum for the Education and Instruction of Deaf and Dumb Persons, which would be the first permanent school for deaf people in the kingdom. The plan is to open it in two years."

The diners applauded Kitty. The viscountess was no longer seen as a blushing girl from the country. She was now recognized as a leading lady of the *ton*.

Louisa picked up the conversation thread. "I do not doubt you shall be successful, Kitty. Your connections ensure your success." Several heads nodded. The political influence the future Countess of Matlock now brought to bear was considerable.

Leading the charge was Bishop Peregrine Abbott, spiritual advisor and educator to Her Royal Highness, Queen Charlotte, a patron of the arts and an amateur botanist. The Queen doted on the Viscountess Hopton after the most astonishing curtsy in court memory.

Lizzy had accompanied Kitty to her presentation, a requirement for Viscountess Hopton as the future Countess of Matlock. Kitty, her natural grace on full display and accentuated by her ornate court dress, dazzled the royals by floating across the great floor. She acknowledged the Queen and the Prince Regent with an elegance never before seen. The royals were awed with her finger signs of answers to their inquiries while Lizzy, standing beside the herald, translated.

In a complete breach of royal protocol, Queen Charlotte left her chair, walked to Kitty, and reverently cupped her face in her hands, shocking the entire royal court and viewing assemblage. The Queen kissed Kitty's forehead, stepped back, and in heavily accented English, announced, "Exquisite, my dear. You are exquisite."

Not to be outdone, her new father, the Earl of Matlock, made his voice much heard on the floor of the House of Lords. He repeatedly lambasted the Poor Law Act of 1597—a piece of legislation pushed through the House of Commons that had made a mockery of disabled persons. He, too, doted on his newest daughter.

Behind the scenes, a quiet but powerful influence convinced the undecided and the misinformed of the mendacity of those hardliners who were unwilling to take the word of a lady or accept that a female may pursue a change in fiscal policy.

The broadsheets continued to tout the investiture *suo jure*[21] of the Duchess of Grafton. The proclamation was repeatedly trumpeted by the palace and its sycophants throughout the Season. Misogynistic barons and earls stood little chance of denying Her Grace's agenda. She educated them to accept the inevitable. Which they did.

The few holdouts claimed that the existing laws provided relief for the lame, impotent, old, and blind—that they made economic provisions for people dependent on charity. Such feeble excuses collapsed beneath the intelligent, cogent persuasions of Her Grace, the Duchess of Grafton, Theodosia Cavendish Manners-Sutton.

Lady Hurst rose to signal the separation of the sexes. The men stood to honor their ladies. If one looked closely, three sets of male eyes followed three sets of female figures as they exited the room. Said figures were silhouetted by the dusky evening light. Said light presented said figures to their greatest advantage.

The men took their time cutting and lighting cigars.

"I had thought to engage the services of your executive officer, Major Carstens, but he continues to remain out of town," remarked Darcy.

"Jane."

"Hopton is correct. Miss Bennet seems to have made quite the impression on that dashing young officer," Hurst explained.

Both Darcy and Richard turned and looked at him, the expressions on their faces identical. Hurst shook his head.

"Apparently, he may soon resign his surname for hers." Hurst, amused by their somewhat skeptical looks, defended himself with a smile. "I am only relating the news from Bennet's most recent correspondence."

While he enjoyed his cognac, he decided to allow his friend Bennet the privilege of informing his sons-in-law that Carstens would be required to become the future *Mr. Bennet* if he wanted to inherit Longbourn. The Courts of Chancery were most inflexible regarding

21 A Latin phrase, used in English to mean "in her own right," encountered where a woman holds a title through her own bloodline or accomplishments.

the conditions of inheritance codicils.

The men settled into their chairs, shared small talk, and enjoyed their familial camaraderie.

"Darcy, your father insinuates your situation has much improved since you employed a new under-steward."

Darcy mock grimaced at him, turned to his cousin, and offered an explanation. "Elizabeth has taken over the ledgers, investment strategies, and tenant management. She completes the work in less time than I ever could, and she has increased our profits to an unforeseen level."

"So, what do you do with your time, Darcy?"

Darcy looked away from his host, but Hurst caught the sheepish look on his face.

"Our son cannot remain away from the stables. My days are now filled with Bennet and his 'horsey, horsey, horsey' fixation."

Hurst snickered with Richard.

"Nurse Darcy!" laughed Richard.

"That would be Groom Darcy, I thank you!"

Hurst and Richard hooted with laughter and toasted their friend's happiness.

The ladies gathered to share their individual motherhood discoveries and delight in the praise of their future generations.

Lizzy mentioned Bennet Fitzwilliam, the Darcy two-year-old heir, and his obsession with horses. Kitty knowingly looked askance at her sister. Louisa smiled.

"'Horsey, horsey, horsey.' Is there not another word in a two-year-old's vocabulary?"

"Whose complaint is that my dear?"

Lizzy laughed and put her hand on Louisa's arm.

"Do not tell Darcy I told you."

Kitty giggled. Louisa laughed.

"We are lucky little Caroline has ceased to fixate on round objects.

Everything found its way into her mouth. I am relieved her elder brother Reggie dotes upon her."

All three ladies chuckled.

Kitty described her little Langston's antics at sneaking into his new baby sister's room throughout the day. He repeatedly claimed she needed her elder brother's protection.

"His father's son."

Louisa sometimes found it difficult to concentrate on the conversation as Kitty was poetry in motion. Blinking, she regained her train of thought.

"Where is your spectacular daughter, Kitty?"

"You shall see her tomorrow at the park."

The men rejoined the ladies. The evening passed in as pleasing a manner as one could imagine. Lizzy played the pianoforte and sang while Kitty held their audience spellbound as she interpreted the music in her unique way—transforming it from a flat sheet of notes to a three-dimensional living, breathing apparition.

The dining-in ended with the confirmation of an afternoon picnic at the park adjacent to Gracechurch Street.

Gracechurch Street

The party reconvened the next afternoon around a large tree in the park, two blocks from the Gardiners' home. The Fitzwilliam family, gathered around a long bench, doted upon a stunning brunette baby girl in the arms of her grandmama. A near twin of the distinguished lady sat to her right.

Hurst and Louisa stopped in front of the merry group and received hearty welcomes. As if on cue, Lady Audrey Fitzwilliam, Madeleine Lambert Gardiner, and baby Lady Lydia Fitzwilliam turned their gazes upon the man most responsible for their reunification.

Three sets of violet eyes crinkled at Sir Reginald Hurst, KCB.

"Extraordinary," whispered he.

Several yards away, Elizabeth sat on a blanket, young Bennet Darcy asleep with his head on her lap. Her skirt, an iridescent blue, provided a comfortable barrier between the Darcy heir and the grass. From afar, he appeared to be lying in a pool of running water. Her hand was on his head, gently scratching his scalp. She sang a love song to her two-year-old heart of hearts.

Darcy, standing with Richard, struggled with his emotions. Next to his wife sat the vision of Lady Anne. Unseen by all but Darcy, the wraith emulated Lizzy's actions. He closed his eyes and tilted his head back. He could feel fey fingernails furrowing his scalp. He sighed.

Richard tapped his shoulder. Darcy turned.

"*Non est dubium*, Cousin."

Darcy turned back and gazed at perfection.

"I never shall."

FINIS

Acknowledgements

I hope you enjoyed reading my first novel as much as I have enjoyed writing it. *Doubt Not, Cousin* was not a solo effort.

In Turkish, the word for village is köy, as in "It takes a village to raise a child." I'm incredibly grateful to be part of the JAFF köy and call many a friend.

I'm extremely grateful to the Meryton Press creative and editorial team: Ellen Pickels, Janet Taylor, and Don Jacobson.

This endeavor would not have been possible without the patience and collaboration of Cherith Boardman, Christin Sprenger, Elin Ericksen, Izabel March, Karen O'Callaghan, Maple Steely, Riana Everly, Sophia Lykke Illner Thorsen, Summer Hanford, Tina Jockin, and Wendy Luther Moreira.

I am deeply indebted to two exceptional individuals: Kimbelle Pease and Tasha Barefield. You provided the diamond polishing to this rock of a manuscript. Thank you again and again.

All errors are solely mine.

So, to my new and hopefully continuous reading audience, I thank you for your time.

With my compliments,
Barry S. Richman

About the Author

Barry S. Richman is a military veteran and corporate logistics professional. While he was recuperating at home after having his wisdom teeth extracted in 2003, he picked up a copy of *Pride and Prejudice* and has yet to put it down.

In the past twenty years, he has read thousands of *Pride and Prejudice* variations. Watching him complete a book every other day, his wife of thirty years suggested he write one.

Doubt Not, Cousin is his first book.

Barry and his "Jane Bennet" live in Los Angeles and Alaçati, a small seaside town in southwestern Turkey.

Made in the USA
Monee, IL
02 August 2023